THE FINAL ROUND

Other books by Bernard O'Keeffe:

No Regrets
10 Things To Do Before You Leave School

THE
FINAL ROUND

Bernard O'Keeffe

**MUSWELL
PRESS**

First published by Muswell Press in 2021
This edition published in 2022
Typeset by M Rules
Printed and bound by CPI Group (UK) Ltd, Croydon CR0 4YY

A CIP catalogue record for this book is available from the British Library
ISBN: 9781838340179
eISBN: 9781838110116

Muswell Press
London N6 5HQ
www.muswell-press.co.uk

In loving memory of Caitlin

1

Saturday 6 April

The towpath is packed, the walkway beside the river is four or five deep, and the balconies of the Lonsdale Road houses are buzzing with parties. The Bull's Head heaves on its busiest day of the year, and this normally quiet area of London is crowded with people, for many of whom this is the only time they ever visit the sleepy 'village by the Thames'.

Occasionally the crews of Oxford and Cambridge are close enough to each other at Barnes for the outcome to still be in doubt, but more often than not one boat is by now so far ahead that there is little prospect of further excitement – it is now unlikely that either boat will sink or that anyone will hurl themself into the river in a protest against elitism. The proximity of the Mortlake finishing line means that by the time the oarsmen pass the Bull's Head and the White Hart, the event has become more of a procession than a contest. In sporting terms, the competition is over, and Boat Race Day is now even more about The Day than The Race.

This does little to dampen the enthusiasm of the crowd,

most of whom have been drinking all day, and when the boats come into sight, rounding the bend below Hammersmith Bridge, there is a surge of inebriated encouragement from the towpath. The vast majority of the spectators may have no connection with the two ancient universities, but this does not prevent them pledging their allegiance to one or the other by loudly crying encouragement or by simply roaring the name of their favoured university with strangely elongated vowels ('Oxfo-o-o-ord!', 'Cambri-i-i-idge!'). Everyone likes to give the impression that they spent their youth strolling through ivy-covered quads or lazing under dreaming spires.

When the crews have passed, the crowds walk away from the river, flooding into the White Hart, the Bull's Head, the Coach and Horses, or the Sun Inn, a pub that marks Boat Race Day by erecting a marquee in its car park and playing loud music late into the night. For one day (and one day only, much to the relief of the locals) Barnes is a party town.

Nick Bellamy stood outside the Sun Inn, facing the pretty village pond. He supped his beer, drew on his cigarette and listened to the loud rendition of 'Hi Ho Silver Lining' coming from the band in the marquee. He checked his watch, finished the rest of his pint in three large gulps and turned right down Barnes High Street towards the river.

The race had finished several hours ago but it was still light, an early evening chill replacing the warmth of the spring sun-shine as dusk approached. Nick tied his college scarf round his neck and, as he made his way through groups of hoodie-clad students drinking from bottles and cans, he wondered why so many made this annual pilgrimage. Was it tradition – some misty-eyed, nostalgic view of the world in which strapping young men from Oxford and Cambridge testing themselves in the choppy waters of the Thames still added up to something significant? Or was it simpler than that – another excuse for people to get together, a yearly event where they could meet old friends and get drunk by the river?

Nick headed away from the crowds, walking along the raised concrete path that ran beside the river. When he reached its end he passed the TV vans and took a smaller track heading to the right. He followed it up a slope, paused at a gate, undid the latch and walked through.

Immediately he was struck by the quiet – he may have been only yards away from the traffic of Lonsdale Road and the Boat Race revelry, but it felt as if he had stepped into a different world. He pushed aside low-hanging foliage as he walked along the path. Nothing was visible through the leaves on either side, but when the bushes thinned he could make out the river to his left. He could also see water to his right – a large lake lying still in the silence. Nothing moved on its dark surface. Nothing rippled. All he could hear was the occasional flap of a bird.

Nick pushed through the overhanging branches, beginning to wonder whether he had heard correctly, whether this was the right place. Then, as he turned a bend in the path, another gap appeared in the bushes to his right and there, in a clearing, he could see a woman sitting on a bench. He picked up his pace.

The woman raised her hand as he drew close. 'I'm here.'

'So I see,' said Nick.

'Glad you made it.'

'A bit out of the way, isn't it?'

The woman looked up at the darkening sky. The light was fading fast. 'I thought we could use the privacy.'

Nick laughed. 'I don't think I'm up for that.'

'You used to be.'

'I used to be up for a lot of things.'

'Didn't we all?' She patted the narrow wooden bench beside her.

Nick sat down and looked into her eyes, searching for the lost years.

'I see you're wearing the scarf,' she said.

'Ironically, of course. Thought you might find it amusing.'

'I do. So . . . As agreed, then?'

'As agreed. Not a word. On my honour.'

'On your honour? That's my worry.'

'You've got it?'

The woman reached into her bag and took out a package.

'All there?' said Nick.

'I counted it all.'

Nick took the package, felt its weight, and shoved it in the inside pocket of his jacket. 'A deal, then.'

'A deal. Worth celebrating, don't you think?' She reached into her bag and pulled out a small bottle of whisky and two plastic glasses. She held up the glasses in her gloved hands. 'Drink?'

'I never say no to a drink,' said Nick.

'You never say no to anything. Or at least you never used to.'

The woman placed the glasses on the bench between them, unscrewed the bottle and poured. She handed a glass to Nick.

Nick held up his glass towards her. 'Cheers!'

'Cheers!' said the woman, clinking her glass against his. 'All sorted.'

Nick patted the package in his pocket. 'Sorted,' he said.

'To old times,' said the woman.

Nick raised his glass again. 'Old times,' he echoed.

The woman was staring at him oddly, as if she were expecting him to do or say something more. She said

4

nothing, fixing him with a steady, expectant gaze, her eyes flashing as light from the road bounced off the water's surface.

Nick took another sip. Why was she looking at him like that? What was she waiting for?

2

Sunday 7 April

Yesterday's crowds were gone, Barnes was restored to its usual state of sleepy tranquillity, and in the morning sunshine a young lawyer took a walk by the river with his wife and daughter. They strolled from the Bull's Head towards Hammersmith, turned right when they reached the gravel towpath, made their way up a small slope and pushed the latch of the swing-to that led to the Leg o' Mutton Reservoir, a nature reserve lying between the river and Lonsdale Road – the perfect place, to those in the know, for a Sunday-morning stroll.

The couple watched their daughter run on ahead as they closed the gate behind them.

'Don't go beyond the bench, Chloe!' shouted the mother. 'And don't go near the slope!'

They knew that Chloe would run ahead to the clearing, where she would sit on the bench and look onto the water for the birds she had recently learned to identify. As she disappeared from view round a bend in the path, they held hands and started to talk about the things that had recently come to matter – his prospects of partnership, her desire for a second child, the likelihood of their trading up their property while staying in Barnes, and the plans for Chloe's future schooling.

Her shout surprised them.

'Mummy! Daddy!'

They looked at each other for a panic-stricken instant and broke into a run.

'Chloe!' called the father.

'We're coming!' shouted the mother.

They ran towards their daughter's cry and as they turned the bend in the path they saw, to their relief, that she was sitting safely on the bench.

'What's happened?' said her mother.

Chloe pointed a finger to the ground in front of her.

'What is it?' said her father.

Chloe said nothing, her arm stretched, her finger extended. Her parents looked where it was pointing.

'Oh my God,' said Chloe's mother, covering her mouth with her hands.

'Shit!' said her father.

They looked at the body lying face up on the tiled slope leading down to the lake.

Its shredded shirt was covered in blood, every part of it bearing large, jagged rips as if a knife had torn through it hundreds of times. Its face, frozen in a wide-eyed death stare, was distended, its cheeks puffed out wide by the scarf stuffed into its mouth and tied round its neck.

The man looked at the scarf and, typically perhaps for a Barnes resident, recognised the Oxford college to which it belonged.

It took him longer to recognise the dead man's tongue lying next to his head like a fat red slug.

3

Melissa Matthews
Requests the pleasure of JULIA and PHIL FORREST at
The 25th Anniversary
Quiz Night
The Ocean Bar

Julia Forrest ran her fingers through her dark bobbed hair and looked at the invitation. 'Twenty-five years!'

'What is?' said Phil, eyes scrolling down his iPad.

'The quiz. It's the twenty-fifth anniversary. Difficult to believe, isn't it?'

Phil looked up at his wife. He did not find the concept so difficult to grasp.

Julia sighed. 'Oh well, I suppose we'll have to go.'

Phil laughed. 'I suppose we'll have to go? Of course you'll go. You always go. That's the thing about you lot. You can't stand each other but you can't miss the chance to remind yourself why.'

8

'What do you mean, we can't stand each other?'

Phil chuckled and turned back to his iPad. 'Well, let's start with Melissa, shall we?'

'Well, no one likes Melissa.'

'There you go. My point exactly.'

'But that's only because she's such a smug bitch.'

'You're jealous. You're all jealous.'

'Nonsense.'

'You moan every time she's on TV.'

'I'm sure I'm not alone there.'

'Just because she's famous ...'

'She reads the news. That's all she does.'

'Reads the news – and the rest. One half of a glamour couple.'

'Yeah, the pretty half. Not too difficult to see how she built her career, is it?'

'And you're not jealous?'

'No.'

'I don't believe you. You and the rest of them. As I said, you can't stand each other.'

'Nonsense.'

'OK then, what about Fay?'

'I've a lot of time for Fay.'

'Really? You don't like her much, though, do you?'

'Can't be easy being head of that school.'

'Exactly. Easy to make mistakes.'

'At least she got where she is on her own merits. No one can say Fay married success.'

'No one can say Fay married anyone. And let's face it, you don't like her because she could have done more to accommodate the daughter of one of her oldest friends.'

'You really think I hold that against her?'

'Melissa's daughter sits the St Mark's entrance exam.

Melissa's daughter gets in. Our daughter sits the St Mark's entrance exam. Our daughter doesn't. Don't tell me that isn't one of the reasons you have it in for Melissa and don't tell me you still can't quite forgive Fay.'

'The more I hear about Fay's school, the happier I am she's not there. Melissa's precious daughter's been in all kinds of trouble. And going to the Dolphin hasn't exactly harmed Helena, has it?'

'You love it, don't you? Bitching.'

'I do not bitch.'

'Gloat, then.'

'I do not gloat.'

'Really? "What a shame that Helena has an Oxford offer at our old college and Lauren doesn't. How nice it would have been for both of them to be there together!" You love it. You may not be on TV. You may not have married someone as successful as Greg Matthews – although you did marry someone a hell of a lot more handsome and who *still* has a full head of hair – but at least you've produced a daughter who's smarter than hers.'

'It's not a competition.'

'Of course it's not. Just an irresistible desire to see everyone else fail.'

'Who wants everyone to fail?'

Julia and Phil hadn't noticed Helena coming into the kitchen. They turned to the voice.

'Boasting again, Mum?'

'Of course not.'

Helena opened the fridge and peered inside. 'Don't count your chickens.'

'You'll be fine.'

'I've got to get the grades, haven't I? Still time to fuck it up.'

'Helena!'

Objecting to her daughter's language made absolutely no difference but Julia liked to persist. This pattern – persistence with little result – had, in recent years, characterised all her attempts at parenting.

'It wouldn't take much, would it? I mean, look at Lauren.'

The last thing in the world Julia wanted was to see her daughter going down the same path as Melissa's. She never wanted to visit any child of hers in the Priory.

'Everything's ... OK, isn't it?'

Helena shrugged. 'All I'm saying is don't make assumptions. Anything could happen.'

'You'll be fine,' said Phil in a no-nonsense tone. 'Just do what you have to do.'

Helena took a yoghurt from the fridge, closed the door with a sigh, and gave them both an exaggerated ironic smile. 'Thanks for that, Dad. I'll just go off and ... do what I have to do, then.'

Phil and Julia exchanged raised eyebrows as their daughter slammed the door behind her. They listened to her thump up the stairs.

'Don't worry,' said Phil. 'In ten years we'll be done – all our kids through the system.'

'Is the first one the most difficult, do you think?'

'Who knows? The way Ellie and Felix are shaping up I think they'll give Helena a good run for her money.'

Julia looked at Phil and wondered, as she did at this time every year when she looked at the quiz night invitation, how things might have turned out so differently. She thought again about Melissa's daughter in relation to her own, and then about their husbands. Phil was definitely the winner when it came to hair (his striking mop of unruly grey curls was the envy of men like Greg, who had turned bald many years ago) and he was also the more handsome. But when it came to material success there was no doubt that Greg and Melissa had experienced it on a scale none of them, not least herself, could ever have imagined all those years ago.

Were there times when she thought what it might be like to be married to someone so rich, to live in that huge mansion, to be so connected to so many of the famous and influential? And were there also times when she felt this strange urge to want some of it for herself, to appropriate and pocket what could, had different decisions been taken, had the dice rolled differently, so easily have been hers?

It struck Fay Wetherby as richly ironic that she should receive Melissa's invitation moments before she was about to field a parental complaint about her daughter. Teaching the daughter of one of your oldest friends would be bad enough, but being her headmistress was proving almost impossible. Had Lauren Matthews been an easy pupil all would have been fine, but, as the nature of the conversation she was about to have and her experience over the last six years indicated, this was far from the case.

There were many advantages to being the head of London's most prestigious girls' school – power, status, influence and money were the first that sprang to mind – but there were also many drawbacks, and at the moment the most significant of these seemed to Fay to be the unrelenting awfulness of the parental body. Who did they think they were? OK, so they paid the fees. OK, so the education of their darling daughters was of supreme importance to their well-being (and also to their daughters', though in Fay's experience this was very much a secondary consideration), but why did they have to be so demanding? Was it not enough for them to have secured a place at what was unquestionably *the* top school in London? Was it not enough for them to know their daughter was guaranteed a plate-load of A*s and a good chance of ending up at Oxbridge?

From what Fay experienced on a daily basis, it clearly was not. What else could explain the string of complaints she dealt with? Complaints that had a habit of trickling through the protective layers of management she had put in place below her and landing in her inbox with a heart-deadening ping, or even worse, as in the case of what she was about to endure, announcing themselves with another turn of her office door handle?

'Mr and Mrs Canning, thank you so much for coming in.' Fay stood up, shook the parents' hands, and gestured them towards the chairs arranged around a circular glass table in the middle of the room, an arrangement intended to make meetings such as this less confrontational than they would be were she to conduct them from behind the barrier of a desk. Mr and Mrs Canning responded with half-smiles, and sat down, keen to dispense with the niceties and begin the fight.

Fay sat down opposite them, immediately wishing she had a desk to protect her. She straightened her back and braced herself. 'Mr and Mrs Canning, it's always difficult when a girl is suspended, and I can understand how strongly you feel about it.'

'Can you?' said Mr Canning.

'Yes, I think I can—'

'Do you have a daughter?'

'No, but—'

Mrs Canning leaned forward. 'Do you have a son?'

'No. I don't have a son.'

Fay gave a tense smile. 'I don't see how whether or not I have a—'

'I know that Phoebe committed a serious offence,' said Mr Canning, 'and neither my wife nor I is here to defend her.'

Fay nodded. They were not here to defend their daughter – they were here to attack her head.

'What puzzles me,' Mr Canning continued, 'what puzzles *us*, and, I think you should know this, what puzzles a large part of the parental body, is why, when there was another girl who seems to have committed exactly the same offence, this other girl was not suspended as well.'

Fay leaned forward, her hands resting firmly on the desk. 'The affair was investigated thoroughly and it was felt there were significant differences.'

'Could you possibly, just so that we are all clear, remind us of what those differences are?'

'We've been through all this before, Mr Canning.'

'Perhaps you don't like to remind yourself?'

'Look, Mr Canning, we all agree that online abuse of a member of staff, in any form, is unacceptable. Your daughter, as I recall, called a member of staff, and I quote,' – Fay looked down at the file on her table and turned over a page – '"a fat poof who is a crap teacher". The other girl—'

'Lauren Matthews.'

'That's right. Lauren Matthews. She wrote, "I agree. Crap teacher." It seems to me quite clear that there is a difference between the two.'

'She was being abusive as well.'

'I really do not want to go over old ground, Mr and Mrs Canning. Lauren Matthews was punished—'

'A detention? Not much of a punishment, is it?'

'But given her previous record it was felt that Phoebe's punishment should be more severe.'

Mr Canning snorted. 'Phoebe's previous record? What about Lauren Matthews' previous record? She's been in all kinds of trouble!'

'There were clear differences between them,' said Fay.

'Oh there were differences, all right,' said Mrs Canning, her voice rising sharply, 'and the biggest difference to us seems to be that, unlike Greg and Melissa Matthews, we are not high-profile media figures and, unlike Greg and Melissa Matthews, we haven't recently made a huge contribution to the Development Appeal.'

Fay leaned back in her chair and let out an exasperated sigh. 'Is *that* what you think?'

'I'm not saying anything,' said Mr Canning.

'It sounds to me as if you are. In fact, it sounds as if you are saying something very specific and I'm not sure I like its implications, Mr Canning.'

'Your decision to suspend Phoebe has damaged her enormously, and it's also damaged us. And what we can't understand is why you seem to have been so selective in the way you have administered what you think is justice. Perhaps there is no connection between your decision and—'

'There is absolutely no connection, Mr and Mrs Canning, and if that is the only reason for this visit, I am afraid you have both wasted your time coming in this morning.'

'All I can say,' said Mr Canning as both he and his wife got to their feet, 'is that if it wasn't Phoebe's A-level year, we'd be taking this further. As it is, we just want Phoebe to take her exams and leave. You've said that this suspension won't affect her university place – not, alas, a place at Oxford – and we're assuming your word on this is to be trusted. But one thing I would like to say, Miss Wetherby, is how glad we are that Phoebe's time at St Mark's is coming to an end.'

Fay held her breath until the door closed and then let out a deep sigh of relief and frustration. Had she been right not to suspend Lauren? Yes, absolutely. Could she understand why it might look questionable? Yes, absolutely. Was she worried about how much the parental body seemed to know and what they might discover? Yes, absolutely.

Chris Turner opened the white envelope as he sat at the kitchen table of his house in Finsbury Park.

'The cow!'

'Who is it this time?' said Kim.

'What?'

'Melissa fucking Matthews.'

Her again. And this time with 'fucking' as her middle name, an accolade achieved only by a special kind of cow.

'The price of a table. She's put it up again.'

'She puts it up every year.'

'But not this much! Charity fascism, that's what it is. As if we've all got enough to give whatever we're asked to whatever ridiculous cause.'

'Why can't you lot just send each other Christmas cards like everyone else? Or have a reunion every ten years or something? Every year you do it! And a fucking quiz, for God's sake! Oh well. I hope you enjoy it.'

'Who says I'm going?'

'You go every year. Every year you open the invitation, moan about the price, moan about Melissa and Greg and their famous friends, and wonder what Nick Bellamy's been up to. Then you say you're not going this year and a few days later I find out you've forked out the money and off you trot.'

'Well, maybe this year I really *won't* go.'

Kim gave a loud laugh. 'Don't be silly. Of course you'll go. And you'll come back saying how Greg Matthews is a crap writer and look at how many millions of books he's sold. And you'll get depressed for a couple of weeks because you haven't even managed to finish your novel, let alone tried to get it published. And then you'll moan about the others . . .'

'I don't moan about the others.'

'Yes you do. All the time.'

'I don't moan about Nick.'

'That's because, unlike the rest of them, he's fucked it up and doesn't turn up any more.'

'Well, maybe he'll turn up again this year. That'd make it interesting.'

'I'll tell you something that will make it interesting.'

'What's that?'

'What about if *I* came along?'

Chris looked at his wife in astonishment. 'Why would you want to do that? You'd hate it.'

Kim waved the invitation under Chris's nose. 'The twenty-fifth! A special occasion. And I'm good at quizzes – I know loads.'

'That's not the point.'

'What *is* the point, then? You don't want me to come along, do you?'

'It's not that.'

'You don't want me intruding on your cosy little world of old pals. Is that it? All those glamorous women.'

'Don't be silly.'

'You're at that dangerous age, aren't you? Fifty looms and there might just be time to revive something from the past ...'

'Nothing like that went on with any of them.'

Kim threw back her head and laughed. 'Of course not! You were up to other things weren't you? Playing in the privacy of your own room. Bless!'

'Please! Not that old chestnut again.'

'Oh, it was a chestnut, was it? I thought it was—'

'You know it's not true. Nothing but another Nick Bellamy story.'

'Still, it's always comforting to think your secret perversions might have started before you met me.'

'Please, Kim, don't ... Look, if you want to come along, that's absolutely fine.'

'Really? Are you sure I won't be an embarrassment to you? A mere teacher at a north London comprehensive?'

'You're Head of History. And you're being silly.'

Kim got up from the table and picked up her bag.

'Do you *really* want to come along or are you just being awkward?'

'I'll think about it today,' said Kim. She gave Chris a good-bye peck on the lips and headed for the door. 'Maybe I want something to take my mind off ... off everything.'

'Harry will be fine,' said Chris.

'Will he?'

'Of course he will. Now that it's been diagnosed, now that we know what it is, we can deal with it.'

'We should have noticed.'

'We did. We ...'

'We should have done something earlier.'

'It's very common, late diagnosis. And it's mild. On the spectrum, but mild.'

'I know, but—'

'He'll be fine. We'll get him the help he needs and ... look, he'll be fine. And if you want to come to the quiz, that's great. You can be on my table. Might be nice to do well for once. Come to think of it, you must know some clever people at school. Ask them along.'

'Not really their thing,' said Kim as she headed through the door. 'And at that price? You've got to be joking.'

Kim shut the door behind her and Chris looked at the invitation in his hand. Something had made him feel uneasy and he couldn't work out whether it was the idea of Kim coming along to the Ocean Bar or her reference to that old story. He hoped she still believed him when he said it was untrue and hoped that he still convinced her when he said he had nothing to hide.

Nick Bellamy almost threw the invitation away. It was sitting in a pile of junk mail and he was about to chuck the whole lot in the bin when the expensive white envelope fell to the ground. He picked it up, recognised the hand, and knew immediately what it was – for many years a similarly addressed envelope had landed on his doormat at this time of year. He opened it and found what he expected. What he had not expected, though, was the handwritten message at the bottom – *Hope you can make up a table this year, as it's a special occasion – the twenty-fifth anniversary! Love, Melissa.*

Could it really be twenty-five years? It seemed only yesterday that he had turned up with a bottle of wine for Melissa's first ever quiz evening. Back then it was just the six of them with their partners in her modest Clapham flat (nothing modest about her now). But as the years went by, the quiz, like Melissa and Greg's wealth and fame, had grown, moving from their flat to a fashionable Notting Hill restaurant and then to the prestigious riverside Ocean Bar, extending its range of invitations to the famous and the wealthy. What had begun as six Oxford friends getting together each year for a quiz night had somehow become part of the London intelligentsia's season. The Melissa Matthews Charity Quiz Night was a big event, and everyone wanted an invitation.

Nick looked at the white card in his hands and wondered why, after turning the invitation down in recent years, he felt the urge this year to accept, to say yes, to get a table together for Melissa's precious quiz night. He knew what it would be like – all the old friends pretending that they still liked each other and that the years had not weakened, if not entirely dissolved, the bonds that had once kept them close. And presiding over all of it would be the glamorous couple – Melissa and Greg, a reminder to Nick of how differently things had panned out for his old college friends and in particular of how well Melissa had done to marry the global bestselling novelist with more money than Nick could shake a stick at.

The more Nick looked at the words 'twenty-fifth anniversary', the more convinced he was that this year he would say yes. He would turn up. More than that, he would turn up and win the fucking thing – he would beat the smartest arses in Melissa's charmed circle of the metropolitan glitterati. He would mark the passing of all those disappeared years by winning the Ocean Bar Quiz. He would carry home the trophy, get his name in the *Evening Standard* and, most importantly, he would show Melissa Matthews that she made a terrible mistake all those years ago. He would remind her of how, despite all the changes they had been through, he would always be important in her life.

And, if he played it cleverly, he would get his hands on some of her huge pile of money. God knows he needed it.

4

Sunday 24 March

Melissa Matthews stood at the front, her long blonde hair framing the blue eyes and high cheekbones familiar to the nation from her TV newsreading. She adjusted the microphone and gave her best to-camera smile.

'Good evening, everyone.'

They were all there: Paul Camden (comedian and chat-show host), Jonny Sinclair (editor of satirical weekly *The Dirt*); Peter Home (world's greatest living playwright); Max Peterson (the prime minister's discredited ex-spin doctor); Annie Green (Oscar-winning actress). Wherever you looked were people who mattered, or who liked to give the impression they did.

Apart, that is, from one table.

Nick Bellamy and his team were initially refused entry – not only because Nick had forgotten his invitation but also because they were all drunk and didn't seem the sort who came to events like this. Melissa was called to the door where she verified Nick as a bona fide guest, before giving him a kiss on the cheek and whispering a quiet warning in his ear.

The level of noise currently coming from Nick's table suggested that her warning had not been heeded.

Melissa tried to ignore it. 'Good evening, everybody,' she repeated. The noise slowly subsided, and heads turned to the top table. 'Good evening, everyone. And welcome to the Ocean Bar Quiz.'

Loud cheers followed, those from Nick's table stopping a good ten seconds after the rest.

'A significant occasion,' continued Melissa, 'because it is the quiz's twenty-fifth anniversary. Its silver anniversary.'

Loud applause filled the room.

'First, the rules.'

Melissa, standing in front of a large screen and an elaborate scoreboard, introduced the format – ten rounds of ten questions, with a joker doubling the points of any nominated round – and handed over to Arthur Manning, celebrated TV journalist and quizmaster for the evening, who launched into the questions with his characteristic blend of sharpness and charm.

As the quiz progressed and alcohol consumption increased, the banter grew louder and the guests more rowdy. Despite claims that this was merely a bit of fun that no one should take too seriously, it was difficult to hide the competitive edge. Accusations of mobile-phone cheating were levelled at those who went outside for a cigarette or headed for the toilets, and scores were questioned and challenged by teams sensing victory within their reach.

Loudest and rowdiest of all were those at Nick Bellamy's table. Arthur Manning's ironic intelligence and consummate professionalism managed, for the most part, to keep them under control, but it was touch-and-go all evening, and Melissa was hugely relieved when the final question had been asked.

What happened, though, as the final scores were being calculated and the winning team was about to be announced, took Melissa and all of the Ocean Bar by complete surprise.

As Melissa sat down, a voice came through the restaurant speakers.

It was a woman's voice, loud and clear, easily heard over the buzz of conversation. But it was not a voice that Melissa recognised.

'Hello everybody,' said the voice. 'It's now time for the final round. A very special extra round of questions for you all!'

Melissa turned to Greg. 'What is this?'

Greg's eyes were wide with surprise.

'This final round,' said the voice, 'is in honour of the six Balfour College friends who started all this, who were there at the very first quiz night twenty-five years ago. This final round is very straightforward. You're about to hear an interesting fact about each of these six people. All you have to do is work out which of them is true.'

Murmurs and laughter spread round the room.

Melissa and Greg were still looking at each other, brittle smiles working hard to cover their concern.

'Is this you?' said Greg.

'Of course not,' said Melissa through ventriloquist lips.

'Are you ready?' said the voice. 'Here they come. Number one. Greg Matthews plagiarised his first novel. True or false?'

All eyes in the restaurant turned to Greg. He faced them with pleading, upturned hands and as broad a smile as he could muster.

'Number two. Fay Wetherby was bribed by parents not to expel their daughter. True or false?'

Fay Wetherby tilted her head to one side, raised her

23

eyebrows and forced a smile. Her years as a headmistress had taught her how to wear an inscrutable expression, and she wore her best one now, nodding ironically to the other members of her team, as if this allegation, impressive in its inventiveness, might even be true.

'Number three. Chris Turner has been blackmailed over a sex tape. Sextortioned. True or false?'

Chris spluttered on his wine, spraying it on the table, causing the members of his team to jump back in shock. 'Sex tape!' he said. 'Chance would be a fine thing.' He guffawed loudly – whether at the outrageous accusation or the wittiness of his response was not clear – and the table joined in. He briefly caught his wife's eye. Kim was laughing too but he could tell that she was far from amused.

'Number four. Nick Bellamy once killed a man. True or false?'

At Nick's table there were whoops of laughter and roars of excitement.

'What?' said Nick, standing up and swaying. 'Only one?'

The whoops became even louder.

'Number five,' said the voice. 'Julia Forrest is a serial shop-lifter, last caught in the act in Harvey Nicks. True or false?'

'What?' said Julia Forrest at her table, her face creased in puzzled disbelief, her hands spread in an appeal to common sense. 'A shoplifter!'

'Maybe they mean shirt-lifter,' said one of her team.

'She can't be a shirt-lifter,' said another, 'that's men.'

'Shopfitter, perhaps,' said another.

'Shape-shifter!'

'Hot shitter!'

As Julia's team drunkenly riffed on the word 'shoplifter' the voice continued.

'And finally, number six. Our hostess Melissa Matthews

has a secret child from a teenage pregnancy. True or false? So which one is it, everybody? Which of these is true?'

Jaws dropped and mouths opened all over the Ocean Bar as gasps of astonishment, ripples of laughter and the occasional handclap punctured the uneasy silence.

'What is this?' said Melissa to Greg through gritted teeth. 'What the fuck is going on?'

'I have no idea,' said Greg.

They both looked out onto the restaurant floor, hearing the buzz of laughter and speculation.

'What do we do?' said Melissa.

Greg moved to her side. 'Pretend it was us,' he said through the side of his mouth. 'Pretend we did it.'

'Pretend we did it? Why would we do a thing like that?'

'As a joke.'

'Are you serious?'

'Have you got any better ideas?'

Melissa took a deep breath. She looked from Greg to the guests and then back to Greg. 'OK, I'll handle it. You go and see the manager. See if he knows what happened. Leave it to me.'

Greg headed towards the bar and Melissa tapped the microphone.

'Thank you!' she said, looking confidently round the room. She was doing her best to look cool, the way she did when the autocue stopped working. 'Thank you!' she said again, louder this time. The hum gradually quietened.

'Well, I bet you didn't expect that, did you?' said Melissa.

'What's the answer?' The loud shout came from Nick Bellamy's table.

Melissa looked in its direction. Nick was on his feet, swaying as he turned from her to the guests. 'Come on, Melissa, tell us which one's true. We all want to know!'

'Ladies and gentlemen,' said Melissa, 'it goes without saying that none of those allegations is true.'

'Bollocks!' said Nick. 'We all know which one's true!'

There was a ripple of laughter from the guests. 'Tell us, then!' came a voice. It was followed by similar cries from other tables.

Melissa waited for silence. It was slow in coming. In her head she could hear the voice's allegations and she sensed the whole room was hearing them too.

'I hope you'll forgive me that little indulgence.' She was almost shouting to make herself heard. 'My little joke. Just a bit of fun and, as I say, please don't try too hard to find out which is true, because none of them is. It was simply a light-hearted way to mark this occasion, the twenty-fifth quiz.'

Nick Bellamy was still on his feet. 'Come on, Melissa. Tell us! Which one's true?'

Melissa ignored him. 'And now, before I announce this year's winning team I would just like to say a few words of thanks. First, thanks to Daisy and all the wonderful staff of the Ocean Bar for lending us their premises for tonight.'

Applause.

'Thank you also to my quizmaster, Arthur Manning, for asking the questions with his usual style and aplomb.'

More applause.

'Thank you to all of you for turning up, and for raising so much money for this year's charity, which, as you know, is Kidsgo, the scheme which provides holidays for inner-city children.'

Another ripple of applause.

'And now the results,' said Melissa. 'In reverse order. In third place, with sixty-seven points, is the Midnight Ramblers. In second place, with seventy points, is String of Pearls. So the winner tonight, with seventy-one points, is the

Crack. Would team captain Nick Bellamy please come up to receive the prize.'

Nick's reprobates were on their feet, whooping and jigging with delight, swigging from wine bottles and waving them around. Nick punched his hand in the air, bowing and waving as he waltzed his way through the tables to the applause of the Ocean Bar guests.

He was, thankfully, not allowed to give an acceptance speech.

5

Monday 25 March

The morning after the Ocean Bar Quiz, Julia Forrest rang Melissa.

'How the hell did you come up with that?'

'With what?'

'That final round!'

'Just a little joke,' said Melissa.

'It may have been a joke, but it shook a few of us up. Me a shoplifter! And Harvey Nicks!'

'They're not true. None of them.'

'Are you sure about that? Your love child, Chris's sex tape, Fay's bribery. Greg's first novel – you know, I always thought there was something familiar about that premise. And as for Nick killing a man, who knows with Nick? Did you see him last night? What the hell was he on?'

'Listen, Julia. Thanks so much for calling.' Melissa clearly wanted to draw the conversation to a close. 'We really should get together soon, shouldn't we? After all, we do live just round the corner from each other.'

Julia knew only too well that they lived just round the corner from each other, but the boundary that corner marked, the one between rich Barnes and super-rich Barnes, was sometimes difficult to cross.

'Let's do that,' said Julia, 'it's silly that we don't see more of each other.'

It may have been silly, but Julia knew perfectly well why. Ever since things started going wrong for Lauren at St Mark's, Melissa had been strangely unavailable when it came to meeting up.

She hung up and turned to her husband. 'Do you really think Melissa and Greg were behind that last round?'

Phil Forrest kept his eyes on his iPad. 'You clearly don't.'

'I was looking at her when that voice came on the speakers. She was flustered. They both were – you could see it in their faces. And the other thing about it is *why*? Why on earth would they do it?'

'It was just a bit of fun.'

'But *was* it? I mean, could any of them possibly be *true?* Of course I'm not a serial shoplifter – that's completely ridiculous, but . . .'

'So why did she say it, then?'

'I have no idea.'

'Well, she must have got the idea from somewhere.'

'Unless . . .'

'Unless what?'

'Nothing.'

Phil looked up from his iPad, a sure sign of his concern. 'Hang on. Is there something you need to tell me?'

'No,' said Julia. 'Of course not. It's just . . .'

'Are you telling me you *are* a shoplifter?'

'Of course not.'

'Are you telling me you *were* a shoplifter?'

'No.'

'You're keeping something from me, aren't you?'

'Not as such, no . . .'

'Not as such? What does that mean?'

'Look,' said Julia in a no-nonsense tone. 'There was this time in Oxford when I was in the Covered Market with Melissa and there was this chi-chi boutique selling jewellery and this bracelet had fallen onto the floor near the door and we both looked at it, and before I knew what was happening, Melissa had bent down, picked it up and shoved it in her bag. She knew that I'd seen her and she gave me this look, as if to say, "Don't say anything."'

'Why have you never told me this before?'

'I've always felt embarrassed about it, and there never seemed an appropriate time, but now . . .'

'But now she's accused you of something she herself has done?'

'I'm saying that she did it once. I don't know if she's done it since. With her money she clearly has no need to and hasn't had the need to for some time.'

'Doesn't work like that, though, does it?' said Phil. 'Shoplifting bears no relation to need. Haven't you read about all those famously wealthy people who've been caught nicking low-cost items? There was that TV woman who killed herself over it. Hang on, I'll find it.' He started scrolling on his iPad. 'But if there's something you need to tell me . . . I mean, we all have secrets. No matter how well you think you know someone, no matter how many years you've lived with them, you can still find something out about them that surprises you.'

'I don't believe this. Are you serious?'

'Just saying.' He held out his iPad. 'Look. Here it is. Lady Isobel Barnett caught shoplifting in 1980. Stole a tin of tuna and a carton of cream worth eighty-seven pence from her village grocer. Fined seventy-five pounds and four days later she was found dead.'

'How the hell did you know that?' asked Julia, taking the iPad from him and starting to read.

'How do you know anything?' said Phil. 'A question we were all asking ourselves last night.'

'Look, it was just one moment a very long time ago. There's no way that Melissa, with her millions, could possibly be a shoplifter.'

'I think you're taking it all too seriously. It was clearly a joke. Everyone was laughing their heads off.'

'You weren't looking at them very closely, were you? Fay Wetherby was shitting herself. She still had that tight-knickered headmistress look about her, but you could tell she was shaken. An accusation of that sort can wreck a school's reputation in seconds. And heads nowadays, they're like football managers. Their jobs are always under threat. And Chris – the look his wife was giving him! I mean we all know about their son and how difficult that must be for them and we also know about this sextortion thing. And, let's face it, Chris has that look about him, doesn't he?'

'And what look's that?'

'The I'm-into-pornography look.'

'There's a look, is there?'

'You can tell.'

'Everyone watches pornography, dear.'

'No they don't. You don't, do you?'

'*I* don't. Of course *I* don't. When I said "everyone", I meant everyone but me. But it's more common than you think – these webcam sex-act scams are on the increase.'

'You seem worryingly well informed.'

'I've read about it.'

'Surely you remember the thing with Chris?'

'What thing?'

'At Oxford.'

Phil sighed. He gave his wife the look he had practised over the years. 'I didn't go to Oxford, remember?'

'I must have told you.'

Phil shook his head.

'He was caught doing something.'

'Tell me.'

Julia shook her head. 'It doesn't matter. I'm just saying that yet again there's something plausible in that accusation. It's the kind of thing that Chris might get up to.'

'You've got to tell me now.'

'OK,' said Julia. 'This is what happened . . .'

But, as she told her husband about Chris's alleged misdemeanour she was wondering what it was that had made her come up with the shoplifting lie and whether she had got away with it.

She was also wondering what everyone else had made of that final round.

When Fay Wetherby heard that Julia was on the line, she was in two minds over whether or not to take the call. Last night had been a huge embarrassment. The quiz itself had been fine, but what happened at the end had been far from amusing. Melissa and Greg might have thought it funny, but Fay could not have been the only one to find the whole thing uncomfortable. She might have managed to smile her way through it, forcing laughs as she lightly dismissed the accusation of bribery, but it had taken some doing.

'Put her through,' she said to her secretary.

'Fay,' said Julia, 'just thought I'd call to see how you are after last night.'

'I'm fine,' said Fay.

She knew she wasn't. Underneath the professional façade she had learned to maintain in all circumstances she was worried, fearing above all what might leak into that evening's *Standard*. She had already checked online but, so far, nothing. A few tweets had thanked the Ocean Bar and Melissa for the great evening and some had even tweeted about the surprise final round, but she had found nothing that detailed the contents, nothing that would set the parental antennae twitching.

'Some way to mark the twenty-fifth,' said Julia.

'Yes,' said Fay, 'I'm not sure that's how I'd have chosen to do it, but each to their own.'

'I won't keep you long,' said Julia, 'but I just wanted to ask whether you think it really *was* Melissa and Greg behind it.'

'That's what I've been assuming,' said Fay, even though she had been asking herself the same question.

'I was looking closely at them when it happened,' said Julia, 'and I could *see* their surprise. I got the sense they were covering it up.'

'If it wasn't them, who was it?' said Fay.

'I have no idea, but I just wanted to share the thought. I mean, I'm not a shoplifter, and as for you taking bribes – ridiculous!'

'Exactly!'

'Anyway, good to see you last night and let's get together soon. Lunch. Dinner. Coffee.'

'Good idea,' said Fay, hanging up and checking Twitter one more time before heading off to the day's first meeting.

'Chris? It's Julia.'

Chris stood in the Finsbury Park kitchen, glass of wine in hand, hovering over the cooker.

'Julia, hi. Recovered from last night?'

'Have you?'

'I think so.'

Chris looked at his wife as she came through the door. The truth was he hadn't yet recovered from last night. If that had been someone's idea of a joke, then he didn't share their sense of humour. As soon as he heard the words 'sex tape' come over the speakers he could see Kim looking at him with that self-righteous, accusatory glare he had become accustomed to over the years. It was the look she had worn throughout the whole round of allegations, almost as if she was pleased it was happening, and it was the look she was wearing now as she pointed at the phone in his hand and mouthed the question, 'Who is it?'

'Julia,' whispered Chris. Her look darkened.

'Just thought I'd give you a call to see what you made of it all,' said Julia.

'You mean those questions at the end? Well, I think the only sensible response is to laugh them off.'

'I agree, especially as none of them is true.'

'Exactly.'

'What I can't work out, though,' said Julia, 'is why Melissa and Greg thought it was a good idea.'

'Yeah. I've been wondering that myself.'

'That is, if it *was* them behind it.'

'You mean . . .?'

'Just an idea. The more I think about it, the more it seems exactly like the kind of thing Nick Bellamy might dream up. The state of him last night!'

'Still, at least he made it this year.'

'Actually, I've been trying to get hold of him but having no luck. Do you have a number for him?'

'I'll have a look and get back to you.'

'Great. And, Chris, given that there won't be another quiz to get us together, maybe we should meet up some time. You, Kim, me, Phil. It would be good.'

'Yeah, let's do that.'

Chris hung up and looked at the phone as if he couldn't believe what it had just told him. He looked at Kim. She was sitting at the kitchen table, her head in a newspaper.

'Let's do what?' she said, without looking up.

'Oh, nothing.'

'Tell me.' Kim's head was still down.

'Just Julia saying we should get together some time.'

'I can't think of anything worse.'

'I know. I think she was just being polite.'

Kim was still not looking at him. Ever since hearing the word 'sex tape' in public she had behaved as if the accusation levelled at him, unlike the others, were true.

Chris knew that it wasn't, but he also knew why she might think that it was.

Melissa Matthews sat opposite Greg at the dining table. Between them was a copy of the *Evening Standard*.

About Town with Forbes

Melissa Matthews held her annual charity quiz last night at the Ocean Bar and marked its twenty-fifth anniversary by springing a surprise. When everyone thought the quiz was over, she produced a final round of questions in which allegations were made about her old Oxford friends, and contestants were invited to guess which of them was true. 'It was spicy stuff,' one guest said. 'Sex. Murder. Bribery. And it got us all guessing.' Melissa Matthews insisted that there was no truth in any of the allegations. 'It was just a little joke,' said the newsreader, 'and I think everyone saw the funny side.'

Among the accused were Fay Wetherby, head of St Mark's Girls' School, Melissa Matthews herself, and her husband, bestselling novelist Greg Matthews. And among the guests at what has become an important event in the London social calendar were Paul Camden, Peter Home and Max Peterson. The quizmaster was Arthur Manning.

'What the fuck are we going to do?'

Greg leaned across the table and took Melissa's hand. 'The most important thing is to keep calm.'

Melissa picked up the paper, read the article again, and threw it to the floor. 'And it's a shit picture of me!'

'We need to be rational about this,' said Greg.

'Who was it? Who on earth would want to do a thing like that, and how the hell did they manage to do it?'

Greg leaned down and picked the paper off the floor.

'It could have been anyone,' said Melissa.

'Well, not quite,' said Greg. 'Whoever did this knows enough about us to make everything plausible.'

Melissa sighed. 'Plausible!'

'Yes,' said Greg. 'Not necessarily true, but plausible.'

'Plausible? So you think it's *plausible* that I have a child from a teenage pregnancy?'

'I'm not saying that. I'm saying—'

'I do not have a fucking love child! OK?'

In the short silence that followed, Melissa and Greg turned to see Lauren standing by the dining-room door.

'Everything all right?'

'Absolutely fine, darling,' said Greg.

Lauren walked towards the table and turned to her mother. 'But you, Mum, do not have a fucking love child.'

36

'It's nothing,' spluttered Melissa. 'Really.'

'It doesn't sound like nothing. What's happened?'

'Nothing,' said Melissa. 'We're just . . .'

Greg picked up the paper and handed it to Lauren.

'So,' said Lauren after a careful scrutiny, 'you played a little joke, did you?'

'That's right, dear,' said Melissa, 'a little joke.'

'And that's why you're shouting "I don't have a fucking love child" at the top of your voice? I don't quite get it.'

'Which bit don't you get?' said Melissa.

Lauren shrugged and put the paper back on the table. 'Shit picture of you, isn't it?'

Melissa picked the paper up again.

'Anyway,' said Lauren, 'I'm going out.'

'Where?'

'Does it matter? Makes no difference now, does it? I've fucked up everything already, so wherever I go and whatever I do isn't going to make much difference, is it? Sorry I haven't turned out to be the wonderful success you'd hoped for, trotting off to Balfour after her parents. Sorry I'm such a disappointment.'

'Please, Lauren—' Greg got up from the table and moved towards her.

'Mum hasn't got a fucking love child and I haven't got a place at fucking Oxford—'

'Lauren!' shrieked Melissa.

'I should never have gone anywhere near St Mark's, should I? Only got in because you're old mates with Fay fucking Wetherby!'

Lauren stormed out.

Melissa threw the paper on the table and held her head in her hands. 'Shit, Greg, this is one hell of a mess.'

'She'll get over it.'

'Not Lauren. This!' Melissa pointed at the *Standard*. 'We need to find out who did it.'

'It'll blow over. Those things – they were plausible, but untrue. I'm not a plagiarist. I could be accused of it, but that's easy. When it comes to stories, there aren't all that many in the world. Most things have been done in some form before. We all know about Chris. Julia and shoplifting . . .'

'We've been through all this. You know she did it at Oxford.'

'And I doubt very much whether Nick Bellamy has killed a man—'

Melissa got up from the table. 'It was him, wasn't it? It was Nick. He's the only one who could do something like that.'

'How can we find out?'

'Call him. See him.'

'And say what?'

'I don't know. Just talk. Hope he found our little final-round joke amusing. See if he says anything.'

Melissa walked to the door. 'In fact, I'll call him now.'

She went into the kitchen, found Nick's number and rang.

There was no answer.

6

Thursday 28 March

Lauren closed the front door behind her and went to the garage to get her bike. She hadn't bothered to tell her parents she was going out. What was the point? They liked to think they were always keeping an eye on her, but their house was so massive they often had no idea whether she was in or out, and the truth was that, despite their claims, they were hardly ever there for her anyway, either literally or metaphorically. Her best chance of seeing her mum each day was switching on the TV at six o'clock, and as for her dad, he may have been physically in the house for much of the time but his mind and attention were always elsewhere, buried in the ridiculous worlds of his novels.

She'd got used to it over the years, but she often wondered whether it was one of the things that had led to all the trouble. The drugs may have led to the eating disorder or the eating disorder may have led to the drugs, but she sometimes thought whatever caused the whole thing could lie in something deeper, something further back in her past.

Whatever the cause, the result was still painfully etched in her mind – that three-week spell in the Priory. It may have earned her fame and notoriety among her peers, and it may have momentarily made her parents wonder whether they were getting things right, but the whole experience was the lowest point in her life, a nightmare from which she knew she had never recovered.

The school hadn't been able to pin anything on her with regard to the drugs. Maybe it was a gesture of sympathy – taking the pressure off her because of her Priory stint. And they hadn't really been able to pin anything on anyone else either. That was the thing about drugs at places like St Mark's. It all happened at parties and outside school – no one was bringing it in or anything, and Lauren knew very well that they often liked to turn a blind eye for fear that they might find so many doing drugs that taking disciplinary action would mean suspending a huge chunk of the student body.

And then there was that social media thing about a year ago. She knew she was on firmer ground with that one. 'Crap teacher' was nothing compared to homophobic slurs, especially in these sensitive times. Maybe it was odd that criticising someone's professional capability should not be taken as seriously, but that's the way it was.

The only good thing she could say about this year at St Mark's was that it was her last. First the whole Oxford thing. And not just Oxford – Balfour bloody College, the one her parents went to. They had made the right noises of course, said all the right things. It didn't matter. She shouldn't take it personally. So what if they had been there. Durham was excellent, in many respects better, especially for her course. Etc. But Lauren knew deep down that they were bitterly disappointed. Their wealth had been able to buy them everything else, but it had been unable to buy them nostalgic visits to Balfour College to see their precious daughter strolling through the quadrangle where they had once strolled themselves.

Sometimes she wished she had never gone to St Mark's. There had been something fishy about the whole process, phone calls from the school just before the results were announced that her mum had taken in private. And other girls who she knew were brighter than her had failed to make it. Helena, for example. The same year at prep school and top of everything. Much to her own mum's pleasure (though she did her best to try to hide it) and much to Helena's mum's distress, Helena had ended up at the Dolphin – not a bad school at all, but not quite top-drawer St Mark's. Good enough, though, to get Helena into Oxford.

Maybe it would all have been different if she wasn't an only child, if she had someone – brother, sister, she didn't care which – with whom she could share all her doubts and misgivings, all the hatred (was that too strong a word?) she sometimes felt for her situation, the questions she had about the way her parents behaved. And talking of parental behaviour, how odd had they been since that quiz night? They had tried to keep it from her, but it had been impossible. Everyone at school seemed to know about Iron-Tits Wetherby and how she had been accused of bribery over expulsions, but thankfully she had heard nothing about the accusations levelled at her parents. She knew them, though – plagiarism and a secret love child. She quite liked the idea of both: the possibility that her father's success, or at least some of it, was based on deception and the idea that she might, after all, have a brother or sister (or half-brother or sister) somewhere in the world.

Yes, they had definitely been behaving very strangely since then, her mother perhaps more than her father. Sometimes she had seemed on the verge of confiding something, of revealing some secret, but each time she had backed off. On the few occasions when Lauren had seen her reading the news (she tried to avoid this as much as she could), she had looked at her as if she were looking at a stranger, as if she was someone she hardly knew at all.

Lauren rode her bike out of Mill Hill, across the road and through Barnes Common towards the pond. Cycling round like this helped calm her down, helped her sort out her troubled thoughts and her racing mind. She tried not to think of the withheld-number phone calls that had started a couple of weeks ago, the ones she had at first thought were from a cold caller, one of those hear-you've-had-a-car-accident ones or one from somewhere in the Far East whose accent you could never understand. She tried not to think of the way the calls had continued, the caller each time saying nothing and hanging up. She tried not to supply the incidents with her own romantic spin, and imagine it was Rob. And she tried not to flirt with the idea that, despite all that had happened a couple of years ago, despite all the warnings that he should never make contact with her again, he might still want to get back together.

Why, though, would Rob withhold his number? In the narrative Lauren liked to construct, Rob wanted to get in touch but didn't want her to know he was trying. He wanted to speak but kept bottling out.

She took out her phone and scrolled through the numbers. There it was. She had wiped most things to do with him, but had not been able to bring herself to delete his number. Just like she had not been able to get rid of that gift hidden safely at the back of one of her drawers. A special one, said Rob. One that would make you see things. Sometimes she would take it out and look at it, and on a couple of occasions she had come close to taking it – maybe it would make her feel that she was with him again, and give her that sweet release she longed for. But each time she had managed to resist and had put the tablet back safely in its hiding place. She would keep it as a reminder and as a temptation, a test of her will. One day, who knows, she might be unable to stop herself and take it, just as one day, maybe this day, she would give Rob a call.

She looked at his number on the phone in her hand and took a deep breath.

As she did, the phone rang.

She looked at the screen. Withheld number.

'Hello?'

Lauren listened to the silence, expecting the caller to hang up.

This time, though, there was a voice.

'Hello?'

It was a man's voice, but not Rob's.

'Is that Lauren Matthews?'

'Speaking. Who is this?'

'You don't know me, Lauren, but I need to talk to you.'

'What about?'

'I can't tell you on the phone.'

Lauren listened as the man spoke. Her eyes were on the swans and the ducks moving slowly and gracefully across Barnes Pond, but her mind was racing again.

7

Sunday 7 April

Garibaldi woke to the surprise of finding a woman beside him. This had not happened to him much in recent years, so when his leg stretched out in an early-morning yawn and his toes encountered flesh, at first he thought it was the end of a particularly vivid dream. When further gentle toe-probes confirmed that it was indeed a real body, he opened his eyes, looked at the woman's back and tried to piece together his fragmented memories of how she had got there.

Slowly, it all came back. A lot of whisky. A taxi home. And Rachel.

This may well have been the kind of thing that Rachel got up to frequently, but for Garibaldi it was unfamiliar territory and he was unsure what to do. Should he wake her with a cup of tea, or should he wait until she woke up herself? And when she woke would it be more than tea she wanted? He'd seen it often enough on TV and in movies and, although he knew these were a million miles away from real life (where, for example, was the hangover or the morning breath?), he

44

had no idea what Rachel might think on the subject. Waking up next to Kay may not have been easy in those final stages when they couldn't stand any kind of physical proximity but, even in the good days, morning sex had never been on the agenda.

As he weighed up the chances of being called into action, Garibaldi rehearsed his good morning. Casual and relaxed is what he'd go for, a suggestion that last night had been nothing unusual, a regular occurrence in his dynamic social and sexual life.

Rachel stirred. Garibaldi got ready to speak, but before he could say anything his phone rang.

'Hello?'

'Jim. It's Karen.'

'Morning, boss.'

'Where are you?'

'At home.'

'Good. Someone's found a body.'

Great. Sunday morning, he'd just woken up beside a woman for the first time in ages, and someone had found a body.

'Where?'

'Just round the corner from you. By the river. Place called the Leg o' Mutton.'

'I know it.'

Rachel opened her eyes and looked at him. He smiled.

'Are you OK, Jim?' said Karen.

'Yeah. I'm fine.'

'You sound strange. What have you been up to?'

You wouldn't want to know, thought Jim. Or maybe you would.

'Anyway,' said Karen, 'get over there as soon as you can.'

'What do we know?'

'A man. Multiple stabbings. And he's had his tongue cut out.'

'OK,' said Jim. 'I'm on my way.'

Rachel sat up in bed. 'Hi,' she said, raking her hands through tousled hair.

'Hi,' said Jim, his casual good morning now abandoned. 'I'm really sorry about this, but I've got to go.'

'Why? What's happened?'

'Work. Something's cropped up.'

'On Sunday?'

'Yeah, well it's that kind of work, I'm afraid.'

Rachel looked surprised. 'Really? I thought you were a . . .'

Garibaldi held his breath. What had he told her?

'I thought you were an accountant!'

He sighed. 'Yeah. Sorry about that.'

'So you were lying?'

He gave an apologetic shrug.

'I hope nothing else was a lie.'

'No, really. I can explain—'

'And you've got to go to work now, this very minute, on a Sunday morning?'

'I'm sorry.'

'You're not a priest, are you?'

Garibaldi laughed as more of last night came back to him. He looked at Rachel sitting up in bed, curly auburn hair framing her bright-eyed face. Even this early in the morning, so soon after waking, she seemed vibrant and alive. Her smile lit up the room.

'Not a priest,' he said. 'A cop.'

'Oh.' It was the usual tone – a mixture of surprise, curiosity and guilt. 'Why didn't you tell me?'

Garibaldi smiled, spreading his arms. 'It has a strange effect on people. I usually say I'm a teacher but given that you're one I reckoned I'd be found out too easily.'

46

'I see.' Rachel stretched some more, gathering the sheets around her as she sat up.

'So I went for something you wouldn't ask about.'

'Well, good choice.'

Garibaldi looked at the woman in his bed. 'I'm really sorry,' he said, 'but I'm going to have to go.'

'Right.' Rachel got out of bed, still holding the sheet around her. Garibaldi tried not to look at her body but couldn't stop himself. He felt like giving himself a medal.

'I'll get my stuff, then,' said Rachel.

'This seems really rude,' said Garibaldi. 'I'm sorry.'

'Don't worry about it.' She was trying to sound cool, but he could tell she wasn't.

'Maybe we could meet up again some time?'

He'd said it. The date offer. He probably wouldn't have done it so quickly or so directly if the phone call hadn't come.

The pause was long and he braced himself for the polite refusal.

'Yeah,' said Rachel, letting the sheet drop as she walked towards the bathroom. 'That'd be good.'

She paused as she walked past a table and bent down to pick up a CD. 'Townes Van Zandt?' she said. 'I love him.'

Jim couldn't believe his luck. A woman who made him laugh and who had not only heard of, but liked Townes Van Zandt.

How the hell had this happened?

Garibaldi hopped on his bike, pedalled out of the block of flats, crossed the roundabout by the Bull's Head and headed up Lonsdale Road. He soon saw the operations van and the cordon.

DS Gardner met him outside the tape. 'Hi, boss.'

'How is it?'

'Pretty ugly.'

He walked to the tape and ducked through it, taking the offered forensic suit, face mask, latex gloves and overshoes. He put them on and DS Gardner led him through a gate, walking ahead along the path by the Leg o' Mutton lake.

'OK, Milly, what have we got?'

'Male. Found this morning. Young bloke on a walk with his wife and daughter.'

'And what do we know about him?'

'He was out for a walk, his daughter ran ahead and saw the body.'

'Not him. The body.'

DS Gardner shook her head, as if surprised by her own stupidity, and took out her notebook. 'No ID. Three interesting things, though. Number one. Body had a scarf shoved into its mouth. Seems to be a university or college one.'

'A lot of those around yesterday.'

'Sorry?'

'The Boat Race.'

'Yeah, of course.'

'The most tedious sporting event in the world watched by the world's most tedious people.'

'Didn't know you felt so strongly about it.'

Garibaldi pushed away some leaves. 'I feel strongly about a lot of things, Milly. Is it much further?'

'A bit out of the way, boss. Good place for a murder.'

Garibaldi knew the Leg o' Mutton well. The kind of place to warn people from walking in alone.

'Number two?'

'Sorry?'

'You said three things.'

'Number two – he's been stabbed. Stabbed a lot.'

'OK. And number three?'

48

'Number three – the bloke's tongue's been cut out.'

Jim nodded. He had seen many dead bodies but not, as yet, a severed tongue. He was glad he had skipped breakfast.

They walked past a couple of PCs and through the entrance to the tent erected over the murder scene. Garibaldi looked down at the body. The scarf was still in its mouth and the tongue lay beside it, a tiny red blob like a piece of spat-out meat. Strange how something that felt so big in the mouth should look so small on the ground.

'We're waiting for the pathologist,' said DS Gardner.

Garibaldi looked at the Leg o' Mutton lake. He knew little about birds, but he was pretty safe on ducks, and he could see a few of those. He may also have caught sight of a woodpecker in the trees but he wasn't sure, and he thought the bird on one of the wooden islands was a heron, but that was only because it was standing on one leg. It was a pretty place – close to the river on one side and the busy Lonsdale Road on the other, but sufficiently hidden from view to make it a popular haunt over the years for drug users, weirdos, and pupils from a nearby school who liked to pop in for a crafty lunchtime smoke.

Garibaldi looked down at the severed tongue then up again at the lake and trees. No attempt been made to hide the body. It wouldn't have taken much to roll it into the water, to delay discovery for a while, yet whoever had done this had simply left it on the slope at the edge of the lake, its feet resting in the rushes.

Why this particular place? Why the scarf? And why, most disturbingly of all, the tongue? Was it part of some religious ritual or simply a statement that the man had been killed for something he had said?

'Bit out of the bloody way, isn't it?' Martin Stevenson squeezed through the tent entrance. 'Hi Jim. Sorry I'm late. What have we got?'

49

Garibaldi raised his hand in greeting. Stevenson displayed the two qualities he valued in any colleague – a high level of intelligence and the ability not to take anything too seriously. If only his boss and his sergeant were the same. The 'sandwich' – that's what the station wags liked to call them. DCI Karen Deighton above, DS Milly Gardner below, and him in between. The filling. Whenever anyone made the gag he liked to point out that when it came to food he, being a Garibaldi, was more of a biscuit man.

'Hmm,' said the pathologist. 'A tongue, I see.'

As ever, Stevenson spoke of the body's features as if they were items on a mouth-watering menu.

'Come across that one before?' asked Garibaldi.

'A traditional form of killing and torture in primitive societies and religions, of course, but the first time I've seen it.'

'What do you reckon?'

'Can't tell yet. That's a lot of stab wounds.' He looked at the corpse as if congratulations were in order.

Garibaldi's phone rang. 'Hello?'

'Where are you?'

Kay. He had completely forgotten. 'Shit. I'm sorry. I'll be right there.'

He knew he couldn't rush off straight away, so he stayed where he was, giving the impression that he was fully immersed in the scene, his detective brain whirring into overdrive, silently asking the relevant, probing questions. Usually, you had to look hard for anything that might provide a way into the story. This scene was different. The college scarf, and the small, severed organ of speech stared at him like a once-upon-a-time opening begging to be continued.

After what he considered a decent period of observation and chin-stroking, Garibaldi said his goodbyes to Stevenson, told DS Gardner he'd see her at the team meeting, cast a final eye over the scene, stripped off his protective forensic gear and headed for his bike.

A couple of minutes later he was in Caffè Nero sitting opposite the woman he had been married to for twenty-five years.

8

Sunday 7 April

'We need to talk about Alfie.'

Of course they needed to talk about Alfie. Ever since Kay and her more-money-than-sense partner made the ludicrous decision to send him to a private school for his sixth form, they were always needing to talk about Alfie.

'He's been in a terrible mood these last few weeks,' said Kay.

The last few weeks? Alfie had been in a terrible mood ever since he started at St Snot's. Whenever Garibaldi spoke to his ex-wife, the words 'I told you so' were never far from his lips.

'Anything in particular that might be causing it?'

Or just the usual? Like being taken out of a school where he was happy and doing well and being put into one where he had to start all over again with a bunch of rich kids.

'A couple of things,' said Kay. 'First, I think there might be a girl.'

'A girl?' said Garibaldi. 'Well, that's good, isn't it?'

It had come out wrong, as if he was relieved his son was straight.

'I don't know that it's doing him any good,' said Kay.

'Is she from the school?'

He liked to call it 'the school'. It made it clear that he still regarded it as a bone of contention.

'I don't know for sure, but I think so.'

Garibaldi could already imagine her – a beautiful, poised St Snot's girl capable of breaking his son's heart. He thought of Rachel and resisted the urge to tell his ex-wife about last night.

'And the second thing,' said Kay, 'is that he's rethinking his university plans.'

'What do you mean "rethinking"? He's got those offers!'

Garibaldi had already been planning his trips to Birmingham (firm) or Reading (insurance).

'I know.'

'He can't not go!'

How could he not want to go? How could he not want to get out of his domestic hell (i.e. living with Dominic) as soon as possible?

'It's not that he doesn't want to go,' said Kay.

'What is it, then?'

'He doesn't think his offers are good enough.'

'Not good enough? That's absurd.'

'He says that all the others are off to Durham or Bristol, even Oxford or Cambridge . . .'

The words 'I told you so' flashed in neon across Garibaldi's mind.

'And you're OK with that?'

'All I want is for him to be—'

'No, Kay, please! All you want is for him to be happy? If that's what you want you'd have listened to me and left him at his perfectly good school . . .'

'It's not that simple.'

'Seems simple enough to me. What the hell's got into him?'

'I know you're not comfortable with the whole university thing.'

'What do you mean?'

Kay laughed loudly. 'Come on, Jim. Whenever anyone mentions university I can see you tensing up. I can see you getting ready to deliver the old story. It's like whenever anyone asks you why you became a cop.'

'The old story?'

'You know what I mean.'

Garibaldi gave a slow nod. He knew what she meant.

Some nights, even after all those years, he heard again, in troubled dreams, the knock on the door and the policeman's words, felt again the comforting arms of his big sister around him. Time had passed, but the pain and sense of loss, far from receding, had grown more and more acute, as if it was only with age and maturity that he could begin to comprehend the enormity of what had happened.

'Look, Jim, if Alfie wants to change his plans, he changes his plans. Simple. End of.'

He hated it when she said that. Like she was in some soap.

'You should have listened to me,' he said.

Not quite 'I told you so', but close enough.

'I did listen to you.'

'Didn't act on it, though, did you?'

'I'm not going over all that again. I did it. End—'

'You and Dominic did it.'

'It was an opportunity I couldn't turn down.'

'Yes you could.'

'The money was there, so – look, Jim, why the hell are we going through this again? There's nothing more to say.'

'We're going through it because Alfie has suddenly decided that Birmingham and Reading aren't good enough for someone from St Snot's.'

'It's not called St—'

'Typical of places like that.'

Kay looked at her watch. 'Can you have a word with him at the weekend?'

'Can I have a word? Of course I can have a fucking word! What do you think I'll do?'

'There's no need to swear.'

'There's no need for a lot of things. It doesn't stop them happening.'

Garibaldi wondered whether this would be a good moment to let her know about Rachel. Deciding he couldn't do it without seeming like he was making a point, and uncertain what that point might be, he kept it to himself and did his best to keep his cool for the rest of his time in Caffè Nero.

But every time he looked at Kay he thought of Rachel, and every time he heard Kay speak he saw the severed tongue lying beside the corpse.

9

Monday 8 April

As DCI Deighton briefed the team, Garibaldi tried not to think about Rachel. He'd been thinking about her a lot over the last twenty-four hours, and he would be the first to admit that his mind had not been as fully focused as it should have been on the body by the Thames. By now he would usually be turning the details over in his head, imagining scenarios, constructing narratives, considering approaches and ideas that would pass others by. Thinking outside the box. Thinking beyond the corpse. Or, as the team around him liked to call it, Being a Smartarse.

Instead, he was thinking about Rachel.

'Right, let's get going.'

DCI Deighton, the top slice of the sandwich, stood at the front of the room addressing the team. Beside Garibaldi sat the bottom slice, DS Gardner, and behind them were the DCs assigned to the case that they were already calling the Tongue.

'We have the post-mortem results,' said DCI Deighton.

Was it too early to give Rachel a call? He didn't want to seem too needy, too desperate, but then it wasn't often you slept with a woman like that and still felt good the morning after (OK, it wasn't often, in recent times, that he slept with a woman at all), and he'd never met a woman who'd heard of, let alone liked, Townes Van Zandt.

'And they're not,' said DCI Deighton, 'what we might have been expecting.'

Garibaldi sat up, his mind now back on the case.

DCI Deighton pointed at the picture of the corpse behind her.

'As you can see, multiple stab wounds, scarf shoved in the mouth and next to the head, on the ground, the tongue.'

She picked up a picture – a close-up of the stab wounds – and held it in front of the team.

'Multiple stab wounds and incised wounds of neck, trunk and upper extremities. Stab wounds penetrating right back into chest cavity and right lung. Another stab wound at lateral right chest, with one penetrating into right lung, and multiple wounds of upper extremities. The width, depth and shape of the wounds suggest a single-bladed knife with a serrated edge. Maybe a kitchen knife. The weapon has not yet been found, though search of the area and of the Leg o' Mutton Reservoir continues. As you can see, though, the number of stab wounds suggests that this was a vicious, frenzied attack. But there's no bruising to suggest resistance or defence.'

She held up a second picture. A close-up of the severed tongue.

'Forensics on the tongue have thrown up nothing of significance. The knife that caused the stab wounds is the knife that sliced out the tongue. The saliva is that of the deceased.'

Another picture. The scarf.

'The scarf of Balfour College, Oxford. One of the more

distinguished Oxford colleges, with a worldwide reputation. And this, despite the fact that it produced our current home secretary. The doc reckons the scarf was put into the mouth after the tongue had been cut out. So whose scarf is it? Was it the victim's? Was it the killer's?'

DCI Deighton paused and looked at the room. 'Any questions so far?'

No one spoke.

'Dr Stevenson's conclusion about the cause of death is not the one we might have expected. It looks as though the victim was viciously stabbed to death. But no.' She took a sheet from the file and read. 'Pink lividity evident during the examination. Alkali burns of the gastrointestinal tract. Analysis of stomach contents and blood. All confirm that the cause of death was poison. Cyanide.'

Garibaldi sensed the surprise around him.

'Dr Stevenson,' continued DCI Deighton, 'thought there was something fishy about the corpse when he was at the scene. It was the smell he got when he bent near the face. The smell of almonds. So it seems that whoever this is was poisoned and then stabbed. Which might explain why there are no signs of a struggle or of resistance.'

DCI Deighton pointed at the map of the area pinned to one of the boards behind her.

'The Leg o' Mutton, as you can see, is a little out of the way. So far door-to-doors have produced nothing, and I think they're unlikely to, mainly because there aren't that many doors near the scene.' She turned to point at a detail on the map. 'There is an entrance from Lonsdale Road visible to some of the houses opposite. Someone might have seen something, but it's unlikely. No CCTV anywhere near the crime scene, though there is one at the junction of the High Street and Station Road. Time of death is reckoned to be between six p.m. and nine p.m. on Saturday the sixth of April, the evening of Boat Race Day. Body was found at ten a.m. on Sunday the seventh by a man out for a walk with his family. He's a lawyer. He's given a statement. No reason to suspect he is in any way involved, but he is still part of our enquiries. Any questions on any of that?'

'Boss?'

'Yes?'

Garibaldi turned to DS Gardner. He sensed what was coming – a statement of the obvious or an unhelpful question.

'So we have no idea who he is?'

She had delivered both – a statement of the obvious phrased as an unhelpful question.

'Still no ID,' said DCI Deighton, 'and that's what we all need to get going on. Who is he? The story should run in the *Standard* tonight and the nationals tomorrow, so let's see what that coughs up. And I have no doubt it will be on TV. They'll love it, of course. Boat Race murder. Oxford scarf. Severed tongue. They'll have a bloody field day.'

'And this tongue,' said DS Gardner, 'what are we supposed to make of it? Did he say the wrong thing?'

DS Gardner was on fire.

'The cutting of the tongue,' said DCI Deighton, 'is in many cultures a religious punishment for speaking an insult. Sharia Law, for example. Militant Muslims have used it as punishment for speaking out against Islam. Not that this is necessarily linked to militant Muslims. But it may well be a symbolic gesture. Who it's intended for, we, of course, have no idea. And the same's true of the scarf. Is that a message? If so, what's it saying and who's it for?'

DCI Deighton paused and looked at the team. 'Any more questions?'

Garibaldi raised his hand. 'Why would anyone poison *and*

stab? If the poison's done the job, and cyanide does its job pretty effectively, why bother with the stabbing?'

'Yeah,' said DCI Deighton, 'good question. We need to think about that.' She nodded her appreciation at Garibaldi, but he could sense her irritation at not having raised the question herself. 'Right,' she said, 'Let's get out there, then.'

Garibaldi got up from his chair, thinking about university and Alfie and what it is to be clever and know things.

And that brought him back to Rachel and Townes Van Zandt. He had to give her a call.

Back at the flat Garibaldi poured himself a whisky and put on John Prine.

His fiftieth birthday loomed – a significant milestone for anyone, but he sensed he was approaching it with more dread than most, weighing up his life's gains and losses in a dispiriting mental audit, as if it marked his final reckoning. And speaking to Kay yesterday had led him, as it always did, to reflect on regrets and might-have-beens.

Would everything be easier if his parents' Irish-Italian Catholicism had stuck, if he had not already started to reject it when he lost them? He had no way of knowing, but he liked to console himself with the thought that at least his parents didn't live to see him never set foot in a church again or witness the way his life had been so spectacularly derailed.

He poured himself another whisky, turned up John Prine and brought up Rachel's number on his phone. As he did, it rang.

'Hi Dad, it's Alfie.'

'Alfie? All OK?'

'Yeah, just thought I'd give you a call.'

'Good. Glad you did.' He turned down the music.

'You've spoken to Mum?'

'Yeah.'

'Did she tell you about my uni plans?'

'She did mention them.'

Alfie laughed. 'Yeah, well, the thing is I don't really know what to do.'

Garibaldi sighed. 'We can talk about it at the weekend, Alfie.'

'I know we can, but I was just wondering if I could see you before. There are things ...'

'This isn't just about university is it, Alfie?'

The silence confirmed his suspicion.

'Can I come over one evening, Dad? Like tomorrow?'

Garibaldi flipped through his mental calendar. 'What does your Mum say?'

'She's OK with it.'

He would have to check. He'd been caught out like this before.

'Can you put her on then?'

Kay came on the line and Garibaldi felt the familiar sinking of the heart that came whenever he spoke to her. When he hung up he brought up Rachel's number again and dialled. Tomorrow was out and so were Friday and Saturday, so that left three days when he could see her.

The call went to voicemail. He listened to the automated message and paused after the beep, not knowing whether to leave a message. He left it a couple of seconds, then, realising he was breathing deeply, hung up.

10

Monday 8 April

Boat Race Murder

Police yesterday revealed details of a body found near the Thames the morning after the Oxford and Cambridge Boat Race.

The man's body, which has not yet been identified, was discovered on Sunday morning by a family walking in the Leg o' Mutton Reservoir, a nature reserve between Barnes and Hammersmith beside a stretch of the river that forms part of the famous Putney to Mortlake Boat Race course.

Police were called at approximately 10 a.m. on Sunday morning. Evidence suggests that the man, believed to be in his late forties, was murdered some time the previous evening between 6 p.m. and 9 p.m.

DCI Karen Deighton said the victim had been poisoned and that the body displayed multiple stab wounds. It had also been subjected to mutilation – its tongue had been cut out and an Oxford college scarf shoved in its mouth.

'It is a peculiarly savage murder, and we are currently mounting a thorough investigation. Thousands and thousands were in Barnes and its vicinity yesterday and we would ask anyone who saw anything or has any information which may be relevant to contact us on 020 8878 9472. Your information could be vital in helping us understand why this tragic event happened.'

The discovery of the body on the day after the Boat Race, together with the scarf in the mouth, has led to speculation that there is some connection between the murder and the event. DCI Deighton refused to acknowledge any link. 'We are keeping an open mind and exploring all avenues. That it occurred on the day of one of the nation's most popular sporting events and close to its route and that a college scarf was found in the dead man's mouth may or may not be of relevance.'

'My God!'

Julia Forrest held the newspaper towards her husband. 'There's been a murder in Barnes!'

'Sorry?' Phil Forrest looked at her as if he had misheard.

'A murder. They've found a body by the river! In Barnes!'

Phil reached for the paper and started to read.

'In Barnes!' said Julia, again, as though the location of the crime were more shocking than the crime itself. Barnes – regular winner not only of Gardens in Bloom but of London Area With the Lowest Crime Rate.

'I don't believe it!' said Julia.

'A scarf in its mouth and a severed tongue,' said Phil. 'Blimey."

Julia's mobile rang.

'Hello?'

'Hi Julia. Melissa.'

'Melissa. How are you?'

'I'm fine. Well when I say fine ... actually, I'm shocked. It's my day off so I've only just found out. Have you seen the paper?'

'I've just read it.'

'I don't believe it. Just round the corner! And on Boat Race Day!'

'It sounds absolutely horrible. The tongue ...'

'And the scarf!'

'Like something tribal, ritualistic.'

Melissa sighed. 'I've always had my doubts about the Leg o' Mutton. A lovely place with the lake and the birds and everything, but also ...'

'I know. Nice and secluded, but popular with the druggies. Or at least that's what Helena says.'

Julia sensed Melissa's discomfort. Helena had also said that Melissa's daughter was often found there with the druggies.

'Not the kind of place to go to alone, and especially not at night,' said Melissa.

'Exactly. Now this ... I don't believe it. And they haven't identified the body.'

There was a pause. 'Melissa?'

'Sorry. I was thinking. Look, Julia, can I take you up on that coffee?'

'Sure. When's a good time?'

'I was thinking now.'

'Now?'

Julia held her phone at arm's length and looked at it, as if it had acted in a strange way.

'OK,' said Julia, 'I'm free. Where's a good place?'

'How about the Italian opposite the Olympic? In half an hour?'

'Arte Chef in half an hour? OK.'

Julia hung up and walked back into the living room. 'That was Melissa.'

'Talking about the murder?' Phil did not look up from his iPad.

'Yes. Pretty shocked.'

'Her and the rest of Barnes,' said Phil. 'I can already hear the chorus of parents telling their kids they were right all along about the Leg o' Mutton.'

'Melissa wants to see me for a coffee.'

The news was surprising enough to make Phil lift his head and look at his wife rather than the screen. 'The great Melissa Matthews has called *you* to ask you for a coffee? Almost as spectacular a piece of news as the body by the Thames.'

Julia spent the next twenty minutes touching up her make-up and trying on three or four outfits. Meeting Melissa was never a straightforward affair, and meeting her casually and at short notice posed the most difficult problem – needing to look good but also looking as if you have casually strolled out of the house without giving your appearance a second thought. She knew Melissa would look fantastic – she always did – but she also knew she worked hard at it. Tennis, the Riverside Health Club, personal trainers, a rigorous diet. They all played their part in making her look unbelievable for a woman about to hit fifty. And all of this very important for someone so much in the public eye, a woman whom people noticed in the street – another reason why Julia needed to look good when she was with her.

They had always looked different. Melissa was tall while Julia was short. Melissa was blonde while Julia was dark. And Melissa had always been thin while Julia had only sometimes been. She had always been aware of these differences, but as she neared fifty she found herself dwelling on them more and more. Fifty. Julia was not enjoying what came with its approach – not only the fading of the looks but also the compulsion, now that more years were behind than in front, to look back on what you've achieved. Yes, she knew there were important things in life that could not be calibrated, significant spiritual and emotional qualities that should be valued more highly than anything else, but she also knew that, despite their Oxford education and apparent intelligence, they still tended to address the question of how well anyone had done in purely material terms.

She and Phil had done well. Her work as a lawyer and his as a sports journalist had left them, by most people's definition, very well off. To live in a huge Barnes house, to send your kids to prestigious London private schools (OK, Helena hadn't made it to St Mark's but, ha, she had an Oxford offer) was only achievable by those who had done well.

Julia knew this, but every time she sat down opposite Melissa, as she did now in Arte Chef, wearing the fifth casual just-rushed-out-of-the-house-when-I-got-your-call outfit, she ended up feeling inferior.

When Melissa had married Greg Matthews no one knew then the extent to which she had landed very much on her feet. No one could have predicted that he would become a literary (Julia used the word loosely) phenomenon, writing his first thriller while still working as a BBC journalist and, after its extraordinary success, giving up his job to write full time and penning a new book every two years. Sales were phenomenal, and after several big-money Hollywood deals the Matthews were rich beyond anyone's imagination – not City hedge-fund rich, but rich enough to make Julia feel depressed every time she indulged in midlife stocktaking.

Nor could anyone have predicted that Melissa herself would

achieve such meteoric success. Julia was never clear about exactly how it had come about, how her friend had moved from being a behind-the-scenes researcher to a front-of-camera star, but it was difficult not to think (or difficult for Julia not to think) that her rise to fame had been the result of her looks rather than her talent. It was hard now to remember a time when Melissa had not been famous. Of course, not everything had been easy for her – Lauren's time in the Priory must have been hell in ways Julia could not begin to imagine and she respected the way Melissa had got through it, giving the impression that it was no more than a minor ruffling of the polished surface of the successful Matthews world. Sometimes Julia wondered at what cost – if not to herself, then to her daughter.

The Melissa that Julia was looking at now was a million miles from the poised success story. Nervously fiddling with the napkin, darting anxious sideways looks around the café, she looked like the uncertain, self-conscious eighteen-year-old Julia had met thirty years before on their first day at Balfour.

'I'm so glad you could come,' said Melissa. 'I just wanted to have a chat.'

'Glad you called,' said Julia. 'Spontaneous invitations are the best, aren't they? It's always good to be surprised.'

Melissa gave a nervous laugh. 'I hope it wasn't too much of a surprise, and I hope I haven't dragged you away from anything important.'

'Not at all. An evening with Phil on his iPad, Ellie and Felix being difficult, and me watching Netflix.'

'Do you think it went well?'

'What went well?'

'The quiz.'

'Oh, the quiz! Of course. It was brilliant, Melissa.'

'And the final round?'

Julia looked closely at Melissa's face, searching for clues that might reveal what lay behind the question.

'Very funny,' said Julia. 'And what was so clever about it was that any of them could possibly have been true.'

'Really?' said Melissa.

'Yes, really,' said Julia. 'Remember the shop in the Covered Market?'

'Of course I do, but it was a one-off, Julia. I can't believe you've done anything like that since, and even that wasn't strictly speaking shoplifting.'

'Wasn't it?'

'It was lying on the floor.'

'But even so, that's why the allegation was so clever. You know, and I know, that it *could* be true. It's not so absurd that it can be dismissed easily. The same with Chris and the sex tape. I mean, we all know about Chris.'

'A long time ago, though,' said Melissa, 'and even then there was an element of speculation. It was Nick who spread the story, remember?'

'And then there's Greg's plagiarism.'

Melissa laughed. 'Obviously nonsense!'

'But plausible and also, conveniently, difficult to prove. And as for Fay's bribery . . .'

Julia let the sentence trail off, sensing Melissa's reluctance to be drawn into discussion of their daughters' schools. She was ashamed at how much she was enjoying her friend's momentary discomfort.

'Which leaves,' said Melissa, moving the conversation on quickly, 'my love child!'

'I can only speculate about that,' said Julia, 'as it's from a time before we knew each other. But these things happen and I know you come from a Catholic family, so . . .'

'Exactly. And now you're going to say you wouldn't put it past Nick Bellamy to kill someone.'

'Well, we all know about his temper, his fights. Not beyond the bounds of possibility, is it? That's why it's all so clever.' Julia took a sip of her coffee.

'Have you spoken to the others about it?' said Melissa.

'Fay and Chris. I couldn't get through to Nick.'

'I tried Nick as well. So Fay and Chris – what did they make of it all?'

'They thought it was funny too. A good way to mark the occasion.'

Melissa took a couple of deep breaths and tightened her lips. She looked as if she was about to say something, but stopped herself,

Julia leaned forward. 'Is everything OK, Melissa?'

Melissa shook herself and straightened in her seat. The vulnerability had gone and, with it, the sense that she was about to tell Julia something important, that she had wanted to do more than catch up and talk about the quiz.

The more Julia thought about it, the more she was convinced that Melissa was keeping something from her.

11

Tuesday 9 April

Garibaldi looked at the photos spread out on his desk. A scarf. A tongue. A body. And not a clue who it was.

He was thinking about Rachel, wondering why he hadn't got round to giving her a call. What was stopping him? Nerves? The fear of refusal (despite the fact that she had said she wanted to see him again)? Or was it something deeper, like him not, maybe, being ready for this kind of thing at all?

Not for the first time since the case opened, Garibaldi's mind was not fully on the job. They were getting nowhere. House-to-houses and interviews had so far delivered nothing, and there had, as yet, been no response to the news coverage. Nothing had helped with identification, and crime-scene forensics had not come up with anything of significance. The weapon had yet to be found, and he was still waiting for something from the CCTV footage. He still had no idea why the victim had been poisoned as well as brutally stabbed, and he was baffled by the scarf and the tongue. It seemed more than a murder – it was a message as well. And it seemed specifically linked to Boat Race Day.

'Boss?'

Garibaldi turned. DS Gardner was standing behind his desk.

'Missing person,' she said. 'We've just had a report that matches.'

'Who from?'

'A woman who says she was due to meet her brother yesterday and he didn't show. She's not heard from him for the last seven days and he didn't get in touch to say he couldn't make the meeting.'

DS Gardner held out a sheet of paper. Garibaldi took it and scanned the details. 'Liz Steele.'

'Lives in Hammersmith. Reported it there. From her description it could be the one.'

Garibaldi sighed with relief. Maybe this was the break they needed. 'Let's bring her in.'

Liz Steele looked as if she hadn't slept for days. Her eyes were dark and hollow, her face gaunt, and she kept wringing her hands as if she were trying to wash something off them.

'When did you last see him?' said Garibaldi.

'About two weeks ago.'

'And when did you last hear from him?'

'We spoke about a week ago, mainly to fix up a date to meet. I try to keep in touch, to keep an eye on him.'

'And when were you expecting to see him?'

'Yesterday. We were going to go out for a meal. I'm used to him changing his plans at the last minute or not showing up, but he'd always let me know. I left it a couple of days, thinking he'd get in touch, but when there was nothing after a week I thought I'd better report it, in case . . .'

'You did the right thing,' said Garibaldi.

71

'I kept ringing his phone, but no answer, nothing.'

'Do you have his number?'

Liz handed over a sheet of paper.

'And do you have a recent photo of him?'

Liz reached into her bag, pulled out several photos and handed them over.

Garibaldi looked at them and recognised him immediately.

'Mrs Steele,' said Garibaldi, 'I'm afraid I may have some bad news.'

Liz Steele took it as well as could be expected. She had feared as much. Her brother had been unpredictable his whole life, but this was the first time he had not shown up without letting her know, and she knew it meant that something terrible had happened.

After tea and consolation, Garibaldi went with her to the mortuary.

Liz nodded slowly when the face was revealed. She had been briefed by Garibaldi over what to expect but he knew that nothing could prepare you for the horror of the unveiling, the stark confirmation in a distended, pallid face that your beloved has not only died, but has been taken away in the most savage of circumstances.

Garibaldi fixed up a time to talk further to Liz about her dead brother and left her in the hands of the family liaison officer.

When Garibaldi got back to the flat, Alfie was already there, lying on the couch, remote in hand, watching *The Simpsons*. Garibaldi knew he should be pleased to see him. He should be looking forward to an evening listening to his son unload his problems and relishing the chance to treat him to gems of paternal wisdom. But the truth was that ever since the split with Kay part of him had come to enjoy being alone. At first the thought of being by himself had terrified him, but as the weeks had passed he had been surprised by the way solitude and quiet, far from unnerving him, had provided some kind of comfort.

'Good day?' said Alfie, a parody of the dutiful wife.

Should he tell Alfie what his day had really been like, what it had been like taking Liz Steele to the mortuary to identify the body of her dead brother? Should he tell Alfie what it was like to spend your waking hours, and not just those spent in the office, mulling over the details of murder, wracking your brain to find a way into something that at first seems insoluble?

Should he tell him how much he enjoyed it?

'It was OK. How about yours?'

Alfie shrugged. 'I don't know what to do.'

'About what?'

'Everything.'

They were into it straight away. Garibaldi had hoped the heavy stuff might wait until after a takeaway and a couple of whiskies.

Alfie flicked through the channels and stopped when he found football highlights.

Garibaldi pointed at the screen. 'And so another QPR season splutters to an indifferent mid-table finish.'

'You know what? Maybe we should stop going. I don't see the point.'

This was serious. Being uncertain about university was one thing, but having doubts about whether or not to go to every Loftus Road home game was another thing entirely. Garibaldi knew it was all his fault. He could have taken him along to Chelsea or Fulham, or even hopped on the Tube to Arsenal and exposed his son to the joys that come with supporting a team that wins, more often than not, and occasionally lifts trophies. But some things are unquestionable. His own father had taken him, and so he was taking Alfie.

He smiled as he remembered the line from Larkin – 'man hands on misery to man'. That's what he had done – handed on the misery of being a QPR season-ticket holder to his son. And he didn't regret it one bit. Those times he sat with his own dad were some of his most treasured memories. Maybe, in years to come, Alfie would feel the same.

Garibaldi sat down, kicked off his shoes, pulled over a stool and put his feet up. 'You don't see the point of it, eh?'

Alfie made a noise somewhere between a grunt and a snort.

Garibaldi kept his eyes on the TV. Words came much easier when it seemed you were doing something other than having a conversation.

'I know what it's like,' said Garibaldi. It was a high-risk strategy – a parent saying they knew what it was like to be seventeen, mainly on the basis that at some time in the past they had been seventeen themselves – but he felt brave enough to try it.

'Really?'

'Yeah. Really. When—'

'Dad, please!'

'Please what?'

'Not the "when I was seventeen" number. I know all that. I know what happened to you and how tough it was. This isn't about you – it's about me.'

He had got what he expected. 'OK. So why don't you tell me what's going on?'

Garibaldi listened as Alfie unloaded. Much as he liked to think that his son's current state of mind resulted from the move of school, he knew, deep down, that the greater blame lay in the events of two years ago. He also knew that nothing he could say or do would make them any easier to handle.

'I've rethought a few things recently,' said Alfie.

'Recently?'

'Yeah, since I've . . .'

'Since you started at the school?'

'No. More recent than that. I'm seeing things a bit differently. And, you know, Birmingham, Reading . . . Maybe I could do better?'

Garibaldi took a couple of breaths. 'What's made you think this?'

'All these kids at school, they have this sense of, I don't know, the world being theirs for the taking, of needing to aim as high as you can, and there've been some comments . . .'

'Comments?' Garibaldi couldn't stop himself. 'What kind of comments?'

'Nothing specific, just this kind of expectation. Like, I've got this friend.'

This friend? Was this the girl Kay had mentioned?

'And she's, like, going to Oxford, and I sort of feel . . . as if . . .'

'Has this friend said anything?'

'No. She . . .'

A girlfriend then. Alfie's effort to hide it had been half-hearted, as if he wanted Garibaldi to know but didn't want to tell him directly.

'I just get the impression that people think I could do better.'

'So you're thinking Birmingham isn't good enough? There's nothing wrong with Birmingham. Or Reading, come to that.'

'I'm thinking maybe I should take a gap year.'

A gap year. Garibaldi's stomach heaved. If anything epitomised the kind of crap Alfie had been exposed to since moving to St Snot's, it was the very notion of a gap year. Rich kids 'travelling', going to the furthest reaches of the world and treating it as some kind of emotional playground intended to further their 'development'. And, while there, meeting other rich kids from schools like theirs who have gone there to do exactly the same.

'And what would you do on your "gap year"?' Garibaldi's pronunciation made the quotation marks clear.

'I don't know. I'd find something.'

'And if you took this year out,' said Garibaldi, avoiding repetition of the offensive phrase, 'what would you do about your offers?'

'I'd scrap them and apply again. Or maybe I wouldn't go to uni at all . . .'

Alfie's eyes stayed fixed on the football highlights. Garibaldi looked at him, and, not for the first time, saw himself.

'OK,' said Garibaldi. 'Here's my last word on the subject. Hold on to your offers and wait for your results. You can always pull out then if you want, but give yourself that time to think about it. And if the results are really good – better than you're predicted, better than what Birmingham have asked for by a long way, then maybe you might want to think about going round again, consider aiming higher. Yeah, who knows? Oxford, Cambridge, whatever. But please don't do anything until then. And remember – there's nothing wrong with Birmingham. Or Reading.'

Alfie said nothing – no nod, no grunt – and Garibaldi wondered whether his words were as powerful as those of his girlfriend, whether his influence as a father could ever match the influence of a teenage love.

'And now,' said Garibaldi, picking up a pile of takeaway menus from the table and standing up. 'What do you fancy?'

He chucked the menus onto Alfie's stomach. Alfie looked at him, his expression one of puzzlement and confusion, as if the prospect of having to decide between Indian, Chinese, Thai and pizza was as challenging as making a decision about university.

Pizza it was, and when he had ordered, Garibaldi persuaded Alfie that he should watch *The Sopranos* with him. It was years since he had seen it himself and it was time to revisit.

'Look on it as part of your education,' he said, as he prepared himself for Tony and the ducks. 'Your real education, that is.'

When Garibaldi went to the door fifteen minutes later he was surprised to find that it was not the pizza delivery.

It was Rachel.

Garibaldi's mouth fell open.

Rachel smiled. 'Have I caught you at a bad time?'

Garibaldi sensed he was blushing. 'Er ... no. Not at all. Great to see you.'

'I was waiting for you to call and was going to call myself, then I realised I was in the area, so, what the hell, let's see if you're in. And you are.'

Over Rachel's shoulder Garibaldi could see the delivery man coming up the stairs.

'We're having pizza,' he said, a schoolboy again, fumbling awkwardly. 'My son ...'

'So it is a bad time, then?' said Rachel. 'I knew I shouldn't have—' She stood to one side to let the delivery man through. Garibaldi reached out for the pizzas with one hand and handed over the cash with his other, all the while looking at Rachel, a woman who liked Townes van Zandt and whose eyes sparkled in a way that made it impossible not to invite her in.

'Why don't you join us?'

'I've eaten,' said Rachel, 'but I could murder a drink.'

Garibaldi stood back and ushered her in. Closing the door behind him, he led her into the living room.

'This is Rachel,' he said to Alfie. 'Rachel, this is Alfie, my son.'

Rachel gave Alfie a big smile and a cheery hello. Alfie may have taken his eyes off the screen to greet her, but if he did, the movement was so quick that Garibaldi missed it.

'I'll get some plates,' he said as he headed into the kitchen.

All he could hear from the kitchen was *The Sopranos*. Rachel and Alfie seemed to be saying nothing to each other, and when he carried in the plates he realised why.

Alfie had gone.

'I'm so sorry,' said Rachel. 'I really shouldn't have come, should I?'

'Did he say anything?' said Garibaldi.

'Nothing. He just looked at me, picked up his bag and his jacket and left.'

Garibaldi went to the window. He looked out and saw Alfie walking away. He threw open the window and called out, 'Alfie! Alfie!'

Alfie didn't turn. Garibaldi called again, but his son was now out of sight.

'Sorry about that,' he said, closing the window and turning to Rachel. 'He's going through a rough patch.'

'It's all my fault,' said Rachel, 'I'm sorry.'

Garibaldi looked at the pizzas. 'Sure you're not hungry?' he said.

'I might be able to squeeze something in.'

He tried to get through to Alfie but with no luck, and although he knew he should ring Kay to check he had got home safely he couldn't bring himself to do it, couldn't face the prospect of having to explain.

So he sought comfort and solace in Rachel. She seemed happy to provide it.

12

Boat Race Body Identified

The murder victim found in Barnes the morning after
Boat Race Day has been identified as Nick Bellamy, 49,
of Hammersmith.

The body was discovered in the Leg o' Mutton Reservoir
next to a stretch of the Boat Race course between Putney
and Mortlake. It had suffered multiple stab wounds and, in
a macabre and shocking twist, its tongue had been cut out
and an Oxford college scarf stuffed in its mouth.

DCI Karen Deighton said, 'This is a savage and disturbing murder. We ask anyone who may have seen
anything suspicious in the area on the evening of the
Boat Race or anyone who has any information which
may be of relevance to contact the police on 0208878
9472. We have no evidence that the murder is in any
way connected to the Boat Race itself and are pursuing
several lines of inquiry.'

The severing of the tongue is in many cultures torture or punishment for something the victim has said. DCI Deighton said they had no evidence as yet of anything Bellamy may have said to provoke such a horrific murder, and again urged the public to come forward if they had any relevant information.

A source revealed that the college scarf was that of Balfour College, the alma mater of several prime ministers and the current home secretary, and the college that Bellamy himself attended between 1988 and 1991.

The murder has shocked the affluent, leafy area of Barnes. 'The Boat Race is about as exciting as it gets round here,' said one local resident, 'but now we've had a murder. I can't remember anything like this happening before.'

The Leg o' Mutton is a nature reserve, built many years ago on the site of a reservoir. Recently eclipsed by the more prominent Wetland Centre, it remains a favourite with locals, though its secluded location has also made it a favourite for other activities. 'I warn my kids against going there,' said another resident. 'Full of druggies.'

The Boat Race commands a huge global audience and attracts hundreds of thousands of spectators to the banks of the Thames each year.

Fay Wetherby flicked through the *Evening Standard* when it landed on her desk each afternoon. She liked to check for references to the school (there had been several in recent years, not all of them complimentary, and she had sometimes been the last to discover them). She also liked to check for any gossip about parents. Given the high-profile nature of much of the St Mark's parental body, this was always a possibility.

Today, though, it was something else that caused her to choke on her coffee, spluttering sprays onto the pile of papers in front of her.

Nick Bellamy.

Only a couple of weeks ago she had seen him at the quiz. And now he was gone. Not only gone, but dispatched in such a horrible way. The tongue. The scarf. The scarf she had herself worn all those years ago.

Fay started to shake. She looked at the coffee-stained papers in front of her. On top of the pile was her speech to the parents of the next round of university applicants. Could she address them in this state? Her mind spun with possibilities. Should she contact the police and tell them she knew Nick, or could she leave that to one of the others?

Maybe it would be wise to keep out of it for the time being. She took herself back to that night at the Ocean Bar and saw Nick swaying at his table, coming up to accept congratulations as captain of the winning team. She heard again that final round, Melissa's sad attempt at a joke, and heard again the allegations. Nick Bellamy had once killed a man. So maybe it was true? Live by the sword, die by the sword.

She wiped the papers with a tissue and breathed deeply to calm herself. The police were bound to find out everything now the events at the quiz and the content of the final round were known. She may have heard nothing over the previous weeks about that accusation, but that didn't mean people weren't talking about it, and Nick's murder meant the chances of the allegation coming under close scrutiny were now increased. Unless, of course, it put the focus onto the allegation about Nick and diverted attention away from the others. Nick Bellamy had killed a man. She heard the words again, now imbued with a sinister significance. Yes, maybe that's where the police would focus their attention. It was a slim hope, but she clung on to it. If she kept her head down and kept quiet, it might all blow over.

Fay picked up her papers, checked herself in the mirror and headed off yet again to address the ambitious parents of overachieving children. She knew they would find out soon enough about her connection to the body by the Thames. Tongues would wag, or continue to wag, heads would nod around London's fashionable dinner tables, and she would need to tread carefully. Treading carefully was something she had learned to do well in her years as St Mark's head but, given what might come her way in the wake of Nick's murder, she might now need to do it more carefully than usual.

She closed the office door behind her, unable to shift the image of her old college scarf stuffed into her dead friend's mouth.

'Julia? It's Melissa.'

'Hi.'

'Have you heard?'

'Heard what?'

Julia waited for Melissa to speak. 'Melissa?'

Still nothing.

'Melissa?'

'It's . . .'

Melissa broke off and Julia heard a sudden intake of breath followed by a sob.

'Are you OK, Melissa?'

Julia heard deep breaths, then Melissa's voice again. 'I have some bad news.' Her voice shook with emotion.

'What is it Melissa? What's happened?'

'It's Nick.'

'Nick? What's happened?'

'He's dead. Murdered. That body by the Thames, it's him.'

'What?'

'It's in the *Standard*. And it's been on the news. Thank God I didn't have to read it. I don't think I could have.'

Julia looked at her copy of the paper. It lay on the table unread. She picked it up and started to flick through.

'Have you got a copy?' said Melissa.

'Yes,' said Julia, her eyes resting on 'Boat Race Body Identified' and dancing down the page.

'Read it,' said Melissa.

Julia scanned the words, conscious of Melissa's suppressed sobs at the other end of the line. 'I don't know what to say,' she said when she reached the end of the article. 'It's incredible. I never thought—'

'Why would anyone do that?' said Melissa. 'Why Nick?'

'He was at the quiz. We all saw him.'

'What do we do?' said Melissa.

'What do you mean?'

'I can't take it in. I can't work out what to do. I mean – don't we need to tell the police? They want information.'

Nick Bellamy once killed a man.

Julia remembered the voice coming through the PA. She saw again the look of panic on Melissa's and Greg's faces as they passed it off as their joke and she recalled everyone's reactions to that final round, each individual doing their best to make light of the accusation levelled at them.

Nick Bellamy once killed a man.

And now this.

'And the scarf!' said Melissa. 'The Balfour scarf! Why?'

'We have to tell them.'

'You're right,' said Melissa. 'The police. We have to tell them. I'll call them now. Talk later.'

Melissa hung up, and Julia sat down at the kitchen table to read the article again.

Melissa switched off her phone and turned to Greg. 'What the fuck do we do?'

Greg sat at the kitchen table, stroking the side of his face, something he was in the habit of doing when he was pondering a particularly tricky plot problem.

'We have to tell the police,' said Greg. 'It would look odd if we didn't.'

'But—'

'We know him and we saw him a few weeks ago. We're connected.'

'But if we see the police,' said Melissa, 'we'll have to tell them everything.'

'What do you mean "everything"?'

'The quiz. That final round. Remember what it said about Nick?'

'Hardly likely to forget, am I?'

'What will the police make of it?'

'We have no option. We have to come forward and tell them everything – otherwise it'll look like we've got something to hide.'

'But we have got something to hide. Or rather there's something we've *been* hiding.'

Greg looked at her thoughtfully, his hand stroking his cheek again. 'You're right. We have to tell them that as well.'

Melissa laughed. 'Really? And then everyone will know, and then what do we do?'

'Melissa, love, listen.' The three conversational tricks that Melissa hated most – using her name, calling her 'love', and telling her to listen. It was a sign that he was rattled. Underneath the cheek-stroking cool, Greg was as scared as she was.

'No, you listen, Greg.' Touché. 'So we tell the police about the quiz, and we tell them we've no idea who pulled that prank, but we've been pretending it was us. Then what happens? They know what was said and they investigate. And what will they investigate? OK, they'll look at Nick and whether he killed a man, but what about the others? You remember them, right? Well, think about it. Think about what's likely to happen when they get going on those.'

Greg got up from the table. 'So what? None of them are true, are they?'

'Aren't they?' said Melissa. 'Are you sure about that?'

'Well, maybe it'll be a good thing. Having the police on the case is a good idea – maybe the only way we'll find out who sabotaged your quiz.'

Melissa picked up the *Standard* and read the article again. 'He had a Balfour scarf shoved in his mouth, for fuck's sake. Where do you think that leaves us all? I'll tell you where – right in the police's lines of enquiry.'

'A lot of people went to Balfour, love.'

'But look at it. The whole thing. It's like one of your bloody novels!'

Greg came towards Melissa and put his hands on her shoulders. 'It's ridiculous,' he said, 'but it's not that ridiculous.'

'And the tongue,' said Melissa. 'You don't think they cut out his tongue because . . .'

'We all know what it means,' said Greg.

'OK,' said Melissa, 'so he said something. Maybe what he said was . . .'

'*He* said something? You think that final round was him?'

'It could be, couldn't it? And if it was . . .'

'And if it was, who would want to kill him?'

'Exactly.'

'And who would want to kill him like that? That's what

I don't get. A Balfour scarf? Who would want to make it all so obvious? Who would want to lead everyone in that direction?'

Melissa sighed. 'What a fucking mess.'

'Come on,' said Greg, lifting her out of the chair. 'We need to call the police.'

Chris was watching *Match of the Day* when Kim came in from work. She threw her bag onto the couch and slumped into the chair in such a way that Chris had no need to ask how her day had been. He pressed pause and went to the kitchen to make a cup of Earl Grey and find a slice of carrot cake.

When he came back to the living room Kim had taken control of the remote and switched to *Coronation Street* on catch-up. Chris knew not to quibble. Kim's re-entry from school was a tricky time and needed to be handled carefully. One wrong move and the bomb would detonate – that's why, whenever possible, he tried to be out when she returned.

Today, though, he had made a point of being in. He had news to deliver.

'Here you are.' He put the tea and cake on the table beside Kim's chair and sat back down. 'I've got something to tell you.'

'Oh yeah?' Kim took a bite of cake and kept her eyes on *Corrie*.

'Remember Nick Bellamy?'

'Of course I do. The wild one. The only one of that lot who isn't completely up himself.'

'He's dead.'

Kim's head turned from the screen. 'What?'

'Murdered.'

'What?' Her cake-filled mouth fell open.

Chris lifted the *Standard* from the table and passed it to Kim. He took the remote from her and switched off the TV as she read it.

'They've all been on the phone. Julia. Melissa. Fay. No one can believe it.'

'Oh my God,' said Kim, still reading, her mouth dropping open again. 'The tongue!'

'Yeah,' said Chris,' 'and a college scarf, *our* college scarf, shoved in his mouth.'

'Who would do that? I mean *why*?'

'And, if you remember, he's the one who once killed a man.'

'Sorry?'

'The quiz. Remember?'

Kim looked at him vacantly, as if she couldn't take anything in. 'What?'

'That joke at the end. The allegation. Maybe it was true. He was always up to no good. Losing his temper, getting into fights.'

Kim looked baffled.

'Everyone's in a real state,' said Chris. 'And we should probably get in touch with the police.'

'The police? Why?'

'Because we know him and because they want information.'

Kim shook her head slowly. 'I don't believe it. Cutting out his tongue? Why? And the scarf!'

'We all wore that scarf.'

'Yeah, tell me about it.'

Chris snatched the paper out of her hands. 'What do you mean, "tell me about it"? This is no time for your—'

'What I mean is, it's a bit fucking weird, isn't it, killing him, cutting out his tongue and shoving a Balfour—'

'He was one of us. Our age. *My* age!'

87

Kim looked round the room as if searching for something sensible to say. 'If you go to the police they'll find out everything.'

'What do you mean?'

'They'll find out he was at the quiz, and they'll find out about that joke at the end. They'll find out about all those accusations.'

'What's the problem? None of them are true.'

'Of course not, but they'll—'

'They'll what?'

'They'll investigate.'

'I've told you. There is no fucking sex tape, all right?'

Chris looked at his wife. She was biting her lip, as if weighing up more than whether or not she believed him. For someone who had hardly known Nick, she looked surprisingly distressed.

'I need your support, Kim. That's all I want, your support. Things have been difficult enough already and now this . . .'

Kim reached for the paper and read the article again. Chris picked up the remote, sat down and flicked the TV back to the football, wondering whether he should do what Melissa had suggested and contact the police, or whether he should wait for them to get in touch with him.

He decided to wait.

13

Thursday 11 April

Garibaldi yawned and rubbed his eyes. It had been a tricky few days since Rachel's surprise visit and Alfie storming off. First of all there had been the worry about Alfie. Should he have checked he was home earlier than he had? That was definitely Kay's view on the matter, and she had made it clear in a painful phone call, one in which she had been unable to disguise her curiosity about Rachel, referring to her as 'some woman' or 'your friend', even on one occasion as 'your lady friend'. Alfie had clearly told her everything. He had learned the trick of playing them off against each other while they were still together, but he could do it to even greater effect now that they lived apart.

'You let him walk out by himself into the night and you didn't even check he had got home safely!'

He had taken the call just after Rachel had left. He was tired from the night's exertions but he was happy – they had spent a lot of time talking, and he was in no doubt that his first impressions had been right. Rachel was one beautiful and clever woman, and hearing his ex-wife's voice screaming down the line only confirmed how lucky he was to have found her.

'Anything could have happened to him!'

'It's not a long way, is it?' said Garibaldi. 'Barnes to Putney's no great distance.'

'It's not the distance! Do you know where he walked late last night? He took a short cut to the bus across Barnes Common. Do you know how dangerous that is?'

Garibaldi knew all about the dangers of Barnes Common. The last murder in Barnes (a long time before the tongue-and-scarf man) had been in that very place.

'Look, he got home, didn't he?'

'Oh, he got home all right, but he was totally traumatised.'

'I still don't know why he left.'

'Maybe you should have called him up and asked him.'

'I did. He wasn't picking up.'

'I'll tell you why he left. He left because someone arrived. He hadn't expected that – he wasn't ready for it.'

'I wasn't ready for it either. It was a complete surprise.'

'Look, Jim, I don't really want to know about your private life.' Garibaldi smiled. Her turn to lie now. 'But when it's affecting Alfie I think I have a right to know. I don't care if you have the kind of life where you frequently get that kind of surprise, but if it's upsetting Alfie then you need to think about it. He came to you midweek because he wanted to talk, because he needed you, and you let him down.'

Kay hadn't said it, but Garibaldi heard the word 'again'.

'I'll make it up to him at the weekend.'

'Make it up? That's you all over. Fuck it up and then promise to make it up. It doesn't work like that, you know.'

'I'm sorry. What more do you want me to say?'

And with that Kay had hung up.

Now, at the station, his actions last night and his

conversation this morning seemed even worse. The passing hours had thrown their horror into sharp relief and Garibaldi yet again found himself wondering why, when he was trained to make the right calls and to consider everything anyone did carefully and logically, he had a habit of doing the exact opposite when it came to his own behaviour.

The only thing that could cheer him up was Rachel. What a night. Guy Clark. John Prine. Steve Earle. Gram Parsons. Emmylou Harris. She loved them all, and she had gone through his CDs picking out her favourites. Whisky. Country music. Rachel.

No wonder he hadn't worried about Alfie as much as he should have. And no wonder he felt so odd this morning.

DS Gardner walked up to his desk. 'We've had a call, boss, about the Boat Race body.'

'Yeah? Who is it?'

'An old friend of Nick Bellamy's. She's on her way in.'

Garibaldi recognised Melissa Matthews immediately and Melissa Matthews could tell that he had. She wore the air of someone who knows that people look at her and who would be disappointed if they didn't. She also had the kind of confidence you would expect from someone who delivered the truth to so many. It was a confidence borne not just of class, but of culture and education – and it irritated Garibaldi enormously.

'Thank you very much for coming in, Mrs Matthews. I understand you're a friend of Nick Bellamy.'

'That's right.'

'Maybe you could tell me how you know him and any-thing else you think might be of relevance.'

'Sure.' Melissa took a breath. 'I've known Nick since we were at Oxford together.'

'When was this?

'We went up to Balfour in 1988 and graduated in 1991.'

Went up? Garibaldi stopped himself asking.

'Then we all moved to London to start our careers, but we'd meet up as a group occasionally.'

'And Nick Bellamy was in this group?'

'I'm getting to that.'

Garibaldi got the impression that Melissa Matthews was used to talking uninterrupted. This may have been something that came with the territory of newsreading, but he sensed that in Melissa Matthews' case it went back further than that.

'There were six of us,' said Melissa. 'Me, my husband Greg, Fay Wetherby, Julia Forrest, Chris Turner. We ended up getting together each year for a quiz night. A bit of fun. Bring a bottle and a game of Trivial Pursuit. I don't know how it happened, but over the years this quiz night grew into something bigger—'

Garibaldi reached for a sheet of paper on his desk and held it up. 'The Ocean Bar Quiz.'

'Exactly. That's what it became. As we – Greg and I – got to know more people – me through TV, Greg through his writing – we extended the invitations, and I had the idea of making it a charity thing.'

'And I see that Nick Bellamy's team won it this year.'

'You're getting ahead.'

Not only was Garibaldi interrupting, he was ruining her chronology.

'Nick came along over the years, but then a few years ago he stopped turning up.'

'And why was that?'

'The rumour was that he had hit hard times. Lost his job. Booze, some say. Drugs maybe. We weren't in touch, so I really don't know, Detective ...'

'Detective Inspector Garibaldi.'

'Garibaldi? As in . . .'

'As in the great Italian nationalist. And the biscuit. So Nick Bellamy turned up this year?'

Melissa nodded. 'He did. Although he was in a bit of a state.'

'What do you mean?'

'He was out of it. All over the place.'

'But good enough to win?'

'I don't know where he got his team from. They all seemed out of it as well – they were making a hell of a noise. But they certainly knew their stuff.'

Garibaldi pointed at the article. 'And I see this was the twenty-fifth.'

'It was.'

'So tell me, Mrs Matthews, do you have any idea who might have wanted to kill Nick Bellamy?'

'None at all. The whole tongue thing makes you think he was killed for something he said. And the scarf.'

'Do you think this murder could be linked to his college friends in any way?'

'You mean, did one of us kill him?'

'I'm not saying that.'

'That's what it sounds like, and I can't believe it for one moment. I mean, if it was one of us, why would we do that with the scarf? If someone commits a murder they don't deliberately leave a big clue like that, do they?'

'Exactly,' said Garibaldi, 'which makes the scarf very puzzling.'

Melissa Matthews turned to one side. Garibaldi looked at her closely. There was a slight quivering of the lip, a telltale furrow of the brow. It was the first sign of her cool cracking. She looked as if she was on the verge of saying something.

'Look, Detective Inspector, there's something I need to tell you.'

Garibaldi leaned forward. Melissa pointed at the article on the desk. 'That article in the *Standard* Diary from a couple of weeks ago mentions something that happened at the end of the quiz.'

Garibaldi picked it up. 'Ah yes, I was going to ask you about that. The final round. Some kind of joke, I see.'

'Yes. Some kind of joke.'

'And a lot of accusations. What were they, exactly?'

'That's not important.'

'I think that's for me to decide, don't you?'

Another flash of irritation hardened Melissa's face. 'The thing is . . .' She trailed off, as if she had changed her mind about telling him. Garibaldi raised his eyebrows, inviting her to continue. 'Look,' said Melissa, 'what happened was a voice came over the restaurant speakers saying that this was a surprise extra round. And then it came out with these supposed facts about each of us – each of the six who had been at the quiz since it began all those years ago, the six of us who were at Balfour together.'

'Can you tell me what they were, Mrs Matthews?'

'I can, but there's something I need to tell you first. When the voice came on everyone was surprised. They had no idea what was happening, but they found it all very funny. Then when it was over I told everyone that it was my joke, my way of marking the twenty-fifth quiz in a humorous way.'

'I see,' said Garibaldi.

'The thing is, though, it wasn't me at all. I didn't have a clue what was happening. I looked at Greg and he had no idea either, but he said I should pretend it was me so that's what I did. I think I got away with it but I could tell there were plenty who had their suspicions.'

94

'So if it wasn't you, who was it?'

'I have no idea.'

'And why would they do it?'

'Again, I have no idea.'

'Can you now tell me what these allegations were?'

'OK. That my husband, Greg Matthews, plagiarised his first novel; that Fay Wetherby, Head of St Mark's Girls' School, took a bribe not to expel a pupil; that Julia Forrest is a serial shoplifter; that Chris Turner has been blackmailed over a sex tape; that I have a secret love child from a teenage pregnancy. And that Nick Bellamy . . .' She paused. 'And that Nick Bellamy once killed a man.'

Garibaldi leaned back in his seat. 'That Nick Bellamy once killed a man?'

Melissa nodded.

'And are any of these true?'

'Not that I know of.'

'Not that you know of?'

'I mean . . . no. Of course not.'

'And you think that Nick Bellamy's murder could in some way be connected to these allegations?'

'I don't know.'

'What if Nick Bellamy was behind it? Would that explain the severed tongue?'

Melissa shook her head. She did not look like the kind of woman who often struggled to find the right words, but she was struggling now.

14

Friday 12 April

Garibaldi sat in the Bush Theatre café cradling a cup of coffee. It was one of his favourite places. He liked its space and quiet, the way it seemed like a library. Books lined the walls, and most of the large tables were occupied by young people tapping away at their laptops. They may have been checking emails and social media, but Garibaldi liked to think they were engaged in serious academic study. It helped him indulge in his favourite daydream, the one where he had left the force and was a mature university student. Sometimes in this dream he was studying Italian or philosophy, but most often he was studying English.

Despite the chalked sign – 'No one admitted wearing football colours' – that appeared outside the entrance every time QPR were at home, he and Alfie had started coming here on match days. When he first saw the sign he had been outraged, seeing the desire to keep out plebeian football supporters as yet another example of the exclusivity of the theatre-going folk. He asked the man behind the bar about

96

it, but his response that it was all to do with licensing failed to convince him – he still found it richly ironic that a theatre keen to 'open its doors to a diverse audience' should want to shut them to a vital (and profitable) section of the community it claimed it was keen to embrace.

So on match days Garibaldi and Alfie shoved their scarves in their jacket pockets and marched confidently into the Bush, pleased to see other Rangers supporters doing exactly the same, exchanging knowing winks as they enjoyed a civilised pint looking out on to the bustle of the Uxbridge Road.

Garibaldi fished a paperback out of his pocket and started to read. He never went anywhere without a book – a habit that made him a figure of fascination and subject to much ridicule at the station. 'What's it now?' was a question often fired at him, and Garibaldi was always happy to oblige. Today it was Graham Greene's *The End of the Affair*. Part of his ongoing project to work his way through the greats.

'Excuse me.'

Garibaldi looked up. 'Mrs Steele? What can I get you?'

'Cappuccino, please.'

Garibaldi put his book away and went to the bar.

'Thanks for coming,' he said when he returned to the table with the coffee, 'and I hope you don't mind me asking you some questions about Nick. I know it must be very painful.'

Liz nodded and took a sip of her coffee. 'That's fine. Whatever I can do to help.'

'I'll get straight to the point,' said Garibaldi. 'Do you have any idea who might have killed your brother?'

'No idea at all. Things were always happening to Nick. Part of his charm, I suppose, but also part of his problem. Whenever you saw him he would more often than not begin by saying, "You'll never guess what's happened," and he was right. You never *were* able to guess what had happened. You always worried that he'd lost his temper again and got into a terrible fight.'

'He had a temper?'

'Always had it. Ever since he was a kid. He was always in fights at school. I never knew what caused it. But as I say, things were always happening to Nick. Sometimes you wondered whether what he was telling you was the truth, but it always made for good entertainment.' She broke off and stared into the distance as if struck by a sudden realisation. 'Strange to think that he'll never call me up or come round to see me and tell me any more of his stories.'

'Are you his only sibling?' said Garibaldi.

'Just me. Big Sis. That's what he called me. Big Sis. We lost our parents some time ago, inspector ...'

'Inspector Garibaldi.'

'It was twenty years ago. Nick was in the City, doing very well for himself, earning a lot of money. That's when Dad went. A heart attack. And then, only two years afterwards, Mum went. Cancer. And I suppose I became more than Big Sis after that.'

'Where did you grow up?'

'Here. London. Hammersmith. You could call it West Kensington if you wanted to sound posh, but it was a Hammersmith council flat. Mum and Dad both came over from Ireland after the war. Dad worked at the Post Office and Mum was a cleaner. I don't know if anyone uses the term working class any more – I don't know if it means anything, but that's what we were. Nick was bright. Top of his class at primary school, and then off to the grammar school. No one has a good word to say for grammar schools now, do they, but they did all right for Nick and me. We did well by them.'

'And from there to Oxford?'

'Yeah. Nick, not me. I went to Leeds. And then into

teaching. I wanted to give something back – which is not something you could ever say about Nick.'

'What do you mean?'

Liz took a sip of her coffee. 'Oxford changed him.'

'What do you mean?'

'When he came back at the end of that first term he was different. He'd obviously mixed with posh people, rich people. He was rubbing shoulders with people from a very different background and it showed. Mum and Dad noticed it but they didn't know what to say. I noticed it but I didn't have the guts to tell him. He didn't *know* that he was acting any different – that's not how it works – but he was definitely behaving differently. He was more interested in money and the right clothes and doing the right thing. Don't get me wrong – he was still our Nick from the flats, he wasn't walking around talking like Little Lord Fauntleroy or anything, but something had happened.'

'And was he like that all the way through Oxford?'

Liz nodded. 'And beyond. He partied hard at Oxford. Did enough to get his law degree but ran up huge debts. He wasn't worried, though. He didn't want a career in law, he wanted to follow the money, and in his last year he landed a job in a bank and he knew that his debts could be cleared. So he left Oxford and worked in the City and he started making money. I don't know how much, but it seemed a lot to me and it wasn't as though he kept it to himself. He was generous with it, especially to Mum and Dad. They were delighted he was doing well but I always thought that, underneath it all, they looked at him and wondered at what he had become. They never said anything about it and then, of course, we lost them. It's never easy losing a parent, is it, but to lose both so close to each other – I'm not sure it's the kind of thing you can ever recover from. Do you understand?'

Garibaldi nodded. She could have no idea how well he understood.

'Anyway, we both had our work and I guess we both threw ourselves into it as a way of coping. And Nick seemed to be OK. I made a point of calling him and seeing him, but I knew he had in many senses drifted away – the process started at Oxford and it just carried on. He kept in touch with all his friends from there and a lot of them went on to be big successes in whatever they were doing. Melissa Matthews, the TV presenter, her husband . . .'

'Greg Matthews the novelist.'

'Exactly.'

'I mean, it's not as though everyone he knew from there was a big success. I'm sure there were loads who went on to do decent, hardworking, low-profile things.'

'Like teaching?'

Liz chuckled. 'Like teaching. But after the loss of our parents I think Nick went even further from what he was . . .'

'Did he marry?'

'Yeah. He slept around a lot, I think, then as the millennium loomed he decided it was time to settle down. He married another banker, but it only lasted a couple of years. I thought it might be just what he needed but it didn't work out – I never really found out why. And then he was back to his old ways. Quite a few women, some long-term, some not, and then when he lost his job his world just . . . folded. Everything he had aimed for, built himself up for just disappeared. It wasn't too much of a problem because at first he managed to find other jobs. But he kept losing them. He was in freefall . . .'

'Where's his ex-wife?'

'She went to America, I think. I'll have to check.'

'And her name?'

'Sophie Wickham.'

'And do you have the names of any other of his women?'

Liz shook her head. 'I can't remember.'

'Do you have any idea why Nick lost his job?'

'He never told me, but I thought or assumed he might have done the usual and got into a fight. Either that or it was alcohol or drugs. Or maybe it was all of them.'

'Alcohol or drugs. Any evidence of that?'

'Nothing specific, but Nick was always the addictive type. He definitely drank. I know that. But I didn't realise how much until he told me that he was trying to get off it, that he was seeking help. As for drugs, I know he smoked the occasional joint and I had my suspicions about cocaine. As for anything else, I have no idea, but over the last few years he didn't have a regular job at all and was keeping some odd company.'

'Odd company? What do you mean?'

'He moved into a flat in Hammersmith, just by the bridge. An ex-council flat. Funny, isn't it? What goes around comes around and all that.'

'In my end is my beginning,' said Garibaldi.

'Exactly.'

'Tell me, what do you know about the Ocean Bar Quiz?'

'I know it's a Melissa Matthews thing and I know Nick goes along.'

'Apparently he hadn't turned up for a few years.'

'Really? I had no idea.'

'But he did go along this year, and this year he won.'

Liz gave a wry smile, as if acknowledging how little this victory now amounted to.

'Do you also know that this year there was a surprise final round of questions in which allegations were made about Melissa and her Oxford chums?'

'Including Nick?'

'Yes. A voice came on the restaurant speakers and gave a fact about each of the six friends and the audience had to guess which one was true. The allegation about Nick was that he had once killed a man.'

Liz's eyes opened wide. 'What?'

'That he'd killed a man. Do you have any reason to believe that it could be true?'

'Well, no. I can't believe it. There were lots of things about Nick that I never knew, but kill a man? OK, he had a temper. OK, he got into trouble every now and then. But kill a man?' Liz shook her head slowly. 'No, I can't believe that.'

Garibaldi finished his coffee. 'Thanks very much, Mrs Steele. That's been very helpful. If anything else occurs to you or if you remember anything you think might be of interest, just give me a call, OK?'

Garibaldi handed her his card.

'I will,' said Liz. 'I can't believe Nick would have killed a man,' she said. 'But then I can't believe that he's been murdered. And in such a savage . . .'

Liz started to sniffle. Garibaldi took out some tissues and handed her one.

'Do you have *any* idea who did it?' said Liz.

'At this moment, no.'

Garibaldi got up from the table and walked with Liz to the door. He left the Bush and headed right, walking beside Shepherd's Bush Green towards the bus stop at the top of the Hammersmith Road. Tubes gave him claustrophobia and he always felt you learned more about London and its people by travelling by bus.

The fact that he was the only detective in the Met who couldn't drive had nothing to do with it.

As he passed the Empire he stopped at the board outside to

see what was coming up. He scanned the acts to see if there was anything he could take Rachel to, but it seemed the good old days of the Empire had gone. He didn't recognise any of the names.

Garibaldi hopped on the 72 and headed back to Hammersmith. From there he walked over the bridge and down onto the towpath, deciding that walking back to Barnes would clear his head and give him time to think.

He still had no clear sense of what Nick Bellamy had been up to, but he was beginning to feel a peculiar affinity with him. He, like Bellamy, was the son of immigrants, an Italian father and an Irish mother. He, like Bellamy, was born in a council flat (Fulham in his case) and he, like Bellamy, was clever enough to get into grammar school (the Catholic London Oratory). He, like Bellamy, had also lost his parents, even if his had been lost much earlier and in a much more dramatic way. And, who was to say that, had things turned out differently, he might not, like Bellamy, also have ended up at Oxford?

As he walked by the Thames, sparkling in the bright spring sunshine, Garibaldi imagined himself in a Balfour scarf. With lines from one of his favourite Larkin poems running through his head (the ones about long perspectives open at each instant of our lives linking us to our losses), he walked westwards towards the Leg o' Mutton Reservoir.

15

Friday 12 April

'You don't seriously think that was true, do you?'

Chris Turner looked at his wife doing her final preparations before leaving for work.

'I don't know what to think,' said Kim. She shoved a file into a bag, slung the bag over her shoulder, and headed for the door.

'It was a joke,' said Chris. 'They were all jokes.'

Things had grown worse between them. They hadn't been in a good state before, but now they were plumbing new depths, and Chris couldn't work out why. An obvious explanation would be that Kim was still angry at the sex-tape allegation, but Chris found this difficult to believe. After all, it wasn't as though this was entirely new territory for them (the specifics might have been different, but the general idea was familiar), so maybe it was the public airing of the private dirty laundry that had upset her so much. But why should it? It was the first – and last – time she would ever go to the Ocean Bar Quiz and she didn't have much time for anyone who was there, so why the fuss? Chris sensed it was something more than this and kept coming back to the idea that it was the news of Nick's murder that had caused the dramatic deterioration between them. But, yet again, why should this matter to her? OK, news of any death is upsetting, and news of a murder particularly so, but it wasn't as though she knew Nick. She had no time for his Oxford friends and Nick, despite his differences, was one of them.

Even Harry, who, for obvious reasons, was never the first to pick up on anyone else's feelings, had noticed Kim's changed mood.

'What's wrong with Mum?' he had said the evening after the *Standard* article.

'Mummy's heard some bad news,' said Chris. 'We all have.'

Harry had then wanted to know all about the bad news and Chris had told him, knowing no detail could be spared in Harry's habitual quest for the literal truth. Chris had ended up telling him everything – the stabs, the tongue, the scarf.

'He doesn't need to know all that,' Kim had said when she came into the living room in the middle of the conversation.

'I think he does,' said Chris, giving Kim the look that said he was the one who spent most of his time at home, ferrying Harry to and from school, the one who saw his needs close up. It was the look that reminded her he was pursuing a freelance journalistic career from home not because it was what he would ideally like to do but because it fitted in well with Harry's needs and her career. It was a look he delivered frequently.

'So what are you going to say to the police?' said Kim.

'About what?'

'They're going to find out about those allegations, aren't they?'

'I guess so.'

'And given that one of them was that Nick Bellamy killed a man they're going to investigate. They'll want to talk to you.'

'I have nothing to hide,' said Chris.

'So you've never done anything like that?'

'What do you mean "anything like that"?'

'You know what I'm talking about.'

Chris knew exactly what she was talking about. 'There's nothing. Honest. There is no tape.'

'You know what?' said Kim, heading for the door. 'I really wish I hadn't gone to that bloody quiz.'

'No one forced you.'

'I should have left you and your Oxford mates to get on with it like you always have.'

Chris said nothing. He couldn't remember the precise moment when what he had always regarded as Kim's admirable social and political commitment had shrivelled into chippy bitterness. Maybe it had always been there and he had simply failed to notice it, or maybe it was something that had grown gradually over the years. When they were young he had been proud of her ideals and values, and he enjoyed being out with her in company, proud to be her partner. He shared her views and looked at the world in the same way – that's why they were together.

When he thought about it coolly and rationally, Chris could see why Kim had no time for his old Oxford friends, coming to the conclusion that he didn't really have much time for them either. That was why, over the last ten years or so, he had limited his contact to the once-a-year quiz. He could quite easily have severed his links entirely, but something kept him participating in this yearly ritual, and he had continued to fork out, with increasing reluctance, the ridiculous money charged by Melissa for one of her tables. Given this year's events, and Kim's surprise attendance, maybe next year would be a good time to knock the whole thing on the head.

'You do believe me, don't you?' said Chris.

Kim, still standing by the door, tilted her head in a way that suggested she was unsure. 'What I don't get is why Melissa would think it a funny or – and this is more worrying – a plausible allegation to make about you. What does she know?'

'Look, we've been through all this. Looking at that stuff – it's normal. Look at the stats. Eighty or ninety per cent of men watch porn.'

'That doesn't make it OK, does it?'

'And you know what?' said Chris. 'Quite a high percentage of men watch porn with their wives! So I don't know what you're being so fucking righteous about.'

He had lost it. He knew from the volume he was speaking at (it was close to a shout) and from the territory he had moved into that his attempt to underplay the whole thing and let it blow over had failed. This was a row. An old row.

'And what percentage of men seem to prefer online sex to real sex?'

'Not that again.'

'Don't pretend it's not a problem.'

'It will sort itself out. It'll pass.'

'I think it passed some time ago, don't you?'

'OK, so what do you want to do about it?'

'You need help.'

'I've already seen someone about the—'

'About the porn? Well, that didn't work, did it? Maybe we need help. Both of us.'

'Look, things are tough at the moment with—'

'With Harry? Things have always been tough with Harry. At least since he was diagnosed we've known there are things we can do about it. I'm just running out of patience, Chris.

Your job isn't the most secure, my job is bloody hard work and not brilliantly paid, and Harry's going to need more help.'

'And we're going to need to pay for it. Is that what you're saying? What happened to your principles?'

'*My* principles? Why don't you have a look at yourself first and then think how it all feels for me. Sometimes I feel like I'm a poor substitute for you. A real-life disappointment. Not as exciting as the screen when it comes to sex and a genuine let-down after your high-flying friends.'

'You're being ridiculous.'

Kim opened the door. 'I'm off.'

'Haven't you forgotten something?'

Kim looked towards the kitchen table to see what she had left behind.

'Kiss?' said Chris.

He walked to Kim and gave her a light peck on the lips, their usual morning farewell. He felt Kim's reluctance and sensed the emptiness of the gesture.

He went back to the table, sat down, and picked up the *Standard* that had lain open at the page about the murder ever since he first read it.

He thought back to that moment in Oxford and didn't know whether to laugh or cry.

He remembered Nick barging through the door and the way news soon spread round college. And he remembered the embarrassment.

The bloke caught fucking the teddy bear.

'Dad!'

Chris turned as Harry came into the kitchen. 'Come on,' he said. 'Time for school.'

16

Melissa thought she would feel better once she had been to the police, but her interview with DI Garibaldi had left her feeling more unsettled. First there was the worry that, having told the police the final round was not her and Greg's doing, she should be telling the others as well. Then there was the feeling that the murder of Nick Bellamy could be linked to what happened at the quiz, and then there was the nagging unease about the allegation that she had a secret child from a teenage love affair. She had been right to insist on its falsity, but she knew only too well why it still made her feel uncomfortable.

The most unsettling thing of all, though, was Nick's death. She may have lost touch with him over recent years, but she remembered what there had been between them, and the loss hurt. They may not have been together long at Oxford – it started and finished in their second year – but there had been something special about it, an intensity she had seldom experienced since. Nick was different. He may have lacked the grace and polish of many of their contemporaries, but his rough edges, far from being unattractive, contributed to his peculiar charm. Everyone liked Nick, and Melissa had felt lucky to have him as her boyfriend for those two Oxford terms.

She had also been right, though, to end it when she discovered his infidelity. As the second year became the third and as they all headed towards finals, Melissa could see that Nick was changing – his edge had started to lose its charm. How right she had been to take up with Greg in that final year. She, like everyone else, had no idea what fame and fortune he was heading for, but there was something reassuring and comforting about Greg's normality after the extremes of Nick Bellamy. Looking back thirty years later, it was impossible not to be pleased to have made the decision to marry him four years after graduating.

And yet she had always been keen to know what Nick had been up to. They had kept in touch when they graduated and moved to London to start their careers – the occasional lunch at first and then sometimes dinner – but Melissa had decided not to tell Greg about them. She knew he would only have been suspicious and, as the years passed, her reasons for keeping the liaisons quiet had not only been entirely vindicated, they had become even more compelling. Now that Nick was gone, those reasons were even stronger. She knew she could never reveal why his death had hit her so hard.

'Penny for them?'

Melissa looked up at Greg. He was watching football with a half-finished *Times* crossword on his lap.

'Sorry,' said Melissa, 'I was miles away.'

'You mustn't dwell on it,' said Greg. 'You've told the police, now let them get on with it.'

'But shouldn't I tell the others as well? They're going to

find out from the police that it wasn't me after all. Wouldn't it be better coming from me?'

Greg looked down at his crossword as if Melissa had just given him a lead on a clue. Melissa reached for her phone. She knew it was time to come clean.

About one thing, at least.

Julia was not surprised when Melissa rang her with the news.

'I had a feeling,' she said. 'It just didn't seem *you* somehow. And although you did brilliantly and convinced everyone it was all your little joke I could tell by looking at you that you weren't comfortable with it. And I could hear it in your voice.'

'I need to tell you, Julia, because I've been into the police to say I knew Nick and I've told them about the quiz. So they know all about that final round and, as it involves all of us, I guess they'll be wanting to talk to you about it as well.'

'So should I go in to see them, then?'

'Up to you. Just thought I'd give you the heads-up.'

'I'm still puzzled, though. If it wasn't you, Melissa, then who was it?'

'I've been wondering whether it could have been Nick.'

'Nick? What makes you think that?'

'It's the kind of thing he'd do.'

'But if it was Nick, why would he make that allegation about himself?'

'That he killed a man? I don't know. The whole thing's so crazy – I can't make sense of it.'

'So do you think, then, that Nick's murder is linked?'

'It could be. That might explain the tongue.'

'But to get back to the police. They know about all the allegations?'

'They do,' said Melissa. 'I had to tell them.'

When Julia hung up she turned to Phil. 'So I was right.

111

That joke wasn't Melissa at all. And she's gone and told the police.'

Phil held his hands out in a gesture of helplessness. 'So let the police get on with it.'

Julia's mind was spinning as she nodded her agreement. She couldn't get Nick Bellamy out of her head. She kept seeing his face again, not as it might have appeared in death, nor as it had appeared during his outrageous performance at the quiz, but as it had been all those years ago at Oxford – youthful, animated, attractive, and never more so than when it had been above her as they made love in the narrow college bed.

She knew it still rankled with Melissa. Despite her success and despite the way her marriage to Greg had catapulted her into the kind of lifestyle she could not have dreamed of all those years ago, Melissa still looked back on that act of betrayal with bitterness. It may have been over thirty years ago, but Julia knew it was why Melissa still found their relationship difficult. Recent events – Helena's Oxford offer and Lauren's failure in particular – might have made things even more strained, but Julia knew that what Melissa had never really recovered from was her discovery all those years ago that, while she was still going out with him, Nick had slept with her friend.

Not once, but several times. And Julia had never admitted to anyone how much she had enjoyed it, how much she had been shocked, and thrilled, by the things he had done.

'I had to tell them everything,' said Melissa.

When Fay heard that Melissa was on the line with 'serious news' she had delayed her meeting with a disgruntled member of staff to take the call. 'So they know all about those allegations, then?'

'They do.'

Fay's fingers started to drum the table, a habit that showed she was anxious and one she had tried to curb over the years. She knew what had triggered it – the thought of the police looking closely at her professional conduct.

'I can't tell you how much of a shock it was to hear that voice come over the speakers,' said Melissa. 'Greg and I had no idea what the hell was going on and then Greg said, "Pretend it's us." It's a long time since I've been on stage, Fay, and—'

'You did very well. No one had any idea you were covering up.'

Fay was lying. Melissa's announcement may have been greeted with laughter, but she could not have been the only one in the room to have had doubts.

'And we have no idea at all who was behind it?'

'No,' said Melissa, 'and we have no evidence that it was in any way linked to Nick's murder.'

'But the tongue,' said Fay, 'and the scarf in the mouth . . .?'

'I know. It connects it to all of us.'

'So you think one of us killed him?'

Melissa laughed. 'Of course not.' She paused. 'The thing is, none of those allegations are true, are they?'

'No. Of course not. And if they're not true, why would anyone kill him for making them? And, come to think of it, what's the point in killing him when he's already spoken?'

'Punishment?' said Melissa. 'Revenge?'

'Or maybe,' said Fay, 'whoever did it was worried he knew more.'

'But we have no evidence that it *was* Nick. And don't forget what was said about him. He had once killed a man. What if that's the allegation that's true? Again, revenge.'

Fay's fingers were tapping again. She thought of Nick Bellamy lying dead by the Leg o' Mutton lake. Every time she thought of his mutilated body, its tongue cut out, she felt his body against hers again, and sensed his tongue probing her own as they made love all those years ago in that college bed. How many times had they done it? How many nights had they spent together in those final days at Oxford? She couldn't remember, but she could still recall the passion and the excitement, the way Nick had made her feel things other men had been unable to, excited her in a way that almost convinced her she preferred men to women. Almost, but not quite.

Chris came off the phone and walked upstairs to the spare bedroom he shared with Kim as a study – he used it during the day, but it was mostly Kim's in the evening.

'Guess who that was on the phone,' he said. 'Melissa.'

'About Nick Bellamy?'

Kim was at the desk marking and in the middle of writing a comment.

'Sort of,' said Chris, 'but it's more about that final round of the quiz. Melissa's just told me it wasn't her at all.'

Kim's hand paused. 'What?'

'Nothing to do with her, apparently.'

Kim kept her head down. Her pen stayed still. 'What do you mean nothing to do with her? She said it was her little joke.'

'Well, she was lying.'

Kim kept her back to Chris.

'Why on earth would she lie?'

'I have no idea.'

The pen in Kim's hand raced across the page. 'I don't know – you and your friends. Murder. Lies. What's next?'

Chris moved closer to the desk. 'It's not something to joke about, is it?'

Kim carried on marking. 'Who said I'm joking?'

'Look at me, Kim.'

Kim turned reluctantly, raised her eyebrows and looked closely at Chris in a way that unsettled him. The pen in her hand suddenly looked like a dangerous weapon.

'This is serious,' said Chris. 'Nick's been murdered and the police are going to pursue the connection between his murder and that quiz. And they are going to be very interested in those allegations.'

'Including the one against you.'

'Which is untrue.'

'Which is, as you say, untrue. So you've got nothing to worry about, have you?'

'I'm worried that they'll think maybe it was one of us who killed him.'

'*You* didn't kill him, did you?'

'Of course I didn't!'

'But you think one of the others did?'

Chris paused for a moment. 'No ... I ...'

'You're not sure, are you?'

'All I'm saying is the police are bound to see a possible connection.'

'And all I'm saying, given that you're innocent of all charges, is why don't you let me get on with marking – and I'm sure Harry's got some homework you could help him with.'

Kim turned back to her work.

'You're missing the point,' said Chris. 'The police will ask questions, they'll probe. And what if Nick *is* responsible for that final round?'

He was suffering. He had not been sleeping well, waking in the middle of the night with images of Nick and the Ocean Bar dancing through his head, and during the days he had

115

been too tired and distracted to settle to his work. His mind kept returning to that allegation.

Kim wasn't helping. She had already turned her back. Chris looked at it, his lips tightening in an angry frown. His wife's reaction to what he had just told her – his revelation that someone else had come up with those questions – had been strange. She wouldn't discuss it, let alone offer Chris any sympathy and support. There was something about her manner that left him feeling there were things she was choosing not to say, thoughts she was keeping to herself. And he had a strong sense that they were not good ones.

Greg Matthews had never expected to be so successful. His time at Oxford had not marked him out as one destined for future fame and fortune. He had got on with his work, dabbled in drama and journalism (never starring in any plays or editing any of the prestigious publications), and dipped a half-hearted toe into the Union and student politics, but had never thrown himself about with the energetic and unreflective commitment to self-promotion and ego-boosting that was the mark of those on their way to being their generation's future household names.

By the time he left Oxford, though, Greg had set himself up nicely. In his final year he had not only managed to secure a traineeship at the BBC, he had also started going out with Melissa Barker. Melissa had managed to land a job in television (unlike Greg, she *had* starred in plays and she *had* edited the university newspaper) and the two of them headed to London to start their post-university life. Unlike many university relationships that withered once they had moved from the cloistered collegiate quads to the rough-and-tumble streets of the real world, Melissa and Greg's survived. The two moved in to a flat in Clapham and, four years after graduating, married.

Greg had started writing a year after he began at the BBC, squeezing in a couple of hours both early in the morning before he went to work and late at night after Melissa had gone to bed. He told Melissa he was writing a novel, but kept to himself what it was about, only revealing this once he had completed a first draft and passed it to her for her comments. A couple of months later he had something he was happy with and he asked colleagues at the BBC for advice about where to send it. This threw up a few literary-agent contacts and he sent his manuscript off to them, expecting to meet with either silence or disappointment. Nothing prepared him for the speed of response from one of them. Soon he had been signed up, and after a round of further edits and revisions, his work was being sent to publishers.

What If . . . was a spectacular success. 'A literate thriller in the le Carré mould,' said *the Times*. 'The emergence of a bright new talent,' said the *Guardian*. 'Brilliant,' said the *Telegraph*. What happened over the next few years was beyond Greg's wildest, most optimistic dreams. *What If . . .* became a number-one bestseller not only in the UK, but in other countries as well, and when Hollywood paid big money for the film option, Greg had become a rich man. Much as he enjoyed his work at the BBC, he realised that he could now afford to write full-time and that is what he did, starting work on another novel as soon as he handed in his notice. Over the next ten years he produced four more novels, each of them doing as well as *What If . . .*, each of them being optioned, and some of them even making it to the screen.

Melissa loved Greg's success. The money it brought enabled them to move houses several times, ending up in Barnes because it seemed almost like 'living in the country'. Greg enjoyed his success as well, but far from encouraging him to stop or take things easy, it had the strange effect of pushing him on to even greater efforts. While Melissa devoted a lot of time to spending the money he earned, he devoted his time to making more of it. His work was his life and he could not have been more delighted or surprised about the way things had turned out.

Now, though, as he sat in the study of his Barnes home he felt far from comfortable. Ever since that quiz night something had been nibbling away at him, and over the weeks the nibbles had become more painful. First there had been the question of who had pulled that prank at the Ocean Bar. Then, being a thriller writer obsessed with detail, there had been the question of how they had managed to do it. And after that had come Nick's murder. His own novels were full of murders and killings, but none had been as bizarre as Nick's, and it had unsettled him in ways that surprised him. What unsettled him even more, though, was the way his thoughts kept coming back to the allegation that he had plagiarised his first novel.

It was this, more than the brutal murder of an old friend, that was making it difficult for him to hit his daily word count.

17

Monday 15 April

DCI Deighton stood at the front of the incident room. Behind her, in the middle of the whiteboard, in large black letters, was the name 'Nick Bellamy'. Around it were pictures – of the body, the stab wounds, the scarf and the tongue – and a map of the Leg o' Mutton nature reserve.

'So,' she said, 'we now have ID.' She pointed at the name. 'Nick Bellamy. Forty-nine. Lived at Bailey House, a block of flats on the estate near Hammersmith Bridge. Both parents dead. One sibling, an older sister, Liz Steele, reported him missing and identified the body. We also have a bit more on him from one of his friends, who came in when she heard the news.'

Garibaldi's mind was less on the words of his boss than it was on Rachel and how to take things further. Her unexpected visit had been more than worth the domestic fallout it had produced, but what should he do next? Should he simply ask her round again, or did he need to ask her on a proper date? And if it were to be a date, where should it be?

For a girl who liked Townes Van Zandt maybe it should be a concert, but then for a girl who liked Townes Van Zandt it would have to be something good.

'So.'

DCI Deighton's emphatic tone brought Garibaldi back to the case. He looked at the board as she added some names to it. 'Melissa Matthews, Greg Matthews, Chris Turner, Fay Wetherby, Julia Forrest.'

'Oxford friends.' She pointed at the picture of the scarf. 'And that is the scarf of Balfour College, the Oxford college they all attended from 1988 to 1991. No DNA matches on it. This scarf does, of course, suggest a connection to Nick Bellamy's friends, all of whom featured in the surprise final round of questions of the Ocean Bar Quiz.'

As DCI Deighton explained the nature of each allegation, she wrote key words beside each name – 'love child' by Melissa's, 'plagiarism' by Greg's, 'sex tape' by Chris's, 'bribery' beside Fay's and 'theft' by Julia's. Finally she wrote 'killed a man' beside Nick's.

'Was it all a joke?' she said. 'We don't know. Is it linked in any way to the murder of Nick Bellamy? We don't know. Could one of them have killed Bellamy? Possibly. The cutting out of the tongue would suggest that he was killed for saying something. Did he come up with those allegations? If he did, could he have been killed as revenge for what he said, or to stop him saying more? Are any of the allegations correct? In short, we've got a lot of questions to ask and we need to get out there and ask them. Did anyone see Bellamy at all that afternoon and evening? Ask in pubs. Ask in shops. Finish house-to-houses along Lonsdale Road all the way up to the Leg o' Mutton. Look at CCTV of the Boat Race crowds. We need to find out all we can about Bellamy – from his sister, from his flat and from his friends. Bank records. Credit cards.

And we also need to know who was on Nick Bellamy's team. Melissa Matthews said she had never seen any of them before. A rowdy bunch who knew their stuff. We need to find out who they were and what they know.'

She turned to the two DCs sitting at the back. 'I want all you can find on these,' – she pointed at the names on the board – 'anything on our database. Anything that might connect to any of those allegations. Trawl social media. And I also want all you can get on what Nick Bellamy did for work. His sister said he'd had a load of temporary jobs but she was pretty vague. And we also need to look at other similar murders – other cases where the victim's tongue has been cut out. Anything we can learn from them.'

She turned to Garibaldi. 'And, DI Garibaldi, I want you to search Bellamy's flat and pay a visit to these five.' She pointed at the names on the board again. 'With Uber Gardner, that is.'

The Uber joke had been funny once but Garibaldi had stopped laughing long ago. There were many things that might stop him rising further through the ranks, including what had happened to him two years ago, but Garibaldi had a hunch that the biggest thing could be his inability to drive – or rather his refusal to do anything to remedy the problem.

Over the years he had become used to his colleagues' bafflement and it no longer bothered him. Garibaldi, the non-driving detective. It added to the sense that he was someone who liked to do things differently. And he liked that.

DS Gardner strapped on her seat belt and drove off. 'What do you make of it all, then, boss?'

Garibaldi was fond of DS Milly Gardner. The hours she had spent driving him round and the way she never forgot to ask how he was and what was going on in his life (never intrusively and always with the most innocent of intentions) had encouraged a strong bond between them. Despite her inability to see beyond the obvious, or maybe because of it, Garibaldi felt protective towards her.

'We need to look at this quiz and these allegations.'

'And what do we know about Melissa and Greg Matthews?'

'Greg Matthews is a hugely successful thriller writer. He wrote *What If . . . .*'

'Really? That was great. Have you read it?'

'I have, yes.'

Anything and anyone was Garibaldi's guiding principle when it came to reading, but he was always discriminating, sifting the good from the bad, the well written from the clunky, the ones likely to last from those instantly disposable. That was why he had only read one Greg Matthews novel.

'What did you make of it?' asked Milly.

Garibaldi had come to learn that it was not always a good idea to let everyone know what he was really thinking. In team meetings and in discussion of cases he often failed to stop himself, but when it came to car conversations with Milly he always did his best to rein himself in.

'It was OK,' he said. 'He knows what he's doing all right, and it's certainly made him a wealthy man.'

'Kevin read them all. He loves them. Or is that loved them?'

Garibaldi nodded and said nothing. Ever since Milly's traumatic break-up with Kevin two months ago he had learned to tread carefully whenever her ex-boyfriend's name was mentioned.

They drove down Station Road, took a left, turned right into Mill Hill and pulled up in front of a huge Gothic mansion.

'Some house,' said DS Gardner as they got out of the car and walked to the door.

Melissa Matthews welcomed them and ushered them into

a huge living room, where Greg Matthews stood by a grand piano in front of French windows that opened onto a beautifully maintained garden.

He stepped forward and introduced himself. Garibaldi shook his hand, introduced DS Gardner, politely declined offers of tea or coffee, and accepted the invitation to sit down. Melissa and Greg Matthews sat on the sofa, affectionately greeting the cocker spaniel ('Jarvis') that bounded in from the garden, sitting him down between them, as if they were all posing for a Sunday newspaper profile – 'bestselling novelist Greg Matthews at home in Barnes with his wife and cocker spaniel ("Jarvis")'.

'Thank you so much, Mrs Matthews, for coming into the station and giving us information about Nick Bellamy. We're here to follow that up and ask both you and Mr Matthews a few more questions.'

'Anything we can do to help,' said Greg.

'First of all, some facts,' said Garibaldi, taking out his notebook. 'Nick Bellamy was at Oxford with you from 1988 to 1991. You were all at Balfour College.'

'Correct.'

'And you were close friends.'

'Depends what you mean by "close",' said Melissa.

'You knew each other well, you hung out together, you socialised. You were more than mere acquaintances.'

Greg and Melissa both nodded.

'And when you all left Oxford you remained friends?'

'We kept in touch,' said Melissa. 'We all started jobs – we were in TV, Nick was in a bank – but we met up every now and then for drinks, for dinner. You know how it is when you start out.'

Garibaldi didn't, but he nodded anyway. 'And you started this quiz?'

'That's right,' said Melissa. 'At first it was just something that a small group of us did.'

'Who was in this group?'

'I told you at the station.'

'Tell me again, Mrs Matthews.'

Melissa Matthews was not used to being told what to do, and Garibaldi sensed her resentment.

Melissa sighed. 'Me, Greg, Nick, Chris, Fay, Julia. It started at our flat in Clapham and that's when I had the idea of setting up a bigger evening, for more of our friends. I thought it would be nice to broaden it and raise some money for charity. I've always been interested in charity, Detective Inspector. And luckily I've been able to do more of it in recent years.'

Garibaldi sighed inwardly. It was people like Melissa Matthews who were responsible for the horrors of Comic Relief and Red Nose Day.

'Each year the quiz grew a little bigger until we needed to move premises. For the last ten years we've been at the Ocean Bar. We've invited more people, but at the heart of it has always been the six of us from Balfour.'

'And the six of you have gone every year?'

'Yes. Apart from Nick, that is. He stopped turning up a few years ago. No reply to the invitation. Nothing. Then this year he was back.'

Melissa sniffled and reached for a tissue. Greg rested a comforting hand on her arm.

'When you say a few years, Mrs Matthews, can you be more precise?'

'I don't know. Three, four years? Something like that.'

'Do you have any idea why he stopped coming?'

'Not really. No one seemed to know, but there was the predictable speculation.'

'And what was that?'

'Drugs. Drink. Trouble. Nick was never far from any of them.'

'I see. And when you say "trouble" . . .?'

'I don't mean anything specific. All I'm saying is that you never knew with Nick.'

'Never knew what?'

Melissa flashed an angry glare. 'Never knew what he was up to,' she said, pronouncing each word carefully and slowly as if to indicate she was getting tired of the questioning.

Garibaldi continued. 'And do you have any idea why Nick decided to make a return this year?'

'I have no idea.'

'And how did he seem on the evening of the quiz?'

'Loud. Completely out of it.'

'Out of it?' said Garibaldi. 'With what?'

'I'm afraid I didn't run a test on him, Inspector . . .'

'Inspector Garibaldi.'

'He had bought a table and brought along guests who I didn't know, and they won the quiz.'

Greg leaned forward. 'The behaviour at the quiz can be rowdy – you know, lots of banter et cetera, but this lot were particularly noisy. In fact, if I'm being honest, I wouldn't be surprised if they were availing themselves of a little narcotic help. Not to mention digital help. The smartphone has killed the quiz in many ways. I'm not suggesting their frequent trips to the toilets were in any way suspicious – neither for the consumption of substances or the use of a phone, but . . .'

Garibaldi jotted down a note. 'Can we talk about this final round? Do either of you have any idea at all who might have done it?'

Greg cleared his throat, as if he were about to deliver something considered and important. 'The obvious starting point would be Nick himself. It sounds like the kind of reckless thing he might get up to – it seems that he had gone off the rails and, let's be honest, he had never really been fully on them, had he? So who knows? He may have wanted to make a point – what point I'm not quite sure – but maybe he wanted to cock a snook at the whole thing.'

Garibaldi raised his eyebrows. He couldn't remember the last time he had heard the phrase 'cock a snook' and he wasn't entirely sure what it meant. He made a mental note to look it up.

'And that could be why he was murdered,' said Greg. 'Someone didn't like what was said about them.'

'Would that be enough to kill him, though?' said Melissa.

'Who knows?' said Greg. 'But the severed tongue suggests he was killed for something he said, which fits with him being the man behind the questions. And the scarf seems to link the murder to Balfour, and so to all of us. But the question to ask is, if it was one of us, which I cannot for one moment believe, why would they leave such a big clue, one that makes the connection so obvious?'

Garibaldi swivelled his head from one to the other. He was unsure which he was enjoying the least – Melissa's insufferable smugness or Greg's knowingness. Just because she read the news didn't mean she knew everything and just because he wrote thrillers and was skilled at handling the twists and turns of fictional plots didn't mean he had a similar grasp of real-life problems.

'I have two questions about this final round of questions,' said Garibaldi. 'The first is whether any of them is true.'

He looked from one to the other. For all their polished veneer, he could see that they were rattled.

'Maybe,' said Garibaldi, 'we could take them one at a time. First of all you, Mr Matthews.'

He turned to a page at the back of his notebook. 'Plagiarism?'

Greg gave a derisive snort. 'Nonsense! What was it, exactly, that I plagiarised, and what, exactly, do you mean by plagiarism? You can't answer a generalised accusation like that – you need detailed specifics. Anyone familiar with copyright law' – he gave Garibaldi a look to suggest that he was not such a person – 'would know that it is a very tricky area. The other thing to bear in mind is that there are no such things as new stories. In one sense everything has already been said and done – all you do is say or do it in a slightly different form. And the final thing is that people *do* often come up with the same idea at the same time. How often do people think there's something zeitgeisty going on because you have three films about the same kind of thing coming out at the same time? How often do you have writers getting pissed off because they're working on something and then they see that something's come out that is doing, if not exactly the same thing, then something very similar that could result in the very accusations you've just mentioned? In short, I have engaged in no conscious act of plagiarism.'

Greg gave Garibaldi a look that suggested there was nothing more to say on the matter.

'So that's a no, then?' said Garibaldi, hoping the brevity of the comment, together with its tone, would let Greg know that his answer had been unnecessarily long-winded.

'And Fay Wetherby?' Garibaldi consulted his notebook again. 'Taking a bribe.'

Melissa took this one. 'Fay is a woman of great integrity,' she said, 'and I don't believe it for one moment. Our daughter is at St Mark's . . .'

'Really?' said Garibaldi, scribbling down a note. 'Which year?'

'Her final year. A levels.'

Garibaldi thought of Alfie. He needed to speak to him again.

'St Mark's, as you must know, is an extraordinarily demanding school. High-achieving girls. Opinionated parents. A difficult school to be head of, and Fay has done a remarkable job there.'

'And your daughter?' said Garibaldi.

'Lauren,' said Greg.

'How has she enjoyed her time at St Mark's?'

'Is that relevant?' said Greg

'I don't know. You tell me.'

'Like all girls,' said Melissa, 'she's had her problems.'

Garibaldi said nothing and waited for them to fill the silence.

Melissa cleared her throat. 'She was unwell a few years ago.'

'Unwell?'

'Yes, she had a stint in the Priory.'

She said it as if it had been an extended spa session.

'When you say unwell?'

Greg leaned forward. 'A kind of depression.'

'Can you be more precise?'

'We thought it was anorexia at first. She was eating so little, she was so thin. But then we discovered there was something else. It was drugs.'

'What kind of drugs?'

'Cannabis,' said Greg. 'Skunk.'

'I see,' said Garibaldi. He paused. 'So why, exactly, did she need to go into the Priory? Was she addicted?'

'We needed help,' said Melissa. 'We needed to get her away from that school, away from her boyfriend.'

'Her boyfriend?'

'Yeah. Rob. A terrible influence on her. In fact, if it hadn't been for him, I don't think she'd have had those problems at all.'

'Tell me about this boyfriend.'

'He's at Dolphin Boys. Or he was, the last I heard. I wouldn't be surprised if they've kicked him out by now. He supplied the stuff.'

'So Lauren was seeing a lot of this boy, then?'

'Too much,' said Greg. 'As Melissa said, if it weren't for him . . .'

'So it wasn't exactly rehab, then?'

'Lauren was all over the place,' said Greg. 'She needed to be somewhere safe, somewhere where she could be looked after.'

'And she couldn't be looked after here?'

'Of course she could,' said Melissa, 'but we're busy people.'

Garibaldi turned to Greg. 'You're at home, though, aren't you?'

'Just because I'm at home doesn't mean I'm not working.'

'And tell me, Mr and Mrs Matthews, how did St Mark's handle Lauren's illness?'

'They were very good,' said Greg.

'Was any disciplinary action taken?'

'No,' said Melissa. 'It was felt inappropriate.'

'Inappropriate? How?'

'It was felt not to be a school matter, more a family matter.'

'But she had been taking illegal drugs?'

'Not at school.'

'And you're both, of course, friends of the head, Fay Wetherby.'

'That is completely irrelevant,' said Greg.

'Was Fay Wetherby involved in Lauren's case?'

'She took an interest, yes.'

'I see. And has Lauren been involved in any other disciplinary issues at the school?'

'There was something else,' said Melissa. 'Again, all a fuss about nothing.'

'And what was that?' said Garibaldi.

'Some online stuff,' said Greg, 'you know, a bit of banter that was misconstrued.'

'And Fay Wetherby dealt with it well?'

'Yes, she did. As I said, a woman of great ability and integrity.'

'I see.' Garibaldi looked at his notebook again. 'So, what about Chris Turner and a possible sex tape?'

Greg and Melissa both laughed, their nervous tension released now that the spotlight had shifted onto someone else.

'Something funny?' said Garibaldi.

'Look,' said Greg, 'whoever made that suggestion must have known Chris from long ago. It's always been a joke with him, ever since Nick walked in on him at college and he was ...' He broke off and smirked at Melissa. 'There's no other way to put this, I'm afraid. He was pleasuring a teddy bear.'

Garibaldi leaned forward. 'Sorry – when you say "pleasuring" ...?'

'Sexual intercourse.'

'With a teddy bear? Teddy bear as in cuddly toy?'

Greg laughed. 'Specially adapted for the purpose.'

Garibaldi looked towards Melissa. She was laughing along with her husband. He looked at DS Gardner. She couldn't suppress a smirk.

'How very *Brideshead*,' said Garibaldi.

Greg gave an approving nod, as if surprised by the literary allusion. 'Exactly. That was the joke at the time – and it was very, very funny. Not for Chris, of course. Soon the news was all over college and he had to live with it for the rest of his time there. In my view he never really recovered. So whoever made that allegation knew about Chris and the way everyone joked about his strange sexual preferences.'

'So you're saying that he could well have been blackmailed over a sex tape. Sextortion.'

'I think you'd better ask Chris about that,' said Melissa.

Garibaldi consulted the notebook again.

'Which leaves Julia the shoplifter. True?'

'Very silly,' said Melissa immediately. 'As if she should need to!'

'That's not quite how it works, though, is it?' Greg turned to his wife. 'It's not about needing. It's often something else that makes you do that kind of thing.'

Garibaldi was reeling from Greg Matthews' smugness. Was there anything the bestselling author did not know?

'So there are no grounds at all for thinking that Julia Forrest might be, or have been, a shoplifter?'

'None at all,' said Melissa. Something about the speed and certainty with which she answered made Garibaldi look at her more closely.

'And presumably,' said Garibaldi, glancing briefly at his notebook again, 'the same can be said about your teenage pregnancy and secret child?'

'Absolutely,' said Melissa with the same conviction.

'Where did you go to school, Mrs Matthews?'

'Is that relevant?'

'Again, I don't know, but the allegation says this happened at school so it might be worth knowing.'

'You mean you're actually going to *investigate* this shit?' said Melissa.

'That's my job, Mrs Matthews, that's why I'm here. And if by "this shit" you mean the brutal murder of Nick Bellamy, then I think it's my duty, and in everybody's interests, to investigate things as carefully and as professionally as I can.'

He looked from Melissa to Greg, both of whom coughed nervously and shifted in their seats. Garibaldi loved it when he had the chance to play the moral card, to remind people like this that when it came to the law, they were not above it.

'I went to Marlborough,' said Melissa.

She said it as if she were flashing a label guaranteed to win approval and admiration.

'And where's that, exactly?' said Garibaldi. He knew precisely where it was and what type of school it was, but enjoyed feigning ignorance as a way of not playing by Melissa's rules.

'In Wiltshire. A boarding school.'

'I see. So a private school, then?'

He deliberately chose not to refer to it as a 'public' school, avoiding one of the English language's more absurd contradictions.

Melissa nodded. 'And you?' said Garibaldi turning to Greg.

'St Paul's.'

'I see,' said Garibaldi. He was more than familiar with the prestigious school's ugly buildings and sprawling playing fields beside Hammersmith Bridge. 'And, while we're on the subject, do you know where Nick Bellamy went to school?'

Greg leaned forward. 'Look, I really don't see how these questions are relevant.'

'Maybe they're not,' said Garibaldi, 'but you never know what you need to know, do you? So the idea of relevance is, let's say, problematic.'

'Nick went to a grammar school in London,' said Melissa. 'He liked to remind us of the fact. His London roots, where he grew up, that kind of thing.'

'I see,' said Garibaldi. Another glance at the notebook. 'OK, the other thing about these questions – why those particular allegations? Why would whoever did this choose those particular things? Is there any logic, or would you say they are completely random?'

'I think,' said Greg, 'they just wanted to raise a laugh.'

'Really?' said Garibaldi. 'So the idea of Nick Bellamy having killed someone and a headmistress taking a bribe are funny, are they?'

'OK,' said Melissa, 'they're not funny. In fact, some of them are a little, I don't know, unsettling.'

'Unsettling?' said Garibaldi.

'No one thought they were true,' said Greg. 'Everyone was laughing.'

'What I mean by unsettling,' said Melissa, 'is that they got people thinking they might be true. Everyone was speculating. If one of them *were* true, which one was the most likely?'

'OK,' said Garibaldi, shutting his notebook. 'Just one further question and then we'll leave you. Do you have any idea how this stunt was pulled? How did whoever was behind it manage to get it onto the Ocean Bar speakers?'

'We were in quite a state, as you can imagine,' said Greg, 'and as we had told everyone it was our joke, we had to be careful about making a fuss—'

'We asked the manager,' said Melissa, 'and he had no idea.'

'Hang on,' said Garibaldi, 'so did you tell the manager that it wasn't you, that someone else had done it?'

'No,' said Greg.

'So what did you ask him?'

'I asked him if anyone had interfered with the sound system and he said he didn't know. So I asked him to ask his staff and to get back to me if they knew anything.'

'And did he get back to you?'

'No.'

133

'And did you get back to him?'

Greg sighed. 'It was a difficult situation, and I didn't really want to push it.'

'Someone had sabotaged your quiz with a practical joke, which your wife has just admitted was unsettling, and you didn't want to push it?'

'We wanted to forget about it,' said Greg. 'Draw a line. And to be perfectly honest, Detective Inspector, I'm not sure how knowing who had got to the PA system would have got us very far. I'm not a detective.'

'But you do write thrillers,' said Garibaldi.

'And how is that relevant?'

'I'm surprised you weren't more curious about how it was done.'

'Oh I was curious all right, but you must understand, Detective Inspector, that we were taken completely by surprise. Somehow finding out how that voice got on the speakers slipped down our list of priorities.'

'Do you feel the same now that Nick Bellamy's been murdered?'

Greg Matthews gave a weary sigh. 'That assumes the murder is linked to the quiz.'

'And is it?'

'You tell me.'

'The thing is,' said Melissa, 'as far as the Ocean Bar was concerned, we were the ones who played the trick.'

'But now that you've told everyone that it *wasn't* you . . .?'

Melissa and Greg looked uncomfortable.

'And tell me, Mrs Matthews, where were you on the evening of Boat Race Day?'

'What? You mean I'm a suspect?'

'That's not what I'm saying. I'm just asking you where you were.'

'I was at home. I'm not a great fan of Boat Race Day in Barnes. So I stayed well away from it all. So, yes, I was here.'

'The whole evening?'

'Yes, the whole evening.'

'And you, Mr Matthews. Where were you?'

'I was here as well.'

'Well, thank you for your time,' said Garibaldi, getting up from the chair. 'I think maybe I should pay the Ocean Bar a visit.'

18

Monday 15 April

Nick Bellamy's neighbours all expressed shock at his murder but could shed no light on what he had been up to in the weeks preceding it. He had, they said, kept himself very much to himself since moving onto the estate a couple of years ago. Some said that he often seemed to be away, and none could recall any regular visitors, or even seeing him in the company of others. One neighbour said that he saw him sitting at the bar of the White Horse more often than he saw him around the flats.

Nick Bellamy's flat also yielded few clues. As Garibaldi looked round the sparsely furnished living room, he sensed it had not been lived in much. There was no sign of a land-line or computer, either of which would have given some sense of recent contacts and activity. An old-fashioned CD/radio player sat on the living-room table and there was a full bookshelf (an odd combination of recent thrillers – Greg Matthews' not among them – and classics: Dickens, Dostoevsky, Virginia Woolf, Graham Greene). A TV sat in the corner, and newspapers (mostly the *Guardian*, with dates from the last two months) were stacked up in the corner. There was nothing on the walls.

In one of the bedrooms the bed's sheets were crumpled, showing no signs of having been slept in recently, and in the other the bed was not even made up. In the kitchen a few dishes lay in the washing-up bowl but there was no impression that this was a place where meals had been regularly cooked or eaten – no food in the fridge and bare cupboards. Everything about the place felt cold and sterile, and Garibaldi was reminded of another Larkin poem (why was Larkin, that most miserable of poets, the one that he came back to most?), 'Mr Bleaney', and the rented room described as a coffin-like 'hired box'.

The search of drawers and cupboards looked as though it would also throw up nothing until DS Gardner called Garibaldi into the bedroom.

'Look at these, boss,' she said, as she held out a pile of paper towards him.

Garibaldi took them and examined the top one. It was a William Hill betting slip – £100 to win on a horse at Chepstow, dated in the month before Bellamy's murder. He looked at the slip below. Another William Hill slip – this time £50 on a horse at Redcar. He riffled through the pile. They were all betting slips and none of them for a stake less than £20.

He turned to DS Gardner. 'Are you a gambler?'

'Not really. Are you?'

'Grand National and the Derby. I remember my Dad asking us all to pick a horse and going down the bookie's.'

'It's all online now.'

Garibaldi pointed at the pile of slips. 'Not for everyone, it seems. Tell me, is that a lot of money to be putting on horses, or is it quite normal?'

'Seems a lot to me.'

Garibaldi flicked through the pile, pausing to look at a few more slips. 'Nothing less than twenty quid here. I mean, I know it's a long time ago, but fifty pence each way was more my thing.'

'Yeah,' said DS Gardner. 'That was a long time ago.'

'So what does this tell us? That Nick Bellamy liked a flutter. From what we know, that seems to be the least of his vices.'

'They all have one thing in common though, boss.'

'Yeah, and what's that?'

'They're all losing bets.'

'How do you know?'

'Because if they had won he'd have taken them along to collect his winnings.'

Garibaldi nodded, trying to give the impression that he had already reached the same conclusion. The truth was that DS Gardner had surprised him with a flash of insight.

'Did you find anything else?'

'Not really. But I did find this.' DS Gardner held a piece of paper towards Garibaldi. 'I think it could be interesting.'

Garibaldi took the paper. It was a list of names. At the top was written: *Darren – Film, Steve – Music, Bill – Sport, Fred – History, Don – Science, Colin – Current Affairs. Phil – Bit of Everything. Me – the Rest.*

'What do you reckon?' said DS Gardner.

'I think you've just found Nick Bellamy's Ocean Bar quiz team.'

'Really? And where do you think we'll find them?'

'I think The White Horse might be a good place to start.'

The White Horse could be reached only by those who knew exactly where they were heading. Tucked in a corner of the Hammersmith Bridge estate between two of the blocks of flats, it looked uninviting. Once he had pushed open its doors, Garibaldi discovered that it was just as uninviting inside.

The pub was empty apart from two men, sitting at opposite ends of the bar, and a barmaid. One man had his head buried in a paper, the other was looking at his phone. Each lifted their head to look at Garibaldi and DS Gardner as they came in, but quickly turned their attention back to phone and paper. The barmaid stepped off her stool and stood behind the pumps with eyebrows raised.

Garibaldi rested his arms on the bar and made a show of looking at the ales on offer. He turned to DS Gardner. 'What would you like?'

'Diet Coke, please.'

'Sure?'

'I'm driving, remember?'

'Of course.' Garibaldi turned to the barmaid. 'Diet Coke and a pint of best bitter for me.'

While the barmaid sorted out the drinks, Garibaldi glanced round.

'You looking for someone?' said the barmaid.

Garibaldi perched on a bar stool and gestured for DS Gardner to do the same.

'I am, actually. I'm looking for anyone who might know – or have known – Nick Bellamy.'

Garibaldi's eyes shot quickly to each end of the bar to gauge the drinkers' responses. They showed absolutely none.

'Terrible news,' said the barmaid. 'Can't believe it.'

'You knew him, then?'

'He was a regular. Every night. A lot of lunchtimes as well. I can't believe what happened. I mean who on earth would do that to him?'

Garibaldi shook his head. 'I know. The whole thing's horrible.'

'I mean the stabbing's horrible enough, but the tongue?' The barmaid grimaced as she made a loud 'yuk'. 'And the scarf!'

'I can't tell you how shocked and horrified I was,' said Garibaldi, turning to DS Gardner, who was shaking her head slowly in disbelief. 'We were both completely devastated, weren't we?'

Garibaldi turned to the drinkers. 'Did either of you know him?'

They both looked up and nodded.

'What do you want to know about him?' said the one with the paper.

'And who are you?' said the other.

Garibaldi had decided as soon as he walked into the pub that he would keep his identity hidden. 'I'm an old friend,' he said. 'And I'm trying to sort a few of his things out.'

'What things would those be?' said the barmaid.

'Actually, it's not so much things as people. I'm trying to track down some people he knew.'

'Why's that?' said the man with the phone. 'I can't believe he's left them anything.'

'Yeah? Why do you say that?'

Both men laughed. 'I thought you said you were a friend of his.'

'Yeah,' said Garibaldi, 'but it's been a long time since I've seen him. What's he been up to?'

'How long have you got?'

'So he didn't have much money, then. Well, that figures.'

'And why's that?'

'Because he always was a gambler. Ever since I knew him.'

The man with the phone climbed off his stool. 'Well, if

there's any money floating around, there are a few in here who'd like to see a bit of it.'

'What do you mean?'

'He owed.'

'I see.' Garibaldi took a sheet of paper out of his pocket. 'Are any of these among them?' He read the list. 'Darren, Steve, Bill, Fred, Don, Colin, Phil.'

The man with the phone laughed. 'That's our quiz team.'

'Your quiz team?'

'Yeah. Hammersmith and Fulham Pub Quiz League. Nick was in it. Clever fucker he was. They don't know how they'll replace him.'

'I see. And where would I find them?'

The barmaid leaned forward. 'They're in most evenings.'

'So if I came back I'd be able to have a chat with one of them.'

'Yeah.'

'OK,' said Garibaldi, nodding to DS Gardner. 'I'll pop back one evening, then.'

Garibaldi and DS Gardner left the White Horse and headed for the towpath, walking away from Hammersmith towards Putney Bridge. They were only yards away from the estate and yet, as they passed luxury riverside developments, they seemed already to be in a different world. Garibaldi had always loved London's diversity, the way you were never far away from a place that was emphatically different. One minute you were among grim blocks of flats, the next you were heading for the Ocean Bar. All that, though, was changing. Property prices had already forced out the young and, as the older generations passed away, Garibaldi could see a future in which the city was a homogenous mass of wealth and privilege, in which there was no longer a place for London's White Horses.

The Ocean Bar had been a haunt of the wealthy and the privileged for many years. When Garibaldi and DS Gardner arrived at lunchtime it was, as ever, busy, and warm enough for some of the wealthy and privileged to be sitting at outside tables. The manager, dark and wiry, with a nervous energy and a strong Italian accent, greeted them animatedly and ushered them into his office, where he offered them tea or coffee or something stronger.

'We're fine, thanks,' said Garibaldi. 'On duty and all that.'

'So,' said the manager. 'How can I help you? I understand you want to know about the quiz night.'

The manager's words tumbled out quickly in a way that made it difficult to work out what he was saying.

'That's right. The quiz night run by Melissa Matthews.'

'A wonderful night!' said the manager, excitedly throwing his arms about in a way that reminded Garibaldi of Manuel in *Fawlty Towers*. 'So many people having a good time – and such lovely people. A lovely evening! And Mr and Mrs Matthews so good. Such good work for charity.'

'I don't know how much you remember of that evening,' said Garibaldi, 'but there was a bit of a surprise at the end.'

'I remember,' said the manager. 'Mrs Matthews said it was her little joke.'

'But it wasn't,' said Garibaldi.

'Sorry?'

'It wasn't her little joke.'

'No?'

'No. It wasn't Mrs Matthews at all and what we need to know is who it was and also how whoever it was managed to do it. As I understand it, the questions came from the restaurant sound system. Can you show us how your system works?'

'I'm not an expert on these things, I'm afraid. We don't use it very often – we're not really that kind of place, you understand. But sometimes, when there are special functions here, we find it useful. For a special event a guest may ask to play something through it from their iPod or something.'

'So it's computer-based.'

'I don't really know. I'm not an expert.'

'But if someone wanted to play something through your system how would they do it? Through their iPod? Through their phone?'

The manager shrugged.

'I think so. To be honest, I've never used it myself. Someone else sorts it out.'

'And who would that be?'

'Usually one of the waiters.'

'Is there a CD facility on it at all?'

The manager shrugged his shoulders. 'Why don't I show you it? I think that's better than me trying to explain.'

Garibaldi followed the manager out of his office into the restaurant area, past a long bar, and round a corner to the entrance to the kitchen. He pointed at a surface where, next to the coffee-making machine, was the sound system. When it came to technical matters Garibaldi was also far from expert, and he was pleased when DS Gardner stepped forward, bent down to peer closely and spoke with authority.

'Quite a basic set-up,' she said. 'No Bluetooth, nothing wireless. Could still use an iPod on it, or a USB or a memory card. It's so old-fashioned you can even use CDs.'

Garibaldi nodded as if he understood. If there ever were a Luddite assault on the digital world, he would be in the vanguard wielding a huge hammer, but he had learned that such opinions were best kept to himself.

He turned to DS Gardner. 'So on the quiz night, whoever played that final round through this would have used an iPod, memory stick or CD?'

'Looks like it, boss.'

The manager gave another extravagant shrug of his shoulders. 'I really have very little to do with this. As I say, we use it so rarely.'

Bustling waiters emerged from the kitchen and hurried past them, ferrying plates. Garibaldi craned his neck to see what was on them.

'Are you hungry?' said the manager. 'I can get you—'

Garibaldi raised his hand. 'Tell me,' he said, pointing at the music system, 'on that night, who would have had access to this?'

'None of the customers. They wouldn't go near it. The loos are there.' He pointed to the other end of the long bar. 'Only anyone behind the bar or anyone going in and out of the kitchens would be able to get to it.'

'So we're talking about the waiting staff.'

'I guess so,' said the manager.

'And how many were working that night?'

'I'll have to check, but it would have been a full house. It wasn't an ordinary evening, so I guess we would have had about ten.'

'Can you give me a list of all those who were working here that night?'

'Of course. When would you like it? I could send it to you.'

'It would be very helpful if you could do it now, actually.'

The manager looked put out.

'I know it might be inconvenient,' said Garibaldi, 'but we're investigating a murder.'

'A murder?'

'Yes. A man who was at the quiz at this restaurant – in fact, the man who won it – was found dead last Sunday. You may have read about it.'

The manager clearly hadn't. His face froze, as if suddenly

struck by the implications of the word 'murder' being connected in any way to the words 'Ocean Bar'.

'So if we could have names and contact numbers of all who were working that night, it would be very helpful.'

The manager nodded and walked through the bar. Garibaldi leaned towards DS Gardner. 'We need to speak to every waiter and waitress who was working that evening. Did they see anyone near the sound system? Did they see anyone in that area as the quiz was drawing to an end?'

The manager came back, holding his hands out in apology. 'I'm sorry,' he said, 'we need a bit of time to go through our records. Can I email them through to you?'

Garibaldi tilted his head to one side, expressing his disappointment.

'As soon as you can, please,' he said, getting up from the table. 'One final question. Did Mrs Matthews say anything else about the surprise round?'

'No. As I said, just that it was her little joke.'

Garibaldi and DS Gardner went to the door that led to the river, and left the restaurant, walking through the outside dining area to the towpath.

'What do you make of him, then?' said Garibaldi as they headed back to Hammersmith Bridge.

'I may be wrong, but I think he's hiding something.'

'You know what? I think you could be right.'

DS Gardener smiled. 'Where to now, boss?' she said. If she wasn't relishing the prospect of ten interviews, she was doing her best to hide it.

19

Monday 15 April

'How did you find out about Nick Bellamy's murder?'

Julia Forrest flicked back her bobbed hair and held a plate of biscuits towards Garibaldi. He raised a declining hand. She offered them to DS Gardner, who did the same.

'Melissa rang me. Told me it was in the *Standard*. I couldn't believe it.'

'Do you have any idea who might have done it?'

Julia shook her head. 'None at all. The scarf seems to suggest that it's linked to us – his college friends – but then I can't believe any of us would do that. We're all, you know, pretty civilised.'

Garibaldi chuckled. 'History is full of civilised people who show themselves capable of the grossest acts of violence.'

'I'm well aware of that, but this seems preposterous. And if it was one of us, why the hell would they shove a Balfour scarf in his mouth? It's like saying, "Come and get me, Mr Policeman."'

'Do you think his murder is in any way linked to what happened at the Ocean Bar Quiz?'

'You mean those questions at the end?'

Garibaldi nodded.

'That's assuming that Nick was behind it and that he was killed for what he said. That the severed tongue was some kind of symbolic gesture, a message.'

One thing Garibaldi was learning about this group of Oxford graduates, and it may well have been the case with all Oxford graduates, was that they thought they were clever – certainly clever enough to have a go at detection.

'And do you think it was Nick behind it?'

'I don't know.'

'But you do now know that it wasn't, as she had claimed at the time, Melissa? So if it wasn't her, who was it?'

'I don't believe it was any of us. I just don't see it.'

'And these allegations, accusations, jokes, whatever you want to call them. What do you make of them?'

'Everyone seemed to find them amusing.'

'Did you?'

'I laughed, yes, but like everyone else I was asking myself what the hell was going on.'

'What did you think was going on?'

'At first I didn't know – then when Melissa said it was her little joke I thought OK, so it was her joke, but even at the time I thought she wasn't telling the truth.'

'And why did you think that?'

'I could tell from her manner. I could see that she and Greg were flustered. Most of the guests were pissed, so they might not have noticed, but I was pretty sober and I was looking at her when the voice came on – I could see she was surprised. She's usually so smooth. Newsreader smooth. The pair of them – they always seem to have everything under control.'

'Can we talk about these allegations?'

'Of course.'

'If you played the round as you were asked to, which of them would you say is the most likely?'

Julia threw back her head and laughed. 'Don't be ridiculous!'

'I'm not.'

'Do you really expect me to do this?'

'Yes I do.'

'It was a joke!'

'All I'm asking you, Mrs Forrest, is to tell me which of them you think is the most plausible.'

Julia looked at Garibaldi and DS Gardner in disbelief, like a schoolkid presented with an impossible maths problem. 'This is preposterous!'

'Shall I go through them one by one?' Garibaldi turned a page in his notebook, realising as he did that he had been through the final round so often he no longer needed to.

'Maybe we should start with you, Mrs Forrest? Shoplifting?'

'Of course not.'

'You have never shoplifted?'

It was not a long hesitation, but years of detective work had sensitised Garibaldi to the tiniest details of body language. He picked up not only the slight pause but also the way her eyes had momentarily shifted to one side.

'I am not a shoplifter, Detective Inspector. Harvey Nichols! Get in touch with them. Ask them.'

'And you have never been caught shoplifting?'

'I've told you.'

'OK. And what about the others?'

'Chris Turner and a sex tape? You never know with men, do you? As you say, violence often lurks below the civilised surface, and the same's true of perverse sexual behaviour – you find it in places you wouldn't expect. Greg Matthews and plagiarism? I think it highly unlikely. If it's an obvious case,

148

given his fame and high profile, I'm sure we'd have heard of it before. Fay and a bribe? Again, unlikely. If you're head of that school you know that everything you do is subject to the closest scrutiny. That's not to say it doesn't happen, of course. Melissa and a teenage pregnancy, a secret child? How would anyone know whether or not that's true? I didn't know Melissa before Oxford and nothing she said about her schooldays suggested it might have happened.'

'That doesn't mean it didn't,' said Garibaldi.

'Of course. And finally, did Nick Bellamy kill a man? If you'd asked me a few weeks ago I would have dismissed it as nonsense. No, not nonsense, as extremely unlikely. But now that someone's killed him, it takes on a horrible plausibility, doesn't it? Especially when you think of the way he was always getting himself into trouble.'

'What kind of trouble?'

'He had a terrible temper. He was always getting into arguments and fights . . .' Julia broke off, fighting back tears. 'I'm sorry. It's been such a shock.'

'Of course it has,' said Garibaldi, 'take your time.'

'Look,' said Julia, 'Nick's been murdered, so maybe the allegation about him is the most likely. Maybe it's linked.'

'Tell me about this group of friends. Did you – *do* you all get on?'

'Does any group of friends get on? We met a long time ago, we've gone our different paths since. It's not as though we hang out together all the time. We've all grown up and moved on. Had kids. You just drift apart.'

'And yet you all go to this quiz every year.'

Julia nodded. 'It's become a kind of tradition.'

'So there were, or are, no real issues among you?'

'Issues? What do you mean?'

'Tensions. Differences.'

'There are tensions and differences in any group of friends, aren't there?'

'Tell me about Melissa.'

'What do you want to know?'

'Well, of all of them, she lives the closest to you. In fact, she lives here in Barnes. I expect that of all of these friends she's the one you see most of?'

Julia clasped her hands in front of her. 'I can understand why you might think so, but we don't really see much of each other at all. As I say, you drift apart.'

'But you must see her more than the others?'

'I guess I do, but, you know, it can be difficult.'

'What can be difficult?'

Julia took a deep sigh. 'Look, the thing about being at college together and the thing about keeping in touch over the years is that although you remain friends you also remain rivals. Competitors. It's what schools and universities do to you. You're constantly weighing yourself up against each other and it all becomes a kind of race. How well is everyone doing? How do you judge everyone's choices, everyone's success? How do you measure that success? Nothing's ever said explicitly, but everyone wants to do better than everyone else and everyone takes some satisfaction in others' failures.'

'Schadenfreude.'

Garibaldi enjoyed Julia's momentary surprise at his use of the word.

'Exactly. Schadenfreude. But I stopped playing that game with Melissa years ago.' She cast her eyes round the living room and spread her arms as if displaying what was on offer. 'Look, I'm doing OK. I work as a lawyer and Phil is a highly paid journalist. We're well off. But Melissa and Greg are well off in a completely different way. You know you can't compete. But the funny thing is that just when you think the days of competing might be drawing to an end, when you might stop getting out your yardstick to measure your contemporaries, along come kids and you start competing through them. And the race starts all over again. Schools, exams, universities. Melissa and I have daughters the same age, both about to do their A levels and go to university. And I think Melissa has found that difficult at times.'

'Can you be more specific?'

'Well, it started with schools. Both Helena and Lauren applied for St Mark's.'

'Where Fay Wetherby is head?'

'Exactly. Lauren – Melissa's daughter – got in, Helena didn't. I'm sure it was an absolutely fair decision. I'm sure that the connections counted for nothing – that has to be the case in this accountable, transparent world, doesn't it? And Helena has done very well at the Dolphin, thank you very much. As for Lauren, it's been a complete nightmare – I do pity Fay having had to deal with all that.'

'What was the nightmare?'

'Well first of all there was a spell in the Priory.'

'What was that for?'

'I never knew exactly, but the rumour was drugs. Apparently a group of them were using, but nothing happened to Lauren, and rumour has it she was guilty as hell.'

'So hang on,' said Garibaldi, 'this allegation about Fay Wetherby accepting a bribe for not expelling a pupil?'

Julia's face froze, as if she had walked into an ambush. 'Yes, I mean, no . . .'

'You said it was unlikely, but you've just outlined a scenario in which the allegation, if not true, would certainly seem to be *plausible*.'

Julia was flustered. 'No, I mean. Look . . . let me get back to Melissa.'

'No hang on, Mrs Forrest, this is important. I'm beginning to wonder whether you might not be telling me the whole truth about things.'

'What do you mean?' The indignation was clear.

'Tell me more about Melissa.'

'Sorry, Detective Inspector, what do you think I have not been truthful about?'

'The other allegations.'

'I see. So I *am* a serial shoplifter, am I?'

'I'm not saying that.'

'What are you saying, then?'

'Please, Mrs Forrest, one thing at a time. Melissa. Tell me more about your race . . .'

'Our race?'

'Your competition.'

'Last autumn Lauren and Helena both applied to Oxford.'

'To Balfour?' said Garibaldi.

'Yes. To Balfour.'

What was it about these people? So keen to carry on the tradition, so keen to see their offspring repeat their own journey, travel the same tracks of privilege.

'And what happened?'

'Helena got an offer . . .' Julia found it difficult to hide the signs of a smile. 'And Lauren didn't.'

'I see,' said Garibaldi, 'and has this been an issue between you?'

'As with everything else, it's all fine on the surface, but you know it's bubbling away underneath. Melissa was perfectly polite about it – she made the right noises, congratulated Helena, said how happy we must be, and gave the usual crap about not having put any pressure on Lauren, and how all you ever want for your kids is for them to be happy. But I could tell. I've seen enough of them over the years to know

152

how upset she and Greg would be. Astounded that with all their wealth and power and influence they couldn't get what they wanted for their daughter. Prep school. St Mark's. But no Oxford. Still, they can always send her to America, can't they? Playground of the rich.'

'But if she's thinking this, she's kept it to herself?'

'Absolutely. And I'm not singling her out. That's the way it is with these ambitious west London parents. It's the jungle we're in. Polite on the surface but there's a Darwinian ferocity in operation that you need to be wary of. And I do, sincerely, wish Melissa all the best.'

'To return to Balfour for a moment, Mrs Forrest. Do you have any idea why the killer chose to shove a college scarf in Nick Bellamy's mouth?'

Julia spread her hands. 'I have no idea. As I said earlier, if the killer actually went to Balfour it seems unlikely they would plant a clue like that. So maybe the killer laid a false trail, deliberately moving the focus in that direction.'

'One final thing, Mrs Forrest. Where were you on Boat Race Day?'

'Boat Race Day? You mean where was I when Nick was murdered? I was here. I went out to the shops in the day. Early, to avoid the crowds. And then I stayed in. It's not a great day to be out in Barnes.'

'And your husband. Where was he?'

'With me, I think. He may have played golf – I can't remember. He sometimes does on a Saturday. Hang on, does this mean that you think I might have . . .?'

'I'm just asking the question, Mrs Forrest. I have to.'

Garibaldi shut his notebook and stood up, nodding to DS Gardner, who stood up as well.

Julia showed them to the door. 'Do you have any ideas at all about this, Detective Inspector?'

'I do have some ideas, Mrs Forrest, yes.'

'What are they?'

'All in good time.'

But the truth was Garibaldi had no ideas beyond the ones Julia Forrest had just expressed.

He still had some thinking to do.

20

Monday 15 April

DS Gardner drove Garibaldi back to Hammersmith, parking again on the north side of the bridge. A short walk westwards along the river took them to the Dove, where they sat outside, tucking into toasted sandwiches and looking out onto the Thames sparkling in the spring sunshine. DS Gardner sipped a lime and soda but Garibaldi, enjoying one of the benefits of never being the driver, treated himself to another pint.

Garibaldi looked at Milly and yet again wondered how, in the wake of Milly's break-up and in his pre-Rachel single state, they had managed to avoid a bout of comfort sex. Milly was attractive – dark hair framing her face in a way that reminded him of Audrey Hepburn in *Breakfast at Tiffany's*, and he hoped he wasn't looking too bad himself for a man hitting fifty. OK, he drank a bit, and his eating habits weren't the best, but he did go for the occasional jog by the river and he did still have a full head of hair.

Over the years in which Milly had been driving Garibaldi, an intimacy had developed between them. There was something about sitting side by side, facing forwards and not looking each other in the eye that made frank conversation easy. When Garibaldi had hit troubled times, he had found a sympathetic ear in Milly. She had seen the way he suffered before his time off and his split with Kay, and when he had made his return she had been beside him, both literally and metaphorically. In a similar way, Garibaldi had been there for Milly when she discovered that boyfriend Kevin had been screwing around behind her back. They were used to listening to each other.

Was it so ridiculous to imagine that something might happen between them? Milly was his junior, a good twenty years younger, and he knew all about the need to separate the personal and professional, yet this fantasy refused to go away. In the same way occasional notions about himself and DCI Deighton – only six years his senior – proved difficult to shift.

Life could be interesting in the middle of the sandwich.

Milly wiped toast crumbs from the corner of her mouth. 'Where to next, boss?'

'Fay Wetherby at St Mark's, and then it's up to Finsbury Park for Chris Turner.'

'Ah, the sex tape!'

Milly licked her lips and gave Garibaldi a wink.

Could it be that she *did* find him attractive? Had he been so caught up in his own problems that he had missed the signals?

'And then I need to get back early to see Alfie.'

This wasn't true. He had to get back early because he was going out with Rachel.

'How's he getting on?'

'Ever since he went to that school, Milly, it's all gone wrong. He should have stayed where he was – he was happy and he was doing well. But along comes Mr Fancy Pants Big

Money Fuckwit Dominic and suddenly it's an option too good to turn down. I did my best, but in the end I didn't have the heart for the fight. They're not good, these places. They're like Larkin's mum and dad.'

'Sorry, boss?'

'They fuck you up.'

Milly looked at him blankly. 'Right. Well, I'm popping to the loo.'

Garibaldi watched her walk through the bar and thought of his parents.

Garibaldi and DS Gardner sat at the round table in the middle of Fay Wetherby's office. Little in the room, or in Fay's manner, suggested that this was the office of the head of the country's most prestigious girls' school. The décor, like Fay herself, suggested a breezy, down-to-earth informality. From the outside the school may have looked traditional, its early twentieth-century red-brick towers and arches looking down imposingly as you approached the entrance, but inside, the girls, scurrying round with not a uniform in sight, gave the place an air of laid-back purpose – at odds with the popular perception of the school as a hotbed of neurotic ambition and eating disorders.

Fay Wetherby epitomised the sense of no-nonsense modernity, her black pencil skirt, white shirt and lilac cardigan making her seem a million miles from the headmistresses of Garibaldi's youth.

'Thank you for finding the time, Mrs Wetherby.'

'Not at all. And it's Fay, please. Certainly not Mrs.'

'I like to err on the side of formality.'

'Well, if you're happy using the term Ms, feel free to, but I think Fay would be better, don't you?'

Garibaldi nodded, deciding to avoid using any appellation

at all rather than give in to Fay Wetherby's demands. She may not have looked like your typical headmistress but she was clearly capable of behaving like one.

'How can I help you, Detective . . .?'

Garibaldi resisted inviting her to call him Jim. 'Detective Inspector Garibaldi.'

'Obviously you're here about poor Nick Bellamy. I can't tell you how upset I was when I heard.'

'Indeed. How well did you know him?'

Fay shrugged. 'Difficult to answer. I knew him well years ago – or, when I say knew him well, I mean in the way that when we're young we think we know people well. We might not know them well at all. And then, as the years passed, I saw less and less of him.'

'Once a year at Melissa's quiz.'

'Exactly. That's what it became.'

'And he dropped out and then made a return this year. Tell me, what did you make of that final round of questions? You know now that it wasn't Melissa behind it. Who do you think it might have been?'

'I have no idea. It's tempting to think it was Nick and to think his murder's connected to it, but I don't think so.'

'Why not?'

'Because that logic would suggest that one of us killed him, and I don't believe that for one moment.'

'Why not?'

'We're not that kind of person.'

'What do you mean by that?'

'Stabbing. Cutting out the tongue. The scarf. It's horrific.'

Garibaldi nodded. Yet again, a highly intelligent Oxford graduate displaying extraordinary naivety. Did none of them realise how the world worked? Had they blinded themselves to the brutal inhumanity everyone is capable of?

'So you can't think of anyone who might want to do that to Nick Bellamy?'

'I can't think of anyone who would want to do that at all. But I'd lost touch with Nick. I have no idea what was going on in his life.'

'So when you heard in that final round that he might have killed a man, did you believe it?'

'I didn't believe any of the accusations. It was clearly a joke.'

'Or you thought it was a joke. That's what Melissa Matthews said it was, but of course we now know that this wasn't the case. Did you believe Mrs Matthews at the time?'

'I didn't know what to think. Like everyone else, I was surprised.'

Garibaldi leaned forward. 'If you were playing that round now, which one would you go for?'

'Sorry?'

'It said one of those facts was true. Which one do you think it was?'

'But none of them were true!'

'But if you had to guess?'

Fay shook her head in a very headmistressy manner. 'I am not here to play games, Detective Inspector.'

'Nor am I, Miss ... This is a murder inquiry and I am taking this very seriously indeed. And I would be grateful if you could answer my question. Which of those would you think most likely to be true?'

Fay Wetherby was clearly not used to being spoken to like this. Garibaldi sensed her discomfort. 'Shall I take you through them again?'

'No, I remember them, but really ...'

'Take your time.'

'OK. Well, can I start with mine?'

'Please do.'

'Absolutely, one hundred per cent untrue. A ridiculous idea. It's not just that I would never, ever consider, let alone actually *do* such a thing – it's also that such a thing nowadays would be impossible. Everything now is open, accountable, transparent. Any decision I make as head is subjected to the closest scrutiny, and if anyone thinks I have in any way acted in the wrong way, there are well-established channels through which to investigate and, if possible, challenge my decision. The idea that I could take some kind of backhander in return for changing my judgement on a disciplinary issue is, frankly, preposterous. Sometimes I wish I had that kind of freedom–'

Fay held up her hands, acknowledging her mistake. 'Sorry, let me rephrase that. I don't mean the freedom to take bribes, I mean the freedom to do things with a little less scrutiny, a little less accountability.'

'So that's a no, then,' said Garibaldi. He caught DS Gardner's eye and saw her suppress a smirk.

'As for the others . . . Greg Matthews and plagiarism? Can't believe it. We'd have heard about that one before though, as I know from experience, plagiarism can be notoriously difficult to prove. Melissa and a child from teenage pregnancy? It's possible, I suppose. After all, none of us knew her then, but I can't help feeling she couldn't have kept it quiet for so long. Someone would have found out. Chris Turner and the sex tape? Have you seen the figure for the percentage of men who watch porn, who engage in that kind of activity? It's very high, so how is this possibly big news, how is this something that Chris should in any way be worried about? We're not living in the Victorian age, you know. We accept that people do things in their private life that have a right to remain private . . .'

Garibaldi leaned forward. 'That may very well be the case,

but the fact is that in these sextortion cases men – and yes, it is predominantly, though not exclusively, men who are involved – do not want their activities made public. Despite what you say, people still want to keep things hidden. There's still shame attached.'

Fay nodded, accepting the point, but clearly irritated that it had been made. 'Which leaves,' she said, 'Nick Bellamy having killed a man. Perhaps the most plausible, but, still, I think, very unlikely.'

'You've left one out.'

'Have I?'

'Yes. Julia Forrest and shoplifting.'

Fay looked flustered. 'Well, it's equally ridiculous, isn't it?'

'I don't know. Is it?'

'Of course.'

'So which of them all would you go for if pushed?' said Garibaldi.

'I refuse to play this game.'

'One final question. How well do you get on with the others – Melissa, Greg, Julia, Chris?'

'As I said, we haven't seen a good deal of each other in recent years and it's not as though we're on the phone each week. But we get on when we're together. We've all gone in different directions, of course, but you know what it's like when you get together with friends from the past – you regress, you go back to the time when you had things in common in an attempt to pick up where you left off. It doesn't always work, but maybe it's the best way to avoid difficulties.'

'And I see that Lauren Matthews is a pupil here,' said Garibaldi.

'Yes, in her final year.'

'And how has she been as a pupil?'

Fay gave an I-know-what-you're-up-to nod. 'You've been asking around, haven't you, Detective Inspector?'

'It's my job.'

'Lauren Matthews has had her personal problems. She was ill in her GCSE year.'

'Ill in what way?'

'I'm not sure it would be appropriate for me to reveal details of her illness.'

'This is a police inquiry.'

'Even so, I feel uncomfortable about it. Let's just say she spent some time in the Priory.'

'And why was that?'

'I'm not absolutely sure of the details.'

'And her disciplinary problems?'

'She's had a couple – one lower down the school and one earlier this year.'

'What did they involve?'

'The recent one was online activity. The earlier one was drug-related.'

'I see. Was she suspended in either case?'

'There was no clear evidence, so no.'

'I see. Could I ask to see the files?'

'Is that relevant?'

'I won't know until I see them.'

'I'll dig them out. Everything will have been recorded and I have nothing to hide, but I really can't see how any of this is useful.'

'Let me be the judge of that.'

'Anything else I can help you with?'

Fay Wetherby had clearly had enough.

'One last question if I may,' said Garibaldi. 'I understand that Julia Forrest's daughter applied to St Mark's and didn't get in.'

'That's right. Disappointing for Julia, I know, but these things happen. Entrance exams are tough and results don't lie. She was well below the cut-off point.'

'And it's all decided purely on the exam result?'

'No, there's an interview as well. We take a good deal of care over the admissions process. It's not merely a matter of academic ability, it's a matter of making sure that the girl is right for the school.'

'And Julia Forrest's daughter wasn't right for the school?'

'It was some time ago, Detective Inspector. I can't remember the details. But there will be a record of it all. In these days of appeals and in this litigious climate we are meticulous in our record-keeping.'

'And did Julia get in touch with you to plead her case?'

'No. She knew there was no point.'

'She didn't get in touch as an old friend to ask a favour?'

'Do you mean did she try to pull strings? Of course not, Detective Inspector. Those days are long gone. It's a fair and open playing field nowadays.'

'Really? And Melissa's daughter did get in?'

'She did better in the exams and interview. That's what happens.'

'The good ended happily, the bad unhappily,' said Garibaldi. 'That's what exams mean.'

'Sorry?'

'Oscar Wilde.'

'Of course.' Fay couldn't hide the fact that Garibaldi's reference had eluded her.

'And I understand that Lauren Matthews applied to Oxford this year and didn't make it? To Balfour, I believe.'

'That's right. Not a surprise, though. The whole Oxford entrance thing has become insanely competitive, and schools like this sometimes ... Well, they're under pressure to get more in from other educational backgrounds. You must have read the newspapers. The story surfaces every year. Not enough state-school pupils at Oxford. Quotas. Positive discrimination. The papers love it.'

'Perhaps they want to make it fairer?'

'It's not that simple.'

'It never is, is it?'

'And when Lauren Matthews didn't make it into Balfour College, did Melissa get in touch?'

'I rang her to say I was sorry.'

'Melissa didn't ask you to intervene or anything?'

'Intervene? As I said, Detective Inspector, those days are gone. It's a different world. The idea that I could get on the phone to Balfour and that it would make the slightest difference is nonsense.'

'Even as a former student of Balfour yourself? As an alumnus? Or should that be alumna?'

'Alumnus will do, I think, and no, not even as a former student.'

'Well, thank you, Mi ... We'd best be off. But if you have any further thoughts on Nick or on anything, do give me a call.'

Garibaldi handed her a card and headed off with DS Gardner to take the long drive to north London.

21

Monday 15 April

Whenever Garibaldi hit north London he felt he was getting a nosebleed. He was OK on the Westway or on the Embankment heading east towards the City, and he was OK in Soho and the West End. Take him beyond Regent's Park, though, heading up through Camden Town, and he was in a different country. And when he reached the heights of north London, the hills of Highgate and Hampstead, he had landed on a different planet. North London was like the past – they did things differently there.

Chris and Kim Turner were not quite different-planet north but Finsbury Park was close enough, and Garibaldi, a west London boy through and through, felt his usual unease. As DS Gardner navigated her way to the Turners' terraced house, nestling between the park and Crouch End, the homing instinct that made him long to be back in the flat terrain where the Thames, source of the city's lifeblood, was never far away kicked in.

Chris Turner was at home by himself. In theory, he was

working, but he was quick to confess to Garibaldi that he hadn't been getting much done. The hours when Kim and Harry were both out of the house at their respective schools were the ones when he should be productive, but these were the hours when he was vulnerable to seductive work-avoidance strategies.

'It's not easy being a freelance,' he said as he ushered Garibaldi and DS Gardner into the living room.

Garibaldi sat down on the sofa, politely declining the offer of tea and coffee. He looked round the room. It was a far cry from the Matthews' and Forrests' Barnes homes. No elements of show, no attempt at *Country Life* décor, and it contained more books than both Barnes homes put together. Kim Turner may have been a book-loving English teacher, but the range on the shelves – history, politics, philosophy, fiction – together with their random arrangement, seemed more a reflection of the lively, magpie mind of her journalist husband. It was an intellectual's house.

'You think with all that time you'll get more done,' said Chris, 'but the fact is you get more done when you're squeezing work round other commitments. Like that old saying. If you want to get something done, give it to a busy man.'

'Parkinson was right,' said Garibaldi.

'Sorry?' said Chris.

'Work expands to fill the time available. Parkinson's Law.'

Chris sat down in an armchair opposite. 'So this is about poor Nick,' he said. 'I still can't believe what happened.'

'How well did you know him?'

'I used to know him well, but that was a long time ago. We lost touch.'

'So you all keep saying.'

'All?'

'Your friends. Your Oxford friends.'

166

'It's what happens. When you're at college you're very young.'

Garibaldi smiled at the use of 'college'. Most people said 'university' or, in more recent years, 'uni'. 'College', he had discovered, far from suggesting the speaker had been at a college of further education or some specialised place of learning, was a coded way of saying Oxbridge.

'And,' said Chris, 'you drift apart. College is a kind of fairyland where for three years you live in a vacuum. The rules of the real world don't apply, and in this strange, unreal place you can choose who or what you want to be. The differences are somehow unimportant. You leave them behind at the college gate. That's why you can get on and be friends with people from very different backgrounds. But then, back out in the real world, those differences that you hadn't noticed for so long gradually reappear and you realise that maybe you didn't have all that much in common after all. It was being thrown together for three years in the most artificial and cloistered world that made you think you were all such buddies.'

'That's quite a long answer to, "How well did you know him?"' said Garibaldi.

'I'm sorry. It's just that since Nick died, since he was murdered, I've been thinking about it quite a bit. And thinking about writing something, of course. In my line of work, thinking about something is usually linked to the possibility of turning the thoughts into something more rewarding.'

'What kind of things do you write?' said Garibaldi, his eyes taking in the range of books again, looking for some unifying thread.

Chris shrugged dismissively. 'All kinds,' he said. 'I used to be on the staff of the *Independent*, but when that folded or, rather, when that responded to the challenges of the digital age and the rapid decline of print media, I wasn't offered a job in the brave new online world – or in the slimmed-down replacement. So I've been taking what I can get. Feature articles mostly, the occasional opinion piece. I've even done some book reviews.' He gave an awkward smile, as if embarrassed by the confession. 'What I like most, though, are political things, not party political, but things that reflect on some aspect of the way things are.'

Garibaldi nodded, but he wasn't sure he understood. It sounded as though Chris Turner was prepared to write anything that would pay well, and was merely dressing it up.

'So you've lost touch with them all, then?'

'Well, not entirely. There were Christmas cards – in the days when everyone still sent them, that is – and there was also the quiz.'

'Which you went to every year?'

Chris nodded. 'Each year with increasing reluctance. They've all done well – apart from Nick, that is, but that's a different story – but they'd all, I don't know, embraced a very different life from mine. TV, the law, head of a public school, even Greg's bloody novels. I felt a long way from that kind of thing and each year it felt more and more awkward, more and more as if the differences were becoming greater as the years passed.'

'Can you be clearer about these differences? What exactly do you mean?'

'Our views, our attitudes. They all danced along holding on to the coat tails of New Labour because it was what everyone did, but they were never . . .'

'So you're talking about political differences?'

'Sort of. My wife teaches in a tough north London comprehensive. She's always found my Oxford friends somewhat questionable.'

'She disapproves of them?'

'She just thinks I don't have an awful lot in common with them any more.'

'And so she disapproved of the quiz, then?'

'I always invited her along, but she never came. Until this year, that is.'

'And why did she come this year?'

'I have no idea. I think all along she was quite fascinated by it. You know how it is. The more someone moans about something, expresses their hostility towards it, as Kim did to the whole quiz thing over the years, the more you wonder whether they're actually, underneath it all, attracted by it. Like those romcoms where the man and woman hate each other at first and go on and on about it and you know that they're going to get together at the end.'

'Beatrice and Benedick,' said Garibaldi.

'Sorry?'

Much Ado About Nothing.'

The look Chris gave him was the familiar one. There were things a mere detective was not expected to know.

'Of course. And just like that other Shakespeare line, from *Hamlet*: "The lady doth protest too much." Maybe that's what was going on with Kim.'

Garibaldi couldn't stop himself. 'That's actually a misquotation.'

'What is?'

'"The lady doth protest too much." Not a misquotation so much as a misunderstanding. "Protest" there doesn't mean make a protest. It means "promise".'

Chris's look had now changed to one of total bafflement.

'So what did Kim make of it all?' said Garibaldi. 'What, more specifically, did she make of that final round?'

'Ha!' said Chris. 'Wasn't that ridiculous?'

'I don't know. You tell me. Let's start with what it said about you.'

'You cannot for one second believe that's true! A sex tape! Sextortion!'

'I've heard the story about the teddy bear, Mr Turner.'

Chris spluttered. 'And you believe that as well, do you? My God!'

'So it's not true?'

'Of course it's not. It was so long ago. I just don't believe this!'

'What happened, then?'

'OK, I had a teddy bear, right? It was an ironic, post-*Brideshead* gesture, the kind of thing you think is clever when you're an undergraduate. And Nick Bellamy came into my room when I was in bed, sleeping off a hangover and I had the bear with me . . .'

'You were in bed with your teddy bear?'

'Look, Inspector, you're investigating a murder, not what I was doing in my college room thirty years ago.'

Garibaldi smiled. 'You never know how things might be connected, Mr Turner.'

'Anyway, I was doing nothing, absolutely nothing. Nick Bellamy throws open the door, laughs, goes out, and the next thing I know everyone round college is talking about the bloke who was caught fucking his teddy bear! I never forgave Nick for it, but that was Nick. Always one for a story. Always making things up.'

'Someone said the teddy bear was specially adapted for the purpose.'

'I don't believe it! There was nothing unusual about this teddy bear. It wasn't a sex doll!'

'So it was all made up? Not an element of truth.'

'Complete fabrication. I was in bed. The teddy bear was

beside me. That's it. Unfortunately the said teddy bear is no longer with me. I lost it when it went into therapy.'

'I see. And you said you never forgave Nick for it . . .'

'You know what I mean.'

'You held a grudge?'

'Well, yes, but look – it's not stayed with me over the years. It's not as though I'd kill him for it!'

'I wasn't suggesting you would. Tell me – given that Nick was always making things up, do you think he could have been the man behind that final round?'

'Who knows? We know it wasn't Melissa.'

'Did you think that at the time?'

'I had my doubts. I think everyone did. As to whether it might have been Nick, I see where you're coming from. The tongue and everything. But why would he do it?'

'Why would anyone do it? To get back to those allegations. Do you watch porn, Mr Turner?'

'Do I have to answer that?'

'Why would you not want to?'

'OK, then. No. I don't.'

'Have you ever watched porn?'

'Yes, but only for the purposes of research.'

'What? An article you wrote?'

'I never wrote it. I just did the research.'

'I see. And when you were doing this . . . this research, did you ever engage in any activity via webcam?'

'Look, inspector, I've told you that allegation is completely untrue. What is it about that that you don't get?'

'OK, Mr Turner, what about the other allegations then?'

Chris shook his head. 'I have no idea. Maybe Nick killed a man. Maybe Greg plagiarised. Teenage pregnancy? Fay taking a bribe. They're all equally unlikely, and at the same time . . .'

'At the same time what?'

'None of them is absolutely impossible. But who knows? The thing about secrets is there's a reason why people want to keep them hidden.'

'You seem to be changing your mind.'

'No. I'm just thinking.'

'Here's another question, Mr Turner. If one of these *were* true, which one would you expect it to be?'

Chris burst into laughter. 'Are you taking this seriously, Inspector?'

Garibaldi kept a poker face. 'More seriously than you could possibly imagine. Which one, Mr Turner?'

'I'd probably go for Greg and the plagiarism, but you have to understand that is motivated entirely by professional jealousy. He's been so bloody lucky. Everything just fell into his lap. And his novels – have you read them, Inspector?'

'I'm afraid I have. One of them.'

'Exactly.'

'And do you have any reason to believe that Greg Matthews might have plagiarised his first one?'

Chris looked away and shook his head slowly. 'I have no idea. I really don't.'

Was Garibaldi imagining it, or did Chris Turner seem uncomfortable?

'And do you have any idea who might have murdered Nick Bellamy?'

'No idea at all.'

'Can we go back to something you said earlier, Mr Turner? You said that Nick made up that story about you at coll . . . at university, and you said that he was always making things up. What did you mean by that?'

'Nick was a great storyteller. Whenever you met him he'd say, "You'll never guess what's happened." Things were

172

always happening to Nick – it was only after a while that you realised what he had said was not always the truth, or certainly not the whole truth. He became a real figure, a real character at Oxford, the centre of attention. I think he took those three years as a chance to reinvent himself in some ways. He played on his working-class background quite a lot, but only as a way of gaining access to another lifestyle. It became his ticket, if you like. And he realised that one of the ways to get on was to be a character, to be the man with the stories. I can still see him rushing into the bar and shouting out, "Guess what, I just walked in on Chris Turner fucking his teddy bear!" and I can imagine him supplying every imagined, lurid detail. The more I think about it, Inspector, the more I think it maybe *was* Nick behind that final round. Things had changed for him; things had not turned out as he wanted. I don't know the details, no one seems to, and maybe this was his final hurrah, his final act of storytelling.'

'And maybe one of you killed him.'

Chris shook his head. 'I don't think so. I really don't.'

'What time does your wife get back from work, Mr Turner?'

'Depends,' said Chris. 'She's late tonight. Parents' meeting.'

'I'd like to talk to her. Could you ask her to give me a call?'

Garibaldi handed Chris a card and got up to leave. DS Gardner got up with him.

'Thanks for your time,' said Garibaldi. 'If you think of anything that might be relevant or of interest, do get in touch, won't you?'

'I will.'

As DS Gardner drove Garibaldi back south, he mulled over what he had learned today. He felt no nearer to any truth, no closer to any breakthrough. Was there a connection between the quiz and Nick Bellamy's murder? Was the scarf in the mouth a lead or a red herring? Had the tongue been severed to make it seem like retribution for words spoken out of turn or had it been cut out in a frenzy, the state of uncontrolled hysteria suggested by the nature and number of the stab wounds?

Garibaldi sighed. He needed to know more about Nick Bellamy.

22

Monday 15 April

Whenever Garibaldi told anyone he lived in Barnes, they assumed he was a man of great wealth living in a huge house. To most people this is what Barnes was – a place for the rich, a place you lived in if you were tempted by a move to the country but wanted to stay in London. Sandwiched between Hammersmith and Richmond, nestling beside a loop in the Thames, Barnes felt like a country village. It was more than the Saturday farmers' market, more than the Barnes residents' penchant for green wellies and dog walking, more than its sense of community. There was something about its very physical appearance – the village pond, the picture-postcard Sun Inn, the independent shops, the quiet leafy avenues – that made it seem like a throwback. Just as a ferry from the mainland to the Isle of Wight could make you feel you were back into the 1950s, so could a bus south from Hammersmith Bridge, followed by a right turn at the Red Lion, make you think you were back in some gentler, more innocent time. This was no place for urban hipsters or metropolitan cool. It may, at one stage, have been a place for the artistic and the intellectual – a south of the river, low-voltage version of Hampstead – but extraordinary rises in property prices had, over the previous decade, driven such residents out. Mammon had very swiftly displaced the mind, and Barnes was now almost exclusively the preserve of the rich. Garibaldi winced every time he passed the young bankers and lawyers parading their wives and dogs, pushing kids in over-large buggies and speaking with loud weekend-dad voices on Saturday mornings.

When people thought of Barnes they didn't think of Rutland Court, a block of flats nestling behind the high-street shops, and Garibaldi's home for the last two years. When his marriage to Kay ended, he had moved out of the marital home in Mortlake (their combined income from his police salary and her accountant salary had made a decent three-bedroom semi just within their range) and into the two-bedroom flat. The rent, like all London rents, was ridiculous, but he could just about manage it, and he enjoyed living there, the neighbours being a more mixed bunch than you would find in the surrounding streets or in the area of Putney where Kay now lived. Dominic's money had not only facilitated Alfie's disastrous move of school but had also enabled Kay to move into an area whose residents, in her more reasonable years, she would have joined Garibaldi in mocking.

When Garibaldi got back to Rutland Court that evening he put on Emmylou Harris (the voice that always soothed), poured a whisky, tried to forget about Nick Bellamy and thought about the evening ahead – and his chat with Alfie. Then he thought about Rachel.

Garibaldi looked at Alfie stretched out on the sofa, remote in hand, flicking from channel to channel. 'Been going out much?'

'What does that mean?'

'It means have you been going out anywhere? You know – parties, that kind of thing.'

Alfie gave as much of a shrug as was possible from his supine position.

'It's always good to get out.'

How pathetic did he sound? Could anyone give a better impression of a father trying, and failing, to connect with his teenage son?

'Look, Dad, you don't have to keep trying to have these chats with me. I know you're feeling guilty, but—'

'I don't think that's very fair.'

'All I'm saying is you don't need to feel guilty.'

Garibaldi knew this wasn't true. He had more than enough to beat himself up about.

'You make it sound like you don't want to come round here.'

'Of course I want to come round here. But just because Mum gives you a call and says I'm in a state doesn't mean you need to go for another big chat number.'

'Don't want to bottle things up, Alfie. It's always better to talk things through.'

Garibaldi sipped his whisky. Maybe if he had talked things through when he was seventeen he might have avoided what happened thirty years later.

'Ever since I went to that school . . .'

Garibaldi tensed. Any sentence beginning like that was unlikely to end well.

'The thing is,' said Alfie, 'I know it's a good school, but everyone's so different.'

Why had he not put his foot down more firmly? Why had he not been clearer about where, exactly, Dominic should shove his money?

'And last year was a complete nightmare.'

'Does that mean that this year hasn't been so bad?'

'This year's nearly over, Dad. One more term and I'm done.'

'That's good, isn't it? It means you're nearly through.'

'Yeah, I know. And in answer to your question, yes, I am going out a bit more.'

'Parties?'

He couldn't believe he had said it. What on earth did he sound like?

'Yeah, that kind of thing. I'm actually going out later tonight.'

'A school night?'

'You sound like Mum.'

'Anywhere nice?'

'Seeing a film.'

'Oh yeah? Anything good?'

Alfie named the film, but it meant nothing to Garibaldi. He had long ago stopped keeping up with the latest releases. He was still trying to catch up with all the stuff that, over the years, had passed him by.

'Who are you going with? People from school?'

He chose the plural carefully.

'No. Different school.'

'Oh?'

'And she's . . .'

He'd said it. That was the moment.

'She's at the Dolphin.'

Alfie's face had changed. The corners of his mouth were resisting the impulse to stretch out into a smile.

'Right,' said Garibaldi. 'And is she in her last year as well?'

Another pathetic question, but he needed to keep the conversation going.

178

'Yeah. I met her at a party. That's the thing about these private schools – everyone seems to know everyone else.'

Garibaldi couldn't believe it. After months of taciturn non-communication in which nothing significant was said for fear of slipping into discussion of the things that were really important, the things that scared Garibaldi to death, Alfie was opening up to him.

'Don't let me keep you, then, if you're going out.'

'Yeah,' said Alfie, getting up from the sofa, his expression still a battlefield, the entrenched sadness still resisting the invading optimism, but much less effectively than when he had first arrived. Garibaldi could imagine him smiling properly by the end of the evening.

He saw Alfie to the door, and gave him a farewell hug. For a fleeting moment he considered telling him that he too had a date lined up, but decided against it.

23

Tuesday 16 April

Garibaldi had not been inside a church for a long time and, as he sat in the pew, feeling the wooden bench beneath him and resting his feet on the kneeler, he was unable to resist the pull of the past. Soon he was sitting with his sister between his parents at Sunday-morning mass, seeing the light shining through the stained glass, smelling the candles, hearing the organ music. And when he caught the scent of the lilies he was next to his parents in a different sense, sitting at the front of the West Kensington church beside their two coffins, about to bid an unbearably painful goodbye.

It was a moment he had revisited in his mind many times, most traumatically in his recent illness, but today's memories, occurring in a Catholic church, had a particular power, and he found himself unable to stop the tears.

In an effort to distract himself, he turned his attention to those in the congregation. There were not many there, but the Oxford friends had made it, all standing together in a pew on the right-hand side. Melissa Matthews, Julia Forrest and Fay Wetherby were all dressed in elegant black, splashes of colour in their scarves acknowledging that Nick would have been the last in the world to expect total solemnity at his departure. A dark-suited Greg Matthews stood beside his wife, head bowed for much of the time, and at the end of the pew stood a tieless Chris Turner.

As Garibaldi looked at them, he saw in their faces the harrowed lines of those who were not so much reflecting on the death of their friend as contemplating the inevitability of their own. Nick Bellamy may not have been the first of their generation to die, but his demise, and its brutal, dramatic nature, had clearly touched them all. Garibaldi had sensed it in all his interviews, but he could see it again now. He could also (was he imagining it, perhaps, or was he indulging himself in such thoughts to take his mind off his own pain?) see guilt. On each face were the signs of someone who could easily be hiding something.

'Nick was not an ordinary man.'

Garibaldi turned to the front. Liz Steele had begun her address.

'From his early years there was something that marked him out as different, as special, and Nick kept that quality throughout his life. He was full of energy, full of life, and that's what makes his death at such a young age, and in such horrific circumstances, so difficult to bear. But I know that Nick, on an occasion such as this, as we say our last farewell, would like us to remember what was good about his life. And that's what I would like to do now.'

Garibaldi looked at Nick Bellamy's sister with admiration. Not only was she holding herself together, she was speaking with great poise.

'Nick was clever. Nick was fun. Nick was charming. He was also never far away from trouble, but only because he was always open to experiences and always prepared to stand up for what he thought was right.'

Garibaldi drifted off again, trying to recall who had spoken at his parents' funeral. He couldn't remember. So much of that day was back with him, but that particular part remained blank. Our memories were strangely selective, as Liz Steele was currently demonstrating in her brother's eulogy.

Melissa tried not to look at the coffin. Every time she did, she felt herself going, so she kept her eyes turned elsewhere. She knew it would be difficult, but she had no idea that it would be as difficult as this. It wasn't just the thought of Nick's body inside the box – a body that had been mutilated but one she could not, despite her best efforts, stop herself seeing in the naked prime of its youth. It wasn't just the thought of the final curtain that awaits us all. No. It was her inability to stop thinking of Lauren, all that she had been through and all that, if her suspicions were correct, she might be about to go through again. Was it because she was her only child that she thought about her so much and cared about her so intensely? She knew it was more than that, just as she knew it was more than a devastating sense of all that her daughter had suffered. Drugs. The Priory. Not Getting Into Oxford. She knew it was wrong to capitalise that third item, to give it as much weight as the first two, but she knew it was a moment that had struck Lauren hard. And Greg hadn't made it any easier. He came out with all the right platitudes – it really didn't matter, the whole Oxford thing was overrated, don't look on it as some judgement of you as a person – but Melissa could see he meant none of it and she had no doubt that Lauren knew that as well. That was the thing about Greg. He may have been a bestselling novelist and he may have been highly intelligent, but when it came to some things he was curiously deficient.

There were blind spots, Achilles heels. In bed, for example. Where to start? Greg's problem exactly. Melissa knew it was entirely inappropriate to have such thoughts in such a context, but she thought again of Nick Bellamy as he had been at Oxford and started to remember him as very much alive.

She shook the thought away and the worries about Lauren flooded back. She had never been an easy child, but Melissa had genuinely thought that after her spell in the Priory, after she stopped seeing her drug-pushing boyfriend, the one who had got her into the mess in the first place, she would be OK. And, generally speaking, she had been. There had been the little spat over online teacher abuse, but that had been minor and Melissa had remained cautiously optimistic. Recent events, though, and her recent behaviour, suggested such optimism had been misplaced. Lauren now seemed to be slipping back into trouble.

As Melissa braved a look at the coffin, her agitation increased. This time, though, it was not at the thought of Nick Bellamy's body, but at the thought of the things she had to keep to herself, the secrets that might go with her in a box like Nick Bellamy's. She thought of her childhood Catholicism. None of it had stuck and nothing about the ceremony was making her think of returning to embrace it. Apart, that is, from confession. Suddenly the healing effects of the confessional seemed very attractive.

Was it so wrong to feel relieved that Nick Bellamy was no longer with them? Was it hard-hearted and insensitive, given the appalling circumstances under which he had left the world, to think that the world might be a better place without him? Greg Matthews stood beside his wife, trying hard not to have these thoughts, but they kept returning. What exactly was it about Nick that he had found so difficult? Could it be the fact that Melissa had been out with him before they got together? Was it anything other than the recognisable feelings of unease about your partner's ex? Maybe not, but sometimes Greg sensed that his feelings about Nick might be disproportionate. He had made a pile of money, was, by anyone's definition, hugely successful and yet the very thought of Nick Bellamy made him feel inadequate. And what was Nick Bellamy, when it came down to it? Some jumped-up kid who made a name for himself as a Jack the Lad, someone whose appetites led to his own downfall, someone who had moments of success but who ruined it all by his own tendency to self-destruct. So why the anxiety? Greg had given it much thought and had come to the conclusion that it wasn't Nick Bellamy so much as what Nick Bellamy represented, a kind of energy that he himself, for all his worldly success, might lack.

And yet Nick Bellamy's death had not made Greg's life any easier. If anything, it had made it considerably worse. From the moment the body had been identified, life in the Matthews household had become difficult. Melissa, for all her charms, had never been easy, but he had sensed her becoming less so in recent weeks. Nothing obvious, but there nonetheless. And when it came to Lauren he didn't know where to start. She showed all the signs of being on the slippery slope again, of reverting to the behaviour that led her to the Priory. Going out at night during school weeks. Not letting them know where she was going. Coming back in the early hours. Looking awful. Avoiding his eye. It pained Greg to think it, but he was worried that she might not even get the grades for Durham. It still irked him that Balfour had turned her down and it irked him even more that his conversation with the Balfour principal, followed by offers of generous donations, had led to nothing. When it came to dealing with Lauren he had, of course, said all the right things, and made all the right noises. If only Melissa had done the same. But it had hit her so hard that she had been unable to hide her disappointment. And Julia's daughter getting in had made it even worse. He knew what these women were like, especially Melissa and Julia. They might have got older but they hadn't really changed – they were still the bright young Oxford undergraduates competing for the prizes. So when Lauren had made it into St Mark's and Julia's daughter hadn't, that was fine. Melissa could handle that one, all right – she knew how to land a telling blow in every conversation. But when the shoe was on the other foot – or the glove was on the other hand – she hadn't found it at all easy.

Despite having known Nick Bellamy in one sense of the term for a very short period of time and with great intensity, Fay Wetherby felt that in most other senses of the term she had hardly known him at all. And yet, here at his funeral, she was distraught in a way she could not have anticipated. She had been to a fair number of funerals over the years and the demands of her job had taught her to keep her emotions in check on public occasions, but she was finding this occasion particularly difficult.

Maybe it was the brutal circumstances of his death. Maybe (and she was sure she was not alone here) it was the way the passing of one of her contemporaries reminded her of the slenderness of the thread by which her own life dangled, the brevity of her own time on earth. Or maybe it was the way his murder (still frustratingly unsolved) had become linked to his Balfour friends and, more specifically, to those accusations in the quiz night final round. If Melissa didn't do it, then who did? And how far would investigations into the truth of those allegations go?

Fay knew that there had been mutterings among the staff

and the parental body. It was still the case that no one had said anything directly to her on the subject, but that didn't mean she wasn't being scrutinised more closely than usual. And, yes, she had things to hide. Was there anyone in the world who didn't?

Fay looked at Melissa, Greg and Julia beside her in the pew. As soon as she had heard that both Lauren Matthews and Helena Forrest were applying to St Mark's, she had feared it could only lead to trouble, and her fears had proved to be well founded. Lauren Matthews had been an absolute nightmare. And now, if her head of Year 13 was to be believed, showing all the signs of slipping back into it all again. Would Melissa and Greg want to talk about it? She hoped not. She couldn't wait for today to be over. Nor could she wait for the day when Lauren Matthews left St Mark's.

Fay looked again at Nick Bellamy's coffin. Maybe, when it was known who had killed him and why, everything might blow over. Maybe, when they knew who was behind that wretched quiz night, she might start to sleep more easily.

As the organ played, Chris looked up at the crucifix and contemplated suffering. If someone had told him when he was young that life, rather than getting better as the years passed, would become more painful, he would not have believed them. How full of optimism had he been back then. How full of optimism had they all been. Looking along the pew, he thought back to his first day at Balfour, the day they had all met. They must have known that a day like this would come, but it was the furthest thing from their minds. They were too intent on living, on making the most of what lay in front of them to consider how quickly it would all pass. And over the years, if they were anything like him, they would all have suppressed the thought, too involved in the intensity

186

of the moment, of hoping, of looking forward, to consider a time when their best years might be behind them and their own final farewell would be approaching. Was this gathering the moment when that truth became unavoidable?

As far as Chris was concerned, this occasion was not so much one of realisation as one of confirmation – he had sensed that his best was behind him some time ago and he knew that things were now unlikely to improve. He loved his son to bits, but dealing with him was not easy. And he wasn't earning enough from his writing to provide the help that Harry needed. On top of that, things with Kim were difficult. In and out of the bedroom. Maybe if she hadn't come along to the wretched quiz things wouldn't be quite so bad. Maybe she wouldn't have been so affected by Nick's murder. Why *did* she come? After so many years of absence, so many years of making snide comments about his Balfour friends, why did she choose to subject herself to it this year? If he were being honest, he would admit that her presence had ruined the whole evening. He hadn't been able to relax at all, ever conscious of the way Kim was looking at, and judging, all that she saw. And then as soon as the word 'sex tape' came over the PA everything tumbled out. Him and that fucking teddy bear. Him and his porn problem. Him and not getting it up with Kim. It all came to the surface.

Julia couldn't stop herself thinking of the times she had slept with Nick Bellamy at Oxford. There was so much about it she had enjoyed. Not just the physical thrill – though that had been considerable – but also the thrill of illicit appropriation, the thrill of theft. The fact that Nick was, at that time, still with Melissa, had made the whole thing that much sweeter. Maybe, over the years, her tendency to want what wasn't hers, to lay claim to things to which she had no right, may have had its roots in those moments with Nick. She looked along the pew to Greg and Melissa. Was it anything more than their worldly success that she envied? Was there any explanation, other than her own mean-mindedness, her own vanity, for her feelings of guilty pleasure at the difficulties they had experienced with Lauren?

There were many things in Melissa's life that she sometimes coveted, but her family was not one of them. How pleased she was that Helena, though not perfect by any means, had turned out OK, or comparatively OK when it came to the kind of things that could end up happening to teenage girls. And how pleased she was that she didn't have Greg Matthews as a husband. He may have earned shedloads of money through his books, but anyone could see that when it came to the important things in life, like being fun and interesting and sexually attractive, he was sadly lacking. How odd that a looker like Melissa should end up with someone like that. If Melissa had known when they got together at Oxford that Greg was going to be as rich and successful as he had turned out to be, she might have understood it, but back then no one had any idea of what lay in store for him. This had always puzzled Julia. To move from someone like Nick to someone like Greg was a huge leap, and she found it difficult to think that there had not been times over the years when her attentions might have wandered beyond the confines of the marital bed. Julia's infidelities had taken place only in her imagination, and she had stayed true to Phil, but was she silly to think that other women did more than think about it? And was she wrong to think that, given the mismatch in her marriage – Melissa attractive and lively, Greg far from either – Melissa might have been more tempted than most? Julia leaned forward and glanced sideways to see the couple standing side by side. They did look like an odd pair and, yes, Greg Matthews was dull. She sometimes thought that all the excitement, all the thrills he could offer had been put into his books.

She thought of Nick's body in the coffin and imagined what it must have looked like as it lay by the Leg o' Mutton lake. She thought of Nick's tongue and for some strange reason couldn't stop herself speculating about what had happened to it and whether, for the purposes of burial, it had been restored to its owner's mouth.

It was a crazy thought, but it somehow calmed her down and stopped her crying.

24

Tuesday 16 April

Garibaldi pushed open the doors to the White Horse and walked to the bar.

The barmaid smiled. 'What can I get you?'

'Pint of best bitter, please.'

'You're the one who was in here asking after Nick Bellamy, aren't you?'

'That's right. And I was wondering ...' Garibaldi looked round the bar at the early-evening clientele. 'I was wondering if any of his quiz team were in.'

The barmaid nodded to one corner. 'That's one of them over there. Steve.'

'Great.'

Garibaldi looked to the corner. Steve sat behind a half-empty pint of Guinness, his head buried in a newspaper. He looked familiar and Garibaldi wondered whether he had seen him at this morning's funeral.

This visit had not been part of his plans, but sitting in his flat and feeling nervous about the night ahead, he had, impulsively and without too much reflection, leapt on a bus from Barnes Pond and come up to Hammersmith on the off-chance. Maybe it was nerves – the need to do something to take his mind off that night's date with Rachel. And even if there was no one to ask about Bellamy it would at least give him the chance of a pint before heading back over the bridge to Putney.

He took his pint over to where Steve was sitting. 'Excuse me. I was wondering if I could have a quick word.'

Steve looked up from his paper.

'About Nick Bellamy.'

'Nick?'

'Yeah. I'm an old friend.' Garibaldi paused and looked at Steve as if he had suddenly recognised him. 'Hang on, did I see you at his funeral yesterday?'

'Could have done. I was there at the back. We were all there.'

'All?'

'The team.'

'What team's that?'

'The quiz team.'

'I see. Well, look, as I say, I'm an old mate of Nick's. Shocked of course, like everyone, but I wanted to have a chat with someone who knew him, because there are a few things I'd like to know.'

'You're not a copper are you?'

'No. Why? Was Nick in some kind of trouble?'

'Always in trouble. Always short of money and prepared to do anything to get it.'

'Really? I knew him a long time ago. Thought he might have calmed down by now.'

Steve laughed and took a sip of his drink. 'No chance.'

'So when you say trouble . . .'

191

'Don't ask,' said Steve. 'Nick had all kinds of problems, but I reckon the biggest one was gambling.'

'Yeah. As I remember, he did like a bet.'

'I can't say I knew every detail of his life – he kept a lot of it to himself – but ask away.'

'Do you mind?' Garibaldi pointed at the seat.

'Go ahead.'

Garibaldi put his pint on the table and sat down, 'It's about the Ocean Bar Quiz. I read about it in the news reports and I just wanted to know a bit more about it.'

'Why do you want to know about that?'

'Because he often talked about it. In fact, he asked me to be on his table one year, but I couldn't make it. Actually, if I'm being completely honest, I couldn't afford it. I know it's for charity and all that but that was a lot of money to pay for a seat at a quiz night. How much did you have to fork out this year?'

'Fork out? We didn't have to pay anything. Nick just wanted us all to do it.'

Garibaldi raised his eyebrows. 'Blimey! So he paid for all of you. That must have set him back a bit. I didn't know he had that kind of money.'

Steve threw back his head and laughed.

'What's the joke?' said Garibaldi.

'Nick and money! If Nick ever had any money then he'd borrowed it or won a bet. Guess which was more likely. Most of the time he had nothing, because he was always asking for it.'

'He was still gambling, then?'

'Gambling?' Steve shook his head from side to side and sighed as if the word itself could not adequately describe what Nick had been doing. 'Let's put it like this. He had a serious problem. Addicted? Yeah, I'm pretty sure he was. Funny, isn't it, you pick up on drink addiction – or at least you do if you know the bloke, because you see him in your local boozer and play with him on the pub quiz team – and it's pretty easy to pick up on someone with a drug problem. But gambling? It's as much of a killer.'

'How much of a problem was it for Nick, then?'

Steve shrugged. 'You can't tell. I mean, I don't often go into the bookie's, but whenever I passed Paddy Power and looked in I'd often see him on the machines. Then there's online stuff. And the thing is, it's everything. You can gamble on absolutely fucking anything. The days of it being horses and dogs are long gone.'

'I see,' said Garibaldi. 'Well, I suppose there was always an addictive streak to Nick, but back in the day it was more alcohol and drugs. Oh, and sex, of course.'

'Sex?' Steve laughed again.

'What's so funny about that?'

'Just reminds me of that quiz night.'

'Sex reminds you of the quiz night? Blimey, that must have been some quiz.'

'Nick kept going on about all the women in the room he'd slept with when he was at Oxford. He liked to go on about that as well – being at Oxford. Wanted everyone to know he was clever. Anyway, he went on about the woman who ran the quiz, the newsreader.'

'Melissa Matthews?'

'Yeah. He said he slept with her many times. And some others as well, some teacher or headmistress.'

'Fay Wetherby?'

'Maybe. I can't remember. You seem to know an awful lot about these women.'

'Yeah, well I was at Oxford with Nick myself.'

Garibaldi had not planned the lie, and was surprised at how easily it came.

'I see.'

'Yeah. I knew them all. That's why I'm so interested in that quiz night. Because they were all there. Did he mention a Julia at all?'

'I can't remember. Look, we were all a bit out of it, if you want to know the truth. Not so out of it that our brains weren't working but, you know, we'd taken some stuff to sharpen us up.'

'Tell me, do you remember what happened at the end of the quiz?'

'What do you mean? When Nick went up for the trophy?'

'No, before that. There was this joke round of questions.'

'Oh yeah. I remember now. That was funny.'

'Can you remember how Nick reacted when he heard them?'

Steve gave Garibaldi a cool, measured look. 'You sound a bit like a cop, you know that?'

'Sorry. It's probably because I'm used to asking questions of people, being a teacher.'

Another lie that had come very easily.

'It's just that you have to be careful round here. Especially with someone like Nick.'

'Yeah?'

'He liked an argument, Nick. Had a temper on him.'

'Tell me about it. So, those allegations at the end. What did Nick make of them?'

'Oh, yeah, I remember now, of course I do. That Nick killed a man! And other stuff about sex. Yeah, Nick thought it was hilarious. Couldn't stop laughing. Yeah, I remember now. He stood up and said, "What do you mean, a man? It was loads more than one!"'

'And what did he make of the others? You see, they were all about the people we knew at Oxford.'

'He just thought it was funny. He couldn't stop laughing. In fact, as soon as he knew that we'd won, he just couldn't stop smiling and thanking us all for everything, for winning the quiz.'

'And why was he so keen on winning it, do you know?'

'He didn't say. Just wanted the team to come along and win it. Which is exactly what we did.'

Steve reached for his pint and finished it with two large gulps.

'Can I get you another?' said Garibaldi.

'Very kind of you.'

Garibaldi went to the bar wondering what else he could ask about Nick Bellamy and the quiz night.

If the claim that Nick Bellamy had slept with both Melissa Matthews and Fay Wetherby at Oxford were true, then Garibaldi needed to consider its implications. Neither had mentioned it, but then they might have felt no need to. Maybe sleeping around was what everyone did in their university days. The truth was that Garibaldi was uncomfortable thinking of the number of women Bellamy might have slept with. Whenever he did, he felt strangely inadequate, unable to resist a sneaking admiration for the dead man's exploits and conscious that his own love life had been dull by comparison. Whenever he counted, he never troubled the fingers of a second hand.

Tonight in particular, he wanted no thoughts of inadequacy.

He had thought very carefully about where to go. He and Rachel might have slept together a couple of times, but in many senses this occasion was more important. This was a proper date, a chance to explore each other in a different (and, at their ages, maybe a more significant) way. This was taking things to a new level.

He raised his whisky. 'Cheers!'

Rachel raised her bottle of Corona and clinked it against his glass. 'Cheers!'

Patty Nelson specialised in the departed, the country greats who are with us no more, weaving their songs with anecdote and narrative. Hank Williams. George Jones. Merle Haggard. Jimmie Rodgers. Guy Clark. Johnny Cash. Patty Nelson did them all, and when he discovered she was playing the Half Moon, he knew this was where his first proper date with Rachel should be. It could have been the movies or it could have been dinner, but this seemed the most grown-up option, the natural choice for a woman who had not only picked up his Townes Van Zandt CD the morning after they slept together, but had nodded with warm-hearted approval.

'She's great, apparently,' said Garibaldi. 'And the thing about her is she's a real tribute act. She only covers those who have gone.'

'It's difficult liking country music sometimes,' said Rachel.

'Why's that?'

'It's like that old joke – what do you get if you play a country music song backwards?'

'You sober up, your wife comes home and you get out of jail,' said Garibaldi.

Rachel laughed. 'Yeah. All that suffering. The white man's blues.'

'Three chords and the truth. But it's not an obsession. I do like other kinds of music.'

'I know,' said Rachel.

'How do you know?'

'I've stayed at your flat twice,' said Rachel.

So she'd been counting as well.

'Any self-respecting woman needs to check out a man's music collection very carefully.'

'I thought I was the detective.'

'Everyone's a detective.'

'And do I pass the test?'

'You pass all kinds of tests.'

'Well, thank you, miss. Do I get a gold star?'

'I wouldn't go that far.'

Nothing had come of the few women Garibaldi had been with since he split with Kay. He had been too wary, too frail, too obviously scarred to come close to any kind of commitment. Was he coming close now? And was that why he felt like he was blushing?

'Room for a bit more classical, perhaps.'

'Classical?' said Garibaldi. 'Never really got into it. Apart from the obvious, that is. For me it's background stuff. Or Last Night of the Proms. I know I'm wrong and I know I should really spend more time finding out about it.'

'It did strike me as a little odd. You seem so incredibly educated in other respects.'

'I'm not sure if that's praise or criticism.'

'It's praise. When we first met I couldn't believe how much you knew about things, especially how much you've read.'

'I'm sorry about that. If I'd known you were an English teacher I wouldn't have gone on about books.'

'And if I'd known you were a policeman I'm not sure I would have gone home with you.'

'Just as well I said I'm an accountant, then.'

'Do you often do that? Pretend you're something you're not?'

'Don't we all?'

'I mean "pretend" as in say you're not a policeman. I mean, I never like saying I'm an English teacher.'

'Why's that?'

'Because it always gives the wrong impression. I'm either

197

bossy, or I'm someone who couldn't find anything better to do with my life.'

'What about someone who wants to devote themselves to helping shape the lives of the next generation, inculcating them with the right sense of values and a discriminating, enquiring mind?'

'Well, that as well, of course.'

'Anyway, I'm glad I didn't tell you I'm a policeman. It could have ruined the evening. And, no, I don't always do it. Only when I'm nervous.'

'Nervous? That's not what you expect from a policeman, from a detective.'

'Everyone gets nervous,' said Garibaldi. 'Even those who don't appear to. In fact, those are often the worst.'

'How long have we got before she's on?'

Garibaldi looked at the clock on the wall. 'About half an hour, I reckon. Time for another drink.' He pointed at Rachel's bottle. She nodded and Garibaldi got up from the table.

Rachel reached for his arm. 'Maybe when you get back we could do the history thing.'

'The history thing?'

'Our stories. Ten minutes each. Birth. School. Work. Marriage. Kids. The whole thing. Love, death and the American novel.'

'OK,' said Garibaldi. He headed for the bar, wondering where he should begin and how truthful he should be.

'What I don't get,' said Rachel after listening to Garibaldi's account, 'is why you didn't go to university.'

'I couldn't get my head round anything when I lost my parents. And I think that's why I hit that trouble a couple of years ago. Suddenly, bam! I'd never talked about it properly, never allowed myself to acknowledge what a horrible huge fucking disaster it was. Maybe it was a delayed breakdown, maybe things had been simmering for all those years and then suddenly they erupted. They had to. They needed some kind of release.'

'And why the police? If you don't mind my saying, you don't seem to me the typical policeman. You're too ...'

'Go on, say it. Write off both me and the whole police force in one sentence.'

'What I mean is you're too ... intelligent, educated.'

'You've done it! Two birds with one stone.'

'What I mean is, I would never have guessed you didn't go to university.'

'Look, I joined the police because at the time it seemed like a good idea. I didn't want to move away from my sister. I knew I wasn't going to get decent A levels because my parents died so close to the exams and I was all over the place, but I didn't want to take my A levels a year later. I wanted – I needed – to *do* something, and I saw this ad. I can still remember what it said – "Be a Force For Good". OK, I was vulnerable, but it struck a chord. Something so *bad*, so horrible had happened to me that I wanted to do something that might have the opposite effect. I was brought up a Catholic – what do you expect with an Irish mother and an Italian father? – but I'd turned my back on it. When my parents died I didn't suddenly return to it, but I thought about it all again. I was only seventeen. You think when you're seventeen that you're pretty clear about what you do and don't believe, but you're not. How can you be? You've hardly started living, so who are you to decide about things as big as religion and decide with such certainty? As I say, I was all over the place and this idea of the police – I don't know where it came from, I really don't, but it took hold and the idea wouldn't go away. It sounds like the road to Damascus, but it wasn't that simple. Why not be a policeman? Why not? And why not a detective? Yes, the old cliché – reading too much Sherlock Holmes and thinking you could use your mind to unlock mysteries. Silly, I know, but I was young. So I did it. I joined the police. Was it an act of rebellion, turning my back on education, on the conventional escape routes for a working-class lad from Hammersmith? Maybe. Was it some crazy form of grief? Maybe. Or maybe it was an act of atonement? "Be a Force For Good."'

Garibaldi paused and took a sip of whisky. 'But don't think I haven't looked back on that decision and wondered whether it was the right one. I've thought of jacking it in and going off to university every year since I joined. And it's still an option. I'm pushing fifty and I've never been more seriously tempted by the idea of doing what I didn't at the age of seventeen. Going back to school and starting all over again . . .'

Garibaldi looked at his watch. 'Ten minutes and thirteen seconds,' he said. 'Your turn.'

He sat back and listened.

Nothing he heard made him change his mind about Rachel. If anything, it made him like her even more and, after a great evening of Patty Nelson country, he was pleased to take her back again to Rutland Court.

25

Wednesday 17 April

Garibaldi waited until it was 8 a.m. on the East Coast before he called New York.

'Is that Sophie Wickham?'

'Speaking.'

'It's Detective Inspector Garibaldi from the London Metropolitan Police here. I'm sorry to bother you, but it's about your ex-husband.'

'Which one?'

'Nick Bellamy.'

'Oh.' There was disappointment in her voice, as if Garibaldi had made the wrong choice.

'I don't know if you've heard, Mrs Wickham, but Nick Bellamy died recently.'

'What?'

'He was murdered.'

'Oh my God.'

There was a long silence.

'Are you OK?'

'I'm sorry. I—'

'Sorry to deliver such bad news.'

'I had no idea. No one told me, but then, why would they? I've had no contact with him for years.'

'I hope I haven't called too early, Mrs Wickham. Is it OK to ask you a few questions?'

'Sorry, this is all too much. *Murdered*, you say?'

'Yes, I'm afraid so.'

'But I don't understand. Why?'

'That's what I'm trying to find out. There were some strange circumstances surrounding his murder.'

'What do you mean?'

'He had been stabbed, but was also poisoned. His tongue had also been cut out and a college scarf stuffed in his mouth.

'What the fuck!'

'When did your marriage end, Mrs Wickham?'

'God. So long ago I can't remember. When was it? 1996 I think. Yes, that was it. He spent all summer watching Euro 96, singing "Three Lions" and treating me badly. Yes, it's all coming back to me now, unfortunately.'

'When you say treating you badly . . .'

'He cheated on me. Had been cheating on me the whole time, but then, that's what he was like. We should never have got married at all, but you know how it is when you're young. He was a charmer, but he was also completely and utterly unreliable. Looking back on it, I'm surprised it lasted as long as it did.'

'And how long was that?'

'Two years.'

'Mrs Wickham, I'm sorry that I've had to give you this news, but can you think of anyone who might have wanted to kill Nick Bellamy?'

'I felt like killing him myself all the time, but I was here on the day in question.'

Garibaldi smiled.

'Is he *really* dead? Murdered? I can't believe it. I know we're all going to end some time but, shit, you don't expect to go like that, do you? Look, no, seriously, I have no idea of anyone who might want to kill him, and to kill him like that . . .'

'In our investigations, someone has suggested that Nick Bellamy might have once killed a man himself. Do you believe that?'

'Nick? No, I don't believe that. I mean, he was always getting into trouble, and he had lots of rows with people, but kill a man? No, he wasn't like that.'

'Maybe not while he was married to you, but at some time after, perhaps. Did he seem to be the kind of man who might have it in him to do that?'

'Who knows? Most men are assholes, aren't they? They're capable of all kinds of shit, so I wouldn't put it past him. Yeah, he had a temper. Yeah, he got into trouble. But I never thought he was getting up to that kind of thing.'

'What kind of thing *was* he getting up to, then?'

'Screwing around, mostly. And he probably did drugs. We all did.' There was another pause. 'Shit! It's kind of early over here, officer, and this is difficult to take in.'

'Well, look, Mrs Wickham, I'll give you my number and my email address, and if anything occurs to you, please do get in touch.'

'OK, sure. You know, now I think about it, there was always something odd about Nick, something I never quite got.'

'What was that?'

'It's not that I thought he'd killed a man, or that he ever would, but there *were* times when I thought he might be hiding something, that he might have some kind of secret.

203

I suppose you think it about all guys when you have a sense that they're screwing around, but with Nick I sometimes thought it was something more. There were times when he looked like he was on the verge of telling me something but he always stopped before he did. There was this sense that I didn't know him fully. Well, clearly I didn't. I thought we were in love, but we split after two years of marriage.'

'Do you have any idea at all what it might have been that he was hiding?'

'I don't know. Probably something that happened at Oxford. He was like the rest of them. Never got over the goddamn place.'

'Do you have any evidence for that?'

'Not really. I didn't really take to his Oxford friends. High opinion of themselves.'

Garibaldi nodded in agreement. 'Well, Mrs Wickham, thanks for your time, and as I said, if anything . . .'

'Sure thing, officer. Shit! Is he *really* dead?'

As soon as Garibaldi hung up, he called Nick Bellamy's sister.

'Detective Inspector Garibaldi here.'

'Oh, hello. Have you made any progress?'

'A bit, but no breakthrough. I have a few questions for you. Is this a good time?'

'It's fine.'

'The last time we met you said you thought it unlikely that Nick would have killed a man.'

'I still do. He did some crazy things and I know he wasn't always entirely sober, but I just can't see him killing someone.'

'I asked because it was an allegation made about him at that quiz. Along with other allegations about his friends. All of them suggested things that they might have wanted to keep secret. Now I know this is a silly question, because the definition of a secret is that no one knows about it, but can you think of anything that Nick might have wanted to keep a secret, or do you have any memory of thinking that he might have been keeping something from you?'

'I'm not sure I do. There was so much about Nick I didn't know.'

'Was there anything he confided in you, opened up about?'

'Not really. We spoke frankly about things but he never . . . You can never know anyone totally, can you? Even your brother. You can always be surprised.'

'I spoke to his ex-wife in New York earlier. She said there were times when Nick seemed on the verge of some big revelation.'

Liz Steele laughed. 'But that was Nick! He was always on the verge of some big revelation! Something was always happening to him. Looking back on it, I'm not sure those somethings were always true, but—'

'What do you mean, not always true?'

'He had a habit of making things up.'

'Do you have any examples?'

'There were so many. Like he'd say he met famous people on planes and at parties and later he'd tell you he hadn't.'

'And why do you think he did this?'

'I've often wondered. I think for Nick life had to be a big exciting story and he had to be at the heart of it. And as I said to you before, it all started when he went to Oxford.'

'Thank you, Mrs Steele, that's very helpful.'

'Is there anything else I can tell you?'

'I'll be in touch if there is.'

Garibaldi hung up and looked at the phone in his hand, asking himself a couple of questions. If Nick Bellamy's sister and ex-wife were right in suspecting that he had harboured a secret, what was its nature? And did Nick Bellamy's love of dramatic misrepresentation and invention of stories mean that the final round was his brainchild?

26

Thursday 18 April

Melissa had perfected the art of separating her professional and personal lives. When you read the news to millions, when your job involved being subject to such close scrutiny from so many, you could not afford a slip-up, and much of her success could be attributed to the way she hardly ever made a mistake, the way she always remained cool. No one in her line of work could avoid mistakes completely, but Melissa liked to think that if anyone had been keeping records she would be found to be the newsreader who made the fewest.

Every time she went on air she managed to clear her mind of all thoughts other than those to do with the job in hand. It was almost like yoga or meditation. Whenever the light came on, whenever the autocue started rolling, Melissa entered a world of intense focus and concentration, and nothing intruded on it. No matter how tough things were, no matter how much shit she had to deal with, as soon as she was in front of the camera, she was in the zone. Even when Lauren had been in the Priory, even when every day in her daughter's life seemed to throw up a new problem, Melissa had managed to keep every aspect of her job running as smoothly and as professionally as anyone could hope for.

Which was why what was happening to her now took her completely by surprise. Ever since the Ocean Bar Quiz and the discovery of Nick's body, Melissa had found it more and more of a struggle to keep things together in front of the camera. For the first time in her career, thoughts leapt into her head as she was reading the news. And not just thoughts – images too. On screen would be footage of the prime minister with a visiting dignitary, and what Melissa would see was Nick Bellamy's body, tongue severed, scarf in mouth. She would be reading the latest Brexit nonsense and through her earpiece she would hear again that final round of allegations. She would be reporting on some earthquake or disaster and the one that she would see or hear would be the disaster that was her daughter, worse than she had ever been and in free-fall as her exams approached.

As far as she knew, the problem was completely internal and Melissa hoped no one had noticed.

One evening, though, after she had neatly straightened her papers on the desk, smiled at camera, said her goodnight and unclipped her earpiece, and as the theme music played, her producer sidled up to her.

'Everything OK?'

Melissa looked at him with what she hoped was a confident smile. 'Why do you ask?'

'There were times when, I don't know, your mind seemed elsewhere.'

It was the first time in her career Melissa had been accused of this, and it stung.

'Really? Was there a particular moment, anything specific?'

Her producer shrugged. 'Nothing particular, no. Just thought I'd ask.'

Melissa reassured him that all was well but took it as a warning. No one knew how difficult she was finding things at home, how worried she was about Lauren. No one knew how much else she had to worry about. And no one knew how important it was that she kept it that way. No one was to know anything. Even Greg. Especially Greg.

Melissa had no idea what to do about Lauren. It was only a couple of months until she finished her A levels and left school, but Melissa's worry was that she might not make it that far.

'I don't know what's happened to her,' she said to Greg when she got back later that night.

'Look, love, it's just the stress of exams.'

'It's more than that. Something's happened. She was absolutely fine and then, almost overnight, bang, she was a changed girl. What happened to her? It's drugs, isn't it? She's back on them. I wouldn't be surprised if she's in touch with him again.'

'We need to keep calm. Confrontation isn't going to help. She needs to get through her exams and then . . .'

'And then what?'

'We don't want her back in the Priory, do we?'

'Of course not.'

'Well, maybe we should ask her if there's anything . . .'

'We've asked her so many times. And we get nothing back. It's either a huge row or she goes back into her shell. We can't win. But we have to do *something*! I don't know, sometimes I think it might have been easier if . . .'

Melissa trailed off.

Greg was on it instantly. 'Easier if what?'

'Nothing.'

'No. Tell me. It might have been easier if what?'

Melissa sighed. 'If she hadn't gone to that fucking school, if she hadn't applied to fucking Oxford, or if she had and she'd got in . . .'

'You can't blame that.'

'Why not? What else do we blame?'

'As you said, maybe she *is* back on drugs.'

They turned as they heard the front door open. They said nothing, listening to the footsteps to work out their daughter's direction.

When Lauren appeared in the doorway, Melissa and Greg did their best to smile reassuringly. Lauren stood there looking from one to the other, fixing each of them with a vague, distant stare, but saying nothing.

'Everything OK?' said Melissa.

It was a ridiculous question. Everything was clearly far from OK.

Lauren stood there, still saying nothing.

'Not long now,' said Greg.

Melissa's question may have been ridiculous, but it was nothing compared to Greg's offering.

'Not long now until what?'

'Until it's all over,' said Greg.

'Until what's all over?'

Greg shrugged his shoulders, a man who made his living from his use of words now seeming to have spent all of them.

Melissa moved towards Lauren. 'Look, we're just concerned about you, that's all.'

Melissa held out her arms, a gesture that simultaneously offered help and suggested helplessness.

Lauren jumped back as if she feared her mother's touch. 'Get away!' she screamed. 'Just leave me alone, will you?'

Greg stepped forward. 'Lauren, love—'

'Just fuck off! The pair of you. Just fuck off!'

'Tell us what it is,' said Greg. 'Tell us how we can help.'

'You can't help.'

'But we want to,' said Melissa. 'We need to.'

'Why can't we help?' said Greg.

Lauren looked at Greg. Then she looked at Melissa. 'You can't help because I *know*.'

Greg and Melissa exchanged nervous glances. Greg moved towards her.

'Don't touch me. Don't come close, either of you. And for fuck's sake just leave me alone!'

Lauren turned, opened the door and stormed out, making sure the door slammed loudly behind her.

Greg and Melissa stood looking at the closed door like a pair of confused sitcom parents.

'What does she mean?' said Greg, his eyes still fixed on the door. 'What does she know?'

'I have no idea,' said Melissa, but as she spoke the words images flashed through her mind again and showed no signs of stopping.

27

Friday 19 April

'Boss.'

Garibaldi turned to see DS Gardner standing by his desk holding a sheet of paper.

'I've interviewed all the staff at the Ocean Bar. In terms of front of house, there were ten waiting staff, two bartenders and the receptionist.'

'Any joy?'

'Nothing. The waiters all said they were rushing around like the proverbial blue-arsed, but even so they would definitely have noticed someone putting something on the machine. No one else saw anyone going near the system, though a couple said that diners sometimes do walk that way by mistake.'

'Why's that?'

'They sometimes think that's the way to the loo, when the loo is actually at the other end of the bar.'

'So guests could have gone near that machine and not necessarily been thought of as suspicious?'

Milly consulted her sheet. 'I did ask that, but they said they normally realise, or are told, before they reach that turn for the kitchen.'

'Hang on,' said Garibaldi, 'so, although no one says they saw anyone near that sound system, it is still possible that someone, even a quiz-night guest, could have accessed it?'

Milly shook her head. 'I think it very unlikely.'

'Even at the very end of the evening? It happened when the dinner was over.'

'I know, and I asked about that as well.' Garibaldi could hear the resentment in her voice, the feeling that her interviewing technique was coming under close scrutiny. 'When dinner was over and coffee had been served, apparently a few of them were taking a breather.'

'A breather? Where?'

'There's a place out the back where they go for cigarette breaks.'

'And how many of them were doing that?'

Milly looked at her sheet again. 'Five of them.'

'So there were only five waiters still out the front?'

Milly nodded. 'And none of them saw anything?'

'No.'

'OK,' said Garibaldi. 'Well done.'

'There is still one I need to catch up with. She left the week after the quiz night.'

'Any idea why?'

Milly looked at her notebook. 'Bronwen May. She's an actress. Does waitressing there between jobs, and apparently one came up. One of the waiters said she left very quickly and another made some reference to her not getting on with the manager.'

'Not getting on how?'

'I got the sense there might have been something going on between them.'

213

'A relationship?'

'They weren't specific, but they did say that they had a huge row the week before.'

'Interesting,' said Garibaldi. 'Needs following up. Where does she live?'

Milly consulted her notes. 'North London.'

Garibaldi sighed.

'I'm sorry to be late, but I've had a nightmare day.'

'No problem.' Garibaldi gave an understanding smile. 'I know how it can be.'

Kim Turner put down her bag. 'I hope Chris has been looking after you.'

Chris got up from his chair and pointed at the tea and biscuits. 'I've been feeding him the freelancer's diet, the one that puts the pounds on as you try to earn them. Talking of which . . . I'll be off for my run and leave you to it. You won't be needing me, will you?'

Garibaldi shook his head.

'Where's Harry?' said Kim

'Upstairs,' said Chris. 'Doing his homework, I hope.'

'And all OK today?'

Kim exchanged a look with her husband – a shorthand look that invested 'OK' with all kinds of nuance.

'Yeah,' said Chris, 'I had that meeting, remember, but Charlotte picked him up and brought him home. And she did some cleaning when she got back – she's just left, actually. Which reminds me – we need to pay her.'

Chris gave his wife a peck on the lips as he walked past. Kim looked surprised, as if the update on domestic detail and the show of affection was a display put on for the visiting policeman.

'Take your time, Mrs Turner,' said Garibaldi when Chris

had shut the door behind him. 'I know what it's like when you get in from a demanding job.'

Kim took off her coat, sat down in the chair and reached for a biscuit. 'I suppose you do. Not everyone does nowadays, and as for Chris . . .' She rolled her eyes in exasperation, as if explaining the differences in their working lives was beyond her.

'When I think what teachers get paid and when I think what these journalists get paid for writing . . . Well, OK, some of them do a good job, but some of them . . .'

'I'd like to ask you about the Ocean Bar Quiz, Mrs Turner.'

'Of course, please do.'

'As I understand, it was the first one you've ever been to.'

Kim laughed. 'And the last.'

'So why did you choose to go along this year?'

'It's a question I've asked myself a lot since that evening. I suppose curiosity is the only answer. Every year when that invitation arrives, Chris says he's not going. Every year he says he's fed up with the whole thing. Then after a couple of days he changes his mind. And when he's changed his mind he says, "You can come along if you want." But he says it very half-heartedly, knowing full well that it would be the last thing I'd want to do. And this year I decided to call his bluff.'

'And why did you do that?'

'As I say, I'm not sure, and I've regretted it quite a bit. Especially when I found out about Nick Bellamy and how he was killed. As soon as I heard that, I regretted it even more.'

'Why did that add to your regret?'

'Well, I'm assuming there's a link between his murder and what happened at the quiz. Maybe someone killed him because of what he said, or because of what he might say.'

'You're making a lot of assumptions, Mrs Turner.'

'Am I? I thought—'

'First of all, we have no evidence that Nick Bellamy was the man behind those allegations. And secondly, we have no evidence that, if he was, his murder is connected to them. And the danger of your assumptions is that they end up placing the blame for Nick Bellamy's murder firmly at the feet of Chris and his Oxford friends.'

'I'm sorry. I thought that the tongue and the scarf suggested the connection.'

'It might appear that way, but they are still assumptions.'

Kim looked away, like a kid in her class who'd come up with the wrong answer. 'I see.'

Garibaldi leaned forward, resting his elbows on his knees. 'Do you think any of Nick's Oxford friends could possibly have killed him?'

'Well, no. I've not really thought about it. I mean, it's unlikely.'

'Yet if your assumptions are true, that's something you would need to consider.'

'Yes, I see.'

'Tell me, Mrs Turner. How does, or how did, Chris get on with his Oxford friends?'

'Tolerated them, I suppose. They were all close when they were there, but then they drifted apart over the years. It's always the way. And Chris felt a bit differently politically, I guess.'

'Politically? In what way?'

'He wanted to be a journalist but, unlike others, he had some principles and tried to stick by them. He didn't want to churn out any old rubbish for the cash and that's why we've ended up where we are, and his friends, or some of them, have ended up where they are.'

Garibaldi looked round the book-lined living room. 'You've hardly done badly for yourselves, have you?'

216

'It's all relative, isn't it? But Chris looked at Julia being a big-shot City lawyer and at Melissa on TV and Greg writing those shit books, and Fay at that snotty school. St Mark's! I mean – what Fay Wetherby needs to do is come and have a look at my school and see the difference. Same city but worlds apart.'

'And what did Chris think of Nick Bellamy?'

'Poor Nick! I can't believe it. Do you have any idea at all who might have done it?'

'Let's stick to the questions for the moment, shall we?'

Kim held up her hands in apology. 'OK. Nick and Chris. Well, Chris never really approved of the way Nick chased money in the City, but of all of them, I think he had most time for Nick, despite everything—'

'Despite what, exactly?'

'I don't know – maybe it's the fact that Nick was so different from Chris. So much wilder, more exciting. Things happened to Nick in a way they never happened and never would happen to Chris. Don't get me wrong, I love Chris, of course I do, but he's very much on the safe side. Nick wasn't. Walk on the Wild Side. That was Nick. Anyway, Chris liked him. And I think he was sad when they lost touch. In recent years he didn't see him much at all – as with all the others, it was just once a year at the quiz, but when Nick stopped turning up he had no contact with him at all.'

'So you wouldn't say Chris is close to the others?'

'Not at all. And to be honest I think he's come not to like them very much. Especially Greg.'

'Why's that?'

Kim sighed. 'Like all journalists, Chris thinks he's got a novel in him. I'm sure he's right. There probably *is* a novel in him. The problem is he's taking one hell of a long time getting it out, and he knows it. Then there's also the likelihood that, when he does get it out, it won't be very good and no one will like it. And there's Greg Matthews. First effort a bestseller and then, bang, one after the other, he churns them out. It drives Chris insane.'

'I see,' said Garibaldi. 'And what do you think of Chris's friends?'

'I'm not part of it, am I? I didn't go to Oxford, and I didn't go to Balfour. So when I first met them – and I did see them in the early years after university – I didn't really take to them. I was fascinated by Nick, perhaps, in the way that many were, but the others?' Kim threw her hands into the air.

'And what did you make of that round of allegations?'

'What do you mean?'

'What did you think of them?'

'Did I think they were true?'

'Yes.'

'Well, no, not really.'

'Not really?'

'I mean, they were a joke. It was obvious they were.'

'So no element of truth in any of them?'

'I can't say. I mean, I don't really know them, do I?'

'But you found them amusing?'

'Yes. They were hilarious.'

'Even the sex-tape allegation about your husband?'

'Look, it's an old joke. Everyone knows about the teddy-bear story, so this whole thing about Chris being kinky is well established. That was the thing about those allegations. You knew they weren't true but you also thought they could be.'

'So Nick Bellamy could have killed a man?'

'Who knows? As I say, I don't really know them well, but from what I heard, Nick Bellamy could be pretty wild.'

'Pretty wild? In what way?'

'Chris said he had a temper. Kept getting into fights.'

'So maybe killing a man might not be out of the question, then?'

'Unlikely, but who knows. And the same's true of the others. Fay Wetherby and bribery? All headteachers become corrupt. It's true of state schools and it's even more true of private ones. Greg and plagiarism? They all went to Oxford. They know how to build a successful career by nicking other people's ideas. Julia and shoplifting? Let's face it, we've all been tempted, we've all come close. For most of us it might be slipping in an unscanned Waitrose curry for a Saturday night, but I reckon everyone's stolen something in their lives. Even you.'

Kim paused and looked at Garibaldi as he trawled his own history of petty theft.

'As for Melissa, I believe it. We've all shagged around and I bet she started early. That sort always do. So, as I say. Hilarious.'

'You may find it hilarious, Mrs Turner, 'but we're talking about the murder of Nick Bellamy. That's hardly funny, is it?'

Kim looked taken aback, as if the murder had slipped her mind. 'Of course, I know, but ... So you mean if Nick was behind it ...'

'An assumption, but one it's difficult not to consider.'

'Which would explain the tongue. But if it was one of them, why would they do that with the scarf? It's like they were letting you know it was them.'

'Exactly. But, as with all these things, it may not be that simple.'

'I don't get it,' said Kim after a pause.

'At the moment,' said Garibaldi, 'neither do I.'

Garibaldi started to get up. 'How old is your son, Mrs Turner?'

'Harry? He's twelve.'

'How's he doing?'

Kim looked defensive. 'He's fine. Just fine. It's tough, though. He's on the spectrum.'

'I see,' said Garibaldi.

'Do you?' said Kim.

Garibaldi felt momentarily embarrassed. Did he see? Probably not. As far as he was concerned, everyone was on the spectrum. It was simply a matter of how far.

28

Monday 22 April

Melissa Matthews walked to the front door of her Mill Hill mansion to pick up the post. Not much came by mail nowadays and she would usually expect to find nothing of great interest, but this morning, as she bent down to pick up what looked like the usual pile of junk mail, bills and magazines, one envelope caught her eye.

No postmark. No stamp. Just her name in large, Gothic handwriting.

Melissa opened it.

The same large handwriting covered the writing paper.

Just to let you know that you're next, bitch. And I know what I'll stuff in your mouth.

She turned it over, but there was nothing on the back. She looked again at the envelope, and then at the words on the page. Her hand went to her mouth.

'Greg!'

No answer so she called louder. 'Greg!'

Her husband was in his study, doing his usual morning

stint of 2,000 words. Melissa heard his footsteps and held out the letter towards him as he came into the hall. He took it and read, turning it over to look at the back before reaching out for the envelope. He looked closely at it and then looked up at Melissa.

'Shit,' he said.

'Yeah. Shit,' said Melissa.

'So, any progress?'

DCI Deighton stood at the front of the room, addressing the team. Garibaldi looked at her, wondering whether this was how Rachel addressed her classes.

'OK, let's deal with the allegations. Who's on Julia Forrest?'

DC McLean put his hand up. 'Checked Harvey Nichols, obviously. No official reports of her being caught shoplifting. Checked all other similar department stores. Nothing. And there's nothing from the questions I've asked at the law firm she works at. Obviously a law firm would be hot on any kind of lawbreaking by its employees. Nothing on any databases.'

'Greg Matthews?'

DC McLean put his hand up again. 'I've read all the reviews of his first novel.'

'Have you read the novel itself?'

McLean shook his head.

'I have,' said Garibaldi. 'Don't bother.'

'But,' said DC McLean, 'I've read all the reviews and not one of them mentioned plagiarism. I've been in touch with his publisher and his agent and they were both pretty dismissive of the whole plagiarism idea. They said it's impossible to prove.'

'Exactly,' said Garibaldi. 'I always thought J. K. Rowling ripped off Ursula Le Guin's *The Wizard of Earthsea* trilogy and

Jill Murphy's *The Worst Witch* series, but no one ever took me seriously.'

There was polite, uneasy laughter. No one knew how to respond when Garibaldi was being clever about books or making references and quotations they didn't quite understand.

'But,' said DC McLean, 'I decided to look beyond his first novel.'

'Very brave,' said Garibaldi.

'And when I found reviews of his second novel there was one in . . .' He opened his notebook and flicked through the pages. 'In the *Literary Magazine*, which said that the plot was very familiar.'

'All plots are familiar,' said Garibaldi, 'there's nothing new there.'

'But this one said – hang on, I wrote it down – here it is. It said that "the similarities between Matthews' *Fathoms Deep* and A. J. Bardsley's *Poseidon* are remarkable. Coincidence? Zeitgeist? Or has Matthews been influenced more than he realises, influenced to the extent of lifting not only the plot but huge chunks of the novel's driving ideas?"'

Garibaldi looked at DC McLean approvingly. This was promising. The allegation was about Matthews' first novel, but maybe it really applied to his second.

'So what have you done about it?' said DCI Deighton. 'Have you got hold of both books?'

'Well, no . . .'

'More importantly, have you got hold of whoever wrote that review?'

DC McLean flicked through his notebook again. 'Hang on, I wrote it down here somewhere, because I was going to contact him.'

Garibaldi shook his head impatiently. McLean had been

shaping up well but had now relapsed into his customary inefficiency.

DCI Deighton looked round the room. 'OK – Fay Wetherby.'

DC Hodson put up her hand. 'It's been difficult to find out anything concrete. It's a strange place, St Mark's, and no one really gives anything away. I have, though, contacted the parents of girls expelled from the school over the last five years and asked them about their treatment. Parents whose kids have been kicked out of a school tend not to think highly of whoever was responsible for it, so there was a lot of bitterness towards Fay Wetherby from the ones I spoke to.'

'Did any of them suggest any kind of corruption on the part of the head?'

'A lot spoke of unfairness, but there was no suggestion of Fay Wetherby having been unduly influenced in any way. Though one of them did say they had some reservations about everything to do with St Marks.'

'Anything specific?'

'One of them said, "Don't look at how they kick them out but at how they let them in."'

As soon as the words were out Garibaldi thought of Melissa and Julia's daughters both sitting the entrance exam.

'OK,' said DCI Deighton. 'Thanks. What about Melissa Matthews' love child?'

'Me again, boss,' said DC Hodson. 'I've contacted Marlborough and they have no record of it. It's a boarding school, so there's no way that kind of thing could happen without them knowing.'

'Maybe she had the child in the summer holidays,' said DS Gardner.

'Maybe,' said Garibaldi. 'Or even after she left school.'

'She went straight from school to Oxford,' said DC Hodson.

'Still possible,' said Garibaldi. 'University terms start in October. School would have been finishing in July. It might not even have been showing when she left.'

'I've contacted adoption agencies but no luck, and I've tracked down some of Melissa's contemporaries. None of them could remember anything that might tally with a pregnancy and a child, though one of them did say that the idea didn't surprise her at all.'

'What did she mean by that?' said Garibaldi.

'It would seem that Melissa Matthews was sexually active in her teenage years, particularly in the sixth form. Apparently there was a lot of it going on.'

'Boarding schools for you,' said Garibaldi. 'Not much else to do in the evening. Tracked down any of the boys?'

'I'm on it,' said DC Hodson.

'Which leaves Chris Turner and the sex tape,' said DCI Deighton. 'Who's on that?'

DC McLean raised his hand again. 'That's me. Well, no joy on any actual sex-tape. Until we have access to whatever technology he uses – laptop, tablet, phone – we won't be able to know. So all I've done is try to find out more about Chris Turner, and I haven't come up with much. You told us the story about him and the teddy bear at Oxford, but I've had no luck on the teddy-bear front. None of them is talking.'

The room laughed loudly. DCI Deighton looked at DC McLean and smiled. She liked to let them know she had a sense of humour.

DC McLean glanced at his notebook. 'Seems he's been happily married to his wife for many years, and if he gets up to anything strange in his spare time he's kept it to himself. The chances are he watches porn.'

'Why do you say that?' said DCI Deighton.

'Because statistics suggest that most men do. Without

access to phone records, financial transactions, credit-card statements, it's difficult to get anything specific. He seems to be a hard-working journalist and, as far as you can tell, he seems completely straight.'

'No one's completely straight,' said Garibaldi. Everyone turned to him, waiting for an explanation. None came, so they turned away, accepting it as yet another gnomic Garibaldi utterance.

'It all comes back to Balfour,' said DCI Deighton. 'And the question to ask is why anyone would make the link so obvious? Are we wrong to be pursuing it? Is it a false trail? The fact is, we still need to find out more about Bellamy. We need to know more about what he was up to round here. Was he into drugs – taking, dealing, whatever? DS Gardner, if you could do house-to-house on the estate where his flat was and DCs McLean and Hodson, if you could make some enquiries in Hammersmith. If he was local in his activities, someone is bound to know him. DS Gardner, carry on trawling everything – banks, cars, anything. Nick Bellamy must have left traces. All we need to do is find them.'

'One more thing,' said Garibaldi. 'A member of the quiz team from the White Horse said that Bellamy claimed to have slept with Melissa Matthews and Fay Wetherby.'

DCI Deighton raised her eyebrows. 'When they were at Oxford?'

'He didn't say. Bellamy had a habit of inventing stories, so we should take it with a pinch of salt. But by all accounts it sounds like he had an active sex life.'

'If he did sleep with them, what's the significance?'

'If it's true,' said Garibaldi, 'it depends when he did it. At university's one thing, more recently is another. It could be something else they want to hide.'

'Easy enough for them to deny, and difficult to prove,' said

DCI Deighton, 'but it's a good question. What exactly *was* Bellamy's history with those women?' She looked round the room. 'Anything else?'

She opened a file and pulled out several newspaper clippings.

'The press are still interested.'

She held the clippings up, leafing through them one by one and reading out the headlines.

'"Who is College Scarf Boat Race Beast?"; "Oxford Link to Severed Tongue Murder?"; "No Leads in Toff Tongue Torture Killing?"'

DCI Deighton put the clippings back in the folder.

'We need results. It's a high-profile case and we need to make progress. So let's all get out there and do it.'

Garibaldi was leaving the room when his mobile rang.

'Detective Inspector Garibaldi?'

'Speaking.'

'It's Melissa Matthews. Something terrible's happened.'

'What is it?'

'I've received a note, a threatening note.'

'Right,' said Garibaldi. 'I'm on my way.'

DS Gardner drove to Mill Hill with the light on and the siren blaring, not because they were needed, but because, as she had once confessed to Garibaldi, they still gave her a childish thrill. Garibaldi had given her a baffled look, giving not a hint of the fact that, even after so many years, they had exactly the same effect on him.

Greg Matthews answered the door and showed them into the living room, where Melissa sat on the sofa, the letter and envelope lying on the glass table in front of her. Garibaldi walked towards the table and Melissa reached forward, picked up the letter and envelope and handed them to him.

Garibaldi read the letter, holding it close to his eyes as if looking for revealing clues, and then did the same with the envelope.

'This has come as something of a shock,' said Greg. He stood behind the sofa where Melissa sat, knees together, hands tightly clasped. Greg put a reassuring hand on her shoulder.

'No stamp,' said Garibaldi, turning the envelope over in his hands, 'and no postcode. Tell me how you found it, Mrs Matthews.'

'It was with the pile of post on the doormat.'

'Do you have that pile of post?'

Melissa pointed to the table and Garibaldi walked over to it.

'This is all very alarming isn't it?' said Greg. 'That's a threat. A clear threat. Do you think Melissa – we – do you think we're safe?'

Garibaldi leafed through the bundle of mail. 'I don't know, Mr Matthews. I really don't know.'

'But . . .' Melissa started to speak, but trailed off. She looked as if she was trembling. 'It has to be linked to Nick, doesn't it? That reference to . . . to the mouth.'

'Did this letter arrive *with* the post?' said Garibaldi.

'I don't know,' said Melissa. 'It was in the pile when I picked it up. I can't tell you how much it's freaked me out. That handwriting, like a child's, so innocent and yet so threatening.'

'When you say in the pile, Mrs Matthews, do you mean *in* the pile or do you mean *on* the pile?'

'I can't remember. I just bent down to pick them up and there it was.'

'But can you remember seeing it resting on the top of the pile?'

'No, I mean . . . Maybe. I really can't remember.'

'Does it matter?' said Greg moving from behind the sofa and standing opposite Garibaldi.

'Well, yes it does. It might help to know whether it was hand delivered or whether it came through the post.'

Greg pointed at the envelope. 'But there's no stamp, so it must have been delivered by hand. It couldn't come through the post without a stamp.'

'Couldn't it?' said Garibaldi. The importance of post and letters had declined so rapidly in recent years that he was struggling to remember what happened to letters without stamps. 'I think, Mr Matthews,' he said, 'that if something is sent through the post with name and address but no stamp, the mail will deliver it but the recipient will be asked if they want to take receipt of it. If they do, then they have to pay for the postage and maybe an extra charge – I can't remember.'

'Nor can I, Detective Inspector, and I would much rather we were talking about the implications of the bloody thing rather than how it got here.'

'Would you now?'

Greg Matthews currently had the look of someone capable of far more than plagiarism. Garibaldi stared at him coldly.

'Do you have CCTV here?'

'Yes,' said Greg. 'You need to.'

'And do you have CCTV trained on the front of the house, on the path leading to the door, the one that the postman – or whoever delivered this note – might have used?'

'Do you think they'd deliver it themselves?' said Melissa. 'Wouldn't they get someone to do it for them?'

'I don't know,' said Garibaldi, 'but it would be very helpful if we could look at the footage from your cameras.' He turned to DS Gardner. 'Can we arrange that?' DS Gardner nodded, and scribbled down a note. 'We will also need to take the letter and envelope away for fingerprinting.'

Melissa nodded. Her hands were still tightly clasped and she was biting her lip.

'This is significant, though, isn't it?' said Greg. 'This must be a clue.'

'And what do you think it tells us, Mr Matthews?' Garibaldi gave the smile of an unimpressed teacher.

'It tells us that someone is threatening to kill Melissa.'

Melissa gave a nervous whimper and reached for a tissue.

'And that it's from whoever killed poor Nick.'

'It seems that way,' said Garibaldi, 'but at this stage we can't be absolutely sure of anything.'

'What should we do?' said Greg. 'Do we need protection or something? It's pretty damn alarming, thinking that some-one is going to . . .'

'I think we should try to stay calm,' said Garibaldi.

'It can't be . . .' Greg paused.

'Can't be what?'

'It can't be one of the others. Chris, Fay, Julia. I mean that's impossible. Why would they? And it can't be connected to that quiz. Not any more. Not now.'

'And why's that, Mr Matthews?'

'Well, if Nick was killed by someone who thought he had made those allegations and wanted to silence him, that's one thing . . .'

'But those allegations weren't true,' said Garibaldi. 'And if they were, wouldn't it be too late to silence Nick? He'd already spoken.'

'Yes, OK, but they might have been worried that Nick might know more.'

'None of them *were* true, were they?'

'No. Of course not.' Greg looked flustered. 'What I'm saying is that *if* that were the motive of Nick's killer, that can't be the same motive for threatening to do the same to Melissa.'

'Unless they think that Melissa might know things as well. Don't forget that your first reaction to that voice in the Ocean Bar was to pretend that it was all Melissa's doing. For a long time that's what everyone was led to believe.'

'But I said it wasn't me,' said Melissa. 'I told them all.'

'What I don't get,' said Garibaldi, 'is why anyone would want to kill, or threaten to kill, someone over allegations that are clearly not true.'

'We don't *know* that, though, do we?' said Melissa.

'Don't we?' said Garibaldi. 'A teenage pregnancy and a secret child?' He looked hard at Melissa. 'A plagiarised novel?' He turned his gaze to Greg.

'Of course we do,' said Greg.

'But a couple of thoughts occur to me,' said Garibaldi. 'What if those allegations aren't true, but are *close* to being true?'

'How can they be *close* to being true?' said Greg.

'Truth is never as absolute as we think, is it?' said Garibaldi. 'As Oscar Wilde said . . .'

'Rarely pure and never simple.' Melissa muttered the words into her tissue as she wiped her nose. 'We're educated people, Inspector, we don't need your lessons.'

Garibaldi, calm until now, felt his anger rise. 'And the other thought is that if this is all about allegations, whether true or not, if this is all about someone knowing something, then we mustn't assume that it's only one person who has that knowledge. Maybe Nick Bellamy did know things, but maybe others know those things as well. So if, Mr Matthews, we are going down that particular avenue, then it is possible to see this' – he pointed at the letter in his hand – 'as part of the same thing.'

'But *I* don't know anything!' said Melissa.

'That may very well be the case,' said Garibaldi. He

motioned to DS Gardner that it was time to go. 'If, as ever, you have any further thoughts on this, do let me know. In the meantime we will require CCTV footage and we'll need to fingerprint the letter.'

'Will I be safe?' Melissa looked at Garibaldi with large, pleading eyes and then turned to her husband. She swivelled her gaze from one to the other, a little girl asking for the men's protection.

'Can't you provide some sort of security?' said Greg.

'I'm afraid our resources are stretched as it is, Mr Matthews.'

'We're happy to . . .'

'Happy to pay? I'm sure you are.'

'I don't know what to do,' said Melissa. 'Whoever this is, they could be anywhere waiting for me, and I just think of Nick and what they did to him. What should I do?'

'Be careful,' said Garibaldi, 'and if you suspect anything, anything at all, get in touch immediately.'

'Is that all?' said Greg. 'Can't you do anything else?'

'I'm sure you'll do all you can, Mr Matthews, to keep your wife safe. I would suggest that for the moment you make sure she is not left alone and that she doesn't go out alone. And if you can't be with her, I would suggest that you make sure someone else is.'

Garibaldi turned as he heard footsteps in the hall.

A teenage girl stood in the doorway.

'Lauren!' Melissa got up and went towards her daughter.

'What's happened?' said Lauren.

'It's nothing,' said Melissa. 'Nothing to worry about.'

'If it's nothing to worry about then why are they here?' Lauren nodded at Garibaldi and DS Gardner.

'We'll explain later,' said Greg.

'Explain now.'

Greg and Melissa exchanged a nervous glance.

'Your mother's received a note,' said Greg.

'What kind of note?'

'A threat,' said Melissa. 'It seems that it's from—'

Garibaldi stepped forward. 'We're investigating it. We don't know who it's from, but we will look into it.'

Lauren turned to her mother. 'What's it threatening to do? Kill you?'

Melissa nodded.

'So it's from whoever killed Nick Bellamy, is it?'

'We don't know,' said Garibaldi. 'It seems that way, but we need to look into it.'

'Fuck me!' said Lauren.

'Lauren!'

'No. Fuck me! Haven't you got more to worry about than me swearing? A threatening note! As if I haven't got enough to fucking worry about!'

Lauren turned and stormed off, thumping up the stairs.

Greg spread his arms wide in apology. 'I'm sorry about that.'

'Please, don't apologise,' said Garibaldi. 'It must have come as a shock to her.'

'She's not been herself recently,' said Greg. 'We think it's what's been going on and the stress of exams. She'll get through it.'

Greg looked at his wife but Melissa was looking away, biting her lip and trying to look as though she agreed.

'We'll be off, then,' said Garibaldi, leading DS Gardner to the door.

'Thank you,' said Greg, but his thanks were half-hearted, as if he was still disappointed that the police could not provide live-in twenty-four-hour protection.

Garibaldi and DS Gardner walked down the drive to their car. When they reached it, Garibaldi turned to look at the positioning of the CCTV cameras. They were trained on the route to the front door and should show whether anyone apart from the postman had put anything through the letterbox that morning.

'They've got their hands full there,' said DS Gardner as they drove back to the station. 'The note's bad enough, but that daughter can't be easy.'

'Yeah,' said Garibaldi, 'she seemed all over the place.'

'That's exams for you. I think there's too much stress on teenagers nowadays, don't you?'

'Maybe,' said Garibaldi, thinking back to his own teenage years.

'Still, I liked the way you took on Greg Matthews over his theory.'

'It just came to me. There's something about them that brings it all out, that sharpens my mind. Know what I mean?'

'Yeah,' said DS Gardner, 'I do.'

Garibaldi looked at her as they sped back towards Hammersmith, very much doubting that she did.

29

Tuesday 23 April

Julia Forrest flicked back her hair and raised her glass. 'Thanks for coming along.'

Chris Turner clinked his glass against hers. 'My pleasure.'

'Greg phoned me to tell me the news and asked if I would let you know. And I thought it might be nice to meet, as I'd quite like to talk about it.'

It was lunchtime. The gastropub round the corner from Julia's City law firm was crowded, but it was the best venue Julia could think of. She didn't fancy the trek up to north London and sensed that Chris wouldn't want to come all the way down to Barnes, so this seemed a good halfway point.

'I'm totally baffled,' said Chris. 'The whole thing. I really don't know what to make of it.'

'Do you think we're all in danger?'

Chris shook his head. 'I can't believe it. There's so much that doesn't make sense. Who sent it? And is whoever sent it Nick's killer?'

'The worrying thing is that logic suggests it's one of us.'

'But that's ridiculous! None of us could have done it.'

'Why not?'

'Because ... Because we couldn't.'

'Why not? Why couldn't we?'

'Because we're not like that, are we? We're not the kind of people who do that sort of thing.'

Julia laughed. 'And what are the kind of people who do?'

'You know what I mean. Are you saying that you think *I* could have done it? Or you're saying that I think *you* could have done it?'

'We must be in the frame.'

'But why? What's our motive?'

'If Nick was behind those quiz-night allegations ...'

'Those allegations! Those fucking allegations. None of them were true!'

'Really?'

'Well, mine wasn't. How about yours?'

'Of course not.'

'But if it was one of us, why draw attention to the possibility by choosing to kill him like that? And then why send a threatening note to another one of us?'

'You're right. It's all too obvious. It's as if someone wants everyone to think it's one of us, to connect it to those ridiculous secrets.'

'Unless it's a double bluff.'

'Exactly.'

Julia sighed. 'I haven't been sleeping, you know.'

'Me neither. I wasn't sleeping much before I heard about the note, but when Greg rang me and told me the news, it got worse. Things weren't great at home before all this started to happen ...'

'I'm sorry.'

'Just the usual stuff. Worries about Harry, and I guess I

haven't been getting on too well with Kim lately. Still, we all have crosses to bear.'

Julia thought of her own crosses: her demanding work as a lawyer, three teenage kids, and a husband who, in his capacity as a sports journalist, spent a lot of time away. Maybe, in comparison to others, they weren't crosses at all. Her job was lucrative, her kids seemed to be doing OK and Phil, while not always with her physically (and even then with his eyes mostly on his iPad) had always been there for her in the metaphorical sense.

Julia leaned forward. 'You know Melissa's had to ask for time off work?'

'Really?'

'That's what Greg said. Apparently she was struggling already, but this has tipped her over the edge.'

'When you say over the edge . . .?'

'He didn't specify, but those were the words he used. Over the edge. And it looks like they've got problems with Lauren as well.'

When Greg had told her the news, Julia had almost regretted ever having wished misfortune on her old college friend.

'Should we be doing anything?' said Chris.

'Like what?'

'I mean, do we need to make ourselves safe, protect ourselves?'

'I don't know, Chris. All I know is that I needed to talk about it. It all seems such a mess.'

'Thanks for coming in, Greg.'

'My pleasure.'

Greg Matthews sat down at the round table and glanced round Fay Wetherby's office.

'When you called me,' said Fay, 'and told me about the

237

threat to Melissa, I really didn't know what to make of it. And yes, I'll admit it, I was frightened. I still am. This whole affair seems ridiculous. I mean, you couldn't make it up.'

Greg, a man who made his living from making things up, nodded his agreement.

'And I suppose the question is whether we should be worried about our safety.'

'That's what I asked the police,' said Greg.

'I'm not surprised. There's obviously a threat to Melissa, but my worry is that whoever's behind this is going for all of us.'

'I can't work it out. If there's a link, what's the connection and where do you start? Someone pranked – if I can use such a term – our quiz with those joke questions at the end and . . .'

'I've never had the chance to ask you, Greg, but what did you make of the final round?'

'What did I make of it? I was fucking annoyed, that's what I made of it. It ruined the evening.'

'But the allegations? What did you make of the allegations?'

'Ridiculous!'

Fay nodded and held Greg's gaze. 'Of course.'

'But on the other hand . . .'

'Exactly,' said Fay. 'Difficult to prove. Difficult to disprove.'

'But the thing is was Nick killed because the allegation about him *was* true? And who has sent Melissa the note? Nick's killer? And if so, why? What the fuck are they trying to do?'

'What are the police doing?'

'Exactly. What *are* the police doing? They seem more concerned about those stupid allegations than they do about finding Nick's killer!'

Fay gave a patient headmistress nod, the one she delivered to anyone in her office whose conversation had degenerated into a rant.

'And how's Melissa taken it?'

'Badly. I've never seen her like this before. You know Melissa, ice cool, always in control. Not any more. She's … Well, it's not a crack-up, it's not a breakdown, but she is definitely in a strange place. She's actually had to ask for time off work. Can you believe that? Melissa!'

'I'm so sorry. Do send her my love, won't you? I'll give her a call this evening.'

'I can understand it, I suppose. If you think about what happened to poor Nick and then you think that whoever did that might be coming after you, it must be terrifying.'

'Absolutely. And how's Lauren coping?'

Greg gave a heavy sigh, exhaling through puffed-out cheeks. 'That's another thing Melissa's had to deal with. Lauren's not coping at all. And that's not down to the note: it started before that. Just when we thought she'd be OK, take her exams, get her grades and head off to … to Durham, something's happened. It was about a month ago, I reckon. There was a change. She had that haunted look on her face again and we were worried. It all looked like it did before and we were fearing the worst. The Priory again. Unable to sit her exams. We have no idea what it was but we're pretty sure she started seeing that old boyfriend again and we're pretty sure that she's back on …'

Greg paused, as if he had suddenly remembered who he was speaking to.

'Shit, Fay, sorry. Is it OK for me to say this? I mean, Lauren's nearly through and everything, but I don't want to …'

'Don't worry, Greg, you can tell me.'

'Really? Look, Fay, the problem here is that you're either my friend or you're my daughter's headmistress. Which one are you? Because I don't think you can be both at the same time.'

'Has it been a problem in the past?'

'Well, there were those phone calls.'

'And which were they?'

'One when Lauren was applying here, one when she hit her troubles, and one when she'd been turned down by Oxford.'

'I don't see that there was anything out of order in any of them. In the first case, a phone call from the head in border-line cases is often appropriate. In the second, it's quite natural for conversations like that to happen between a head and a parent, and the same is true for the third. You're not the only parent who's asked for help in trying to get Oxford to change their decision.'

'And the other things that were said in those conversations?'

Fay gave a knowing smile. 'I have no idea what you're talking about. My memory's not what it was and it will prove to be just as faulty if you tell me more about Lauren.'

'OK,' said Greg, 'it's a deal.'

30

Forensics had found no fingerprint match on the envelope. Melissa's were there. Greg's were there. And, as he hadn't gloved up when he handled it, Garibaldi's were there as well. CCTV had provided no lead – footage from the camera outside the Matthews' Mill Hill house showed no one, apart from the postman, putting anything through the front door letterbox during the twenty-four hours preceding Melissa Matthew's discovery of the threatening note.

Its delivery remained a mystery.

'So tell me,' said Garibaldi, taking a sip of his coffee as he sat in the Mortlake delivery office. 'How long has Mill Hill been on your round?'

Fred Bowles had the look of a man who regarded any question he was asked as a personal insult. 'Dunno. Couple of years now, I guess. Can't say I enjoy it. Bit out of the way. Massive houses, a lot of walking, and they're all really rude.'

'How are they rude?'

'It's the rich, innit? Haven't got the time of day. Not like

241

the old days, or like doing the old estate towards the bridge. Couldn't go five yards up there without someone stopping you and asking how you're getting on. Changing times, innit? No one speaks to you no more. And hardly anyone sends no letters, neither. I remember when everyone did.'

'So do I,' said Garibaldi. 'But the reason I'm here is to ask if you remember delivering this particular letter to the house of Mr and Mrs Matthews on Monday the twenty-second of April.'

'I deliver a lot of letters, you know. I'm not likely to remember it, am I?'

'You might remember this one.'

Garibaldi took the plastic bag out of his pocket and placed it on the table in front of him.

Fred peered at the letter inside. 'Blimey. Bit weird, isn't it?' He bent closer and shook his head. 'No, guv, don't remember this at all. Look at it. Weird writing. And no stamp.'

'That's why I thought you might remember it.' Garibaldi picked up the bag, put it in his pocket and got up to leave. 'What usually happens if you get post addressed to someone without a stamp on it?'

'Depends,' said Fred. 'If you know the house, know the people, sometimes you just slip it through the box, no questions asked. You just do it as a favour and hope nothing comes of it. In theory you're supposed to ask them to pay, because it should be marked from the office as postage due. If there's a return address – and there wasn't one on that, was there? – you should really send it back to whoever sent it. Between you and me, most of us just slip it through the letterbox, no questions, know what I mean? Saves a lot of hassle.'

'And that letter I showed you,' said Garibaldi, 'definitely wasn't in your pile?'

'Well, I can't be definite, can I? When I say no one sends

242

letters no more, that doesn't mean there aren't still a load of letters to handle. Even if it's an odd-looking one like this and even if it's got no stamp, it's not likely I'll remember it. What's this all about anyway?'

'It's connected to a murder investigation.'

'Murder?' Fred's jaw dropped and his eyes widened, stunned at the huge significance his job had suddenly acquired.

'The one on Boat Race Day.'

'Blimey! And you say this letter's connected?'

'It may be,' said Garibaldi, realising as he spoke the words that he was still unclear about the nature of that connection.

Outside the Mortlake office he got into the waiting car (two officers interviewing would have been excessive, so he had left DS Gardner with a coffee and the paper).

'Mill Hill,' he said as he did up his seatbelt.

DS Gardner drove them back to Barnes and parked the car on Station Road. They walked together through the common towards the Matthews' house.

'What we need to work out,' said Garibaldi, 'is how that letter was delivered. It wasn't the postman and no one is shown putting anything through the front door between the time Melissa Matthews picked up one day's post and the time she picked up the post with that letter. The question is whether there's any way of getting it through the letterbox without being picked up by CCTV.'

When they reached Mill Hill, Garibaldi's hopes that their presence would be undetected disappeared when Greg opened the front door.

'Detective Inspector! What brings you here?'

Garibaldi stepped forward. 'Good morning, Mr Matthews. Hope we haven't disturbed you.'

'I'm stuck,' said Greg. 'Thorny plot problem, so I'm glad of the distraction. How can I help you?'

243

Garibaldi pointed at the CCTV camera. 'This camera's shown no one putting an envelope through your letterbox, so I thought I'd come along and see if you could do it without the camera seeing you.'

'I see,' said Greg. 'How much of the footage have you looked at?'

Garibaldi took a deep breath. He resented being told how to do his job. 'We looked at enough, Mr Matthews. Tell me, does this camera move at all, or is it fixed?'

'I don't actually know. Melissa might know more, as she's the one who supervised its installation, but I'm afraid she's out. Gone for a bike ride. She's not been feeling very well lately – ever since this wretched business began, and especially since this note – so she's gone out for some air.'

Garibaldi turned to the camera and looked at it closely, trying to give the impression that he knew exactly what he was looking for. 'Looks pretty fixed to me.'

'I think it's very much trained on the front door,' said Greg. 'Can't see how you could avoid it, unless . . .'

'Unless what?' said Garibaldi.

'No it's silly,' said Greg, 'but you could always throw something over the camera to cover it up.'

'That would have shown up,' said Garibaldi, 'there would have been blackout in the footage.'

'Of course,' said Greg. For a fleeting moment he looked embarrassed at his own stupidity. 'But there's always the chance it wasn't put through the letterbox at all.'

'How would that work?'

'You'd do it from inside the house. It would mean getting into the house through one of the other entrances, and I'm not sure how that could be done.'

'What entrances are those?'

'Maybe I should show you?'

Greg Matthews held the front door and ushered Garibaldi and DS Gardner inside. 'There are three possible ways in. The back door, which leads into the kitchen, the French windows, which back onto the garden, and the conservatory, which has a door leading into the utility room.'

Greg Matthews showed them each of the possible entrances, ranking each in terms of likelihood. 'So,' he said, after he had walked from the conservatory into the utility room, 'this one, I think, is the most likely. Probably the easiest door to break open, though I hope you realise, Detective Inspector, that there was no evidence of any break-in.'

'I'm well aware of that, Mr Matthews. I'm afraid the whole thing remains a mystery.'

'You trust the postman, then?' said Greg.

'I have no reason not to,' said Garibaldi. 'Why would he lie?'

'Maybe someone paid him to deliver it.'

Garibaldi shook his head. This was all getting ridiculous, as if Matthews was dreaming up another plot for one of his preposterous novels.

'Hello!'

The voice came from the hall.

'In here, love,' said Greg.

Melissa delivered a classic double take when she saw that her husband was not alone.

'Oh my God!' she said. 'What's happened?'

'They've come to do some further investigating,' said Greg.

'Has something happened? I thought it would.'

If Greg Matthews had not told him that his wife was not feeling well, Garibaldi would have been shocked. She seemed a different person – pale, gaunt, anxious.

'Nothing's happened,' said Garibaldi. 'We're just trying to work out how the letter was delivered.'

Melissa's hands went to her mouth. 'I see. So nothing on CCTV, then?'

'No,' said Garibaldi, 'and the postman doesn't remember it. So we were wondering whether it could have been delivered some other way, maybe from inside.'

'Inside?' said Melissa. 'Surely not. I mean ... are you sure you can't avoid that CCTV camera? I mean, it's very visible. They'd know it was there. Maybe they would slide along a wall or something.'

'Maybe we should try it,' said Greg. 'See if it's possible.' He turned to Garibaldi. 'Why don't you go outside and try to get to the letterbox without being caught on camera, and we can be inside looking at the screen?'

Garibaldi heaved an inward sigh. Was this really happening? Was he about to go outside and act out this ridiculous scenario?

No. He had a better idea.

Garibaldi walked back to the car with DS Gardner.

'Thanks for that, boss.'

'You were brilliant.'

DS Gardner looked at her trousers and dusted them down. 'That wasn't very comfortable at all.'

'But good of you to volunteer.'

'Volunteer? I knew the score as soon as you gave me that look.'

'And what look was that?'

'The one that said if he thinks I'm going out there to take part in some crazy re-enactment, he's more stupid than he looks.'

'Oh, *that* look. Still, you showed it could be done, didn't you?'

'Yeah, by crawling on my belly along the drive and

stretching my arm up to the letterbox. I think I might have done my back in.'

'Why didn't she do it? Why didn't he do it? Why didn't Mr Thriller-Writer-Smarty-Pants do it? Treating us like bloody lackeys!'

'Forget it, boss, it's done. Mrs Matthews doesn't look too good, does she?'

'No. Terrible. Still, it must be an awful strain.'

'Must be.'

'The thing is, Milly, I don't believe for one moment that whoever delivered that letter chose to do it that way. Only someone who knew the exact limitations of the CCTV's range could have done it.'

'So how was it delivered, then?'

Garibaldi had no idea and was pleased, when his phone rang, to avoid having to give an answer.

'Garibaldi.'

'Hello, Detective Inspector, it's Chris Turner here. I was wondering if we could meet. There are a few things I need to tell you.'

31

Thursday 25 April

Chris Turner suggested they talk in a Turkish café round the corner from his house.

'I think it's better here than at home, Detective Inspector. Just in case . . .'

Just in case his wife made an unexpectedly early return from school.

'I hope I'm doing the right thing.'

'Take your time. Tell me whatever you need to.'

'Any news on Nick?'

'A few leads,' said Garibaldi, 'but nothing definite.'

'And the threatening note to Melissa?'

'The same.'

'OK, look. It's about that final round. That accusation about me and the sex tape. The first thing to say is, as I have maintained from the outset, there is absolutely no truth in it. There is no sex tape and I have not been blackmailed by some internet porn scam. However . . .' He paused and took a deep breath. 'That doesn't mean, though, that I haven't had problems with ... with porn. I'm over it now, I think, but there was a time when I was seeking help. No one knows this apart from Kim, of course, and those who gave me the treatment. It was a difficult time for both of us, but I suppose, looking back on it, the most difficult thing of all was recognising that it was a problem and doing something about it. I can't say it did wonders for my relationship with Kim. It's been strained at the best of times, but recently, what with the pressures of dealing with Harry ...' He broke off to take a sip of water. 'Anyway, the reason I'm telling you this is to say that the accusation about me in that final round is absolutely not true, but it *could* be true, it's plausible. So whoever did that round knew that such an accusation about me could not be dismissed out of hand.'

'Can we assume,' said Garibaldi, 'that whoever did it also knew the stories about your sexual tastes at college?'

'You mean the fucking teddy bear? Or rather, fucking the teddy bear? That was complete nonsense. Made up by Nick Bellamy. Totally untrue. How that leads in any way to thinking I'm susceptible to sex-tape blackmailing ...'

'It's not too big a leap, is it?'

'But it wasn't true. If anyone had an excessive sexual appetite at college, it wasn't me – it was Bellamy!'

'What do you mean?'

'Nick fucked everything that moved. The truth is, he screwed his way through Oxford. He went out with Melissa, shagged Julia and had it off with Fay as well, if the rumours are to be believed. Yeah, Nick made me feel very tame by comparison.'

So Steve from the White Horse was right. And Garibaldi was not alone in his feelings of inadequacy.

'And I wouldn't be surprised if he screwed his way through all that followed. There was something about him. Something mysterious. I think that's why everyone fell for him.'

'To get back to the accusation, Mr Turner. You're saying that it isn't true, but could be . . .'

Chris held up his hand. 'There's something else. This thing about Greg Matthews and plagiarism. You may or may not know, Detective Inspector, but one of the things I do, and have done, as a writer is reviewing. I did a lot at one stage – terrible pay, but it's the kind of thing you need to do to get your name out there. In fact, I was once doing so much that I used a pseudonym for some of my work. Went by the name of Tom Bryant in the *Literary Magazine*. And as Tom Bryant I wrote a review of Greg Matthews' second novel *Fathoms Deep*. There were extraordinary similarities to another thriller I'd reviewed several years earlier and I pointed this out in my review.'

'You accused him of plagiarism?'

'Hinted at it.'

'I see. So *you're* the one my DC was talking about.'

'Sorry?'

'We found the review. Or at least one of my team did. They're finding out who you are – or, at least, they should be.'

'The thing is, Detective Inspector, don't believe all that stuff about writers never reading reviews. Greg Matthews will have seen that review and will remember it. They all do. The funny thing is there was no comeback – no complaint or request for a recantation. I know the *Literary Magazine* doesn't have a huge readership, not like the books pages of the papers, but the thing is it was out there and nothing was said.'

'So you genuinely think it was plagiarism?'

Chris nodded. 'I don't know how many there are in the world who have read both *Poseidon* and *Fathoms Deep*. I may well be the only one. The only unfortunate one. But I couldn't believe it when I saw the comparisons.'

'So tell me, Mr Turner, does anyone else know that you wrote it, that you were, maybe still are, Tom Bryant?'

Chris laughed. 'Tom Bryant died some time ago. And no one knows about the pseudonym apart from me and those at the magazine.'

'So what you're saying,' said Garibaldi, 'is that those two accusations to do with yourself and Greg Matthews may well not be true but are close to the truth – almost true and very plausible. Also, whoever did that round knew enough to make it believable. No sex tape, but a man with a porn problem. Not the first novel, but very likely the second.'

'That's right.'

Garibaldi got up from his chair and threw a note on the table to cover the coffees. 'Well, thanks for the information, Mr Turner. Very useful. And you're absolutely sure that Nick Bellamy slept with Melissa, Julia and Fay at Oxford?'

'Not sure about Fay, but the other two – yes.'

'And since Oxford?'

Chris shrugged. 'Who knows? Wouldn't have put it past him.'

Garibaldi left the café and called DS Gardner. They headed back to west London, Garibaldi talking as they went, realising as he did that he wasn't making much sense. He couldn't stop thinking about Rachel and about Nick Bellamy's love life in relation to his own.

'So tell me, Jim, where are we?'

'Three things,' said Garibaldi. 'One. Melissa Matthews has received a threatening note. Threatening to do to her what was done to Bellamy. She found it in her pile of post, but the postman doesn't remember seeing it – and you wouldn't forget it if you did – and CCTV shows no one else putting anything through the Matthews' letterbox in the hours it is likely to have been delivered. Forensics show nothing. Two. Chris Turner has owned up to writing the review of Greg Matthews'

Fathoms Deep that pointed out possible plagiarism. Wrote it under the pseudonym of Tom Bryant and apparently no one knows that it was him. So that accusation at the quiz was close to the truth. Not Matthews' first novel, but his second. He also said that while he has never been blackmailed over a sex tape he's had problems with porn addiction and sought treatment.'

DCI Deighton leaned forward. 'What kind of porn?'

'He didn't specify.'

'You mean you didn't ask?'

'No. Do you think it matters?'

'It could do.'

Garibaldi kicked himself for the oversight.

'And the third thing is Chris Turner also saying that Bellamy slept with Melissa Matthews, Julia Forrest and maybe Fay Wetherby at Oxford.'

'And how is that significant?'

'I don't know.'

'Let's get back to these accusations. If two of them are *nearly* true, what are we supposed to make of the rest of them?'

'Exactly.'

'We need a result soon, Jim. Questions are being asked.'

'Only because it's a couple of well-connected, famous people, ma'am. Only because it happened on bloody Boat Race Day. Only because the home secretary went to Balfour.'

'Be that as it may . . .'

'One murder! There are loads of other crimes out there, you know – kids getting knifed every week and yet all our resources are going on this just because it keeps turning up in the papers.'

'Only because,' said DCI Deighton, leaning forward again in a way that suggested it would be the last time she did and the meeting was about to end, 'we're not getting closer to a result.'

'We're getting very close,' said Garibaldi, but he knew as he spoke the words that they were far from the truth.

When he sat in the team meeting that followed and heard the same old questions and theories, he knew it even more strongly.

32

Friday 3 May

Julia Forrest lay in bed reading. Phil was fast asleep beside her, iPad on his chest. She leaned over, picked up the tablet, switched it off and put it on Phil's bedside table. This had been the pattern of recent weeks. Whereas she had been finding it difficult to get off to sleep ever since the quiz and ever since Nick's murder, her husband had no problem at all, and on the nights when he wasn't working late his snores had provided the soundtrack to her sleepless hours. On the nights when he was working late he would come home in the early hours and find Julia still reading. Sometimes he found her downstairs watching TV or sipping hot milk or camomile tea, drinks that were supposed to help in her quest for elusive slumber but that kept her up half the night peeing.

It was Friday, and Helena was out. Julia's maternal instinct had for many years stopped her dropping off until she heard her returned daughter's footsteps or caught the smell of early-hours toast wafting upstairs. Tonight, when Julia heard the front door open and shut, she reached for the bedside clock radio, face turned to the wall to stop her counting the hours. Half-past one. Why had Helena been out so late? Maybe she was often this late and Julia hadn't registered it, the reassuring thuds of the door and of Helena's feet on the stairs being enough to send her quickly back to sleep. But it was several weeks now since she had experienced that soothing reflex, and tonight, even though she knew that her daughter was safely home, the sleep still wouldn't come.

Phil had urged her to get some pills from the doctor, but she had held out, fearing addiction and hoping she could get through it by other means. But nothing she had tried – breathing, reading, calming chill-out music, yoga positions, a hot bath before bed, even sheep-counting or mind-emptying mantras – made sleep easier to come by or slowed the whirling images. Each night she saw the bracelet she had picked up off the floor in the Covered Market in her student days, and everything else she had been tempted by over the years, reliving the moments when, in all kinds of places, her hand had reached out. Each night she remembered reaching for Nick Bellamy's body, another thing that had not been hers, and each night she saw and felt that body the way she had felt it all those years ago, recalling the peculiar thrill she had never felt since. And each night she saw again a very different image of that body, a scarf stuffed into its mouth, its severed tongue lying beside its punctured torso.

It was two-thirty. The worst time – not close enough to morning to get up and call it an early start, not far enough away from bedtime to give up on the idea of sleep completely.

Julia pulled on her dressing gown and went downstairs. She would sit in the living room and listen to music – some gentle classical stuff might stop these rolling thoughts.

It was when she was adjusting the lamp's dimmer switch, hoping for a soothing half-light, that she heard the noise outside. It was sudden and loud. First the crash against the hedge, and then something or someone stumbling against the recycling boxes. Her hand halted on the dimmer and turned it back to darkness. Was it a cat? A cat wouldn't make that much noise. A fox? More likely. Barnes was crawling with them.

She stood still in the darkened living room, straining to hear more from outside.

Nothing.

She tiptoed towards the window. What if it wasn't a fox? What if there was someone there?

She stood next to the window, her body tight with tension, a picture of Nick Bellamy's dead, mutilated body fixed in her head.

Was that another noise?

She leaned closer to the window.

Something or someone was there.

Was that a footstep?

The pain in her chest and the sound of the smashing window came at the same time.

The next thing she knew she was lying on the carpet. Had she been shot? She touched the front of her dressing gown, but felt only glass – sharp shards against her fingers.

More noise from outside. The footsteps of some-one running.

She tried to get up to the window but the pain stabbed her sharply and she crashed back down.

'Mum?'

The light came on and she turned to the voice. Helena stood in the doorway.

'Mum! What the—?'

She felt Helena's hands on her body.

'Mum! Are you OK?'

She turned to the voice.

'Mum!'

She tried to speak, but no words came.

'What the hell is this?'

Julia turned again but Helena was holding something in her hand.

'It's a brick!' said Helena. 'Someone's thrown a fucking brick through the window!'

Helena pulled a rubber band and held up an envelope. 'This is attached. It's addressed to you.'

Julia shifted herself into a sitting position, glass falling from her dressing gown onto the carpet, and took the envelope. She looked at the front.

Julia Forrest

She tore it open and pulled out a sheet:

You could be next …
And so could your daughter.
Bitch

33

Saturday 4 May

When Garibaldi took Julia Forrest's call early on Saturday morning, he jumped on his bike and cycled across Barnes Green. This was only the third time Rachel had stayed over but the second time a phone call had disrupted their morning. Was someone sending him a message?

Julia was in the living room, still in her dressing gown. Her husband and daughter were with her.

The envelope and the sheet of paper lay on the coffee table. Garibaldi picked them up. Exactly the same handwriting as Melissa Matthews' note – the difference was this one had come through the window attached to a brick rather than through the letterbox. And this one threatened the daughter as well as the mother.

'Take me through what happened, Mrs Forrest.'

Garibaldi listened as Julia gave her account. She was still shaken, the lack of sleep and the shock showing in her face and in her voice. Garibaldi turned over the implications as she spoke. Why had both Melissa and Julia received these notes?

If he assumed they came from the same person, why was that person threatening them? Was it a threat of punishment for what they had done – the damaging quiz allegations or the murder of Nick Bellamy? Or was it a warning? If so, what kind of warning was it? Not to reveal any secrets? It was too late for that. Or was it a warning not to reveal any more?

'It's horrifying, Detective Inspector, but what's particularly disturbing is the threat to ...' She broke off, and pointed across the room to Helena.

'And you didn't see anyone?' said Garibaldi, his head swivelling between mother and daughter.

Both shook their head.

'It was the middle of the night,' said Julia. 'I couldn't see anything.'

Garibaldi turned to Phil Forrest. 'And you heard nothing?'

'I was fast asleep upstairs.'

Garibaldi picked up the envelope and letter, slipped them into an evidence bag, and got up to leave.

'Are we safe?' said Phil Forrest.

'I hope so,' said Garibaldi 'but if you remember any other details, or anything else occurs to you that might be of significance, give me a call.'

Garibaldi cycled back across Barnes Green, hoping he might still catch Rachel before she left. When he got in he found a note – this one in nicer handwriting, unattached to a brick, and signed off with a kiss.

At least something seemed to be moving in the right direction.

Milly Gardner enjoyed the drive to Finsbury Park. It was sometimes good not to be driving Garibaldi. Not that she didn't like him – more that being alone with him in the car wasn't always easy.

She had often tried to work out why. Maybe it was the front-seat conversations they had shared over the years, the revelations they had made that they might have been better off keeping to themselves. She knew every detail of Garibaldi's breakdown and divorce, and Garibaldi knew more than he perhaps should about her own love life and, in particular, her spectacular split with Kevin.

Maybe it was because she was always half-expecting Garibaldi to make a move? Expecting or wanting? She wasn't sure. She knew she would resist, but it would be nice to know he was interested.

Or maybe (and Milly often thought this was the real reason) it was because Garibaldi had the habit of making her feel stupid. The fact that he thought most of his colleagues were stupid made no difference, because when it came to his judgement of her, he had much more evidence to draw on. He never said anything, but Milly had come to recognise the look he gave whenever he was thinking it. It was the look he gave her when she said anything in team meetings, the look he gave her from the passenger seat when she offered her opinions.

Sometimes she wondered why she liked him.

Milly pulled up outside the Finsbury Park block of flats, checked herself in the mirror, and headed to the entrance. She took a lift to the sixth floor, walked to the end of a corridor and knocked on a door. A woman opened it and looked at the warrant card Milly held up towards her.

'Bronwen May?' said Milly.

The woman nodded and Milly followed her in. The flat was neat and well kept, the photos on the mantelpiece and the posters on the walls reflecting its occupant's theatrical interests. Through the windows the north London skyline shone bright and clean.

'You've been difficult to track down,' said Milly.

'I've had a job,' said Bronwen. 'It tends to take over things, especially when it's starting.'

'What kind of job?'

'A small fringe theatre but hey, work is work, and you don't often get the chance to play Rosalind.'

'Rosalind?'

'*As You Like It.*'

Milly nodded as if she understood. If Garibaldi were here, no doubt he would have come up with some smart-arse quotation.

'Well, as you know,' said Milly, 'I'm here about the Ocean Bar.'

Bronwen threw her head to one side and snorted dismissively.

'I see,' said Milly, 'it's like that, is it?'

'I was glad to get out of the place.'

Milly referred to her notebook. 'So can you confirm that you left on the Monday after the charity quiz?' Bronwen nodded. 'And that you were working at the Ocean Bar on the night of that quiz?' Bronwen nodded again. 'And can you tell me why you left so suddenly?'

Bronwen gave a resigned nod, as if the idea of going through it all pained her. 'Look, I'm an actress, right. That's my real job. No one who's an actress wants to be a waitress, but over the years I've done a lot of it – we all have. We need to live, and acting jobs aren't that easy to come by, even for the best. So I didn't really want to be working at the Ocean Bar, but if you're going to be a waitress, that's a pretty good place to be. Anyway, the thing is, I started a relationship with someone who also worked there.'

'Who was that?'

'The manager.'

261

Milly remembered the small, animated Italian.

'At first it was great,' said Bronwen, 'but then I discovered he was cheating on me. More than that, I discovered that he'd been cheating on me from the get-go.'

'And that was what made you want to leave?'

Bronwen nodded. 'I wanted to leave as soon as I found out, but I kept my powder dry until the right moment. And when I got the Rosalind role and knew that rehearsals were starting, I knew I'd have to leave anyway, so I went. I sent Luigi a text on Monday – went something along the lines of "Fuck you and fuck your job".'

'So you just didn't show on the Monday?'

'That's right. Probably made no difference to Luigi Fuckface, but it made me feel a lot better.'

'OK,' said Milly, 'so to get back to the quiz night. You might remember that there was an extra final round of questions.'

'I remember that, yes.'

'Apparently, the questions were played through the restaurant's sound system.'

'That's right. They were.'

'Did you, on that night, see any of the guests, or for that matter any of the Ocean Bar staff – waiters, barmen – go near the machine at all?'

Bronwen shook her head. 'No.'

'No one at all?'

Bronwen shook her head again.

'And were you in sight of the machine at the end of the quiz, just before the voice came over the system.'

'Very much in sight.'

Milly looked up from her notebook. 'You're very confident about that.'

'That's because I was standing right in front of it.'

'And why was that?'

Bronwen looked as if she had been asked a question so obvious she had no need to answer it. 'Because I put the CD in.'

Milly's jaw dropped. 'You put the CD in?'

'Yes. I was told to.'

'Who told you to?'

Bronwen wore the surprised look of someone whose innocent act is suddenly seen as a crime. Her eyes opened wide.

'It was part of the whole thing, wasn't it? That's what I was told.'

'Who told you?'

'My friend.'

'Which friend was that?'

'Charlotte. Another actress. Look, I haven't done anything wrong here, have I? I was told it was a practical joke, and I thought, what the hell, I'm leaving on Monday, I hate the fucking place and I hate that douchebag Luigi so, yeah, I'll help play a practical joke. Why not?'

'So you put the CD in the system?'

'Yeah. I was given precise instructions about when to do it. As soon as the woman got up at the end to announce the results, I had to put it in. Then as soon as it finished take it out, bring it home and throw it away.'

'And nobody saw you do it?'

'Do you know what? I didn't really care.'

'This friend, Charlotte. Why did she want to play this joke?'

'It wasn't her. It was the woman she works for.'

'And who's that?'

'I don't know. All I know is that Charlotte asked if I could do her a favour for the woman she worked for. She explained what I had to do and I thought, fuck it, why not? A practical joke on my last night working at the place? Yeah, go for it.

263

And if it ended up making things difficult for Luigi Fuckface, so much the better.'

Milly was already imagining the look on Garibaldi's face when he heard the news.

'So you don't know who this woman is who Charlotte works for?'

Bronwen shook her head. 'But I've got Charlotte's number if that's any use.'

'Yes please,' said Milly. Bronwen reached for her phone and scrolled down.

'Where does she live, this Charlotte?'

'Just round the corner.'

Bronwen scribbled down the phone number and passed it to Milly.

'That's been very helpful, Miss May. We may be back in touch with some more questions. We will probably want to take a statement.'

'Have I done something wrong?'

'It's too early to say.'

'It was only a joke, wasn't it?'

'It may have been only a joke, Miss May, but it's one that may have led to a murder.'

'Murder?'

Milly knew she wasn't one for keeping up with the news, but she was surprised that all coverage of the Boat Race murder seemed to have passed by Bronwen May. Maybe actresses really did live in another world.

'Good luck with Rosemary,' said Milly as she went through the door.

'Rosalind,' said Bronwen.

Milly headed for the lift, pleased that Garibaldi hadn't been there to correct her as well.

*

Five minutes later, Milly knocked on a door in another block of flats. 'DS Gardner,' she said, showing her warrant card. 'I just called you. It's Charlotte, isn't it?'

'That's right. Come in.'

'I won't keep you long,' said Milly as she sat down. 'I'd like to ask you a few questions about the quiz night at the Ocean Bar.'

'Oh yes?' said Charlotte.

'Apparently you asked your friend Bronwen to help you play a practical joke.'

'That's right. The CD.'

'And you were asked to do this by the woman you work for.'

'That's right. I'm sure Bronwen told you, I'm an actress, but when I'm resting I do some cleaning and nannying.'

'And what's the name of the woman you work for?'

'Kim,' said Charlotte. 'Kim Turner.'

34

Saturday 4 May

Garibaldi sat at his desk thinking about Alfie. His girlfriend might have made him question his university ambitions, but there was no doubt, now the dust had settled, that she was also making him happy. Alfie's last few visits had been so much easier. Rather than slouch in sullen silence, turning from the TV screen only to question the point of everything, he had been bright and cheerful, telling Garibaldi about the films he had seen, the gigs he'd been to, even speaking with optimism about QPR's prospects for next season – a sure sign that he was either in love or insane.

Or maybe the change was not in Alfie, but in Garibaldi himself. Could what was developing with Rachel be making him see things differently? He had no idea where it was all heading, but he definitely felt good about things – better than he had for some time. They had come a long way from the pizza takeaway disaster.

Or was he feeling good because over recent weeks he had heard less from Kay? Alfie now said very little about his Putney life with Dominic and there were times when Garibaldi had been able, momentarily, to forget that it existed.

Things, generally, were looking up. So much so that Garibaldi's mind had drifted from the Bellamy case into a pleasant daydream in which Rachel had moved in with him and Alfie was coming round to introduce his girlfriend.

It took some time for the ringing of the phone to snap him out of it.

'Boss. It's me.'

'Milly. What is it?'

'I'm on my way back from Finsbury Park.'

'And?'

'I've had a breakthrough. I know who arranged the final round.'

'Really? Who was it?'

'I'll tell you when I see you.'

Garibaldi started to speak but the line had gone dead. What was DS Gardner playing at?

Garibaldi's request to Chris Turner that they would like to speak to his wife alone had been greeted with suspicion but, having confirmed that Kim would be back from work by five, Chris had agreed to take Harry out while the interview was conducted.

When Kim opened the door Garibaldi immediately saw the guilt in her face. Having always prided himself on his ability to read people, to detect telltale signs that others missed and to have an instinctive sense of whether or not someone was hiding something, he was disappointed that he had not seen it before. Had her guilt been there all the time, and was he seeing it now only because he was looking at it through the lens of the actress's revelations? And did his failure to see it earlier cast doubt over the way he had been judging everyone else?

Garibaldi and DS Gardner sat down in the living room, declining the offer of a drink. Garibaldi took out his notebook. 'I'd like to ask you a few questions about the Ocean Bar Quiz Night, if I may, Mrs Turner. I know I've asked you about this before, but certain information has recently come to light.'

'Oh? What information?'

'I'll get straight to the point, Mrs Turner. We have interviewed a Bronwen May, an actress who was working as a waitress at the Ocean Bar on the night in question, and we have also interviewed Charlotte Bailey, who I understand does some cleaning for you.'

Kim Turner's face froze.

'And what they have told us suggests that you were behind the whole thing. Is there anything you'd like to tell us, Mrs Turner?'

Kim nodded slowly, as if with each nod the realisation was taking firmer hold.

Garibaldi exchanged a glance with DS Gardner. He waited.

Kim was still nodding.

'Take your time,' said Garibaldi.

More nodding.

'Is it true, Mrs Turner, that you got Charlotte to record the CD and that you got Bronwen to play it at a specified time on the night of the quiz? Think carefully before you say anything, Mrs Turner, but what we would like you to do is confirm whether or not this is the case.'

Kim stopped nodding. 'It is,' she said, looking down at the floor and clasping her hands together in front of her as if she were about to offer up a prayer.

'What we would like to know is why you withheld this from us when questioned earlier, especially as it may be connected in some way to the murder of Nick Bellamy. We would also like to know why you did it in the first place.'

Kim took a deep breath, her head still bent towards the floor, and exhaled loudly.

'OK,' she said, slowly lifting her head and looking first at Garibaldi and then at DS Gardner. 'I guess the game's up, isn't it?'

'Take your time, Mrs Turner, and tell us everything.'

Kim looked from one to the other, rubbing her hands together as if trying to wash away the evidence. 'Can I say first of all that if I thought this might lead to a murder, I would never have done it. Of course I wouldn't. It sounds like a silly thing to say now, but all it was, and all it was ever intended to be, was a joke. A silly joke, perhaps, but only ever a joke.'

'It may have been intended as a joke, Mrs Turner, but some of those accusations were quite serious.'

'I didn't say any of them were true. I said "work out which is true". And that doesn't necessarily mean any of them ...' She broke off and sighed. 'Shit. What am I doing trying to justify myself? Look, it was a really, really stupid thing to do. I know that now, but ...'

'Remind me, Mrs Turner,' said Garibaldi. 'This was the first time you ever went along to the quiz. Why had you never been before?'

'I hated it. The whole idea. Every year, Chris going off to this glitzy affair to meet up with his old chums, to rub shoulders with the rich and famous. I hated it, but this year I thought I'd go. I can't tell you exactly why, apart from the fact that things have been difficult recently. With Harry – it's always difficult with Harry – but also with Chris. Maybe that's why I did it, to get at him. To get at all of them. Shake them up.'

'Shake them up? Why did you want to do that?'

'It's so ... so smug. I wanted to puncture all that pretension and get below the surface, get to the things we're all keen to hide.'

'I see. So you came up with those allegations. Why those in particular?'

Kim looked around the living room as if searching for some means of escape.

'This is terrible,' she said. 'What am I going to do?'

'Take your time, Mrs Turner. There's no hurry.'

'I'm sorry. What did you ask?'

'The allegations. Why those ones?'

'I've made a terrible mistake, haven't I?'

'The allegations, Mrs Turner. Tell me about them.'

'I don't believe I did it! What was I thinking of? What got into me? Look, the thing is, I wanted to make them all nervous, get them guessing. I wanted to make them think that they could be true, so I tried to make them plausible. Unlikely but plausible.'

'So you knew enough about them to do that?'

Kim shook her head in firm denial. 'I don't know them at all. But Chris has spoken about them all so much over the years that I feel as though I do. I've heard so much about them. And you can't turn on the telly without seeing Melissa bloody Matthews.'

'And that irritates you?'

'They get everywhere, don't they?'

'Who?'

'These Oxbridge types. They're all over the place.'

'Were you at university, Mrs Turner?'

'Newcastle.'

'I see.'

Kim threw back her head and laughed loudly. 'You see, do you? What exactly is it that you see?'

Garibaldi shrunk back in his seat. He hadn't expected such a strong reaction to an 'I see'.

'Maybe you could take me through these allegations?'

'Do I have to?'

'Yes, you do. It's important. Why don't you start with your husband?'

Kim laughed. 'Well, that was easy enough. He's had problems in that area for a long time.'

'Can you be more specific?'

'Porn. He had a habit – and I think he still does – so it didn't take much imagination to come up with the idea of a sex tape. For all I know, it might even have happened.'

'When you say porn, Mrs Turner, what kind of porn are you talking about?'

'Nothing extreme, Detective Inspector. No . . .' She broke off, suppressing a sob as she struggled for the word. 'No . . . children.' She looked to one side, trying to gather her composure.

'I'm sorry, Mrs Turner, but I have to ask these questions.'

'I know. I've just realised I'm going to have to tell Chris what I did. Things haven't been good between us recently.'

'In what way?'

'In every way, but especially . . . yeah, well maybe we haven't been too much of a husband and wife recently.'

'I see. Mrs Turner, you must have known your prank was likely to have repercussions?'

She wrung her hands. 'I did, but when I decided to do it I was in a particularly low place. And when Chris said . . .' She trailed off and tightened her lips.

'When Chris said what?'

She turned back to face Garibaldi and shook her head dismissively. 'Nothing. It's nothing.'

'Perhaps we could move on to the other allegations? Greg Matthews?'

271

'Greg Matthews? I knew about Chris's review as Tom Bryant, so all I did was change the novel. Not the second but the first. As for the others, it was guesswork and intuition. For someone who claims not to like his Oxford chums, he's spent a lot of time talking about them. He was always going on about them. For all his political views, for all his apparent rejection of all that it stood for, he spent a lot of time banging on about Oxford and what they were all up to. So all I had to do was listen carefully.'

'Fay Wetherby?' said Garibaldi.

Kim laughed. 'I'm a teacher. I know all about schools. And I've no reason to believe that prestigious London private schools are any less corrupt than the state schools I've worked in, and the ones I hear about. If anything, I suspect they're probably even worse. And one thing I do know about these private schools is that the parents, the paying customers, have these awful attitudes. And I don't believe bribery's out of the question – subtle financial bribery. So I took a punt on it and went for expulsion. I have no idea whether it's true, but it's certainly possible.'

'Julia Forrest and shoplifting?'

'Chris said he heard a rumour once that one of them had lifted something from a shop in Oxford. He only mentioned it once and that was almost in passing and I can't even remember which one of them it was. And it may only have been a rumour, but I never forgot it. The idea of these privileged Oxford undergraduates nicking stuff from shops seemed so absurd. I've got no idea if it was Julia and absolutely no idea whether she's done it since. I very much doubt it. But, there you go, like the rest of them, I thought it was funny. Harvey Nicks. It seemed appropriate.'

'Melissa Matthews and the love child?'

Kim laughed. There was a touch of hysteria in it, as if

272

she couldn't believe the preposterous scale of her invention. 'I have no idea at all. All I know is that she probably slept around in the past. I mean, who hasn't? So who knows? Again, plausible.'

'And finally, Nick Bellamy killed a man?'

Kim's head shook again. 'That's the one, isn't it? That's the one that makes the whole thing look so . . .'

At last the façade cracked. She cried. Quietly at first, but soon the tears were uncontrollable, and she was sobbing loudly.

DS Gardner passed Kim some tissues.

She wiped her eyes and gathered herself. 'I'm sorry. Look, I have no idea whether Nick Bellamy killed a man. All I know, again from what Chris said, was that he was always getting in trouble, that he had a temper. In a way, I wish I'd left him out. Of all the ones Chris spoke about, he was the one I liked most – or, at least, the one for whom I had the least contempt. But there was something Chris once said about Nick that I've never forgotten. He said that Nick had dangerous tastes, that he liked to live on the edge and that some of his appetites were deadly. I asked him what he meant but he couldn't be precise. No evidence, he said, just a suspicion. I've always assumed he was talking about drink or drugs, but it was that word "deadly" that stuck. So that's where it came from.'

Kim looked from Garibaldi to DS Gardner and back again, as if awaiting judgement.

'Right at this moment,' she said, 'I've got two worries. The first is how much trouble I'm in with you, and the second is how much trouble I'm in with Chris. I said things were bad – I can't imagine what they're going to be like now.'

'You haven't told us the truth, Mrs Turner,' said Garibaldi, 'and that's a serious offence. Obstructing the police in their enquiries. As for the accusations, I have no idea, but they could be construed as slanderous.'

'I didn't say any of them was true. All I said was "which one". And it was a question. I didn't say one was definitely true.'

'At the moment,' said Garibaldi, 'we have to consider whether your confession throws any further light on the murder of Nick Bellamy.'

Kim sniffled and blew her nose. 'I really don't know what to say. I feel stupid. Really stupid.'

'One thing before we go, Mrs Turner. You began a sentence just now with "When Chris said . . ." but you didn't finish it. You said it was nothing. What was it Chris said?'

Kim looked at Garibaldi with the wide eyes of a trapped animal.

'Even if it was nothing, we'd quite like to know.'

Kim let out a huge sigh. 'He said something that pushed me over the edge, something that sparked the whole idea. What he said was, "Just because you didn't get into Oxford doesn't mean you have to be so chippy about the place."'

'I see,' said Garibaldi. This time the words met with no response.

He got up from his chair and nodded to DS Gardner that it was time to go. 'You'll need to come in and give a statement,' he said. 'I'll leave you to tell your husband.'

Kim stood up, her face heavy with the realisation that her troubles were about to get significantly worse.

'So where does that leave us with regard to Nick Bellamy?'

Garibaldi looked out of the window as they headed south past King's Cross and the British Library. 'One thing's for sure. If he was killed as punishment for revealing secrets, or secrets that were close enough to the truth to be threatening,

274

or if he was killed to prevent him revealing any more, whoever killed him got the wrong man.'

'OK,' said DS Gardner,' and do we tell the others?'

'I think we do,' said Garibaldi. 'It will be interesting to see how they react.'

'And the other thing I'm puzzled about is whether what she did is actually a crime. I know she lied to us when we asked her about the quiz, but she's not the first who's done that and not the first who'll get away without a charge, but is it actually a crime to come up with that kind of practical joke and make those allegations?'

'Who knows?' said Garibaldi. 'All I can say is that if it's a crime it's not in the same league as stabbing and tongue-severing, is it?'

'Where to now, boss?'

Garibaldi reached for his phone. 'I'll check in with DCI Deighton, and then I think we should pay a few visits to the Balfour pals.'

Fay Wetherby was surprised that DI Garibaldi wanted to see her again. She had started to forget about Nick Bellamy and that awful quiz night. Parents and staff may well have still been talking about the accusation about her professional conduct, but if they were, she had heard nothing and she was beginning to think the storm had passed. The news that Garibaldi was on his way suggested that her optimism might have been misjudged, and she grew anxious as she waited for the detective's arrival, her fingers drumming the table. Had there been a breakthrough? Did they know who killed Nick? Or, more worryingly, had they probed the allegation against her?

'Good to see you again, Detective Inspector.'

Fay motioned Garibaldi to the circular table.

'I won't keep you long, Ms Wetherby. Just want to update you on the Nick Bellamy case.'

'Has there been a breakthrough?'

'On the murder, no, not as yet, but there's been significant progress on another front. On the Ocean Bar Quiz front.'

'I see.' Fay felt herself tense.

'Yes,' said Garibaldi, 'we know who played that practical joke. We know it wasn't Melissa, but we now also know that it wasn't Nick Bellamy either.'

'Who was it, then?'

'It was Chris Turner's wife, Kim.'

'Chris Turner's *wife*?' Fay tried to put a face to her but couldn't. She knew Chris (though she never really had much time for him), but as for his wife, she had no recollection at all. Had she even met her?

'She was at the quiz.'

It came back to her now. The small, mousy woman beside Chris. She must have said hello and shaken her hand when they were introduced.

'Why did she do it?'

Garibaldi shrugged. 'She says it was a joke, but she also says it was because she was fed up with Chris's connection to you lot, the Oxford crowd.'

'Fed up? What do you mean?'

'I'm not sure I fully understand, but maybe it was something to do with your attitudes.'

'Attitudes?'

'Your opinion of yourselves. Your sense of importance. Your privilege.' Garibaldi stopped himself. He was supposed to be speaking for Kim Turner, but he had started talking for himself. 'It may also have something to do with her relationship with her husband. Whatever the reason, she was the one behind it all.'

'But those allegations. I mean . . .'

'Does the news that it was Kim Turner change your reaction to them at all?'

'I'm surprised.'

'What are you surprised about?'

'That she . . .' Fay's years as a head had taught her the trick of never articulating what she was thinking, yet here she was, on the verge of making that very mistake. 'I can't believe she did it. I mean . . . *Why*? What was she hoping to achieve?

'Kim Turner says that she tried to make the allegations plausible . . .'

'Are you saying, Detective Inspector, that there may be some truth in the allegation made against me?'

'Not at all. I just leave the thought with you.' He got up to leave. 'But if there's anything, in the light of this new information, that you'd like to tell me, do get in touch. You already have my card?'

Fay nodded and got up to show Garibaldi the door.

Garibaldi shook the headmistress's hand. 'We still need to find Nick Bellamy's killer.'

'Of course,' said Fay, closing the door behind her.

She leaned on the door and sighed.

Why did she ever accept that generous donation two years ago and involve herself more closely than usual in that year's admissions process? And how had Chris Turner's wife got so close to the truth?

'This is a surprise!'

Julia had not expected to see DI Garibaldi when she opened her front door.

'Have you found out who did it?'

'The murder? Not yet.'

'I mean, found out who threw the brick.'

'The brick? Not yet, Mrs Forrest, but we're making progress.'

Julia showed him into the living room.

'We've also made progress on another front. That's why I'm here. We know who set up that final round of questions at the quiz.'

'Who was it? Nick?'

'No, not Nick. It was Chris Turner's wife, Kim.'

Chris Turner's wife? Kim? Julia tried hard to put a face to the name. She had only met her a couple of times before and nothing had stuck. She must have said hello at the quiz but, if so, it had been no more than a brief greeting.

'I don't understand,' said Julia, 'why on earth would she want to do that?'

She listened as Garibaldi explained, but her mind was elsewhere. She was thinking again of Nick Bellamy's murder, of the brick through her window and the threat to her daughter.

'She wanted to make those allegations plausible . . .'

The word 'plausible' brought Julia's focus back to the quiz. How had Chris Turner's wife managed to hear about an incident from so long ago? And how had she moved from that to such speculation about what might have happened since? OK, so it wasn't Harvey Nichols, and, OK, she had done nothing like that for some time, but she remembered all too well the times she had succumbed. And she knew there was still something in her that coveted what wasn't hers.

'Does knowing who was behind that round change the way you think about it, Mrs Forrest?'

'Should it? No . . . I mean . . .'

'It seems to rule out the theory that Nick Bellamy was murdered in response to that evening's events.'

'Unless the killer got the wrong man.'

'That's a possibility, Mrs Forrest.'

'And my concern, Inspector, is that the killer is still very much at large and posing a serious threat to my safety and that of Helena's.'

'We're on to it, Mrs Forrest. We're on to it.'

Garibaldi got up to leave and paused at the front door. 'If anything occurs to you, anything at all, give me a call.'

Julia took the card from his outstretched arm and closed the door behind him. She stood in the hall, looking at the card, conscious again of how much that allegation had shocked her, conscious that she still had things to hide.

'I'm afraid Melissa's out, Detective Inspector. Charity stuff.'

'Not to worry, Mr Matthews, I'll catch up with her later perhaps.'

Greg was irritated by DI Garibaldi's arrival. He had been on a particularly productive roll and had only answered the door because he was expecting an Amazon delivery.

'We've made some progress,' said Garibaldi.

'On who wrote that note?'

'We're still working on that. I mean on the Ocean Bar. We know who was behind that final round.'

'Was it Bellamy?'

'No. It was Kim Turner.'

'Who?'

'Kim Turner. Chris Turner's wife.'

'What? Why the hell would she want to do a thing like that?'

'It's complicated,' said Garibaldi. 'Resentment, perhaps. Working through something in her relationship with Chris, or something in her past. She is, doubtless to say, full of remorse. She had no idea what it would lead to.'

'That's hardly the point, is it? That fucking woman ruined our evening. And she may even have caused the killing of

279

poor Nick Bellamy! Who is this woman? Who does she think she is?'

Greg was furious. Melissa's twenty-fifth quiz night. All ruined by some jumped-up woman, the wife of someone who never quite made it.

'She wanted to make the accusations plausible,' said Garibaldi.

'Well, she failed there, didn't she?'

'When it comes to the allegation against you, Mr Matthews, I'm not sure she did.'

'What do you mean?'

'Do you remember a review of your second novel, *Fathoms Deep*, in the *Literary Magazine*?'

Greg shook his head, but he already knew where this was leading.

'Think hard, Mr Matthews. It was written by a Tom Bryant.'

'I don't recall,' said Greg.

'I think you do. Well, I have news for you, Mr Matthews. Tom Bryant is a pseudonym. The man who wrote that review is, in fact, Chris Turner.'

Greg sat in silence, letting the words sink in. Chris Turner! That explained an awful lot. He had never understood why they had bothered to keep in touch over the years, even if their contact had only stretched as far as the once-a-year meet up at the Ocean Bar. Their paths had gone in such different directions that keeping up the connection had always seemed absurd. So what if they were at Balfour together? So what if they had once been friends? Things change. Things move on. And if there was one thing of which Greg was now absolutely certain, it was that he would never speak to Chris Turner again.

And as for his snivelling wife . . .

'So that accusation, Mr Matthews, may have been well wide of the mark when it came to your first novel, but when it came to your second . . .'

'It's nonsense, Detective Inspector, and I can prove it.'

'That's OK, then.'

'And what's more,' said Greg, deciding to go on the offensive, 'I am much more concerned about the threat to my wife from a killer still at large, the same killer who most likely killed Nick Bellamy. Perhaps you should focus your efforts more on that than on that pathetic, failed practical joke from some . . . What is she? I don't even know what she does.'

'She's a teacher,' said Garibaldi, 'in a north London comprehensive.'

'Exactly.'

'What do you mean, "exactly"?'

'Look, Detective Inspector, many thanks for letting me know. And I'll tell Melissa what you've told me.'

'Actually, Mr Matthews, I would prefer it if I were the one to tell her.'

'Why? Don't you trust me?'

'It's not that. Not that at all. Do you have your wife's mobile number?'

'Of course.'

Greg reached for a pad of paper and scribbled down the number.

When the detective had gone, Greg went back to his writing desk. But he couldn't get going again.

He kept thinking about that second novel: more specifically, the idea of that second novel being subjected to closer public scrutiny.

Still, at last he now knew who Tom Bryant was. Images of what he had for many years wanted to do to this unknown reviewer had now crystallised into very specific pictures of what he would like to do to Chris Turner and his appalling loser of a wife.

Melissa had told Greg she was on charity business, but the truth was she was walking over Barnes Bridge, intending to walk up to Hammersmith through Chiswick and then back to Barnes. It was a walk she took often, particularly when there were things she needed to think through. And today was one of those times. Today there were so many things to think through that they needed to form an orderly queue so she could deal with them one at a time. But the thoughts wouldn't settle. They were still a swirling jumble and she couldn't deal with them. She was not in a good place, and it was frightening. The most frightening thing of all was that she could see only one way out of it.

The last thing she wanted to do was talk to DI Garibaldi. So when she saw his name on the screen of her ringing phone she didn't answer. She walked over the bridge past the boat-houses and along the promenade by Duke's Meadow towards Chiswick bandstand, where she sat on a bench, put her head in her hands and battled with her thoughts. The phone rang again. Garibaldi. She let it go to voicemail, but when it rang again immediately she realised that DI Garibaldi, like so many other things in her life at the moment, would not go away, and decided to take it.

'Melissa Matthews?'

'Speaking.'

'DI Garibaldi here. I have some things I need to tell you and some questions to ask.'

'About the note?' said Melissa. 'Have you found who sent it?'

'Not the note, no.'

'The killer, then? Have you found the killer?'

She was trying to sound as though she had things under

control, but her questions had tumbled out in a breathless rush.

'I think we should meet, Mrs Matthews. It will be easier that way. Are you in Barnes?'

Melissa looked across the river. She was closer to Barnes than Hammersmith.

'At home?' said Garibaldi.

'No. I'm out shopping.'

'OK. Can we meet somewhere for a coffee? Where's good for you?'

Melissa looked back towards Barnes Bridge. 'I can get to Orange Pekoe.'

'OK,' said Garibaldi. 'Half an hour?'

'Fine.' Melissa hung up and checked her watch. She should just about make it if she went quickly. She set off at a brisk pace, wondering why Garibaldi hadn't asked to see her at home, and then rang Greg to find out if the detective had been in touch with him as well. But Greg, presumably on a creative roll and cruising to his daily word count, didn't answer.

Melissa walked back to the bridge and crossed the river, taking a right towards the White Hart and the tea shop by the roundabout. Her head was still spinning. How had she got herself into this mess? More importantly, how the hell could she get out of it? She could still see only one possible solution and she was trying hard to resist its pull. She was trying very hard.

Garibaldi was waiting at an outside table when Melissa arrived. He stood up when he saw her and suggested that they spoke as they walked rather than stay in the café.

So Melissa soon found herself beside the Thames again, this time on the Barnes side, and heading west rather than east.

'OK, Mrs Matthews,' said Garibaldi, 'what I'm here to tell you is that we know who was behind that final round of questions.'

Melissa's heart jumped. 'Really? Don't tell me – it was Nick, wasn't it?'

Garibaldi stopped walking. 'How do you know that?'

Melissa had dreaded this moment. She had practised her reaction and rehearsed her lines, but that wasn't making it any easier.

'I just knew. It had Nick written all over it.'

'Really? In what way?'

'Only Nick could do something as crazy as that. And only Nick could know what kind of accusations to make.'

'I see,' said Garibaldi, starting to walk again and stroking his chin as if in an act of careful deliberation. 'And how did he know what kind of accusations to make?'

'He knew us from way back, Detective Inspector, he knew what might be close to the truth and he knew what would get under everyone's skin.'

'Was that his motive, then? To get under everyone's skin?'

'I don't know what his motive was, but I do know that it ruined my charity quiz and I'm also pretty sure it led to his murder. Still, what goes around . . .'

'I don't understand, Mrs Matthews. There's absolutely no evidence to suggest that his killing *is* linked to the events of that night.'

'I know, but . . .'

Garibaldi stopped again. 'Are you suggesting, then, that it was one of your Oxford friends who killed him?'

'We've been through all this, Detective Inspector, and I can't answer that question. But I'm glad you've found out it was Nick. At least it means we can move on.'

Garibaldi stayed still. 'There's one thing, though, Mrs Matthews. I haven't actually said that it *was* Nick Bellamy.'

Melissa looked at Garibaldi, the stupidity of her mistake slowly dawning on her. The detective's face blurred and his words became muffled. She hardly heard what he was saying, so numbed was she by the realisation of what she had done.

'The thing is, Mrs Matthews, the person behind that round of questions wasn't Nick Bellamy at all. It was Kim Turner, Chris Turner's wife.'

'Sorry . . .?' She hadn't heard it properly.

'Kim Turner. Chris Turner's wife.'

She heard it now. 'Why on earth . . .?' She struggled to remember the woman on Chris's arm when he had walked into the Ocean Bar. Had she met her before? 'I don't understand.' Her stomach was sick with heaviness, her head working out the implications of the trap she had just walked into.

'Let me explain,' said Garibaldi.

They started to walk again and Garibaldi explained how Kim Turner had pulled the Ocean Bar prank and did his best to explain the complex psychology of her motivation.

Melissa couldn't believe what she had done. Why had she opened her mouth so quickly? Why had she jumped in like that? Why hadn't she waited for Garibaldi to tell her what he had discovered?

She could tell the detective had noticed. How could she recover from her mistake?

'Thanks,' she said when he had finished his explanation. 'That answers one of the questions, at least. I don't know why I assumed it was Nick . . .'

'No. I don't either, Mrs Matthews, but we're all under considerable strain, you especially, what with—'

'Does my husband know?'

'I saw him earlier.'

'And what was his reaction?'

'Pretty similar to yours, I'd say. Couldn't understand why, but was glad to know where the plagiarism accusation came from.'

'And where was that?'

Melissa listened as Garibaldi explained.

'Why didn't he tell me?' said Melissa. 'I had no idea about that review. Why did he keep it to himself?'

'I can't explain why people keep secrets, Mrs Matthews, but I'm sure your husband must have had a good reason.'

'Chris Turner! What a thing to do!'

'Your husband felt the same, but he expressed it more strongly. One other thing, though, Mrs Matthews, before I let you get on with your day. It's about those allegations. I think I understand the ones about shoplifting, sex tapes, plagiarism and bribery – or at least I can understand how and why our friend Kim Turner came up with them. But the other two I'm still not sure about.'

'The other two? Remind me.'

'Do you really need reminding Mrs Matthews?'

Of course she didn't, but she wanted time. She knew what was coming.

'That Bellamy nearly killed a man and your teenage pregnancy. You see, the thing about all the others is that, while they may not be the absolute truth, they're all close enough to the truth to be plausible and to make those they were levelled at squirm. So my question is, how close to the truth are the other two?'

'I really have no idea,' said Melissa. 'As I've told you before.'

She had already made one mistake and was desperate to avoid making another.

'But tell me,' she said, grasping for the initiative. 'Julia told me about that awful incident and that note. Just like mine. So terrifying. And hers through a window. Are we any closer to knowing who sent them?'

'Nothing yet.'

'But can we assume that the same person sent both of them?'

'I think assumptions at any stage can be dangerous things, don't you?'

Garibaldi raised his eyebrows and gave an accusatory stare.

Melissa was reminded of her stupidity yet again, and how she had nearly revealed exactly how close the allegation against her was to the truth.

35

Monday 6 May

When Garibaldi had finished with Melissa Matthews, he headed back to the station. He had been struck by two things in their conversation. The first was how terrible Melissa Matthews had looked, so different from the smooth, polished television newsreader. The second was how easily she had fallen for his trick. He hadn't planned it at all, but as soon as she came out with the idea that Nick Bellamy had been behind the final round, he had simply let her run with it. Why had she been so quick to assume it had been Bellamy behind it all?

He thought of the evening ahead. Jason Isbell at the Hammersmith Apollo with Rachel, and even though it was what she called 'a school night', the prospect of what might follow. It was enough to take his mind off the case entirely.

When he was walking under Barnes Bridge, Alfie rang.

'Hi Dad, where are you?'

'Heading home. Be there in five.'

'Is it OK if I drop round?'

'Sure. Is everything OK?'

'Everything's fine. It's just that I'm going out tonight in Barnes.'

'In Barnes?'

'I'll explain. I was just wondering if I could chill.'

'Chill? Sure.'

Alfie was waiting outside when he reached the flat. Garibaldi gave him a hug and opened the door. Alfie came in, threw his rucksack onto the couch and followed it, flicking on the TV with the remote and stretching out.

'Fancy something to eat?' said Garibaldi from the kitchen.

'I'm eating later.'

Who with? His girlfriend? Was this the time to ask, or would that make him clam up?

'Where are you eating?'

'It's a dinner thing.'

'A dinner thing?'

'Yeah. At someone's house.'

'So it's a dinner party, is it?'

'I guess so.'

Garibaldi came into the living room with his cup of coffee. 'A dinner party in Barnes? How posh.'

'Not really. It's just a friend of my friend.'

'A friend of my friend. That all sounds very vague.'

Garibaldi sat down in an armchair and looked at the TV. It was the usual pattern – talk while looking at something else.

'OK,' said Alfie. 'If you want me to be more specific ...'

'I'm fine. You don't have to tell me.'

'My friend is Alice,' said Alfie. 'And her friend is Helena. They're both at the Dolphin.'

'I see, and you've been ...'

'I've been seeing Alice for some time, yes.'

'So she's the one who ...'

'She's the one who's going to Oxford, yes.'

The one who's cheered you up. The one who's made you rethink your life plans. Not from St Snot's, but with a St Snot's attitude.

'Well, that's great,' said Garibaldi. 'And Helena lives in Barnes?'

'Yeah. One of those massive houses near the pond. I don't really want to go. Not my kind of thing.'

Like father. Like son. Living with Dominic might have done terrible things to him but it hadn't destroyed the genetic link.

'I think it's going to be a weird evening.'

'Why's that?'

'Apparently someone smashed their window the other night.'

'And that's going to make it a weird evening?'

'Yeah, well, they smashed it with a brick and on this brick was a threatening note. '

Garibaldi started. 'What?'

'Yeah. And apparently this girl's really freaked out and so's the mother, so God knows what it's going to be like.'

'And this girl's called Helena?'

Garibaldi kept his voice calm, trying to disguise the level of his interest and surprise. He knew he was playing the policeman with his son.

'And what's so weird about it is that I heard some kids at school talking about it the other day.'

'Talking about what? The brick through the window?'

Alfie nodded. 'Yeah. They weren't talking *to* me. I just happened to be sitting next to them in the common room and couldn't avoid hearing. I mean, they're a bunch of tossers. Loud tossers.'

Loud tossers at St Snot's. Garibaldi couldn't imagine it.

'What did they say?'

'Well, these blokes had all been out on Friday night and it was the early hours of Saturday morning. They were by Barnes Pond on one of those benches, and they were doing stuff.'

'Doing stuff?'

'Drugs.'

'What kind of drugs?'

Slow down. Too much the detective.

'I don't know. Whatever it is a bunch of loud tossers take at the weekend. Weed. Coke. MD. I don't know. And before you ask, Dad, no I'm not taking drugs. And, no, Alice and her mates don't either. So there's no need to be all Mum about it.'

Garibaldi held up his hands, protesting innocence. 'Go on.'

'I don't know why they were there. Maybe they all live round there, I don't know. Anyway, they were definitely doing stuff, because this bloke was talking about it in a really loud voice like he was trying to impress everybody. A lot of that goes on at the pond late at night, but I expect you know that, don't you? Anyway, they were really out of it or whatever and they heard this crash like a broken window. So they all freaked out. Some of them were obviously in a pretty strange state, so God knows what they thought was happening and some of them were worried they were going to get busted, but apparently this bloke who was telling the story ran towards the noise.'

'Why did he do that?' said Garibaldi

'I don't know. He didn't say. Anyway, he ran towards this noise and crashed into a bike. And he fell over and whoever was on the bike came off it. And then they got back on and cycled off.'

'Was that it? Did this boy say anything else?'

'No, but it's pretty weird, isn't it? I hear about this brick through the window from Alice and then I hear someone talking about hearing a window getting smashed at about the same time. The thing is, I don't know whether I should tell them. I mean, if they're freaked out about it they might not want to hear, but on the other hand I don't know if it's an important detail. I mean, I don't know what's happened, whether the police are involved or . . .'

Garibaldi could hold himself back no longer. 'Look, Alfie, there's something I need to tell you.'

Alfie listened as Garibaldi yet again broke the rules, telling his son about the Bellamy case and Julia Forrest's connection to it.

'OK,' said Alfie, 'so now I've got to go and have dinner with the daughter of this woman and I know all that about her. Thanks, Dad.'

'I can't tell you how much of a help you've been, Alfie, and if I were you I wouldn't say anything about it this evening. It would only worry them. But there's one more favour I've got to ask of you, and you're probably not going to like it.'

36

Tuesday 7 May

Jason Isbell at the Apollo had been great, and when Garibaldi woke up beside Rachel the next morning he felt better than he had done for some time – he might even have called it happy. How different this was from that first morning all those weeks ago. So much more natural and relaxed. No worries about what to do or say, a kind of warm comfort that made him cast anxious looks over his shoulder to see if someone was lurking there, ready to snatch it all away.

Last night had been so good that he had almost forgotten about the Bellamy case and Alfie's connection to the Forrest household. Almost, but not quite. There were moments when images of his son in the palatial pond-side mansion had flashed across his mind, and he had wondered whether the brick through the window was featuring in the dinner-table chit-chat.

It was the same this morning. As he woke Rachel with a cup of tea in good time for her to get ready for school, something about what Alfie had told him nagged at the back of his mind. He was tempted to give him a call, but it was too early and, besides, given that Alfie had already agreed to one huge favour, it might be best to leave him alone for a while.

Alfie had only a vague idea of the boy's name, but he had promised to send Garibaldi a text when he knew for sure, and an hour before school was due to finish he delivered. The boy was called Jack Donohue.

'There's no guarantee he'll even be at school tomorrow,' Alfie had said, 'and in the sixth form you sometimes don't have lessons in the afternoon, so he won't necessarily be coming out at the end of the day.'

But Alfie had done his homework, showing great detective potential in finding out Jack's timetable, even calculating the likelihood of his leaving school through anything other than the main entrance.

Garibaldi stood outside St Snot's talking to Alfie and drawing on his years of experience to make sure no one noticed him. His eyes were on his son but his focus was on the students pouring out of the school gate. Looking at them confirmed his feelings about the place, but when Alfie pointed out Jack Donohue, he forgot his reservations and focused on the task in hand. Leaving Alfie checking his phone and doing his best to look invisible, he set off on an old-fashioned piece of tailing.

Jack Donohue was with two other boys. Garibaldi followed them to the bus stop, and when they got on a bus heading to Richmond, he jumped on after them. The three boys headed upstairs, but Garibaldi took a seat by the doors, trying to shut out the irritating loudness of excited schoolkids.

Just outside Richmond Jack Donohue and his two mates came downstairs. All three got off the bus together and Garibaldi followed.

The three walked back down the main road, and when Jack raised his hand in farewell and turned down a road to the left, Garibaldi saw his chance.

He increased his pace. When he was five yards behind Jack he called out.

'Excuse me!'

Jack turned.

'Can I have a quick word?'

Jack paused, and looked at Garibaldi with a mixture of guilt and suspicion.

'You're Jack Donohue, aren't you?'

He nodded.

'I won't keep you long. It's just that I think you may have witnessed an incident the other night and I want to ask you a few questions about it.'

'Why? Who are you?'

'My name's Bill Loveridge. I live in Barnes and what I want to ask you about is something that happened late last Friday night – well, actually, it was more like early Saturday morning.'

Jack's face tightened. It was clear he knew exactly what Garibaldi was talking about.

'You see the thing is, Jack, I live next door to Julia Forrest and on that particular night she had a brick thrown through her window. All very unpleasant. But I have been given to understand that you and some of your mates were there when it happened. To be more specific, you were all sitting by Barnes Pond.'

Jack looked up and down the street as if he was planning an escape or checking to see if anyone was looking.

'It wasn't me.'

'I'm not saying it was.'

'How do you know I was there?'

'Because someone saw you.'

'Who?'

'That doesn't matter.'

'Look. I – we – nothing was going on, all right? We weren't doing anything.'

'I'm sure you weren't, Jack, but I've been told that you actually ran after the person who may have thrown the brick and bumped into their bicycle. Is that true?'

'I didn't hurt anyone, did I?'

'I've no idea, Jack, but what I'd really like you to do is tell me as much as you can remember about the bike and the rider.'

'How did you find out where I was?'

Garibaldi touched the side of his nose. 'My neighbour has a lot of contacts – a lot of influence. The fact is, Jack, I know what you and your mates were doing by Barnes Pond that night and I know who I could tell about it – school, parents, police, even – to make it all very difficult for you. So the deal is I don't say anything and you tell me as much as you can about the bicycle.'

Jack looked hard at Garibaldi, weighing up his options. 'It was dark and it was late,' he said, 'and I'm not sure if I can remember much.'

'Maybe that's connected to what you and your mates were up to. Plays havoc with the memory, you know.'

'Look,' said Jack. 'I—'

'Give it a go,' said Garibaldi. 'See what comes to mind.'

Jack looked up and down the road again. 'I'm not in trouble, am I? I mean . . .'

'Tell me all you remember and I'll say nothing about the drugs . . .'

At the word 'drugs' Jack started and nodded, as if he understood exactly what was at stake. 'OK, we all heard the sound of breaking glass and looked at each other. We were a bit shocked, I suppose, and maybe a bit worried. It was early morning. No one was around, and we were ... Anyway, for some reason I decided to go and see what had happened. I don't know why I did it. Maybe I shouldn't have, but before I knew it, I was going towards the noise. I may even have been running. It's all a bit of a blur, but I was going towards those big houses next to the pond ...'

'The Crescent. Where I live.'

'Whatever. I was running along, and the next thing I know is I've been knocked down by a bike and I'm lying in the middle of the road. And so is she.'

'She?'

'Yeah.'

'It was a woman?'

'Yeah.'

'Did she say anything?'

'That's what was so weird. I mean, maybe I'm not remembering it right, but it was all really spooky the way she didn't say sorry or ask if I was all right. She just got up, picked up her bike, and rode off. No lights. Nothing. If the bike had lights I'd have seen it coming.'

'She said nothing at all? So how do you know she was a woman?'

'She grunted and groaned. I could tell.'

'Even if you'd been taking drugs?' Jack shrugged. 'Did you see what she looked like?'

'It was dark. There were a few lights round the pond, so it wasn't total darkness, but there weren't many and you couldn't pick anything out. And I wasn't really taking much in. I'd been knocked over. I was out of it.'

'Nothing at all distinctive about her, then?'

'I couldn't see her. But the bike ...'

297

'What about the bike?'

'I think it had a basket on the front and I remember some light catching it as she rode it away and thinking it was an odd colour.'

'What colour was it?'

'It looked kind of purple.'

'A woman on a purple bike with a basket?' said Garibaldi. 'Are you sure about this?'

Jack nodded.

'And did you see pink elephants as well?'

Jack didn't seem to find this funny. 'Can I go now?' he said. 'I need to get home.'

Garibaldi didn't hear the boy's words. His mind was spinning with possibilities. A purple bike with a basket? Was he imagining it, or had he seen one somewhere recently?

'Is that it?' said Jack.

'That's great,' said Garibaldi. 'I'll tell my next-door neighbour and see if that helps her.'

'And you're not going to say anything about … about other stuff?'

'No, Jack, I'm not, but I do have a message for you and your mates.'

'What's that?'

'Stay away from it. It's dangerous. All of it's dangerous. Believe me, I've seen it.'

37

Thursday 9 May

'Thank you for seeing me, Mrs Matthews.'

Garibaldi had called in advance, and when he heard that Greg Matthews was at a publishing lunch and wouldn't be back until the evening, he had cycled to Mill Hill. He needed to see Melissa Matthews alone.

He followed her into the living room and sat down on the sofa. Melissa Matthews sat down opposite. She looked gaunt and tense – if anything, worse than when he had walked with her by the river.

'I'm afraid I'm not feeling too good, Detective Inspector.'

'I'm sorry.'

'Yes, everything's very difficult. Ever since ... Anyway, I'd hoped to go back to work, but I don't think I can yet. I'm OK, but things are a bit tricky with Lauren.'

'A bit tricky?'

'She's got worse. We're hoping she can make it through her exams, but she's not in a great state. What a household, eh? Mother and daughter! Still, at least Greg's OK. He's keeping us all together. But tell me, have you made any progress?'

'We might have, Mrs Matthews. What I'd like to do is ask you a few more questions about that note.'

'Certainly. I still keep thinking about it, you know. I've tried to forget about it, but I can't. The worry that I might not be safe, that someone might be after me. God knows what it's like for poor Julia. It's bad enough when the threat is to you, but when it's to your daughter as well ...'

'My first question is about your note, Mrs Matthews. I'd just like to go over what you said about finding it.'

Garibaldi reached for his notebook and flipped it open. He knew exactly what he wanted to say, but on occasions like this he liked to give the appearance of backing up his words with the authority of written text.

'You said, Mrs Matthews, that you picked up the pile of post and I have the words you used here – you said that you found the envelope "in the middle of it". That's right, isn't it?'

'Right that I said it or right that it was in the middle of the pile?'

'Either or both, Mrs Matthews.'

Melissa furrowed her brow as if struggling to remember. 'Now that you mention it, Detective Inspector, I'm not entirely sure. All I remember is picking up the pile and find- ing that ... that horrible thing.'

Garibaldi tapped his notebook with his finger. 'But you said it was "in the middle of the pile".'

'Did I? Well, it's a figure of speech, isn't it?'

'Is it? I'm not sure. Surely you would have remembered if that envelope was on the *top* of the pile, wouldn't you? It would have been the first thing you saw when you bent down to pick up the post. You'd have said something like, "And there, sitting on the top of the pile of post, was this envelope with my name written in strange, large Gothic handwriting."'

'Is this important?'

'It could be. You see, Mrs Matthews, we don't know for sure that the postman delivered it. There's no CCTV footage of anyone coming up to your front door and putting something through your letterbox. It could have been delivered that way but only, as DS Gardner so ably demonstrated, by crawling along the ground on your belly. So it seems unlikely that it came to you that way. My problem is this. If it *was* somehow delivered through your letterbox – and CCTV suggests this could only have been after the postman had made his delivery – then it would surely have been sitting on top of that pile of post. If not literally on top, then to one side, perhaps – there's a chance that it may have fallen differently. But you said quite clearly that it was found *in the middle* of the pile.'

Melissa opened her shoulders and spread her arms. 'As I said, a mere figure of speech.'

'I'm not convinced, Mrs Matthews. My question is, if it was in the middle of the pile, how did it get there? It could only have got there if someone accessed that pile of post from inside the house. Now your husband showed me some of the ways whoever it was could have got into your house and it's possible that's what happened. But I do find that very unlikely.'

Melissa nodded slowly, as if the implications of Garibaldi's words were sinking in. 'So how does this fit in with the delivery of Julia's note?'

'In the case of Julia's note we're not dealing with subtleties. It came through a window attached to a brick.'

'I know that – I mean, do you have any leads on that one?'

'We may do, Mrs Matthews.'

Melissa raised her eyebrows.

'Yes,' said Garibaldi, 'I've managed to track down someone who may actually have been in the vicinity when it happened.'

'Really?'

'Yes. And this person – a boy – actually ran in the direction of the crash and ran into a bicycle heading away from it. It hasn't given us much, Mrs Matthews, but we do know that the person on the bike was a woman.'

'I see. And do we know that the woman on the bike is definitely the person who threw the brick?'

'Not for sure, but given the circumstances it seems likely, doesn't it?'

'You're the detective. You tell me.'

'I'm telling you what we've discovered, Mrs Matthews.'

'And if this woman did do it, are you saying that she also delivered my letter?'

'Again, I don't know, but it's an idea we have to consider.'

The front door opened and a voice came from the hall.

'Hello?'

Melissa stood up. 'Is that you, Lauren?'

'Yeah.'

'What are you doing home?'

Lauren walked into the living room and stopped when she saw Garibaldi.

'Detective Inspector Garibaldi is asking a few questions,' said Melissa.

'Questions about what?'

'About the notes,' said Garibaldi.

Lauren turned from her mother to Garibaldi and then back to her mother. 'Do we know who sent them?'

Melissa shook her head. 'Not yet.'

'What about Nick Bellamy?' said Lauren.

Melissa shook her head again. 'Why are you home so early, Lauren?'

'Teacher's off sick, so no lessons this afternoon.'

'Do I need to check or should I believe you?'

'You can do what you like. It's pretty much all over now, so it hardly matters, does it?'

Melissa shot Garibaldi a glance suggesting that all she had said about her daughter's state had been confirmed.

Garibaldi got up. 'Well, I'd better be off,' he said. 'If anything else occurs to you, Mrs Matthews, you have my number.'

Melissa walked to the door. 'I'll show you out.'

As Garibaldi stepped out of the front door he looked up again at the CCTV camera. He walked towards it and turned to face the house.

'I'm still baffled, Mrs Matthews. Still baffled.'

'Do you know what, Detective Inspector, the more I think about it, the more I think it was a figure of speech. Maybe that letter *was* on top of the pile.'

'Even so,' said Garibaldi, stroking his chin and looking round. 'I'll be back in touch, Mrs Matthews, if anything else occurs to me.'

'Thank you.' Melissa closed the door.

Garibaldi walked down the drive, but stopped halfway, turned back and walked again towards the front door. Had he imagined what had caught the corner of his eye as he had stood under the CCTV camera?

He walked back to the same position and looked to the left of the house. It was as he had thought. The front of a bicycle wheel on the other side of the garage. He walked towards it and turned the corner. Leaning against the garage wall was a bicycle. A purple bicycle.

He heard the front door open and the sound of shoes on gravel coming towards him. He shrank into the garage wall.

Lauren came round the corner and stopped suddenly when she saw Garibaldi.

'What are you doing?'

Garibaldi stepped away from the garage wall.

'Just having a look round.

Lauren took a bag out of the bike basket.

Garibaldi pointed at the bike. 'Is this yours?'

'Yeah. Why?'

'Nice colour.'

Lauren looked at the bike as if she had never noticed its colour before.

Garibaldi leaned towards it, tapped the frame and looked up at Lauren.

'You cycle to school?'

'Yeah. Unless it's raining.'

'I hope you've got lights.'

'Would you arrest me if I didn't?'

Garibaldi laughed.

'Yeah. I've got lights,' said Lauren.

'Good,' said Garibaldi, 'you can never be too careful. Especially at night.'

He tapped the frame again and walked to the front of the garage.

38

Friday 10 May

Garibaldi felt like a dirty old man. He had been standing opposite St Mark's watching the girls come out for fifteen minutes, and in any of those moments he would not have been surprised if a colleague had approached him and told him to move on.

He was standing in front of the main exit, looking at the bright, confident, articulate west-London teenagers heading home and thinking, as each one passed, of the one who had changed Alfie so much. When he saw what he was waiting for – a girl wheeling a bike with a purple frame – he walked in front of it and held up his hand.

'Lauren Matthews?'

As soon as the girl turned Garibaldi realised his mistake.

'No,' said the girl, giving him a what-are-you-up-to look and pushing her bike past him with a suspicious sideways glance. Garibaldi raised his hand in awkward apology and resumed his watch, accepting that there was likely to be more than one St Mark's girl with a purple bike.

The next time he had more luck.

'What do you want?' said Lauren.

'I'd like to ask you a few questions.'

'Do I have to? I've got a lot to do and I'm in a hurry.'

'It won't take long.'

Lauren sighed, shrugged her shoulders and gave an exaggerated roll of her eyes. 'There's nothing I can tell you. Why don't you just leave me – leave all of us – alone?'

The whole of her body showed strain and tension. Garibaldi thought she might even burst into tears.

'There's a café just round the corner. I thought we could go there and have a chat.'

'I really don't see how I can help.'

Lauren avoided Garibaldi's eyes, looking at the St Mark's girls walking past, as if she thought one of them might rescue her.

Garibaldi waited patiently. Eventually Lauren grunted an OK and wheeled her bike beside Garibaldi as they walked to the Shepherd's Bush Road. He waited while she locked her bike, held the door for her and followed her in. He showed her to a table by the window and ordered coffees at the counter. When he turned he saw that Lauren had moved away from the window and was now sitting at the back of the café.

'You've moved,' he said when he sat down.

'Yeah, well, it's bad enough being seen walking along the street with you, but being seen here with you would be worse.'

'Why's that?'

'God knows what everyone would think. They're talking enough as it is.'

'Oh yeah? And what do they say?'

'Can we just get on with it?'

'Look, Lauren, I'm sorry to have met you like this, but I thought it was important for me to see you by myself.'

306

'Why's that?'

'Because it might be easier away from your home, away from your mum and dad. And I don't think you'd really want to come into the police station, would you?'

Lauren's face froze. 'Police station? Why? What have I done wrong?'

'That's what I'm here to discover. Tell me, Lauren, what you know about these threatening notes?'

'I know Mum got one and that Julia got one as well.'

'Has your mum or dad spoken to you about it?'

'About the note? They told me what it said and told me not to worry.'

'Did they talk about how the note was delivered?'

'No.'

'You see, that note couldn't have been delivered through the letterbox. I'm convinced it was put on that pile of post or, rather, *in* that pile of post from inside the house.'

'Who would do that?'

'Exactly. Who would do that?'

Garibaldi examined Lauren Matthews' face as she sipped her cappuccino and licked the froth from her lips. She was an impressive actress.

'Are you aware that the note on the brick thrown through the Forrests' window threatened Helena Forrest as well as her mother?'

'No, they didn't say. I had no idea. Why would anyone . . .?'

'Who do you think threw that brick through the Forrests' window?'

'I assume the same person who delivered ours.'

'That brick was thrown very late one night last week. And I have reason to believe that whoever threw it was riding a bike, a purple bike.'

Lauren's jaw dropped open. 'You think *I* did it! Why on

earth would I do that? Why would I threaten them? Hang on, do you also think that I'm the one who delivered our own note from inside the house? Why the hell would I do that?'

'People often do strange things and they often do them for the strangest of reasons.'

'I'm not the only person round here who has a purple bike, am I?'

'I'm not saying it *was* you, I'm just telling you what I know.'

'But why would I do it?'

'As I said, there are often the strangest of reasons.'

'And what would my reasons be?'

'I don't know. Maybe you wanted to freak them out.'

'"You"? What do you mean "you"? It wasn't me, for crying out loud. My mum might be a crazy bitch, but I wouldn't do that to her!'

'Crazy bitch? That's unkind, isn't it?'

'You wouldn't believe how much of a . . .' Lauren's lips tightened.

'How much what?'

'Nothing. It's nothing.'

'Your mum says you haven't been feeling too good recently.'

'I thought you were here to ask me questions, not enquire about my health.'

'I'm here to get a better picture of things. When did you start feeling bad again?'

'Again? Feeling bad again? Is that what she said? She's just worried that I might not pass my A levels. First not getting into Oxford, then I might not get into Durham. What a disappointment I must be. Still, maybe I can do three years at the Priory and *they* can give me a degree.'

Lauren's hands cradled her coffee cup. Garibaldi noticed her bitten fingernails.

'I think your parents are just concerned about your well-being.'

'Hah!' Lauren said it so loudly that heads turned in the café. 'Well, if they were concerned about that, they should have done something about it years ago.'

'What do you mean?'

'Are you an only child?'

'No.'

'Well, it's not easy, I can tell you. Everything is on you. All that pressure, all that anxiety – it all comes to you. There's no one to share it with, no one to call to talk it through with.'

'Tell me, Lauren, have your parents spoken about what happened at the Ocean Bar Quiz?'

'You mean that final round of questions? Yeah. I know all about that.'

'Have your parents told you that they weren't the work of Nick Bellamy?'

Lauren looked up suddenly. 'What? But I thought . . .'

'You thought what?'

'I thought that's why he was killed.'

'So did a lot of others. But no.'

'Who was it, then?'

'It was the wife of one of your parents' Oxford friends. Kim Turner.'

'Why did she do it?'

'As a joke.'

'But—'

'What did you make of those allegations about your parents?'

'OK, so my Dad plagiarised one of his books. Who cares?'

'And your mum?'

'Ridiculous!'

'Why do you say that?'

'Because it is. A teenage pregnancy and a secret child!'

'Why not? It could be the brother or sister you've always wanted.'

Lauren looked surprised, as if she was giving the idea serious consideration.

Garibaldi gave a reassuring smile. 'As you say, who knows? And they'd be quite a bit older than you, wouldn't they?'

'Where did this woman get the idea from in the first place?'

'We don't know. She says it was simply speculation. She worked on the assumption that a lot of girls, a lot of teenage girls, often make mistakes.'

'But it's like saying that I . . .'

'Yes?'

'It's like saying that I get pregnant now, or got pregnant a few years ago, or . . .'

'Exactly. But as you know, Lauren, these things do happen. Things can happen to you that you don't want or don't expect, as I'm sure you know only too well.'

'All these secrets. Sometimes they're best left as secrets.'

'And sometimes it's better that they're out in the open, don't you think?'

'Look, what do you expect me to say about those things?'

'Surely you can see the effect they've had on your parents – particularly on your mother?'

'My fucking mother! What about me? What about the effect it's had on me? Why don't you just find out who killed Nick Bellamy and who sent those notes?'

'That's what I'm trying to do.'

'Well, it doesn't sound like it.'

'OK. So back to the brick. Where were you on the night it was thrown?'

'At that time of night? I should think I was in bed.'

'I see.'

'No hang on. What night was it?'

'Friday the third of May.'

'Right. I remember now. I wasn't at home that night.'

'Where were you?'

'I was in north London and I stayed the night.'

'Who with?'

'A friend from school. Steph. You can ring her if you like.' Lauren reached into her pocket, pulled out her phone, scrolled through to find the number, and handed the phone to Garibaldi.

Garibaldi took it and made the call. In the confident gushy tones of a St Mark's girl, Steph confirmed that Lauren had been with her that night and stayed over.

'So,' said Lauren, 'does that satisfy you?'

Garibaldi nodded. It would have to. The sceptic in him believed the alibi could have been set up, but for the moment he was prepared to accept it.

'As I said, it wasn't me. And if it was my bike – and that's still a pretty big if – maybe someone else was riding it.'

'Do you lock your bike, Lauren?'

'Yeah.' Lauren fished her keys out of her bag and pointed at a padlock key. 'You just saw me do it.'

'And do you lock it up at home?'

'Not usually, no. Sometimes I wheel it round the back, sometimes I leave it in the garage. I figure if someone wants to come all the way to our house to steal stuff they'll be looking for bigger things than a bike.'

Garibaldi looked at the keys Lauren had put on the table and then up at Lauren. Sun was streaming through the café window, lighting up the table and Lauren's face. As light flashed in Lauren's eyes and bounced off the keys on the table, another light flashed with the same sudden intensity in Garibaldi's head.

311

How had he failed to consider it before?

And could it possibly be true?

After seeing Lauren cycle off, Garibaldi took the bus to Hammersmith, getting off just before it reached the bridge and walking down onto the towpath. It was bright, sunny day and he needed time to think.

He walked westwards towards Barnes Bridge. When he reached the Leg o' Mutton he took a path to the left, went up the slope and pushed open the swing-to gate. Soon he was in the clearing where Nick Bellamy's body had been found. He sat on the bench and looked out at the lake, seeing again the corpse's distended face, the severed tongue and the college scarf. He saw the body lying beside the lake, remembered its shape and angles, and he remembered, as if for the first time, its hands. He had no idea the memory was there, but it now came to him clearly and he again marvelled at the possibility that had come to him as he looked at Lauren Matthews across the café table.

At last things were starting to fall into place, and he was close to understanding exactly what had happened.

39

Friday 10 May

'Dad, this is Alice.'

'Pleased to meet you.'

When Alfie had called him on his way back to Barnes and asked if he could come round briefly and bring a friend, Garibaldi had panicked. A friend could mean only one thing, and his flat was a complete tip. Rachel was coming round that evening and he had been intending to give the place a good tidy in the hour before she turned up. Now he was about to meet Alfie's girlfriend and he would have no time to make it look as though her boyfriend's father wasn't a total slob. He had done his best, but he knew it wasn't enough, and he sensed Alice's eyes darting round with disapproval.

Or maybe it was nerves.

'We're off to the theatre,' said Alfie, 'and thought we'd pop in on the way.'

'Glad you did. What are you off to see?'

'*Twelfth Night*. At the National.'

'Great. I love that play.'

Was this his son? The awkward, alienated Alfie who had been screwed over by his change of school, exposed to ideas and values from which Garibaldi had tried hard to protect him? Was this the boy shattered by his parents' separation but doing his best to hide it, or a confident young St Snot's student aiming high in his university choices?

'Funnily enough,' said Garibaldi, 'we're off to the theatre as well.'

'Coincidence,' said Alfie, 'what are you seeing?'

'Something at the Bush. Can't remember its name.'

'The Bush, eh? You normally only go there on match days.'

'Yeah, my first time in the theatre. Not my choice, though.'

'You're going with ...?'

Garibaldi nodded. 'Rachel.'

So this was it, the big father-son moment. Garibaldi had shown Alfie his and now Alfie was reciprocating.

And they were both off to the theatre.

The play was not to Garibaldi's taste, more a political tract than a piece of theatre, as far as he was concerned, but he kept his views to himself as he and Rachel climbed off the bus at Barnes Pond. They walked to his flat, Garibaldi anticipating the nightcap and all that would follow. Friday wasn't a school night.

Hours later, he was woken from a deep post-coital sleep and a dream about going to Nashville with Rachel by the ringing of his phone.

At first the phone was part of that dream, an urgent call summoning him back to Barnes, but he soon woke to its reality. A glance at the bedside clock radio told him it was five minutes past midnight.

The screen showed Melissa Matthews' name.

He hauled himself out of bed, walked towards the kitchen,

314

cast a glance back at Rachel to check that she was still asleep, and took the call.

'DI Garibaldi?'

'Speaking.'

'I need to see you.'

'What? Now?'

'There are things I need to tell you.'

'It's past midnight.'

'I wouldn't be doing this if it wasn't important.'

'Where do you want to meet?'

'Not here. Greg, Lauren, they mustn't know. I can come to you.'

Garibaldi looked through the door into the bedroom. 'That's not a good idea.'

'I can get to the pond. How about meeting there?'

Garibaldi thought of Alfie's schoolmates sitting on a bench smoking spliffs.

'Not the pond. Meet me by the river opposite the Bull's Head.'

'OK,' said Melissa, 'I'm leaving now.'

Garibaldi went back into the bedroom and started to get dressed. Rachel was sleeping soundly. Should he wake her? Should he leave her a note? Or should he take a risk?

He took a risk and left the flat, wondering whether he was right in his hunch about what Melissa Matthews wanted to tell him.

At half-past midnight, under the pale streetlights, Melissa Matthews looked far from the glamorous TV newsreader. Hugging herself, and sniffling and shivering, not through the early morning chill but through what seemed to be nerves and exhaustion, she nodded when Garibaldi crossed the road towards her.

Cars occasionally passed on their way home or, in the case of the young and adventurous, on their way out, and there was the occasional pedestrian, but they were in no danger of being overheard.

Garibaldi pointed in the direction of Hammersmith Bridge. 'There's a bench further up. Shall we go there?'

Melissa nodded and they walked together along the raised concrete path by the Thames, Barnes Bridge behind them, the lights from the Chiswick side reflected on its dark, silent surface.

'I need to tell you everything,' said Melissa, as they started to walk.

'I could save you the trouble, Mrs Matthews, because I already know.'

'Tell me what you know,' said Melissa. 'Maybe you can save my breath. Maybe I won't have to go through it all again.'

'Let's wait until we're sitting, shall we?'

When they reached the bench they sat side by side, looking out across the river.

Garibaldi took a breath and let out a sigh. It had the air of relief, finality. 'Mrs Matthews, I know what happened with that note.'

'You do?'

He nodded. 'You sent that note to yourself, didn't you? You wrote it, you put it in an envelope and then you put it with the pile of post and pretended you had just picked it up. Maybe you did put it in the middle of the pile or maybe you didn't, and just suffered a slip of the tongue when you told me. And shall I tell you why you sent that note to yourself?'

Melissa looked out across the river.

'You sent it to yourself because you wanted us to think that whoever killed Nick Bellamy wanted to kill you. And that's why you took your daughter's purple bike early one morning and threw a brick with a note attached through Julia Forrest's window. You wanted us to think that whoever killed Nick Bellamy was still around and was still a threat. You wanted to make it seem that it couldn't possibly be you. That's why you were the first to come to the police and say you knew Nick Bellamy. It was all a front, a screen.'

'I knew you'd worked it out,' said Melissa. 'I . . .'

Garibaldi held up his hand to stop her.

'Nick Bellamy needed money to pay off huge gambling debts, and he thought he'd found a way of getting it. You wanted to see Nick Bellamy to buy him off, didn't you? To buy him off for good.'

Another nod.

'Because you thought Nick Bellamy was behind that final round that ruined your quiz. You had no idea at the time that it was the work of Chris Turner's embittered wife. You thought those allegations were all close to the truth, and you knew for sure that the one about you was very close indeed. And you knew that Nick knew that as well. So you wanted to buy his silence. Because you didn't want your secret known. You're a figure in the public eye and the revelation would hurt everyone. Greg. Lauren. But, most of all, you. So you arranged to meet Nick at the Leg o' Mutton nature reserve, where you handed over a large sum of money. And then you poisoned him. Cyanide. A rich, well-connected, powerful woman like yourself wouldn't find it difficult to get hold of some. You poisoned Nick Bellamy. Presumably you thought it would look like suicide. A man for whom everything had gone wrong seeking to end it all. I don't know what happened to the money – I guess you took it off him with what I assume were your gloved hands. I'm assuming you took his phone as well, and disposed of it somewhere safe, probably in the river. You left Nick Bellamy lying dead by

317

the lake, hoping that your secret would remain a secret for ever, that it would go with you to your grave. And what was that secret, Mrs Matthews, that you wanted Nick Bellamy to keep to himself?'

Garibaldi turned to look at her. She was still looking straight ahead, across the river, her face frozen.

'You went out with Nick Bellamy at Balfour before you hooked up with Greg. But it never quite ended, did it? When you left Oxford, you kept seeing him, didn't you? And on some of those occasions you slept with him. There was still something dangerous and attractive about him, wasn't there?'

Melissa nodded.

'And when you became pregnant you knew, didn't you? And Nick knew as well?'

Another nod.

'But Greg has no idea?'

A shake of the head.

'And neither does Lauren?'

Another shake.

'Have either of them ever suspected?'

'I don't think so.'

'And you'd like to keep it that way, wouldn't you? You certainly wouldn't want it revealed by someone else. How inconvenient, how awful that would be. Just think of Greg coming to terms with that. And just think of Lauren. She's had enough to deal with already. And just think of you. Think of what the papers would do with that juicy story.'

Melissa was still looking at him. Lights glinted in the tears on her cheeks.

'Am I right?' said Garibaldi.

'Yes.'

The yes was gentle and accepting, a yes of resignation and defeat. Whatever game she was in had played itself to an end.

She reached out a hand, rested it on Garibaldi's arm and leaned towards him. 'Is there any chance . . .?'

'Of what?'

'Is there any chance of keeping this quiet?'

'I don't think so,' said Garibaldi. 'I really don't think so. A couple of other things, Mrs Matthews. First of all, why the Leg o' Mutton? Why did you arrange to meet Nick Bellamy there, of all places?'

'I needed somewhere out of the way, somewhere quiet. I thought no one would be there on Boat Race night. It's the kind of place that's lovely in the daytime, but you warn your kids about going there at night.'

'And did you warn Lauren?'

Melissa smiled as if remembering an earlier, less troubled time. 'When she was young, yes, but since she hit fifteen, sixteen, there wasn't much point.'

'So she's in the habit of going there, is she?'

'She could be. I don't know. If ever I ask her where she's going when she leaves the house, she never tells me, so I've stopped asking. Maybe she does go there. Maybe if she's back on the stuff, that's where she's been taking it. I don't know. It hardly matters now, does it?'

'And the other question, Mrs Matthews. I forgot to mention the knife. After you'd stabbed Nick Bellamy in a frenzy and cut out his tongue, I'm assuming you threw the knife in the river along with the phone?'

Melissa turned to Garibaldi. 'I didn't have a knife.'

'Really?'

'Yes, really.'

'Do you expect me to believe that, Mrs Matthews?'

'Yes I do, and for one simple reason. It's true. I didn't have a knife because I didn't stab him and I didn't cut out his tongue. I put the poison in his whisky, but that's it. I didn't touch

319

him. When I heard what had happened I couldn't believe it. The scarf, the tongue, the stabbing. That wasn't me. None of that was me.'

'You're telling me the truth?'

'It's all over. Why would I lie now?'

Garibaldi looked across the river at the lights of Chiswick, his mind whirring with possibilities, clicking into overdrive.

'What happens to me now?' said Melissa. Her heavy eyes looked defeated and resigned, their spark diminished to an empty dullness.

'I think this is what happens. Melissa Matthews, I am arresting you for the murder of Nicholas Bellamy. You do not have to say anything, but it may harm your defence if you do not mention when questioned something which you later rely on in court. Do you understand?'

'Yes, I understand. One thing, though. Before you take me wherever you need to take me, can I pop home?'

'I'll have to come with you.'

'Of course.'

'One other thing, Detective Inspector, can I be the one to tell Greg and Lauren?'

'Tell them what?'

'Tell them everything. Let me leave them a note to say I've been called into work as emergency cover at the last minute and that I'll see them tomorrow morning. Then maybe you can go round tomorrow to Greg and Lauren and I'll be allowed to give them a call. I'd like to be the one to call them.'

'If you really think that's for the best,' said Garibaldi.

He got up from the bench and, for reasons he couldn't quite understand, offered Melissa his arm. She took it and they walked by the Thames back towards Barnes.

Garibaldi woke the next morning, unsure whether his encounter with Melissa Matthews had really happened or whether it had been an extension of his dream about going to Nashville with Rachel.

He turned to his left and was surprised to find no one there. He checked the time. Nine o'clock. Where had she gone? He sat up and saw Rachel coming towards him with a mug of tea. He yawned and took it from her outstretched hand.

'You owe me an explanation.'

So she hadn't been asleep when he crept out. Or she'd woken up before he got back.

'I didn't want to wake you,' said Garibaldi. 'You'd only have worried.'

'Did it not occur to you that I might worry more if I woke up in the middle of the night to find you'd disappeared?'

'I'm sorry. It was work.'

'Work at half-past midnight?'

'It's that kind of job.'

'Listen, Mr Garibaldi, if we're going to make a thing of this, we need to have a proper discussion.'

He loved it when she called him Mr Garibaldi. But he loved it more when she spoke of making a thing of this.

'Let me explain,' said Garibaldi.

He had no idea whether Rachel believed him or not, but he told her the truth – not about what was said in his mid-night riverside meeting with Melissa Matthews, but about why he needed to see her then. As he explained yet again the nature of his work and the kind of demands it made, the idea of chucking it in and going off to university had never seemed more attractive.

'Do you forgive me?' he asked when he had finished.

Rachel said nothing, but there was something in her shrug and her smile that made him feel she might.

DCI Deighton was much less forgiving when he called her. 'Why didn't you tell me all this earlier?' she said.

'I was waiting to have it confirmed. I didn't want to come out with another hypothesis. I wanted to nail it.'

'You need to follow the rule book, Jim. You really do. But thank God we've got a result. High-profile crime and a high-profile criminal. God knows what the tabloids will make of this, but at least we've cracked it.'

'Yeah,' said Garibaldi. 'We've cracked it.'

Not quite, he thought as he hung up.

40

Saturday 11 May

Garibaldi was at the Matthews' house very early the next morning.

'What on earth are you doing here at this hour?' said Greg Matthews, bleary-eyed and still in his dressing gown.

'I need to see you. More specifically, I need to see Lauren.'

'Where's Melissa? I thought she would be downstairs.'

'I don't know,' lied Garibaldi. 'I'd like to see Lauren if I could.'

'You'd be lucky. I've no idea if she's even here, and at this hour . . .'

'Maybe you could look.'

Greg Matthews scowled, unhappy at being disturbed in the first place and now at being ordered around. When he had left the kitchen and gone upstairs Garibaldi looked for a note on the hall table. There wasn't one, so he quickly went into the kitchen. There it was, in Melissa's handwriting, explaining to Greg and Lauren why she wasn't there. Garibaldi got out of the kitchen before Greg came downstairs.

'She's on her way, but she's far from awake and far from happy.'

'Maybe that makes three of us.'

'I need a coffee.' Greg walked into the kitchen. Garibaldi followed and saw him pick the note up from the kitchen table. When Greg had read it, he turned it over, as if he was expecting more or something had not been fully explained.

'Everything OK?' said Garibaldi.

'Fine,' said Greg, filling up the coffee machine.

Garibaldi watched while he made the coffee. There was no attempt at small talk, no invitation to sit down, not even a polite enquiry as to whether Garibaldi might want a coffee himself.

When Greg had finished his coffee-making ritual, he turned to Garibaldi, giving him the evaluative look he had become familiar with over recent weeks.

'So, have we made any progress?'

'I think so.' Garibaldi gave a slow, pleased-with-progress nod.

'You mean we know who killed Nick Bellamy and we know who's behind those notes?'

Garibaldi nodded again.

'And are you going to let me know the nature of the progress you've made?'

'I hope so.'

'You hope so? So when should I hope to hear?'

'Later today, if things go to plan.'

'OK, so . . .' Greg Matthews broke off, his eyes looking past Garibaldi towards the kitchen door. 'You're up, then?'

Garibaldi turned to see Lauren standing in the doorway, hair tousled, sleepy-eyed, but clothed, wearing a pair of jeans and a sweatshirt that he thought she had probably slept in.

'I was wondering if I could ask you some questions, Lauren.'

324

'Why? What's happened?'

Greg came towards them. 'Why don't you both go into the living room, Detective Inspector? I'll leave you alone.'

Garibaldi held up a declining hand. 'If it's OK with you, I think I'd like to talk to Lauren outside.'

'Outside? At this time in the morning? That's ridiculous!'

'Maybe so, Mr Matthews, but that's what I'd like to do.' He turned to Lauren. 'Do you need a coat?' Lauren shrugged and went into the hall, coming back with a fur-hooded jacket draped round her shoulders. Garibaldi walked to the front door and Lauren followed.

'Where exactly are you going?' said Greg, following them to the door.

'Just a little walk.'

'So I'll see you soon, then?'

'I think there is no doubt of that,' said Garibaldi, opening the door for Lauren, showing her through and closing it gently behind him.

It was not yet eight o'clock and the early morning was crisp and fresh. Garibaldi walked with Lauren along the path to Mill Hill Road.

'How are you?' he said, not turning to look at her, in driving-with-Milly-face-forward conversation mode.

'Not great.'

'I'm sorry I've got you up and out so early, but it's very important and I need to ask you a few questions. I also want to be out of your dad's earshot.'

'What's happened? Has something happened?'

Garibaldi sensed weariness in the voice.

'I thought we might walk up to the pond, if that's OK with you?'

'Please! Can you just tell me what's happened? Say what you have to say!'

'I need to ask you a few questions, Lauren. There are some things I need to be clearer about. First of all, when did Nick Bellamy get in touch with you?'

'What do you mean?'

'Nick Bellamy, the man who was murdered, the old college friend of your parents.'

'What makes you think he got in touch?'

'Just tell me. Yes or no? And when?'

They had reached the end of Mill Hill. They paused and crossed the road, taking a left and walking beside the common.

Lauren had been silent for some time.

'How much do you know?' she said.

'That's what I'm trying to find out.'

Lauren fell silent again. Garibaldi turned to see that she had started to cry. Her shoulders were shaking and she was wiping her eyes with the sleeve of her jacket.

'What makes you think he got in touch?'

'Just tell me.'

'OK, yes, he did. It was a couple of months ago that he started. Phone calls at first. Then text messages. I had no idea who he was or what he wanted, and I had no idea how he knew my name or how he got my number. I suppose you can get hold of them easily enough nowadays.'

'And what did he say in these phone calls?'

'He said he wanted to meet me.'

'Did he give his name?'

Lauren shook her head. 'No. I mean, he gave a name but it wasn't Nick Bellamy. He called himself Billy. I thought he was a pervert.'

'And what did he say in these phone calls?'

'He said that he had something he needed to tell me that I would be interested to know and that he wanted to meet. Again, I just thought it was a sex thing. I didn't know what to do. He kept calling, and whenever I recognised the number I didn't take it. Then he kept texting.'

'Saying the same thing?'

'Saying he meant no harm and that he was completely sincere and that there was something I needed to know.'

'That must have been quite disturbing for you.'

Lauren sniffled. 'It was. I would have told my parents but . . .'

'Why didn't you?'

'Because he said – on the phone and in his texts – that I shouldn't tell the police and I shouldn't tell my parents. He kept saying he meant no harm.'

'Tell me, Lauren, was this about the time that you started to feel unwell again?'

'Yeah. Maybe that's what triggered it, I don't know. Anyway, I started feeling jumpy again and I . . .'

'And did you start taking drugs again?'

'No, I mean . . .'

'I know I'm a detective but, believe me, your taking drugs is not of great interest to me. You won't get in trouble for it, I just want to have the picture.'

'Yes, I did.'

'And you got back in touch with your old boyfriend who used to supply you?'

Lauren nodded.

'So this man kept calling and texting asking to meet and you kept saying no or not taking his calls. But eventually you agreed to meet him. Is that right?'

'Yes.'

'And why did you do that?'

'In one of the texts he said, "What I want to tell you is something you need to know. I won't rest until I've told you. And when I've told you that will be it. No more from me," and I thought what the hell. I didn't want to go to the police. I couldn't tell Mum and Dad, so I figured the best way to stop it was to see him.'

'So you agreed to meet?'

'Yeah.'

'And where did you meet?'

Lauren wiped her eyes again. 'This is horrible. Do I have to go through all this? I don't feel good. It's early. I feel shaky. I . . .'

'Let's turn off here,' said Garibaldi, taking a path to the right that went through the common.

'We met at the Sun on Boat Race Day. He said it would be a good place to meet because it would be crowded and no one would notice. He said he knew what I looked like – that's social media for you, I guess – but so that I could know who he was he would be the one wearing a Balfour College scarf. Can you believe it? A fucking Balfour College scarf! Anyway, I went along on Boat Race Day to the Sun and there he was. We found a seat in the corner and . . .'

'And then he told you?'

Lauren nodded.

'He told you that he was your father.'

'How do you know?'

'Am I right?'

'Yes. But, I mean, who told you? How did you—?'

'And what was your reaction?'

Lauren turned to him and gave a desperate laugh. 'What do you think my reaction was? What the fuck are you supposed to do when someone tells you something as big, as huge, as that? At first I didn't believe him, but then I listened and I looked at him and I thought about things and I thought, Fuck it, he's telling the truth! I'd never experienced anything like it. Everything changed. I didn't know what to do.'

'Did he tell you why he needed to tell you?'

'He said he thought I should know, but he also said it was something he needed to do. He didn't look great. He was upset. He promised that he would never be in touch with me again unless I wanted it and he said that it was something he had to do because he was going away and he might not be coming back. I think that's what he said. I thought he meant emigrating or something, but then when I heard what happened it kind of meant something else entirely . . .'

They were approaching Barnes Pond. Garibaldi pointed at a bench. 'Shall we sit here?'

Lauren pointed across the pond. 'Let's go to that one. It's where I go to . . .'

'To what? To think.'

'Yeah.'

'So when did you find out that Nick Bellamy had been murdered?'

'When it was in the papers and on the news. When Mum and Dad were talking about it.'

They sat down on Lauren's bench.

'And what did you make of the way he was killed? The scarf, the tongue . . .'

Lauren held up her hands, as if trying to ward off the disturbing image. 'Don't! Please!'

'It was pretty horrific, wasn't it?'

'Please!'

'Who would stab someone so many times? Who would cut out their tongue? And as for the scarf . . .'

'Stop it! Please!'

'Who do you think did that, Lauren?'

'I don't know. Have you found them? Is that what this is about?'

329

'Tell me what you did on Boat Race Day after you had met Nick Bellamy in the Sun.'

'I was devastated. I went home and . . . I didn't know what to do. There was no one I could speak to. I was desperate. I went to my room but I couldn't settle. I needed to do something, but I didn't know what. I was desperate.'

'And were you thinking of doing something desperate to escape from it all?'

'What do you mean?'

'I think you were so desperate when you got home that you thought of the ultimate act of escape. I think you may even have been considering ending it all. That's how upset you were.'

'I didn't . . . I mean, yes, I was distraught.'

'So you did what you often do when you feel like that?'

'What do you mean?'

'You went somewhere you like to go when you need to think.'

'You mean this bench. Yeah, I came here, to the pond. I needed to think.'

'There's no point lying, Lauren. It's too late for that. The game's up.'

'What do you mean?'

'You didn't come here on the evening of Boat Race Day did you? After you had received that shattering news, news that in an instant had changed your life completely, you went somewhere else you like to go when you need to think. But it's a place you go when you need to think and do something else, isn't it? You went on a walk by the river up to the Leg o' Mutton, didn't you? The place you go to take drugs. The place you went with your boyfriend to do drugs, maybe the place you've started going to with him again. So you rolled a joint and went up there. Skunk. That's what it was. Very strong, not like the dope of my youth. Powerful stuff.'

'How do you know all this?'

'I don't. Or not for sure. Not yet. I'm just trying to piece it all together, trying to make sense of it all. Tell me, though, am I right?'

Lauren nodded.

'Would you like to walk with me to the Leg o' Mutton now?'

Lauren started, as though struck by a sudden pain. 'No! No! Please no!'

She had started to shake. Garibaldi rested a hand on her shoulder. 'Hey, it's OK. It's OK.'

Lauren was still shaking. 'No! No!'

There was a flap of wings as the ducks on the pond took fright at the loud shriek.

'Lauren, it's OK. It was only a suggestion.'

'I can't go there. Never! Never!'

'Because of what happened?'

'I keep seeing it. It won't go away. I keep seeing it.'

'Tell me what you see, Lauren. What is it?'

'Him.'

'Nick Bellamy?'

'You don't have to say anything, Lauren. Just nod. Tell me if I'm wrong.'

'Do you have to? It's coming back again, I can see him.'

'I have to, Lauren. I have to know what happened. So you walked up to the Leg o' Mutton in the evening, through the Boat Race crowds, with a joint in your pocket and when you were out of sight, walking towards the gate, you lit up. As you walked beside the lake you got that familiar feeling – distant, remote, strange. Your mind started going somewhere else, away from the harshness of the world, and then something happened, didn't it?'

Garibaldi looked sideways at Lauren. She nodded.

'You came across the last person in the world you wanted to see at that moment. You came across Nick Bellamy. Lying on the ground by the lake. What did you do next? I don't know. But I'm figuring something very, very strange started happening to you. You were already in a very disturbed state, having just heard from this man lying on the ground that he was your father. It had changed, almost destroyed your world, your life. And you were out of it, feeling weirdly detached, and everything must have suddenly gone very strange. Do you want to tell me what you did?'

Lauren started shaking again, hugging herself tightly and rocking backwards and forwards on the bench. 'Please, no! I keep seeing it! I keep seeing it!'

'I don't know where you got the knife from, but I'm guessing it came from home. You may have taken it out of the drawer when you got back, thinking of using it on yourself upstairs. And I'm guessing you disposed of it after the event, when you came down and realised the enormity of what you had done. It hasn't been found, so I assume that, together with so many other things, it's lying somewhere at the bottom of the Thames. As for the tongue . . .'

'Please!'

'As for the tongue, not the kind of thing anyone in their right mind would do, but then, you weren't in your right mind, were you? You were somewhere else entirely and this man had just used his tongue to tell you something that had destroyed your world. So out it came. I have no idea how you did it, but you were frenzied. That explains the number of stabs. And the scarf? How much had Balfour College, Oxford, plagued your life? Your parents and their expectations. Your applying and being turned down. Nick and your mother together there. Into the mouth it went.'

Lauren was sobbing lowly, still rocking back and forth.

'I know how painful this must be for you.'

'You have no idea, no idea at all.'

'I need to be clear about what happened.'

'I have no idea why I did it, believe me. And ever since that night I've kept seeing it, I've kept seeing him. The image has kept coming back. I keep seeing his body, I keep seeing the scarf and the tongue. I keep seeing that fucking scarf! And do you know what the weirdest thing is? With all this stuff going on in my head, with all this unbelievable stuff in my life, I still keep worrying about my A levels ...' Lauren took a deep sigh and turned to Garibaldi. 'So what happens now, then? What happens now that you know?'

'I'm not sure.'

'What do you mean?'

'I'm not sure what happens.'

'I don't understand.'

'The thing is, Lauren, you didn't kill Nick Bellamy. When you came upon him, when you saw him lying there beside the lake, he was already dead.'

'What?'

'He was already dead. Someone else had killed him.'

'Really?'

'Don't pretend, Lauren. You must have realised when you read the news. He had been poisoned. And you knew that you hadn't poisoned him.'

Lauren nodded slowly, then turned to Garibaldi. 'When I read that he'd been poisoned, I couldn't take it in. Then I realised that when I came across him, when the crazy things started happening in my head, he was already dead. Someone else killed him and I did those things, those things that I keep seeing, I did them to a dead man. I did those things to a dead man! But it wasn't me who did it, you must understand that. It wasn't weed. It wasn't a joint. It wasn't me.'

'Who was it, then?'

'It was the tablet."

'What tablet?'

'I had been keeping it, I don't know why, and now I thought, what the hell. I took it when I got home. I was desperate. I got a knife and I took it and I went to the Leg o' Mutton. It was over. Everything. And then when I got there these things were happening in my head and then I saw him. I didn't know if he was real or if I was imagining it. I didn't know if I was seeing things. I didn't know whether I was doing those horrific things or whether I was hallucinating. Something had gone in my head. Something had happened. And then, in the days that followed, I kept hoping you'd find who killed him and that I'd somehow get away with it, that everything would be down to them. That whoever poisoned him would be charged with it all.' Lauren broke off, and looked beyond the pond into the clear morning sky. 'Have you got them? Do you know who killed him?'

Garibaldi paused. Melissa Matthews had asked to be the one who broke the news to her husband and daughter. Would he be out of order to tell Lauren now? She needed to know.

Lauren was still gazing into the sky, hugging herself tightly. Garibaldi leaned forwards, resting his elbows on his knees and took a breath. She was only eighteen and this was too much for any eighteen-year-old to go through.

As he braced himself to tell her, his phone rang. He checked the screen. DCI Deighton.

'Hello, boss.'

'Bad news, Jim, I'm afraid.'

41

Saturday 11 May

Greg Matthews looked dreadful – unshaven, unkempt, with dark hollows under his eyes. It was as if the events of the morning had transformed him completely from a successful, wealthy man to a vulnerable, pitiful wreck. He stood outside the hospital room, a comforting arm round his daughter's shoulder. Lauren Matthews looked like a ghost. Her life and her world had been taken from her and Garibaldi found it difficult to imagine how she could carry on.

'I'm so sorry, Mr Matthews,' said Garibaldi.

'Apparently it was cyanide. I have no idea how she got hold of it. I mean – cyanide! What the hell was she doing with that?'

Garibaldi nodded. He couldn't work out what he should tell Greg Matthews and when he should tell him. He thought back to yesterday evening. He now understood why Melissa had been so keen to go back home before coming to the station. She may have written a note for Greg and Lauren, but she had also done something else. Quite why she should have kept some of the poison with which she had killed Nick Bellamy at the Leg o' Mutton he did not understand and he had no idea where she would have kept it. But he was convinced that Melissa, seeing only one way out, had gone back home to get it.

And then, at the station, having been formally charged, she took it.

'Poor thing,' said Greg. 'It was all too much for her. If only that bitch hadn't pulled that stupid stunt at the quiz! If only ... The stress she was under! I mean, we still haven't found out who sent that note, have we? And then the note to Julia? What progress have you made there, Detective Inspector?'

For someone who made a living out of spinning yarns, of presenting the improbable as entirely believable, of exercising his powers of imagination and speculation, Greg Matthews seemed surprisingly naïve. Could he really have no idea? Had he never suspected his own wife and had he never seen the physical resemblance that had flashed into Garibaldi's head as he sat with Lauren in the café?

'Can we have a quiet word, Mr Matthews?'

Garibaldi led Greg towards a consulting room. He would tell him slowly. He would start with his wife's murder of Nick Bellamy and then he would move on to Lauren.

Then he would give them time to take it in, time to consider how they could possibly start to rebuild their shattered lives.

'They're going to love this.'

DCI Deighton picked up the paper and handed it to Garibaldi. He read the headline.

TV star kills herself after Boat Race murder probe.

'And this is just the beginning,' said DCI Deighton. 'When everything else gets out they'll have an absolute field day. Still, at least we got a result.'

'Yeah, we got a result.'

'Funny, isn't it? All those secrets.'

'And none of them true.'

'But close enough to the truth for them all to worry.'

'And the work of an embittered woman desperate to puncture all that pomposity, that self-importance.'

'A gesture that has led to the death of two people and a living death for two more. What do we do about them?'

'Who?'

'Kim Turner.'

'It was a practical joke. That's all. I don't think she broke any law.'

'OK. And what about Lauren?'

DCI Deighton leaned back in her chair. 'Poor kid. Orphaned at eighteen.'

'Orphaned?'

The word echoed in Garibaldi's head, bringing back unwanted memories.

'Yeah. She lost her father hours after she had discovered his identity, and now her mother.'

'Do we charge her, though? The thing is, she didn't murder Nick Bellamy. He was already dead. She was out of her head, maybe hallucinating even, maybe hearing voices – who knows? So she stabbed him with a knife she thought she might use on herself, she cut out the tongue that only hours ago had told her such devastating news, and she stuffed the scarf which represented so much that had, in her view, gone wrong with her life, into the mouth.'

'She mutilated the dead body of her father while under the influence of LSD. And what will happen when the papers get hold of that?'

'Poor kid. Have you ever thought that . . . no, silly idea.'

DCI Deighton leaned forward. 'Thought what?'

'Lauren needs protection. Melissa Matthews is dead – there's nothing she can say. And for a long time we all thought that whoever poisoned Nick Bellamy also stabbed him and cut out his tongue. We asked the question why poison him and then stab him, but we never answered it. Could it not stay that way? Could we not let the world think that Melissa Matthews did it all?'

'No, Jim. We can't do that.'

'Why not?'

'We play by the book.'

DCI Deighton's words made Garibaldi think again of Melissa Matthews' request to 'pop home'. Had he played by the book then, she would have been unable to pick up the cyanide and might still be alive.

'Really? Why? Lauren will need help. She'll need to talk this through. She may never recover from it. Might this not help just a little? Let Greg and Lauren live with it, give them time to try to understand what's happened. She needs help and she needs it badly. And I don't think having her story splashed over the front pages is going to help her at all. There'll be enough about her mum.'

DCI Deighton paused, as if giving the idea serious consideration. 'Who knows about what she did?'

'Lauren, Greg, and us.'

'Let me think about it.'

'What does that mean?'

'It means let me think about it.'

'We don't need to tell anyone. Our secret.'

'We've had enough secrets, haven't we?'

'She needs a break. And as if she hasn't got enough to deal with, she's got another tricky challenge to face.'

'And what's that?'

'Her A levels.'

42

'That's fantastic Alfie. Unbelievable!'

Alfie raised his pint and looked round the Bush bar, as if inviting more general congratulations.

Garibaldi raised his glass. 'Straight A stars and a home fixture against Hull. Life doesn't get much better, does it?'

'I never thought I'd do it!' said Alfie. 'I mean, after moving school and everything.'

The only bad thing about Alfie's grades was the way Kay claimed they were in some way a result of her and Dominic's decision about Alfie's schooling. Garibaldi's lips were still sore from the biting he'd given them in that phone call.

'Alfie,' said Garibaldi, 'you'd have got those results anywhere.'

'Maybe, but, you know ...'

'So what are your plans?'

Alfie sipped his beer and leaned back in his chair. 'Well, I'm pulling out of UCAS and I'm applying again.'

'OK, makes sense I suppose.'

Garibaldi knew what was coming.

'And I think I'll apply to Oxford.'

'OK.'

'You don't sound very pleased.'

'No, I'm delighted.'

'Mum definitely is.'

I bet she is. And Dominic.

'So that will give you a year off, won't it?'

At least he hadn't uttered the words 'gap year'.

'Well, nine months, really.'

'And what will you do?'

'Get a job and then travel, I guess.'

'Anywhere in particular?'

'I don't know.'

'Ah well, the world's your oyster, I suppose.'

Had he really said that?

'And Alice?'

'She's starting Oxford this year.'

'So you could end up there together?'

'Could do. Who knows?'

Garibaldi looked at his watch. 'Come on. Time to go.'

They finished their beers and stepped out into the Uxbridge Road crowds, taking out their QPR scarves and winding them round their necks.

Garibaldi looked at the blue and white on Alfie's shoulders and saw again the Balfour College scarf stuffed into Nick Bellamy's mouth at the Leg o' Mutton.

'So if you do apply to Oxford?' said Garibaldi, 'do you have to choose a college and things like that?'

Alfie nodded. 'Yeah, but the school helps you. They seem to know all about that kind of thing.'

Yeah, thought Garibaldi. I bet they do.

Acknowledgements

Thanks to: Laura Macdougall, Olivia Davies, Kate Beal, Sarah Beal, Kate Quarry, Fiona Brownlee, Barry Walsh, Barnes Bookshop. Special thanks to Jo, Caitlin and Rory – without them nothing would have been possible.

Read on for an exclusive preview of the second in the
gripping Garibaldi mysteries as our country-music loving,
self-educated copper, and the only one in the Met who
can't drive, takes on his next case, in leafy Barnes.

PRIVATE
LESSONS

Bernard O'Keeffe

Garibaldi unlocked his bike from the railings of Rutland Court and cycled into the High Street. Barnes was up and about, enjoying the crisp September morning. He passed the Sun Inn flower stall and glanced to his right where, beside the pond, loud young parents with loud young kids were feeding the ducks and the swans. He winced. Whenever he heard the young bankers or accountants or lawyers with their braying wives and their children, whenever his ears were assaulted by their high-volume public-parenting, he always asked himself the same question – was he just getting old and grumpy, or were they prats?

He always reached the same conclusion.

He cycled on, checking out the posters outside The Olympic and the window display of Barnes Books, took a right at the lights opposite The Red Lion and headed down Rocks Lane.

He wheeled his bike towards the police cars and the forensic van parked in the car park, locked it to a stand and walked to the taped cordon and the tent. An information board mounted on a wooden stand caught his eye and he paused to look at it. *Welcome to Barnes Common Old Cemetery.* He glanced at the pictures and the map, surprised by how he could have lived so close to the place for so long and know so little about it.

"Sir?"

Garibaldi turned to see DS Gardner in a forensic suit walking through the cordon past a uniformed officer.

"Morning, Milly. What have we got?"

Gardner stood beside him and looked at the board. "Male youth. Twenties."

"Any ID?"

Gardner shook her head.

"Phone?"

She shook her head again.

"What's it look like?"

"Stabbing."

Garibaldi pointed at the information board. "You know much about this place?"

"Not a lot. Pretty spooky, isn't it?"

"Most cemeteries are."

"Yeah, but this one's a different kind of spooky."

Garibaldi walked with his sergeant towards the police tape.

"And what have you been dragged away from on this bright Saturday morning?" said Garibaldi.

"Nothing much. Only Tim."

Gardner had been with her new partner for a couple of months. Still early days, still plenty for her to worry about.

"And you?"

"Nothing much. Only Rachel".

He knew as he spoke the words how little he believed them.

Garibaldi showed his card and nodded to the uniform at the cordon, pulled on a forensic suit hood, shoes and gloves and walked along the gravel path.

Light from above filtered through the branches and the leaves. To his left the ping and thwack of balls on rackets came from the tennis courts. To the right gravestones and memorials were dotted and scattered with no sense of order or regularity amongst low-lying shrubs, bushes and foliage. Some were broken, some had sunk into the ground and leant at an angle, many were green and lichened. The place reeked of abandonment and decay.

Garibaldi had seen many dead bodies, but the mixture of emotions he felt when he was about to see a new one always surprised him. Fear at confronting more evidence of man's inhumanity to man, his capacity for savagery and cruelty. Fear that there but for the grace of God went us all. Fear that whoever killed might kill again. And pity. Pity for the life cut short. Pity for those who would mourn.

But there was also excitement. Not at the thought of what he was about to see but at the thought of what he was about to engage in. Another puzzle. Another challenge. Another chance to bring whoever did it to justice and bring even a tiny amount of comfort to those who grieved.

The fear others might understand, but the excitement he kept quiet about. It might make him seem weird. Or strangely old-fashioned, like he was on some kind of moral crusade, desperate to restore order to a broken world. Both, he knew, were a long way from the truth. It was a lot more complicated than that . . .